PATRIOT JAMES

R.O. Palmer

To Chris,
An avid reader and sister to a good friend of mine.
Enjoy the read.
Best wishes,
RO Palmer

This book is a work of fiction. Any resemblance to actual events or persons, living or dead, is entirely coincidental.

"Patriot James," by R.O. Palmer. ISBN 1-58939-779-7.

Published 2005 by Virtualbookworm.com Publishing Inc., P.O. Box 9949, College Station, TX 77842, US. ©2005, R.O. Palmer. All rights reserved. No part of this publication may be reproduced, stored in a retrieval system, or transmitted in any form or by any means, electronic, mechanical, recording or otherwise, without the prior written permission of R.O. Palmer.

Manufactured in the United States of America.

Dedicated to

Frances Palmer,

who knew there was an author inside me before I could read or write.

Acknowledgments

For inspiration: CJ Smith, Arielle Emmett, Jack Reiling, and David Van Vleck.

For critical input (including virtual slaps to the face): Steve Palmer, Cathey Barbee, the FLC Book Club, and the Denville Mixed Genre Writers' Group.

For editing and more: Sarah Cypher.

For specific information: Bob Farina and Bob O'Hare.

For proof-reading: Meghan O'Hare.

For wisdom: Marshall Palmer.

For suggestions, and encouragement: too many people to list… but all are appreciated.

For all of the above: Sharon.

Patriotism is the last refuge of a scoundrel.

—Samuel Johnson

PROLOGUE

A tractor-trailer rolled to a stop on a Route 287 exit lane, the truck's top less than a foot from a Route 80 overpass. A burly driver squeezed out the passenger side, bumping the door against a concrete side wall that supported the bridge. He hopped into a black Toyota that accelerated around the ramp and sped onto Route 80 West, leaving the truck abandoned in the night, honked at by irate motorists.

The man checked his watch, counting intervals every five seconds. He looked at the driver. It was exactly midnight, Eastern Daylight Time, in Parsippany, New Jersey. "*Un minuto, Dante.*"

The driver nodded.

The passenger punched in eleven numbers on his cell-phone. Two seconds later, the truck exploded, blowing a gaping crater in Route 287 and shooting mangled hunks of the overpass hundreds of feet into the October night. Debris rained down three football fields away, the fireball visible from Manhattan skyscrapers. One chunk of roadway landed on the eastbound passing lane of Route 80, squashing a skidding Grand Am and its driver, Sam James.

One minute later, 800 miles west, a second truck-bomb exploded under another Route 80 overpass—this one south of Chicago. The blast obliterated a rented van carrying employees and customers of the Paulson Electronics Company.

Within several minutes, six other truck bombs demolished Route 80 overpasses at major interchanges across the continent. The explosions killed 461, wounding 939. All eight interchanges were impassable, choking traffic from New Jersey to California. Repairs would take months and cost hundreds of millions. By the eleven o'clock news in L.A., the media had given the attacks an instant label: *I-80.*

* * *

On a Mediterranean hillside, cheers erupted on the patio of a secluded hacienda. Six men celebrated, jabbering Spanish.

"It is confirmed," a drunken voice crowed. "Eight hits. Victory for Sabah Al Khair! A good morning, indeed!" The men cheered.

"Speech, Diego," said a higher voice, one that grated like an untuned violin.

"Yes, speech, Diego," implored another.

Five brothers, all in western clothes and with bags the size of pears under their eyes, gazed at their oldest brother.

The most somber of the party—the one with a stubbly beard—stood and raised an arm until the others were silent. "You want a victory speech?"

"Yes, yes!"

The bearded man frowned. "Wine has made you sloppy—never call me Diego where our work is concerned. The deception must be complete. I am Anwar. And as for victory speeches, do not be fools. There is too much more work to talk of victory. And what of the two cells that failed?"

The five lowered their eyes.

Anwar faced the Mediterranean, reveling in a southerly breeze. "I'll grant that Sabah Al Khair achieved *success* today, but do not claim victory. Just as a venomous snake becomes wary when tormented, so the Americans will become more vigilant."

He paused, aware of the power he held over his family. "Do not misunderstand. I am pleased at what we accomplished. Trucking, the pulse of the United States economy, will be disrupted, and the Americans will be paralyzed, fearful of driving their extravagant automobiles." His voice rose to a crescendo. "Instilling fear of everyday life, that is how we will gain our revenge!"

He placed his hand on the pager-sized device clipped to his belt. "Remember, my brothers, secrecy is the key, and for our next project, the night owl will protect us."

The youngest brother cleared his throat. "Then surely we can be ourselves in the safety of our home?"

"But what if a satellite is taking pictures right now?" Anwar dropped to his knees, gazing east—toward Mecca—smiling at his cleverness. "For the benefit of American spies, join me in Islamic prayer...for the next great blow in our Jihad—clean water." He laughed, and his five brothers laughed and bowed with him.

The rising sun bathed the hacienda's red-tiled roof in golden light. It was a good morning.

1
CYNTHIA JAMES

It was a good morning in Stanhope, New Jersey, yet Cynthia James was ill at ease. For three weeks, she had been depressed—preoccupied with comings and goings and the difference that a few seconds can make. She sat in her kitchen watching a white sedan park in front of her condominium. What might result from *that* car taking that place at this moment? Cynthia thought about her brother's departure from that very space 21 days ago. A lump tightened her throat.

She took a drink of water then leaned her slim torso toward the sliding door, widening one slit between vertical blinds to get a better view out the front of the condo she was house-sitting—a first-floor end unit of the northernmost building in the complex. There was something familiar about the stocky man exiting the car. The driver closed the door and looked at her condo; Cynthia's heart jumped. She recognized Detective Taylor from Chattanooga. As she pulled back, his eyes darted toward the slider a blink before he hurried up the front steps.

She could ignore the doorbell, hoping Taylor hadn't seen her and would go away. She could let him in. Or she could flee. Cynthia was 27 and in excellent shape—she could outrun an overweight, middle-aged man in dress shoes. If the police had found Alexander Gates, Taylor was here to arrest her, and she couldn't let that happen.

In one motion, Cynthia turned and snatched her purse off the kitchen table. She bolted through the living room and bedroom to her back balcony where she slammed the slider closed before leaping over the rail, purse clutched in her hand. It was six feet to the ground, and she cushioned her landing with a sideward roll. On her feet, she sprinted west to the woods fifty feet behind her building. Swerving between tree trunks as if they were slalom gates, she dodged through the forest. After ten seconds, she stopped and hunched behind a boulder, watching, listening, waiting. She saw Taylor snooping around the back of her building, inspecting something below her deck. He must have seen where her feet had pressed grass flat.

Taylor followed her footprints to the woods, then her trail through the trees. She had to move. Watching where she stepped, Cynthia stayed low, easing south toward a ravine behind the boulder's cover. A twig snapped under a careless step. She froze.

Crackling leaves. He was moving her way.

She had car keys and an emergency packet—alternate I.D. and money—that she kept in her wallet. Having parked by the garbage bin, she was now closer to her car than Taylor was. Still listening, she eased the keys from her purse. Keeping low, she crept until she reached an east-west gulley. Without looking back, she sprinted east toward the condos.

Cutting around the back of building number 25, she skidded to her knee, picking up a grass stain before regaining her feet. Seconds later, she was at her Subaru and forced the key into the door lock on her second jab. She hopped inside. The Outback started, and she threw it into reverse, backing up with a screech. Only as she shifted to "Drive" and turned the steering wheel hard left did she peek to her right—to the north—where Taylor huffed around the northeast corner of her building.

She snaked her car down the steep artery that served the entire development. At the stop sign, she rolled through a left turn, accelerating in front of an oncoming Volvo. She ran a yellow light before making a series of lefts and rights that exhausted her local knowledge.

Avoiding Route 80, she wended her way east on back roads, keeping an eye on the rearview mirror. Taylor's white sedan did not appear. When she pulled behind a building to check her map, she thought: don't ever panic again; always think before you act; stay cool.

A half-hour later, Cynthia found herself at a junction with Route 10. She headed east and turned in at the first car dealership she saw. After parking behind the showroom, she took off her sweatshirt, twirled her long hair into the type of bun pictured on her mother's license, and donned mirrored sunglasses. She had enjoyed acting in school plays as a teen; now she sucked in a lungful of courage and took on the identity of a young widow.

This was one lucky day for the beer-gutted salesman on duty. A clueless woman looking years younger than the age on her I.D. wanted to trade a perfectly good Subaru for the cheapest clunker she could drive off the lot—she didn't even haggle over his lowball trade-in offer.

An hour later, Cynthia parked her $600 Chevy at a mall where she bought clothes, toiletries, and a suitcase. Thirty minutes later, she made another trade, this time for a rusting Dodge pick-up.

In Parsippany, Cynthia checked into a motel, paying cash and registering as her mother, Karen Smith. At 2:00 a.m., she drove to an all night diner and used the pay phone to dial Oxford, England.

"Good morning, Stephen. I'm afraid I won't be able to house-sit the condo for the rest of your sabbatical. Turns out I can't handle Sam having been there that night. I'm sorry." It was only a half-lie.

After breakfast, she called a neighbor in Stanhope. No, the police hadn't been asking questions. The only unusual visitor had been a thickset man poking around Cynthia's building the morning before. Cynthia exhaled. If the police had found Alexander Gates, they would have been all over her building. Taylor must have been trying to rattle her. If so, he had succeeded.

The next day she deposited the car dealership check in a new bank account in her mother's name and rented a cheap, furnished apartment in Boonton.

* * *

Cynthia James had long, silky hair the color of dark honey. When photographed, she appeared tense, imperfect features frozen. But when she moved, every part melded like a symphony. Once while running together, Sam described her tapered figure by saying, "Sis, when you run, you flow like a stream rippling over smooth stones."

"Sounds like a line from one of your poems," she had said.

He grinned the way he had when he got his first soaker. "I'll call it *Rippling Water*."

She thought about his way with words as her strides followed a forest path paralleling a brook in Tourne Park. The beauty of the forest was tempered because he would never again write of its sights and sounds. Bushes on both sides curved overhead, giving her the impression of running through a leafy, red tunnel to nowhere. A songbird's early-morning tune made her jealous of creatures that could sing for the joy of singing.

Other runners were rare at dawn, so she paid attention when a short man overtook her with a call of, "On your left." Probably a skier, she thought. Cynthia let him by, but he didn't pull away. Instead, he settled in a few feet ahead, saying, "Mind if we run together?"

"It's a free country." She was conscious of her ponytail bouncing on her shoulders. They ran in silence until emerging onto a sandy beach to the west of a small lake.

"Beautiful morning, huh?"

Cynthia ignored him.

The athletic man, who appeared to be in his mid-thirties, slowed until Cynthia came abreast. "Our meeting isn't an accident. My name's Marco, and I'd like to talk to you about a job."

"I don't have a job for you," she deadpanned.

"Funny. But I have one for you. I'm a headhunter for an organization that wants to hire you."

She tensed. "To do what?"

"To be a patriot," he answered, as if "patriot" were a normal job title.

She snorted. "Sounds like you've been drinking. A little early for that, don't you think?"

"I'm sober as a judge."

"Who *are* you, really? Who put you up to this?"

"I'm dead serious. I'm here to offer you a job."

"First time I've heard *that* pick-up line."

"No line. I'm offering you a job."

"Without an interview...*Marco*?"

"We already know what we'd be getting."

"We?"

"*Patriots for Freedom*," he replied.

"Here's where I turn around," she said at the south end of the beach. She hoped he would take the hint and keep going, but he turned, and they retraced their steps. She took her first close look at him.

Marco was her height, 5'7", with dark curls and a large nose. His voice was melodic, like a tenor's. "We want to train you to become an operative with *Patriots for Freedom*."

"And what do patriotic operatives do? Shoot off fireworks on the Fourth of July?"

"They seek justice for terrorists who facilitated the I-Eighty attacks." Marco answered as evenly as if he had said they sold insurance.

Cynthia glanced around, half-expecting to see a cameraman from some sick reality TV show.

"We know your brother died in the Parsippany explosion. But even if you don't necessarily *want* to seek justice, Cynthia, we're quite sure that you'd be good at it. In fact, we think you already are."

Her eyes narrowed. "How do you know my name?"

"We know a lot about you. We know you've taken justice into your own hands once. Maybe twice. We'll pay you to do it for us."

"Sounds sick."

"What's sick is terrorists murdering your brother, Sam. Listen, Cynthia, terrorists are getting more aggressive, and they're fanatical. The time has passed for sitting back and assuming the government can do everything. Washington's preoccupied with preventing Al Qaeda's next attack. It's time for citizen patriots to take up the call."

"I should join you because they killed my brother?"

"Don't ask me. Ask yourself."

Cynthia slowed, wanting to keep him in front of her as they approached the woods where the path narrowed.

"Does the name Jimmy Taylor mean anything to you?" Marco asked. "He's looking for you. The Chattanooga Police may not have our organization's means, but Taylor's persistent."

For a few moments, there were only the sounds of breathing and feet thumping in unison.

Marco resumed. "You seem to be a good listener, so listen. We do patriotic things in the war on terrorism that the government can't. We think you'll be useful with terrorists who have a weakness for beautiful women."

"How?" she asked with a sarcastic cock of one eyebrow. "By infiltrating Islamic camps?"

"They're not Islamic," he said.

"But the papers say Sabah Al Khair is Arabic for 'Good Morning.'"

"That's what these bastards want us to believe. The name's a red herring."

She stopped and glanced around. "So who are they?"

Marco stopped, too. "It's complicated." He shrugged as if the answer would be too intricate for her to grasp.

"Look," Cynthia snapped, "if you want me to take you seriously, you'll have to level with me. Otherwise…" She started to jog away.

"Hold on."

She stopped and faced him, hands on hips.

"Okay. Here's the deal. The government doesn't know who these guys are, but we do. They invested in a trucking company a few years back and used the profits to buy explosives and ten trucks under a paper front. Documentation was conveniently lost in a fire a few months ago. The Feds picked up on bogus trails and traced the trucks to Islamic groups, not the perpetrators."

"So how do *you* know who they are?"

"We have a surveillance system. I can't tell you about its capabilities, but using leads from the two failed attacks and computer trails, we've identified almost a hundred conspirators who had a hand in killing your brother."

"But who are they?"

"A cult, called *Eighteen Ninety-Eight*, based in Southern Spain. They use Arabic code names so their actions will be blamed on Islamic fundamentalists."

"What do they want?"

"To avenge the Spanish-American War. The organization revolves around one tightly-knit family that lost everything in the year eighteen ninety-eight. It sounds crazy, but what terrorists seem sane?... Anyway, we're their target, and the Arabs are perfect scapegoats."

Cynthia rubbed her forehead, fighting a sudden headache. She ripped a water bottle from a Velcro pad on her running belt and shot a stream into her mouth. Still hot, she squeezed more onto her face and neck.

"These guys are fanatics, Cynthia. You and I would call them crazy. They need to be stopped, but even if we share what we know, the government can't go into Europe to get these people. But patriots can, and we will."

She shook her head.

Marco touched her elbow. "It's a brave new world—horrible and dangerous. You can help make it safer for everyone."

She frowned. "This is hard to believe." For a moment, she measured him, eyeball to eyeball, then she pointed. "You go first. I want to keep moving."

He started running again, and she settled in behind. Neither spoke for a minute.

The path widened, and he dropped back to jog side-by-side. "There are many people in the *Eighteen Ninety-Eight* network. For example, drug dealers in Spain who launder profits through German bankers."

"And you want me to seduce Spanish drug dealers and German bankers?"

"Just Spanish drug dealers—because you speak Spanish."

"Is there anything about me that you *don't* know?"

"Not much." After several strides, he added, "Any questions?"

"You say I've...taken justice into my own hands. How?"

"The first time was your stepfather. You used him to improve your batting average when you were seventeen." He chuckled. "Pretty ironic since it happened in Cooperstown. The 'maybe' was in May, a man named Alexander Gates on the steamboat *Louisiana Lady*, where you were a bartender."

"Oh, really! And what did I do to him?"

"Frankly, we're not sure of the details...yet. What we *are* sure of is that Mr. Gates was attracted to you, and he disappeared. We're pretty sure he's dead."

She said nothing.

"How'd I do?"

Cynthia stopped. "You a cop?"

He stopped, too, turning to walk back to her. "No. I represent *Patriots for Freedom*. I'll cut right to the chase, Cynthia. First, the *Louisiana Lady* went bankrupt so you don't have a job. More importantly, we can protect you so the Chattanooga Police can't touch you. Think about that. And we pay very well. Base salary: ninety thousand a year with all expenses paid. Plus bonuses for successful missions—up to a hundred grand per contract. We want someone motivated—like you. You don't have to enjoy the job, just be good at it. And think about Sam. If that's not enough, think about the families who'll be destroyed by *Eighteen Ninety-Eight's* next attack."

She clenched her fists.

"What do you say, Cynthia?"

The numbers were mind-boggling to an unemployed bartender. Cynthia paced back-and-forth before looking at him. "I'm not saying I'm interested, but where do you get the money for this?"

"We have wealthy benefactors who want justice for I-Eighty."

Cynthia glared. "What if I say no?"

"I don't think you'll say no unless Detective Taylor arrests you before you make up your mind. That would be a pity."

She looked into his dark eyes. "What makes you think I can't keep ahead of one cop?"

"Until recently, he was investigating you in his spare time. Now, he's connected you to Gates through the death of your mother, and he found out you lived in Stanhope. Might that be why you moved to Boonton?"

Cynthia's lips parted, but no words came out.

He continued. "Now the case will likely be reopened so Taylor can use all the resources of law enforcement. He may not be as quick as us, but he'll track you down. Do you want to run forever?"

She examined her Reeboks. "Suppose I was interested. Where's the training?"

He waited until she looked up. "The Jersey shore." His eyes twinkled. "I hear it's lovely this time of year."

She almost smiled. "And after?"

"After training, you'd take periodic trips overseas. The official reason for your travel would be pro-American rallies."

"But instead, I'd be *seeking justice*. Is that what I think it is?"

Marco's eyes locked on hers. "Yes."

Her forehead flushed. Did that mean she was taking him seriously? "What would I tell people?" she asked.

"Officially, you'll be a supervisor of bar and restaurant services. Remember, ninety thousand a year, plus bonuses."

Cynthia softened her expression. "You didn't tell me your last name."

"We're both better off if you don't know."

Cynthia's eyes flickered. "I know who you really are."

"I told you who I am."

"No. You lied. You're the devil trying to buy my soul."

"Is it for sale?"

She stared deep into Marco's eyes.

He blinked. "Here's my cell number and a good faith pre-signing bonus. Take a day or two to think about it." With that he placed an envelope in Cynthia's hand.

"You never explained how you know so much about me."

"We can hear your phone conversations without tapping your line. We can read your mail without opening it—"

"I suppose you can tell me what color underwear I have on."

"It's black." He paused a beat. "That's a joke."

Cynthia wasn't so sure.

When she returned home, Cynthia opened the envelope. Inside was a phone number and $5,000.

2
THE GATES BROTHERS

"I got a job offer today," Cynthia told her boyfriend as she watched him tongue-wrestle linguini. They were one of three couples dining in a family restaurant with red and white checkered tablecloths—good food, no frills.

"Wharlknd," Thomas Gates mumbled before swallowing. "Excuse me. What kind?"

"Catering—with *Patriots for Freedom*," she said, as if it were a Fortune 500 company.

"Never heard of them."

Just thinking about the bizarre offer made her heart beat faster. She jangled the cubes in her glass and took a sip of water. "They were spawned by the Route Eighty bombings to promote freedom worldwide."

He noted a glistening in her eyes but didn't mention her brother—or his. "Worldwide?" Thomas asked, a single strand of pasta hanging from his jaw.

"Yes. There'll be travel. Did I ever tell you I speak Spanish?" He shook his head. "Well, I'll probably go to Spain—after training."

Thomas wiped a napkin across his mouth, leaving a smile behind. "Can I ask how much they're offering?"

"Fifty-five, plus bonuses." She squinted at Thomas, an expression that usually got him to say what was on his mind, but he finished his entrée in silence.

"So what do you think about the job?" she asked after they'd ordered dessert.

"Sounds like a great opportunity, but I'd be lying if I said I wouldn't miss you when you're away."

She felt his foot stroke her ankle, prompting a smile. "On the *Louisiana Lady*, I was gone six out of eight weeks, so we're used to being apart."

"I guess," he mumbled. "You know, you could always move in with me in Manhattan."

She shook her head. "That's not a good idea right now."

Thomas started to ask, "Then when?" but a twitch of her jaw told him not to.

They were comfortable during silence, appreciating each other. Thomas was enchanted by her healthy complexion—the shade of a paper bag, even in November—and exotic, brown eyes, the result of one-eighth Peruvian ancestry. He admired her shimmering hair, which she swirled and pinned so it looked different to him each time.

Thomas was twelve years older than she but didn't look it because he had good genes. She missed his beard, but he looked younger without its salt and pepper flecks. His was a handsome, lovable face, yet she did not love him—she didn't really love anyone. Every time she brooded about this, she wished her family were still alive.

She focused on Thomas's gray eyes. Most of the time, they were intriguing, like a textured painting one appreciates for hours—but when his eyes became suggestive, she saw lust, not desire. A trivial distinction, perhaps, but to Cynthia, haunted by the memory of her stepfather's leer, it made all the difference. She glanced at Thomas's eyes and saw it—lust. For a moment, she was seventeen again, feeling her insides shrivel like burning leaves.

"I'd rather not take a train back to New York tonight," Thomas said. Cynthia knew the code—he was horny.

"Would you like to—"

Thomas was already nodding.

She smiled, reaching for the White Zinfandel. "I'll finish this. You drive."

Thirty minutes later, they were on her bed, the only piece of furniture in the place that wasn't bought at a garage sale. As Thomas unbuttoned her blouse, her head spun, but not too fast. She had gauged the alcohol just right, leaving herself alert enough to go through the motions and numb enough to tolerate the act. She guided his tongue to her ticklish navel, prompting a twitch that encouraged him to remove the rest of her clothes. Once naked, she rolled onto her stomach so he could caress her backside. When he was a few degrees beyond ready, she rose to her elbows and knees. He always took the bait, which relieved her from having to see the hunger in his eyes.

Cynthia saw herself as an infomercial for the Mate-O-Matic, model 27SWF/34-23-33, guaranteed to tighten thighs and satisfy your man, or your money back. *The things she concocted to repress her stepfather's image!* Once she was sweating, Cynthia writhed and moaned, causing Thomas to ejaculate.

"I love you," he murmured into her cheek after they collapsed.

She almost said she loved him, too. "You're sweet," she whispered. At least she didn't lie.

Cynthia recalled how she had promoted the affair for non-romantic motives, but the relationship had germinated, if not blossomed, because she cared for him. But why did she care? There was no one-word answer, unless she lumped everything about him into "sweet." But that was so banal, and Thomas wasn't banal. He was bright enough to articulate his fascination with people. He rarely made her laugh, but who did? In three words, Thomas was "worth caring for," so she endured sex—like traversing a minefield—to get to the caring, the cuddling. That's when she was able to wonder what loving would be like. So she cared because she could imagine loving him. To actually love him, she would have to reveal the ugliness beneath her façade, but she wasn't ready for that.

She was tired of running and could use the money from this crazy job, but did she want to channel her vengeance into vigilante justice? She wrestled with dilemmas to the rhythm of Thomas's snoring. Why was she considering the job? Although she pretended to ponder the question, she knew the answer. She had been waiting—hoping was a better word—for something to snap her out of a ten-year depression.

Ten years.

Ten years of feeling sorry for herself—a decade without fulfillment. She actually thought such drivel, which made her more miserable. She had lived in isolation, protected by her mother, sports, and a shell of self-pity. Her first attempt at something significant had been the pursuit of Alexander Gates. Her heart beat faster. She told herself that was because of what she had done on the riverboat, but that was dishonest—reliving the thrill of the chase excited her.

She pictured Alex Gates's face the first time she saw him in the Louisiana Lounge. He was handsome, but that wasn't what set him apart. He was rich, but that did nothing for Cynthia. He had a voice like a newscaster, but that only amused her. It was his eyes. What eyes! Playful. Giving. Mesmerizing. Cynthia had wanted him to be a monster, but he gazed at her as if she were the most enchanting woman he had ever seen. That was his gift. He made any woman see her beauty reflected in his eyes.

Cynthia had had little practice flirting, and she avoided looking into his eyes as if they were dual solar eclipses. The more she ignored him, the more interested he became—he loved a challenge.

They talked late into the night across the bar. He told her he had to disappear and asked if she would sneak away with him to the Cayman Islands. Danger *and* adventure—intriguing. So she focused on his mouth and nose, smiling without looking into his eyes for more than an instant. Not until that last morning.

A flush warmed her face—she wanted to know more about *Patriots for Freedom.*

The next day, Cynthia called Marco from a pay-phone and they agreed to run in Tourne Park the following morning. When he caught up to her on her usual trail, Marco was frowning. "Detective Taylor's suspicious of the way you disappeared. He's pushing for a warrant."

"And that's gonna make me sign up?"

"Maybe, maybe not, but it's something you should know. We don't want you to get caught. We want you to work for us."

"What if I were interested?"

"Are you?"

"Maybe."

Marco stopped, grabbing her wrist. "This isn't a job for maybes. I have to know for sure. Are you *really* interested?"

Cynthia's mouth was dry, her palms sweaty. This was a moment of truth but not the point of no return—there would be other chances to quit. She returned his stare and nodded. "Yes, but I have questions."

He let go and relaxed his gaze. "I should hope so. We'll pay your rent; provide a maid who'll pick up your mail. The training manager's name is Carole Burns, and her compound's in Stone Harbor. That's where you'll live. Everything'll be provided, so you won't take much, not even your truck."

In a strange way, she would miss the rusted Dodge. They jogged into the woods side-by-side with Marco talking and Cynthia wondering what the hell she was getting herself into.

3

PATRIOTS FOR FREEDOM

Jerry Paulson was a man accustomed to knowing tomorrow's headlines today. He drummed fingers on his mahogany desk, waiting for the 8:00 a.m. briefing. Until then, all he had was *The New York Times*—yesterday's news.

At 6'4", 290 pounds, Paulson surrounded people in an arm-draping style reminiscent of Lyndon Johnson. He had worked for twenty years making Paulson Electronics a leader in high-tech surveillance, becoming one of the wealthiest men in the country. But after two of his executives and four customers died in the *I-80* explosion near Chicago, Paulson found a new focus. He picked up a photo of one of the murdered executives—the youngest vice-president in the company—his only son, Norman.

At 7:50, he took the elevator to the basement for the daily meeting of his war cabinet in the highly-secure conference room known at Paulson Electronics as the Bunker. Impressionist art adorned the walls, but the windowless room was intense—a masculine space that would have looked better with paintings of submarines. There was a photo collage taped on a white board at the far end of the room—family pictures of the murdered executives and customers—a sobering memorial. Paulson pretended to weigh the victims equally, but that was impossible. His eyes focused on the picture of him and his son, arm in arm, eating hot dogs at Yankee Stadium. Beads of perspiration popped onto his brow.

The oval cherry conference table appeared huge with just one person sitting there. Pilar Ibanez, vice-president of Sales and Marketing, thumbed through papers. *I-80* had touched her tragically, too—Pilar's husband was one of the customers lost in the company van—making her Paulson's most committed disciple.

Pilar wasn't beautiful—her nose was hooked and her skin

weathered—but she was sexy. An exotic pulse energized her in a way that made men take a second look—and a third. She caught Paulson peering over her shoulder. His expression changed to that of a father checking what his daughter is reading.

"How are things coming with the women?" he asked.

"We just signed our top prospect. She reports tomor—"

The door swung open, and Duane Root marched in with the air of a general. Root, the V.P. of security, shaved his head and dressed in tailor-made suits, presenting an image of absolute control. His exterior was hard, as if coated in clear plastic. Pilar shivered.

"Good morning, Duane," Paulson said. "Pilar says she's hired her first female trainee. How are you coming with the men?"

Root frowned, an expression indistinguishable from his smile. "You can't goad me into rushing. I agreed to support the patriots only if we can insulate ourselves from all illegalities."

Paulson bristled. "And hasn't Eddie done that with SCOPE?"

At the mention of his name, Eduardo Juarez scurried in like a squirrel and sat down, smiling at Pilar. Out of habit, she smiled back. She knew his SCOPE system would revolutionize surveillance, if not the entire computer industry, so there were advantages to being on good terms with its creator.

"Eddie," Paulson said, jerking Juarez out of a daydream. "How's the SCOPE security for *Patriots for Freedom*?"

Juarez spoke in a soft, rapid cadence. "Great. I put the firewall prototype on the Internet with a reward, but no one's cracked it."

"What about the hardware?"

"Two front-end satellites are up. The other two by the end of January. Every part of SCOPE is testing flawlessly."

Paulson smiled. "Good. Let's get started.... Duane?"

Root handed out the morning security brief. To Paulson's disappointment, there were no surprises for tomorrow's front page, so he browsed down to the heading, *War Cabinet*. "Excellent projections for the women, Pilar. I say we hire four."

Root cleared his throat. "Excuse me, Jerry, but remember, there's no track record for a women's program quite like—"

"What?" Paulson barked. "We agreed on this two weeks ago."

"Abstaining and agreeing aren't the same thing."

Pilar saw Paulson's eyebrow jerk—he had blown a fuse; she shared a darting look with Juarez. The boss's dramatic outbursts had become frequent since I-80—the stress was getting to him.

Paulson stood and exaggerated his enunciation. "No? Then let's go over it again, Duane. Correct me if I say anything you don't agree with."

Paulson gestured and paced as his color rose. "I can't expect you to grieve for Norman the way I do, but Bud Green was an invaluable colleague and one of your best friends. After the tragedy, we all felt compelled to do something to stop these bastards." Paulson was on the verge of hyper-ventilating.

Root braced for the usual tirade—about how patriotic Paulson was for using his personal wealth to fund *Patriots for Freedom* in support of the War on Terror. Blah-blah-blah.

But Paulson refrained. He stopped pacing and calmed—a little. "Agreed so far, Duane?"

Root hated being humiliated by irrational outbursts, but he nodded as if they were discussing the Bunker's carpet. Root exchanged a glance with Pilar—encouraging each other to have patience.

Paulson spread his massive hands. "We put together a list of the men who had facilitated the I-Eighty attacks. We agreed that these accessories to mass murder deserved to die, did we not?"

Again, Root nodded. "Yes, but I suggested we turn our SCOPE evidence over to the government." Before he had finished, Root regretted his answer.

Paulson slammed a fist into his palm. "Forgetting the fact that they're way over-extended with new terrorist attacks, if we go to the Feds, they'll never admit to misidentifying the culprits, and we'll have revealed SCOPE's capabilities before we're ready."

Root shrugged. He would have to wait out the eruption.

Paulson became more deliberate. "In reviewing those eighty-five profiles, Pilar noticed eight or nine targets had a weakness for women. And what did you suggest, Pilar?"

Turning red, she answered in her softest voice. "I suggested that alluring women could get closer to these particular men than traditional operatives."

"What was that quote of yours?" Paulson encouraged.

"I said: there's nothing like a sexy woman to make a man let down his guard."

"And what did you say, Duane?"

Root coughed. "I think I said something like: skimpy clothes would be cheaper than sniper rifles and explosives."

"And what does the financial analysis show?"

Root traced a finger down his spreadsheet, although he knew the numbers all too well. "The women's program is projected to operate at sixty-eight percent of the men's."

Paulson spread his palms up. "Those numbers include the training, correct?"

Root resigned himself to the inevitable. "Yes, even though you insisted on training fresh faces for the women because known pros would increase scrutiny."

"It's *imperative*," Paulson said, "for deaths to appear natural—like heart attacks—so there will be no retaliation." He softened, as if aware of his loss of control. "I understand you're skeptical about unknowns getting the job done. But *we* are committed."

Root chose not to quibble with Paulson's choice of pronoun.

Paulson brushed his lapel, appearing calmer. He turned to Pilar. "How are things going with the legitimate programs?" Everyone in the room knew he was pumping $300 million into *Patriots for Freedom* to mollify media who chastised him for not giving generously to charity.

"On schedule," Pilar announced. "*Patriots for Freedom* has launched missions to South America and Africa and will be making large grants to the Peace Corps, Red Cross, and AIDS research."

"Duane, what's the percentage breakdown: charitable to covert?" Paulson asked. The storm was over.

"Eleven-to-one," Root replied. "Better than our ten-to-one target."

"Excellent. Any problems laundering the covert expenses?"

"No. Every penny, squeaky clean," Root said.

"Good. So we're agreed on hiring four women?" Paulson stared at Root, who nodded. "Done," Paulson decreed. "Anything else? If not…"

Paulson couldn't adjourn the meeting fast enough. Juarez darted out of the Bunker to his lab. Root muttered, "Lifo. Last-in, first-out." Paulson and Root watched Pilar stride away seconds later—each making a show of gathering papers. When she was gone, Paulson draped an arm around Root's shoulder. "Duane, I'm sorry I lost my temper. These are trying times for all of us. I know you have reservations about our methods, but this program's important to me, the company, and America.

"Increased terrorism has the government on the defensive, but *we* can do what the government can't. This is what liberty's all about— being free to be patriots when our safety's threatened."

"That's B.S., Jerry. You want revenge and you're willing to risk the company to get it. That's not patriotism, and it won't bring your son back."

"You speak in clichés, Duane. I react from the heart. That's the difference between us."

Root shrugged away from Paulson's grasp. "No. The difference between us is that you're a dreamer, and I'm a realist."

"Another cliché." Paulson chuckled. "But there's one more

difference."

"What's that?" Root asked.

"I own eighty-five percent of the company."

Root said nothing.

"You can always resign if you're not happy. Otherwise, I suggest you work a little harder on *Patriots for Freedom*." Paulson knew how to leverage his security chief's few insecurities. "You know, Duane, you should be more patriotic—*like Pilar*."

Paulson's inflection obligated Root to respond. "Well, Jerry, I think she's obsessing over work since her husband's death, but that doesn't mean she's more—"

"You call it obsessing," Paulson interrupted. "I call it damn noble patriotism."

"I'm worried about her. She's working fourteen-hour days. It's pretty obvious she's filling a personal void with work. She's burning out. She's more agitated, more intense, more unbalanced."

Paulson delivered his next line with masterful timing. "And more of a threat to you?"

Root's face hardened.

Paulson picked up his briefcase. "Grief hasn't made me blind. With Norman gone, you're thinking about the scramble for power. You're the logical choice to succeed me now, but with Pilar working so hard—and so effectively—you're looking over your shoulder."

Root reddened. "I think she's losing it. Look at the fire in her eyes. That's not normal."

"You might benefit from a little more fire, Duane."

"We all need *less* fire. With no outside board, we're not accountable to anyone but ourselves. Without accountability, even good men are doomed to fail."

Paulson slapped Root's back. "You'll keep us from failing. That's your job, and there's nobody better."

"Then reconsider," Root said. "*Eighteen Ninety-Eight* isn't a worldwide force like Islamic fundamentalism. It's not even a movement like Basque separatists. It's one family and a few—"

"I don't care if they're two rodeo clowns who want longer coffee breaks! They murdered my son and four hundred sixty other fine Americans. The government may not rank these bastards with Al Qaeda, but they will know this: *kill my son, and you mess with me*."

As soon as she exited the Bunker, Pilar hurried to the elevator. She had to keep moving; she had to keep doing. If she stopped pushing herself, she would think about her husband, and emptiness would expand from a pocket behind her navel to a cavern in her chest. She punched the third floor button and looked at her reflection in the mirrored side-wall of the elevator. Minimal make-up, a short bob, conservative suit—the appearance tempered sexuality so she could earn respect. Oh, she still turned heads, but she hadn't resorted to flashy clothes since her college days at Boston University. Then, she had been a Pan-American success story. Those days seemed long ago to the driven executive who exited the elevator.

Striding down the hall to her office, Pilar thought about breaks. Her husband's death had been a bad one—a horrible one. She would have to look to the future by herself. With Paulson's son gone, the next CEO would likely be Root, but...

As she slid into her desk chair, Pilar thought that *Patriots for Freedom* could be a good break. Root was still more powerful than she, but his coolness toward Jerry's pet project worked to her advantage. Paulson was obsessed with the assassins, so if she could turn the female program into a success, she could replace Root as number two.

Pilar buzzed her assistant. "Order my usual for dinner at seven-thirty. I'll be working late tonight."

4

CAROLE BURNS

One week later, Cynthia James exited a taxi in Stone Harbor and carried her suitcase up a curved driveway, pebbles crunching underfoot. Toward the ocean she saw sand dunes, topped with tufts of grass that resembled heads of a Mohawk war party. She checked that the yellow bungalow was indeed number seven before waving away the cab. She straightened her shoulders and knocked three times. The door creaked open before she exhaled.

"Hi, Cynthia! I'm Carole Burns." Carole spoke in a Texas drawl with a smoker's rasp. She was taller than Cynthia and ten years older, but no heavier. Her gritty face was creased like an old road map, yet the blue eyes were friendly. Carole sized up her new charge the way a horse-player handicaps a thoroughbred. "Take off your coat and turn around." Cynthia did as she was told, self-consciously pirouetting in jeans and a pullover sweater. Carole noted that Cynthia was more athletic than voluptuous, with excellent posture. After two revolutions, Carole nodded. "Marco was right: you look better than your picture. I think he picked a winner."

Cynthia's fellow patriot gave a tour of the compound—five acres of ocean-front property bordered with a snow fence and guarded by two terriers, Tumble and Weed. Carole unchained the dogs after introducing them to the new resident. Both dogs reveled in Cynthia's touch, having no interest in what she looked like, which helped Cynthia feel at home.

In addition to the Cape Cod bungalow where Cynthia would be staying with Carole, there was a rambling, five-bedroom Victorian, which they didn't enter because of termite treatments, and a four-car garage/carriage house, which they did. The ground floor of the garage was half gymnasium and half dance studio. Carole flicked on a single light in the corner. The windows were shuttered, which gave the large area the look of a cave. Cynthia scrutinized her reflection in the floor-to-ceiling mirror on the wall with a ballet bar. She looked timid, like a girl on her first day of high school.

Upstairs was a dormitory with six beds, a TV room with a ping-pong table, and two bathrooms. Carole remarked that additional personnel would be arriving soon to stay in the big house and dorm.

After the tour and some paperwork, the first evening was all about rules. Carole and Cynthia sat in the bungalow's small living room furnished with wicker straight from the 1950s. Although the windows were closed, Cynthia smelled salt everywhere.

"My most important rules are the Big Three of Two," Carole said. Cynthia furrowed her brow, and Carole explained. "Rule number one: always have two lethal weapons. Number two: always have two avenues of escape. Number three: always have two backups and know where they are."

"I wouldn't have thought something *against* so many rules would *have* so many rules."

"That's just the tip of the iceberg." Carole plowed on. "Ankles and wrists get taped for all physical activity. You can't afford a sprained ankle if you have to strut your stuff in high heels. I'll teach you the what, when, and why of everything you wear. If you think you're in good shape now, wait 'til I put you through the conditioning program. There'll be acting lessons, of course. And you'll need ballet for grace and balance."

Cynthia smiled because Carole didn't seem the ballet type. "Are you gonna give me Miss America tips on things like how to tape my butt to a bathing suit?"

Carole laughed. "You keep that sense of humor, 'cause when things get tough, the tough get things."

That made no sense, but Cynthia smiled anyway.

Things got tough the following morning. The workday started before dawn with Cynthia wrestling a rubbery octopus that turned out to be a wetsuit Carole tossed onto her bed. After ankle-taping and a two-mile run on the beach, they zipped themselves into wetsuits for a swim in the frigid ocean—all before breakfast.

Carole kept drilling rules into Cynthia's head through morning aerobics, lunch, weight-training, and a massage, then switched gears for a yoga session aimed at flexibility and concentration. By evening, Cynthia was dragging, but the day wasn't over.

While they prepared dinner in the galley kitchen, Carole talked about poison. "I guarantee your first job'll involve poison. In this line of work, you have your body, your clothes and accessories—

sometimes." Carole grinned. "And whatever you can conceal and carry while you're dressed to kill. Pun *intended*. Poisons are small and light; they can be carried in tiny vials—liquids, pills, and powders you can conceal *anywhere*, if you catch my drift." Cynthia nodded as Carole continued. "Sometimes, you'll need access to an antidote, just in case."

"Sometimes?"

"Some poisons don't have antidotes."

"That's comforting," Cynthia mused.

"The ones with no antidotes are the most deadly. Remember, we're out to kill the bastards, not make 'em sick."

And so it went until bedtime. Cynthia crashed at ten, but Carole stayed up to study the contents of a FedEx mailer.

At breakfast next morning, Carole announced, "I've got the specs for your first job. It'll be in Seville."

"An assignment so soon? I haven't even—"

"When cattle need branding, you gotta heat the iron."

"What?"

"Time's a wasting," Carole said. "Now that I know what you need, we'll go shopping, and I'll fill you in."

Cynthia was a step behind. "Shopping?"

"Now that we know what your mark likes, we can dress you to kill."

"Pun intended," Cynthia said.

During the drive to the mall, Carole lectured. "The mark's Alejandro Cabrera. He helped plan the I-Eighty operation. He thinks he's Don Juan, reincarnated, which is why he was assigned to our team. He's a runner; you're a runner."

"How will I meet up with him and...?" Cynthia's voice trailed off.

"And kill him?" Carole finished. "Our people in Spain will work out the choreography. Right now, I can tell you that you'll use a poison delivery system hidden underneath hinged fingernails. You'll dig your nails into his skin so that tiny needles give him two injections, one from the middle finger of each hand."

"You're kidding, right?"

"It may sound crazy, but the nails work. Trust me. The CIA's been using this system for years."

Cynthia forced a laugh. "With needles under fingernails, I'll bet they lose a lot of agents sticking themselves."

"It's only deadly with both injections. You'd have to stick yourself with two needles. That way it's harder to poison yourself."

"Harder?" Cynthia huffed.

"Yeah. This poison's got no antidote."

"That's comforting. And the backup weapon?"

"A collapsible hairpin—almost the same as what you're wearing—that, when released, becomes an eight-inch stiletto. We'll go over the weapons tomorrow." Carole pulled to a stop in the mall parking lot. "It'll take a while for you to become proficient with the nails and blade."

Cynthia frowned, but Carole smiled. "Cheer up, Cynthia. We've got an expense-account shopping spree ahead of us. You'll be fine."

Cynthia was glad her mentor was confident, but Carole wasn't going to be the one with deadly poison under her fingernails.

Shopping for her Spanish wardrobe took Cynthia's mind off the difficulties ahead. Carole insisted on solids only so Cynthia could mix and match everything. Over the next few hours, Carole selected pants, tops, skirts, shorts, dresses, running clothes, and shoes for the job; Cynthia chose her everyday clothing—mostly black.

"Next stop," Carole said. "Victoria's Secret."

Cynthia flashed an "I don't think so" look, to which Carole replied, "You need a few push-up bras in your arsenal. They make a simple Miracle Bra that'll enhance what you've got. Macho guys love the look almost as much as they love zippers. One black and one white should do it." Cynthia shrugged and followed along.

"One more stop—for swimsuits. Bikinis," Carole said after they exited Victoria's Secret. "What colors do you want?"

Cynthia smirked. "Red, white, and blue, of course."

During the bathing suit fitting, Carole marveled at Cynthia's abdomen, which maintained a navel-screwed-to-the-spine taper, even when relaxed. *Oh, to be ten years younger.*

After reviewing the Cabrera file that afternoon, they drove to a North Wildwood bar for a late supper. Carole told Cynthia to wear snug jeans and brand new four-inch heels.

Cynthia wobbled in the parking lot. "I've never worn shoes like this before…and I hope to God I never have to again."

Carole chuckled. "Gotta get used to 'em 'cause some men go ga-ga over compressed calves. If a job calls for you to dress like a bimbo, I don't want you falling smack on your kisser."

Cynthia rocked her hips to one side and pantomimed a chaw of Bubblicious. "For the true bimbo look, shouldn't I be chewing gum, too?"

"The way you're walking, you're not ready to add gum."

Cynthia laughed at herself, and it felt good. "Okay. Give me a minute." She paced back and forth in the lot until she turned smoothly three times in a row. "I'm ready." She stumbled going in the front door but steadied herself. "Loose floorboard," she muttered. Carole laughed.

Despite the footwear, Cynthia enjoyed unwinding with a beer. But there was more to the nighttime session than high-heel practice.

At a booth in the smoky tavern, halfway through the second Coors Light, Carole said, "Tonight, we're gonna work on your smile. You got a sexy smile; you need to use it more." Cynthia flashed a plastic grin, and Carole frowned. "Get serious. I don't mean a painted-on Suzy Homemaker. That wouldn't be you. I mean a cool, challenging smile that says to a man, 'I might be interested, if you show me you're worth my time.' Go for a...taunting look."

Cynthia smiled.

"Better," Carole said. "Think of it as acting. Let's see, we're at a bar...There are guys on the prowl...There's a pool table... Do you play?" Cynthia nodded. "Then let's shoot some pool."

Mugs in hand, they approached the pool table, Cynthia leading. Shifting weight onto one leg, she said, "Do you boys let girls play at your table?" Both men scrambled to welcome Cynthia to their world.

"Ever played before?" said the taller of the two men. He handed Cynthia a pool cue and set her mug aside.

"Let's just say I know how to handle a stick," Cynthia replied, sliding the cue slowly between her fingers. Carole smirked.

The tall man twirled his moustache. "What say you and me team up? I'm Ted. Rack 'em, Freddie. I'll break. How about a dollar a game? What's your name, honey?"

"It's Cynthia, not honey."

"Well. Let's shoot some pool, Cindy."

After three sloppy games of Eight Ball, it was clear that Cynthia was a distraction, causing both men to miss shots they bragged they could make in their sleep. Carole, who *really* knew how to handle a cue, carried Freddie to victory in both games.

As the ladies headed back to their booth, Ted followed. Looking over her shoulder, Cynthia shook her head. "Work on your form, Ted, and maybe we'll play again sometime."

Once they were clear of the men, Carole chuckled. "I'd say you know how to use a taunting smile...and you owe me two bucks."

Cynthia left the tip. They put on their coats and found Ted lingering near the pay phone. "Leaving so soon?" he asked. Cynthia shrugged, a gesture Ted read as an invitation.

Exiting into the cold night, he saw that Carole walked to the driver's door of a Honda. "Hey, Cindy, can I give you a lift? Maybe your friend doesn't want to go out of her way, but I'm going wherever you're going."

Cynthia rolled her eyes then walked to her mentor's side of the car. "How do you want me to play this?" she whispered.

"Your call."

Cynthia hesitated. "No thanks, Ted. I've got a really early class tomorrow."

Ted moved closer. "I'm a pretty good teacher."

Cynthia shook her head in disbelief. "I'll bite. What do you teach?"

"The art of love," he said, taking her hand.

"You've got three seconds to let go, or I'll put my elbow through your throat. One…two…" Her icy stare and rising arm caused Ted to back off at "two."

"And my name's *Cynthia*, not Cindy."

The women climbed into Carole's Honda. "So, Cyn, would you have done it?"

"I told him to bug off, didn't I?"

"No, I mean would you have put your elbow through his throat?"

"I was ready to fight."

"Why?"

"Truthfully? Because I thought Ted was a plant—part of the training. Why else would you say I could leave with an asshole like that?"

"He was just who he seemed—a wolf on the prowl. We need to hit another place. I saw you nursing your beer; you still got some unwinding to do."

They stopped at a bar with no pool table but less smoke. While Carole listened to Willie Nelson songs on the juke box, they drank three beers before Cynthia's conversation fizzled during *On the Road Again*. Carole drove home.

At breakfast the next morning, Cynthia learned that while Ted may not have been part of the training, the beer was.

"You held your alcohol pretty well," Carole said, pouring oat bran. "You started losing motor control after two beers, and your mind got sluggish after three. What that means is that while on the job, you should never have more than one beer or glass of wine, and not more than half a drink of hard stuff. It's important to know your limits." Carole noted Cynthia's pout. "What's the matter?"

"Oh, I'd hoped the second bar was for fun."

Carole punched her pupil's shoulder. "It *was* fun, Cyn, but you have to remember that this is dangerous shit. It's a good thing I like you—more incentive to keep you alive."

That night, after dinner, Cynthia applied false fingernails for the first time—all ten had to be long so the middle nails didn't look out of place.

"Jeez. How do women wear these damn things?" Cynthia said. "They're worse than the heels."

The special nails were activated by sliding a thumbnail into a tiny groove of the hinged cuticle until it clicked. Once activated, pressure on the finger-side of the nail caused the spring hinge to open, exposing the tip of the needle. The tiny syringe was pressure-activated, ejecting liquid only when the hinge was open and the tip met resistance. When pressure was removed, the needle retracted and the nail snapped in place.

"How long does the poison take?" Cynthia asked.

"It'll start to disable nerve impulses in fifteen to twenty seconds. His heart'll seize and stop within thirty. He'll be dead in forty-five—unless you stick yourself first by mistake." Cynthia had no reaction. Carole teased, "That's a joke. Have to keep some levity or this grind'll kill you."

Cynthia stared at her nails, which belonged on a hooker. Her stomach churned; she shook her hands. "Do women like me ever have doubts?"

"Always."

"Do they ever quit?"

"Sometimes. What's on your mind?"

Cynthia tapped her nails on a tabletop. "Maybe I'm not cut out for this."

"I think you are. If you're having second thoughts, wait a few days. If you feel the same way, wait a few more. Don't make a snap decision." Carole picked up an audio cassette from the counter and flipped it to Cynthia. "Meanwhile, memorize this."

Cynthia caught the tape and examined the hand-written label: Bird Calls of Southern Spain. She fell asleep listening to soothing tweets, twitters, and cheep-cheep-cheeps.

5

ROAD TRIP

The next afternoon, Carole took Cynthia on a photo-shoot. In the musty basement of an A-frame cabin on the outskirts of Vineland, a dwarf with oily skin took head shots of Cynthia in numerous hair styles and a variety of wigs. He was a master forger who would create an assortment of false IDs.

After late supper at a diner, the women headed home in a heavy fog. Carole lost her way in the piney woods of Belleplain State Forest.

Pulling onto the shoulder of a dirt road that proved to be no shortcut, Carole banged the dashboard. "Damn! I'm lost. Can you believe it?"

Cynthia chose to treat the question as rhetorical.

Carole cursed again. "This fog is wicked. I'll have to pay more attention to the map. You drive."

"Me?"

Carole scowled. "You *can* drive a car, can't you?"

"But you know the area."

"And I got us lost. I'll navigate, and you'll turn when I tell you, okay?... What are you waiting for?" With a shrug, Cynthia got out of the car. As she walked around the rear bumper, rubbing her hands against the cold, Carole yelled, "Curfew's at eleven!"

Cynthia jumped back as the wheels kicked gravel against her legs. "Very funny," Cynthia shouted, expecting Carole to stop after a few seconds. But Carole kept accelerating, the Honda's lights disappearing in darkness.

Cynthia's insides twisted. If this was a test, she hadn't studied. It was freezing, and all she had on was a black turtleneck, jeans, and Reeboks. Her coat and purse were in the car. She hugged her upper arms and released a series of expletives that were absorbed in the total blackness.

Try to think of it as a game, she told herself—get home by eleven. Pressing the light button on her Casio, she saw it was 9:05. Her fingertips were already numb. The way the temperature was dropping, she'd freeze before curfew.

Walking blindly down the road, she stumbled into the brush. She needed a system. Locating the shoulder with her foot, she shuffled down the edge of the road in the direction that Carole had driven. By sliding her foot to keep contact with the shoulder, she could move at a slow walk. Maybe Carole had killed the lights and was waiting a few hundred yards up the road.

A quarter-mile later, there was no sign of anything but black and more black. Cynthia was resigned she was on her own. Cursing Carole, she kept moving.

Then it started to snow.

She quickened her pace. Five minutes passed before she felt something different underfoot. Blacktop at ninety degrees.

Which way? Guessing they'd been traveling east when Carole ditched her, Cynthia turned right, hoping it was south. Her gait was a cross between a trot and an Igor-like drag. She tucked her numbed fingers under her armpits and shivered.

Her vision should have grown accustomed to the dark, but she still saw nothing, not even the snowflakes that stung her eyes. The only hope was a passing car, but at this hour, on this road...

After two minutes on macadam, Cynthia saw something move. She straightened, froze, and stared. Then something else moved; then a pattern of motion. The falling flakes reflected a light source she couldn't identify. Then she saw a faint glow in the distance. The light was small and fuzzy...Now it separated into two lights, each with a halo—twin moons on a starry night. They were getting bigger, illuminating hundreds, then thousands, of snowflakes.

She had to stop that car. No, she had to get *into* that car. In seconds it would whoosh past. *If only the driver was male.* But even if it were a man, she was all in black, not a reassuring picture. The feeling was gone from her fingers—or were they stumps? She reached up and knocked—more than pulled—out the clip, spilling hair down her back. Then she clawed at the bottom of her sweater.

The driver leaned forward and squinted through the swirling snow. Did he see what he thought he saw, or were the beers playing tricks on him? He slowed his pickup, just in case this was his lucky night.

"Holy shit!" he gawked.

Damned if there wasn't a woman standing in the middle of the road, waving a black flag. And not just any woman, but a long-haired honey wearing nothing above her waist but a bra. He stomped on the breaks, skidding to a stop.

"Help me!" Cynthia cried after he rolled down his window. "Let me in. There's someone chasing me. Please!"

She scampered around to the passenger side without waiting for a response and pawed at the handle with frozen hands. Deliverance—the door was unlocked! She exhaled and hopped in. The interior was toasty; she let the air thaw her icy skin as she draped the sweater in front of a heat vent.

She took a look at her savior—a stereotypical Joe Honky-tonk, with beard, baseball cap, and flannel shirt. He was looking at her sheer cotton bra—more specifically at what the frigid air had done to her nipples.

"Go! Go!" she urged through chattering teeth. From the way the guy was staring, he would drive off a cliff if she asked.

A pair of headlights appeared a hundred yards ahead. "That must be who's chasing you. Hold on!" He shoved the gearshift into first and peeled out. As they blew by the oncoming car, Cynthia saw the driver. It was Carole.

"I'm Carl. Where to, honey?"

"My name's Cynthia. Thanks for stopping. I really need a ride to Stone Harbor." She looked behind to see the Honda turning around. "Uh-oh. We've got company."

He glanced in the rearview mirror then took a third look at her bra. "I'd like to help you, but Stone Harbor's way out of my way."

The corners of Cynthia's mouth curled up, despite her chill. "I'll pay you a hundred dollars if you get me to my house by eleven, with a fifty dollar bonus if you beat that car."

"Beggin' your pardon, honey, but where you got a hundred bucks hidden? I don't see a wallet in those painted-on jeans."

Cynthia unclasped her belt buckle.

Carl stared; the truck swerved. Straightening the wheel, Carl gaped as she wriggled out of her belt.

"Don't stop there, honey."

"Eyes on the road, Carl."

"I'll need to see your money."

She twisted open a secret slit in her belt. "Here's sixty bucks."

"You said a hundred."

"If I'm home by eleven."

He snatched at the bills, but she pulled them away.

Taking another look at her, he said, "I'll settle for a roll in the hay, honey."

"In your dreams. The show's over. You'll settle for a hundred." She pulled on her sweater.

"Hey, what'd you have to go and do that for, honey?"

"If you called me Cynthia instead of honey, I'd have let you look all the way to Stone Harbor. Now just stay ahead of that car." She blew on her burning fingers.

"I could stop and let you out right here."

In other circumstances, she would have complied. Air-freshener wouldn't stand a chance against the stench of cigarettes and beer. But her competitive juices were flowing. She glanced around the shabby cab—frayed everything. He'd do it for the hundred. "Drive. That's the only way to get your hundred bucks."

He moved his right hand toward her thigh. "I can help warm you up while we go."

She slapped his hand, stinging her fingertips. "And I'm a black belt in karate...Carl."

"Okay, we'll do it your way." A moment later, he said, "Who's the asshole chasing you?"

"My roommate. She's a real country gal pisser."

He pushed "Play." A George Jones Greatest Hits CD blasted from the speakers. "I ain't never been beat driving to good ole George."

For the next hour, Carl skidded through corners and sped down straights, pulling away from Carole's chase car. Warming, Cynthia anticipated the thrill of victory.

The pickup stopped in the empty driveway at 10:56.

"Want to come in for some coffee and the rest of your fee?" Cynthia said, handing Carl three twenties.

Carl didn't wait for her to change her mind and followed her footprints up the snow-dusted steps. Cynthia used a key hidden in a light housing to unlock the bungalow. "I'll fix some coffee."

Five minutes later, Carole drove up and parked next to the pickup.

"You're late," Cynthia said when Carole came through the door at 11:02. "Carole, meet Carl, my driver. You owe him a hundred and fifty bucks."

Carl shook his head. "But she already gave me—"

Cynthia jabbed an elbow into his ribs. "I *gave* him bad directions, but he still made it on time. Carole, get the man his money. Without him, I would have missed curfew, so he deserves a big tip, don't you think?"

Carole said nothing as she counted eight twenties and a ten into Carl's sweaty palm. After coffee and a one-man debate on whether George Jones or Hank Williams was greater, Carl visited the bathroom before hitting the road.

"Sorry about that," Carole whispered, "I need to find out early if a girl can keep her wits, especially if she's having doubts. Don't get a swelled head, but nobody's ever beaten me back.

"I was following you with night-vision goggles. When I saw you moving on the main road, I went to where I stashed the car. I was about to get in and pick you up when he came out of nowhere and beat me to it. Damnedest thing."

A smile crept onto Cynthia's lips.

Carole noticed. "Doing a good job feels great, doesn't it?"

Cynthia nodded.

"It'll be like that when you take out murdering scum...only a hundred times better."

Carl exited the bathroom looking nothing like a terrorist.

Cynthia walked him to his pick-up. The snow had stopped. "Thanks for gettin' me a *really* big tip," he said. "Um, you two gals are gay, aren't you?"

Cynthia hesitated. "Ah, yup. Saw right through me. So thanks for the ride." She kissed his cheek.

Carl cranked up George Jones and smiled all the way home.

6

THE AITIES

The next morning, Carole didn't dwell on the wilderness adventure. "We got new folks coming in today."

"How many?" Cynthia asked. "And who?"

"Three Aities."

"Eighties?"

"Yeah, Aities. You're an Aitie. For A-I-T—assassin-in-training—and for I-Eighty."

New personnel arrived in a van at noon. Luncheon introductions were cordial. Carole gave a brief bio of each woman while Cynthia observed her sister Aities, who were each within two years of her age.

Joanie Lee, a well-endowed beach-baby with muscles, spewed jokes in assorted accents, making herself the center of attention from the first toss of the most luxurious blonde hair Cynthia had ever seen. Joanie volunteered her motivation—a brother-in-law died on Route 80 near Cleveland—and she bragged about her expertise in electronics. Cynthia distrusted Joanie and began constructing defenses against her dominating personality.

Charisse White had the most violent history of the Aities. She had been a Los Angeles drug lord's queen, involved in gangland wars for much of her life, some of which had passed in jail. She was still a striking woman with supermodel cheekbones and incredible legs that stretched to her ribcage. Cynthia vowed not to be intimidated by Charisse.

At 5'5", Maria Lopez lacked Charisse's height and Joanie's strength but exuded personality. She slid from fiery Latina to innocent waif as easily as shifting from first to second gear. Carole said that Maria was a makeup wizard and champion gymnast, but Maria diverted conversation away from herself. Her most distinctive features were shadowed eyes that welcomed Cynthia as if she could see Cynthia's skeletons...and accept them. From the first moment, Cynthia and Maria clicked.

Joanie, Charisse, and Maria moved into the large house, chaperoned by Carole's assistant, Jo Bennet, a stout woman in her thirties whom Joanie christened the Closet Nazi. Cynthia would be the first assassin in the field, so she required the most intense training, which included skull sessions with Carole four nights a week. One of the other Aities would move into the bungalow when Cynthia left for Spain.

Carole had named the three-story house Odessa after her home town in Texas, but Joanie called it the Bates Motel because of a spooky turret. A covered porch with rocking chairs sprawled around three sides. On the back, a planked deck abutted a narrow, raised boardwalk to the beach.

The dining room was formal with a huge table, an ornate chandelier better suited to an opera house, and fancy high-backed chairs that Carole identified with some king's name and number. She convened team meetings in Odessa's more comfortable living room, where she began the afternoon session. "Ladies, there's nothing glamorous about hard work. For every hour we spend on appearance and seduction, we'll spend twenty on self-defense, weapons, covert techniques, conditioning, and mental discipline."

Cynthia was glad the coffee table was worn—her feet were not the first to rest on its surface. She glanced at her colleagues. Each was, like herself, dressed in exercise clothes, ankles and wrists taped, hair pulled back, wearing no make-up. Carole was right; there was no glamour.

"We'll make sure you clean up nice and stay feminine because your looking like body-builders won't help us. You have to look non-threatening." Carole glanced at Joanie, who stuck out her tongue.

"Will we get to choose our own clothes?" Joanie asked.

"Sure. As long as they're the same outfits I pick out. I'll dress you all the way from custom body stockings—to keep your DNA to yourself—to poison earrings in case you need to commit suicide. Any more questions, Joanielee?"

There were no more questions, not even from the brassy blonde, so Carole ran them through a vigorous aerobic workout followed by weight training, ninety minutes of yoga, and a written quiz.

That night, Carole left the four Aities to bond. Cynthia felt awkward with Joanie and Charisse, but everyone warmed to Maria, who had a way of making others think things were their idea. It was

Maria who got them talking.

Joanie required the least prodding. She was an army brat who had lived all over the world, mastering languages as easily as tying her shoes. She was a magician with a deck of cards. On the practical side, she was a telephone/electronics expert who bragged of tapping phones and being a cat burglar. Cynthia believed it. Joanie's most recent employment had been as a telephone field technician in Lexington, Virginia. Borderline hyperactive, she had never held a job longer than a year. Joanie was a natural mimic who could imitate the voice of everyone in the compound after one day.

Charisse, direct from a Los Angeles half-way house, was mysterious, with questionable motivation—she didn't have a loved one killed by terrorists—and a chip on her shoulder the size of California. She sulked through much of the first day, yet during the aerobics workout, she blitzed the others with unmatched fury. Cynthia guessed Charisse was the smartest—she answered every question on the quiz correctly in half the time as the others. "Tell me once then leave me the fuck alone," Charisse told Carole. Over the next few months, she would say it at least twice a day.

Maria, from California via New York, had been a starving actress before becoming a makeup artist in Hollywood, but she revealed little else, content to orchestrate the conversation.

After Joanie and Charisse went to bed, Cynthia flipped a pillow at Maria. "You're pretty clever. You got us spilling our guts, but you kept quiet."

Maria beamed. "You learn a helluva lot more by listening."

"How come you didn't ask me the questions you asked the others?"

"I didn't think you were ready to open up—at least not to everyone."

Cynthia had an eerie feeling that Maria could read her mind. "It's my turn to listen," Cynthia said. "Why did *you* join the patriots? You seem too artistic for violence."

Maria's light dimmed as if shades had been pulled over her eyes. "I lost both my fiancé, Joe, and father on Route Eighty—in California. I want to strike back." She flushed. "I need to strike back."

Cynthia almost said she was "so very sorry"—and she was. Instead, she stroked Maria's hand, touching something deeper. Maria brightened. Cynthia felt the spark of an electric circuit connecting; she blinked, as if waking from a dream.

Maria broke the silence. "I must not seem so tough. Sometimes I wonder if I was meant to... But then I think about Joe and Dad, and I know this is right." She slouched. "Whoever heard of a makeup-artist hit-woman, huh? Well, beyond the double-whammy from I-Eighty, I once beat the shit out of a guy who date-raped me. And I was state champion on the uneven bars. At least those are the reasons Marco gave." Twisting her neck, Maria said, "Man, I'm sore from today's workout. You?"

"Want a massage?"

Maria hesitated. "Okay."

"I have a policy," Cynthia said, placing her hands on Maria's shoulders. "I give a backrub to anyone who beats the shit out of a rapist."

"You're making that up, but your hands feel nice." Maria lay face down on the couch while Cynthia massaged aching muscles. "So now you know my sad story," Maria said. "What about you?"

Cynthia deepened the massage. "We seem to have common themes. My brother died on I-Eighty in Parsippany. And when I was seventeen, my stepfather raped me and my mother. I whacked him in the head, and he died. I went ten years without letting a man...you know. I have a boyfriend now—Thomas—but I still... I think the patriots might give me a positive outlet."

Maria mumbled into the cushion. "Lower...there... Mmmmm, that feels good. I *love* what you're doing to me."

Cynthia eased her hands off Maria's back.

"Don't stop."

Cynthia hesitated. "I'm not..."

Maria sat up. "You're just giving me a backrub, that's all."

Cynthia was surprised that she didn't reposition herself farther away from Maria's knee, less than an inch from her own.

"Are you okay?" Maria asked.

"I thought, you know, about touching—about you liking it—and it made me feel kinda strange. I've never..."

Maria smiled. "Ten years without a man, and you never...?"

Cynthia shook her head.

"So, for ten years, your only sex was solitaire?"

Cynthia was astonished at Maria's openness—and at her own answering nod.

"So don't you see the irony? Maria brushed Cynthia's hand. "You think it's strange to be touched by a woman, yet when you go solo, it's a woman's hand that does the touching."

Cynthia flushed. "It's only a substitute for a man."

"Then here's to substitutes," Maria said, picking up her glass, "...when we need them." After drinking, Maria added, "By the way, I can help you with your make-up."

Cynthia scrunched her nose. "I'm from the less is more school."

Maria laughed. "You mean the *none is all* school. Come on; I'll show you."

A minute later, they were in Maria's room. Based on what had just happened—or almost happened—Cynthia shouldn't have agreed, but here she was, scrutinizing a series of black-and-white head shots of Maria.

"So which look do you like?" Maria whispered.

"Hmmm...This one."

"Shhh." Maria pointed toward the wall—Joanie's room.

"Sorry," Cynthia whispered. She pointed to the picture with the least eye makeup.

Both women kept their voices soft as Maria worked.

"So why all the photos?" Cynthia asked.

"I'm a makeup artist who wants to be an actress. And I like to experiment—to make myself look better. You could say vanity is my weakness.... Hold still."

Cynthia studied both faces in the mirror. Her opinion of Maria's beauty was best left un-thought. Her eyes panned Maria's room. It was tidier than her own. The wall decorations were movie star posters—Clark Gable, Gary Cooper, Marilyn Monroe, and Katherine Hepburn.

"Ask me a question," Maria said. "Whatever's on your mind."

"Tell me about J— Oh, I'm sorry."

"It's okay." Maria smiled. "Joe was a great guy—very smart. That's what floats my boat. Good looks are temporary; a great mind turns you on for a lifetime."

Aware of her limited education, Cynthia sensed a confusing drop in her stomach.

Maria added a last stroke of mascara. "There. Take a look."

Cynthia stared at her face in Maria's mirror. The changes were subtle, yet effective. Her eyes radiated a touch of mystery. "You're a magician, Ree."

"All I did was dot a few eyes."

* * *

The next evening after dinner, Carole Burns told Cynthia to sit in a wicker chair. "We have to talk about sexual arousal."

Cynthia's pulse quickened. She thought about the night before. "What kind of place is this?"

"The kind where sex counts. According to your file, you had a major trauma followed by a long dry spell. Am I right?"

Cynthia picked up a ship in a bottle from the coffee table. "I have a boyfriend now."

"And how's the sex?"

"Good," Cynthia lied.

"But you *like* him. What if you had to sleep with a man you didn't like?"

"I won't have to do that, will I?"

Carole looked smug. "Getting turned on is part of being sexy, even if you don't go all the way. Arousal is physical, and you can't always fake it. Experienced men can tell—some can smell it."

"So?"

"So, can you get aroused by a man you hate?"

Cynthia thought about nights with Thomas and shook her head.

"We can help. Here's a sex stimulant." Carole tossed Cynthia a bottle of pills. "We call it X-eighty. It'll warm you up."

And so began research to determine how much X-80 Cynthia should take and how far in advance. She found that fifty milligrams and thirty minutes were optimal, giving her a sense of queasy pleasure, as if she wet her pants.

Combat training started with basics. In the first self-defense session, Carole said to Cynthia, "Grab my wrist with both hands as tight as you can. Got me? Sure?" Then she added, "I don't think so." Carole removed her wrist with such ease that Cynthia was embarrassed. "That's what knowledge of the muscles and joints can do. In breaking hand holds, always pull toward the thumbs. You try it." With minor exertion, Cynthia broke the hold. From then on, she listened closely to everything Carole said about the physiology of fighting.

Alternate afternoons were spent in self-defense sessions. Cynthia learned to use agility and leverage to counter a stronger opponent. In addition to joint-locking Jiu-Jitsu moves, she learned to execute a hard knee to the groin and eye gouges. Cynthia was good, but Charisse was better, warding off attacks as if she had four arms and four legs. Joanie, mimicking Carole's drawl, labeled Charisse, "that dang Octopus."

During combat practice in the gymnasium, the Aities wore more protection than ankle and wrist wraps. Fully loaded, they looked like football players. At first, they complained about the padding, but as bodies were banged around, the Aities were thankful.

Weapons training went beyond the use of poisons. The Aities learned to make fatal thrusts with blades concealed in sunglasses, boots, and hairclips. Maria, quick and precise, was the best with knives, earning the nickname "the Spanish Chef," which Joanie broadcast in a shrill Julia Child impression. With handguns, Joanie recorded the highest range scores, while Cynthia was the best at placing two quick shots from the draw. Doing a fair Paul Newman, Joanie called Cynthia, "The Sundance Kid."

Maria asked Carole, "If we're supposed to seduce and poison the marks, why all the training with guns and knives?"

"Sometimes," Carole said, "things don't go according to plan."

After a few weeks, the routine settled into boredom. It wasn't the training Cynthia found boring, but the life. The day-to-day existence—isolated in a winter seashore hamlet—was duller than cold sand. While Cynthia had no place about which to feel homesick, she was trapped intellectually. There was a degree of brainwashing inherent in training to kill, and that depressed her, too. But every time she thought about hitching a ride to the Parkway, Maria cheered her up, as if she knew what Cynthia was thinking. "Tell me about the book you're reading," Maria would say. Or she'd ask, "Where do you want to be in three years?" They talked about things that convinced Cynthia she was still a cognizant human being—she realized it wasn't Sam that kept her in the training compound. It was Maria, who understood Cynthia as if they were blood-sisters.

So the training went on—both in masculine combat and feminine wiles.

On overall allure, Cynthia rated Maria highest. Ree started with the prettiest features, but her charm went beyond the surface. Through the grace of a gymnast, the vocabulary of an English major, and facial expressions of a comedienne, she was irresistible.

Joanie was sexy but obvious, requiring constant reminders about finesse.

Charisse struck Cynthia as stubborn and aloof.

On the combat side, Joanie attacked quick and hard. When impatience led to mistakes, Carole suggested Joanie perform the exercises more like Cynthia. Joanie would then mimic Cynthia down to the grunts, but she never made the same mistake twice. Where Joanie relied on muscle, Charisse used her head, applying technique and leverage in place of brute strength. In a random fight, Cynthia would put her money on Charisse. Maria worked like a sled dog, but wasn't mean enough to be a pit bull.

Any fleeting notions that the compound was no more than a self-defense spa ended the day Carole first covered weaknesses of the head and neck, including the locations and angles for blows most likely to kill. This went way beyond self-defense. Since the neck was the body's weak point, Carole taught strangulation in detail with wires, ropes, cords, and clothing. At first, Cynthia couldn't bring herself to choke hard enough on the mannequin. On the first day of practice with "real" victims, she was tentative, but by the second day, she was more aggressive. On the third day, Cynthia earned a nickname that stuck.

"Do it again," Carole commanded, glaring at Greg Marks—one of the four male trainers who lived in the garage dorm—after he had been "killed" by Cynthia three times in a row. They took their positions, but Greg lunged at Cynthia a split-second before Carole shouted, "Go!"

Side-stepping, Cynthia kneed him in the crotch. Before Greg could recover, she wrapped her belt around his neck guard, holding it there for the five seconds that defined a kill.

Carole blew the whistle. "Good job, Cyn. Let's do some stretching before we call it a wrap."

Greg rose to his feet while Cynthia coiled her belt then turned away to place it on its shelf. She didn't see his windup. Greg lashed a kick into Cynthia's ribs. Everyone in the gym heard the impact. Cynthia reacted like a wounded animal, whipping her leg as she fell, tripping Greg, who toppled backward. As soon as his head bounced off the mat, Cynthia looped the belt around his neck. He tried to squirm away, but she dragged him. To avoid neck trauma, Greg grabbed the belt, absorbing the torque with his arms. Carole blew the whistle again, but Cynthia kept dragging Greg in the choke. With fire in her eyes, she growled, "He's the one who likes to fight after the whistle."

She released her grip, and Greg lay on his back, helpless, clawing at the belt. Cynthia picked up a pair of handcuffs and snapped them on his wrists. She raised her hands like a calf-roper. "Stop the clock!" Cynthia winced.

"Are you crazy, Cyn?" Carole barked. "Get away from him!" But Carole was glad Cynthia had reacted viciously—it was the mark of a survivor.

Joanie intoned a passable Sean Connery imitation. "The name is Bondage…James Bondage."

From then on, Cynthia James was known as Bond.

7

BUBBLES

On the second Wednesday in April, Carole arranged a field trip to an Atlantic City dance club. After dinner, Carole laid out what Cynthia was to wear: black cocktail dress, gold earrings with matching necklace and bracelet, high heels, pantyhose, and Miracle Bra. Dressed, she saw a different person in the mirror—statuesque and, with Maria's make-up, mysterious. Cynthia told herself that the woman in the mirror really *was* a new person. If she *looked* dangerous, she could *be* dangerous.

Cynthia was anxious as she entered Odessa. This was the first time she would see her sister assassins dressed to kill. Tonight, each woman would have an opportunity to strut her seductive stuff, so Cynthia was curious to see what the others would be wearing. She paced the living room, handling knick-knacks she had never noticed and would never notice again.

Charisse was first down the stairs, and when she and Cynthia saw each other, their jaws dropped. They were wearing identical black cocktail dresses with identical high-heels and jewelry. Even the disco purses were the same. Only the hair-styles were different. Maria descended behind Charisse, wearing the same outfit. After a brief stand-off, the three women protested. Carole laughed. Joanie came down to see about the commotion. After a quick assessment of the identical outfits, Joanie said, "Hey, Carole, don't you think it's unfair to them—dressing them the same as me?"

Charisse put hands on hips, glaring at Joanie.

"Hold your horses, ladies," Carole sniggered. "There's no 'I' in team, hence the uniforms. It's all part of the training. There'll be a little contest during tonight's outing, and I want y'all to have an equal chance."

A contest! Cynthia assessed her competition. All three were different in coloring, builds, and personalities, yet in the matching outfits, their body language was similar. And dangerous. They were rival panthers, circling for the hunt, sensing there wouldn't be enough game to feed them all. The black dresses showed four inches of thigh, and their scoop-necks revealed a hint of cleavage—although in Joanie's case, the hint was a giveaway.

Carole, critically eyeing her charges, smiled when comparing Cynthia to the others. Cynthia's hair was up, accentuating a graceful neck. The dress clung to her figure, highlighting a taut derriere and tapered torso. She moved like a dancer. Cynthia was the star without knowing it.

"Ready, gals?" Carole asked. "Then let's saddle the stove and ride the range."

In the van, she laid out the evening's plan. "Okay, ladies, Greg'll be driving us to a dance club called Bubbles. It's loud and dark, the kind of place where sexual predators are in their element...and horny men go there, too." Carole's joke drew nervous laughter. "That's right, ladies, tonight's exercise will be a true man hunt. Y'all'll go in together, like gals out for a good time. Drink. Dance. Flirt. Whatever. Greg and I'll go in separately, and we'll keep it that way. I'll observe the possibilities for a while, and then I'll sidle up to each of you and point out your mark. Your task'll be to bring back a personal possession of your designated man. How personal is up to you."

"Does semen count?" Joanie asked.

Carole grinned. "The only rule is that all your clothes stay on. Each girl who completes the mission gets all day Sunday off. Whoever brings back the most personal item, in Greg's judgment, will win and get both days off this weekend."

"This is stupid," Charisse said. "Look at us. Don't you think we *know* how to flirt?"

"Then you'll have no problem—it'll be an easy day off," Carole said. "Just so there's no misunderstanding, you're not going to harm anyone. This is a chance to have some fun honing your skills of seduction. And here's a hundred dollars spending money for each of you. Use it for drinks or save it for cab fare, 'cause the van'll leave the parking lot at one a.m. sharp, with or without you."

"Seriously, what qualifies as personal?" Joanie asked.

"Greg?" Carole said.

"Anything that a girlfriend might give her boyfriend. I won't say any more than that."

"So semen's out," Charisse said.

"But not condoms," Joanie replied, impersonating Greg's voice.

Carole clapped her hands. "Ladies!... A few things about the place.

It's very loud. I mean *really* loud. You won't be able to hear yourself think, much less hear people talk from more than a few inches. But that's intentional in clubs like this. It forces people to get close. It allows guys to talk into your ear, smell your perfume, and look down your dress." The other girls looked at Joanie, who vamped.

When Jasper Jordan, head bouncer all in black, saw four uniformed ladies strutting through the double-doors, he whistled. "First time at Bubbles?"

After a "yeah" from Joanie and a nod from Maria, Jasper ushered them inside, taking time to point out the restrooms and ladies' purse lockers. "Point out" was about all he could do, because the rocking music was so loud. Bubbles's gimmick was bubbles—pink bubbles—that were constantly blown into the main room, descending like Candyland snowflakes, before disappearing on contact. Cynthia pictured hundreds of children with bubble soap hiding on the other side of ventilation grates.

After ordering drinks and getting their bearings, the four women cruised the club separately. Cynthia had never approached a man in a bar on her own, but she was an Aitie now, so she would behave like one. She picked out a cute guy and lost track of the other Aities. The guy said, "Hi," to her chest and led her onto a raised, black-and-white checkerboard dance floor where they danced to head-numbing rock music. Within minutes, the others were on the dance floor, too. Cynthia watched her sisters dance. Cynthia had never consciously thought about being attracted to women, but she remembered the backrub with Maria. Was Maria sexier than Joanie or Charisse? Maria's movement was simultaneously vibrant and soothing, her steps hypnotizing. Cynthia realized that she was mimicking Maria's footwork. So were Charisse and Joanie. Cynthia shook her head—Maria had done it again, getting them dancing in unison.

Every eye in the club was on the synchronized babes in black.

Guys started hitting on them as soon as they returned to their table. Within minutes, Joanie returned to the dance floor, grinding with a man dressed like a mobster. Charisse was at the bar with a tall man on each arm. A suave Latino moved in on the table where Maria and Cynthia remained seated. It was too loud to engage in conversation, so Cynthia asked the man to dance, but he shook his head. After a brief delay, he asked Maria. Cynthia might have felt rejected had not a guy in a pinstriped suit swept in, putting his hand on her hip and leaning close to say something to her cleavage. She nodded, although she didn't have a clue as to what he had said. They danced. The suit was a toucher, his hands finding periodic excuses to graze her hips. Cynthia wanted to brush him off—literally. But she didn't.

During the first hour, she limited her alcohol to a few sips. She couldn't tell if the others were doing the same. She tried to guess which man she would be assigned, what personal item she would go after, and how. Was this the kind of place that had private dance rooms? She looked around, noticing dark nooks and unidentified doors. The noise gave her the creeps; she didn't want to be here, but she vowed to make the best of it. She checked her watch: 10:55 p.m.

Carole had been invisible until she materialized next to Cynthia, saying, "Jasper, the bouncer," into Cynthia's ear. Carole walked over to tell Maria something, and then to the dance floor to give Joanie and Charisse their assignments. Joanie was grinding with twins who looked like Brad Pitt, while Charisse had her two men from the bar just as interested on the dance floor.

Cynthia thought about Jasper. He looked like a cast-iron boiler, with a presence that made people respect his space. Yet she would have to get close. Was he married? If so, was he faithful? Knowing nothing, she would have to wing it.

Within minutes, the hunters were comparing prey. As four heads leaned together over the cocktail table, Joanie asked, "Who'd you get?"

"The tall dude in blue," Maria said. "One of the pair Charisse was with."

Laughing, Charisse pointed to the man in the suit who had been rubbing Cynthia. Six eyes then focused on Cynthia.

"The bouncer," she said. This drew some laughs. She furrowed her brow and pointed at Joanie.

"The owner," Joanie said with a flick of fabulous hair.

"Good luck," Cynthia said, leaning in until she was almost nose-to-nose with the others. "I've got some bouncing to do."

Feeling like an actress, Cynthia wended her way through people and bubbles to the entrance where the noise was less deafening. She glided up to Jasper, pressed her bust against his bulk, and said into his ear, "I need to talk to you in private. When do you get a break?"

Jasper's eyes bugged out. "Um-ah...I get fifteen minutes at eleven-thirty, but for you, I can get away right now."

Shaking her head, Cynthia tapped the expensive, gold watch on his left wrist (noting he didn't wear a wedding ring). "No. I'll be back at eleven-thirty." She swiveled to the main room, confident Jasper liked what he saw.

From a seat at her table, Cynthia watched the others work. Joanie was at the bar, talking to the barmaids. Cynthia guessed Joanie was asking questions about the owner, so Cynthia borrowed the idea and went to learn about Jasper. According to the barmaids, the rock-hard bouncer was single with tastes that exceeded his means.

Maria was also at the bar, having wedged her frame between the two tall men. They fawned as much over Maria as they had over Charisse, who was already on the dance floor with her assigned suit.

Joanie danced with the twin Pitts. Within seconds of a tempo change, she stumbled and fell. Cynthia stood and took a step toward Joanie but stopped because the two Pitts were instantly attentive. After the twins carried her to a couch and obtained ice for her ankle, Joanie swore up a storm, demanding to see the f-ing owner and threatening f-ing lawsuits—only she wasn't saying f-ing. Within five minutes, a dapper man in his late forties initiated damage control. Moments later, the man supported Joanie's limp into his office where they could discuss the legalities of dance floor injuries in private. He was looking down, but not at her ankle.

Maria had trouble isolating her mark from his buddy. Twenty minutes later, the three of them left the main room, heading for the exit. Cynthia saw it was almost 11:30, so she followed Maria as far as the lobby. Leaving the main lounge, Cynthia looked over her shoulder and observed that the toucher was swaying with Charisse, and his hands had predictably drifted below her waist.

Jasper was jawing with an unruly patron. Cynthia crossed her arms, which pushed up her bust, and put weight on one leg, trying to look impatient. It must have worked, because Jasper ejected the troublemaker and strode to her side.

"So, what can I do for you, doll?"

"Is there a place we can talk?" she asked, her shapely chest grazing his massive one. "Just the two of us?"

"Yeah." He turned to his fellow bouncers and tapped his watch. They nodded. Jasper led Cynthia around a corner and through a door into a pantry behind the bar.

"Now, what can I do for you, doll?"

"Do you wear boxers or briefs?"

"'Scuse me?"

She smiled, taunting. "Which?"

"Um, boxers. Why?"

"I'll give you fifty bucks for 'em."

"What?"

"It's a scavenger hunt. I need a pair of boxers, and I'll pay fifty for yours. If you say no, some other guy'll get this." She waved a $50 bill so Jasper could smell the ink. "I don't even have to watch you change," she added, scratching his neck with the Grant. She laid the bill on the pantry counter. "Hurry back."

A few minutes later, Jasper returned, boxers in hand, with a grin that looked foreign on his hard face. She placed the bill in his fingers but didn't let go until he mumbled, "Here," and slipped her the rolled-up boxers at thigh level.

"Thanks," Cynthia said. She stuffed the shorts into her purse then walked back to her table. Once seated, she looked for her teammates but saw none.

With time to kill before curfew, Cynthia watched the human species in action. The more she observed, the more she thought Bubbles was an honest place. Not honest in the sense of legality, but honest because the people were open about what they wanted. Most of the women flaunted assets more provocatively than the Aities. The men weren't afraid to act on the inevitable attraction, and the women weren't surprised by the men's advances nor did they pretend the attention wasn't welcome. Whereas modern society suppressed mating urges, this nightclub allowed them to flourish.

One of the Pitts made eye contact, and Cynthia smiled. He nodded—as if the door to the bedroom of his imagination opened—and approached. During small talk that was drowned out by the music, she pictured a labyrinth inside her own head—numerous doors and locks. She asked him to dance. A minute later on the raised floor, his hands caressed her rear. He was being honest, but she was disappointed and thought: why do so many men open the wrong doors? She missed Thomas.

Fifteen minutes later, Joanie exited the office and limped—with the owner's help—to the table where Cynthia and Charisse were people-watching. Joanie wore a man's tie knotted loosely around her neck.

"Goodnight, Rocky," Joanie said as he kissed her cheek.

Once the owner disappeared, Charisse teased, "Goodnight, not goodbye?"

"Ha! I got his tie. Maybe next time I'll get something *more* personal. And you guys?"

Each gave a thumbs-up.

At 1:00 a.m., Carole materialized, yelling, "Time to go, ladies."

"But Maria's not here," Cynthia said.

"She's already in the van."

They trooped outside, Cynthia winking at Jasper as she swept through the lobby.

Greg was in the van with Maria, who kept her eyes on the floor.

Cynthia slid in and rubbed Maria's hand until they made eye contact. Maria's eyes were puffy and red.

After the van pulled out of the parking lot, Carole said, "Okay, it's show and tell time. Joanie?"

"Got the manager's tie right here," Joanie bragged, holding it as if it were a noose.

"And tell us how," Carole said. "This is a learning exercise."

"I asked the bartenders about the owner. They said he was paranoid about lawsuits, so I pretended to hurt myself and threatened to sue. That got me alone with him, and he turned out to be pretty nice. I said I'd drop the suit if he gave me his class ring, but I settled for this."

"And what else did you have to do for the tie?" Charisse goaded.

Joanie puckered. "Aities don't kiss and tell."

Carole said, "Okay, Charisse, how about you?"

"Right here, boss," Charisse said, showing a monogrammed handkerchief. "That honky would have walked on hot coals to get a piece of my sweet—"

"So how'd you get it?" Joanie interrupted.

"He had his hands all over my *sweet black ass*, so I returned the favor and lifted the honky's hanky. He still doesn't know it's gone." Charisse laughed with an air of superiority. "*You* may have to put out to get something personal, Lee, but not Charisse."

The van turned a corner lit with several neon signs. Only then did Cynthia notice Maria's torn pantyhose. As if on cue, Carole said, "Maria, I know you're upset, but you have to tell the others what happened."

Maria spoke softly. "I couldn't get him away from his buddy.... But I got them to agree to go outside. The noise and smoke were getting to me. They'd been bragging about liking a three-way. I thought we'd make out in the parking lot, and I'd lift a lighter or something, but they had more in mind than just..." She faltered before pressing on. "They tried to force me, and when they didn't take no for an answer, I had to fight them off. All I got was this." Maria produced a penknife.

While Cynthia comforted her friend, Carole addressed the group. "What lessons did we learn here? Charisse?"

Charisse answered quickly. "Stay away from threesomes."

"Joanie?"

The blonde looked artificial when caught in genuine thought. After a few seconds, she answered, "You know, maybe I was lucky. My plan could have backfired, too."

"Cynthia," Carole said. "What's your take on Maria's encounter?"

Cynthia stretched her neck and pondered. "She got the penknife and kept her clothes on, so she passed the test."

Carole grinned. Soon the others were laughing. Maria, less shaken, nodded at Cynthia.

Before the laughter died down, Joanie shouted, "Hey, what about Bond?"

Cynthia produced Jasper's shorts. "After your stories, I'm kind of embarrassed. All I did was offer fifty bucks for his boxers. I said it was for a scavenger hunt."

Joanie sniffed the boxers and burst into laughter a beat before everyone else.

Carole quieted the van with a shrill wolf whistle. "Okay, Greg, you've heard the stories. Who got the most personal item?"

Greg blushed. "Everyone did well, but I don't see how anything can top underwear."

Charisse rubbed Cynthia's shoulders. "Way to go, Cyn."

"Congratulations," Joanie said.

Charisse, noticing Maria was quiet, raised her voice to get the others' attention. "Hey, Carole! You have that weepy tape? The one with the long song Maria likes? What's it called, Cry, Cry in My Apple Pie?"

Cynthia chuckled. "That's *American Pie*, by Don McLean."

"Yeah. That's it. You got that one?"

"Matter a fact, I do," Carole drawled, reaching for the console.

"Then pop that sucker in. It'll cheer our girl up."

Maria lowered her eyes and blushed, but by the second verse, she was singing along. When the fourth verse ended, Maria was smiling. Six voices rocked the van with melody and rhymes, all the way to the last Chevy at the last levee.

After Greg parked the van in the compound driveway, Carole announced, "Everybody passed the test, so ya'll'll get Sunday off. Cynthia, you've won Saturday, too. Congratulations! You all did good, and I'm damn proud of you."

Cynthia smiled at her colleagues. Her initial wariness about Joanie and Charisse was long gone, and Maria…well, she was Maria.

In the driveway, Cynthia lingered for a word with Carole. "Maria could have gotten hurt."

"Maybe. Greg followed her outside and was ready for real trouble, but he wasn't needed. Each of you had a wire in the strap of your purse, and one in your bracelet. I was shadowing Joanie and Charisse.

"What about me?" Cynthia asked.

"I wasn't worried about you," Carole said with a twinkle. "If I haven't prepared you to handle a nightclub bouncer one-on-one, it's best to find out now. I'm turning in. 'Night."

The Aities were too wired to go to bed. They sang and danced a reprise of *American Pie* in Odessa's living room before collapsing into overstuffed chairs. It was a good morning, and although Cynthia's body was crashing, her senses remained sharp. She was aware of the timing that made inane banter funny, aware of the tomato and sausage that made cold pizza delicious, aware of the warmth that made Maria's tea comforting.

When Cynthia's eyelids grew heavy, she said goodnight. Outside the door, she passed Charisse who was sneaking a smoke. "Hey, Charisse, thanks for suggesting Maria's song. I know you hate it."

"I don't hate that song. I *hate* asparagus. But next time you trash rap, just think about that Chevy-levee jive, okay?"

Cynthia nodded. "Fair enough. But I saw *you* singing along to *American Pie*."

Charisse shook her head. "Don't be sayin' that out loud. Just 'cause a sister can be white for a night doesn't mean she *likes* that shit."

* * *

Cynthia spent her bonus weekend with Thomas at a bed and breakfast in Cape May. No bars, no discos, no training—and no sex. Abstinence wasn't what Thomas had in mind, but Cynthia complained of various aches and pains, particularly sore ribs. She and Thomas walked, talked, read, and lounged. She was happy that he was willing to be platonic.

On Sunday afternoon, they sat on the beach, huddled against a chilly breeze. "I've really come to love the surf," she said, nuzzling his neck inside the blanket he had wrapped around them. "My boss is a seashore nut from west Texas, of all places, and she's gotten me hooked, too. Can you feel it? The roar. *The power!* I feel like the surf is life itself."

He held her to his chest. "Too tight?" She shook her head and snuggled closer. Sex might not be high on her list of pleasures, but affection was.

"Promise me something," she said.

"Anything," he said, and she knew he meant it—she knew he loved her.

"Thomas, promise that when things warm up, you'll make love to me in the surf. The ocean invigorates me—makes me feel alive. I really want to share that life with you."

Thomas gulped. "Whoa!"

She pulled her face out of the blanket. "Oh. I don't mean to have a baby. I mean to share the *joy of life*." She saw relief on his face. "No need to panic."

"Hey, Cyn, I love kids. It's just way too soon to think about—"

"I know."

Feeling his chest expand and contract, Cynthia realized that someday she would have to open up to him if she ever hoped to love him. She wasn't ready to tell the whole truth, but she had to lay a foundation.

"There's something you should know about my job."

"What's that?"

"Well, it's not quite as simple as catering pro-American rallies."

"Yeah?"

"You can't tell a soul what I'm about to tell you, but it isn't an ordinary job."

"Why am I not surprised?"

"One of the things we do is gather intelligence on enemies of the United States." Her head rocked with his chest as he breathed. When he exhaled, she continued. "I'm training as a support person on one of the surveillance teams. They wanted me because I speak Spanish, I know my way around bars, and I did well on all their tests. They're paying me more money than I told you."

"Sounds dangerous."

"Maybe. They're teaching us self-defense stuff. That's how I got hurt—not playing volleyball."

"What kind of things will you do?"

"I'll watch people, case out places, act as a lookout, monitor stakeouts—that kind of stuff." For the next half-hour she fabricated answers to his questions. The lying came easily; she felt better because *these* lies were closer to the truth. When they kissed goodbye, she responded as best she could to his passion. It was a nice finish to the weekend. But as much as she enjoyed her time with Thomas, she couldn't help wonder: would she ever love him?

8
PAULSON ELECTRONICS

When the war cabinet of Paulson Electronics met in April, the Aities' training was in full swing. The men's program was operational in Arizona, although lagging behind the women's. Duane Root's security team had scouted targets in Spain and established a support network. Pilar Ibanez had created a worldwide organization that was spending millions of dollars on pro-freedom programs around the world. Some of that money was filtering down to the Aities.

Pilar, wearing a green business suit, stood to address the war cabinet in the Bunker. Root noticed changes—hem a few inches higher, stretch blouse, high heels. *What was she up to?* He straightened his back. And his tie.

Pointing to the whiteboard, she said, "You see before you the first-round proposal for early June. Cynthia James will take out Alejandro Cabrera, a planner, in Seville. A week later, Maria Lopez will eliminate Valeriano, a recruiter, in Madrid. Then, Charisse White will target Abdul Mohammad, a bomber, in Casablanca while Joan Lee eliminates Ramon Benitez, a courier, in Madrid. You can see the support team assignments. The schedule is tight, but doable."

The executives listened as Root outlined assignments for the men's team. When Root was done, Jerry Paulson asked for discussion, but there was none. By a show of hands, they approved the plans. The meeting was over in less than ten minutes. As usual, Eddie Juarez was first out, followed by Pilar. As Paulson wiped off the board, Root lingered.

"Still want to talk me out of it?" Paulson said.

"No, Jerry. But I do have some intelligence that I think you'll find very interesting. Tomorrow's news." Root handed Paulson several SCOPE surveillance sheets. Paulson, eyes dancing, scanned the reports until something caught his attention. He sat down and absorbed the information, color rising in his face.

"Thatcher!" Paulson spat. "This means we can go after him. I knew the son-of-a-bitch was involved, and now we can prove it." Paulson thought for a moment and smiled. "I recall that Sir Wilton has quite an eye for young ladies, so we should use one of the girls. Have Pilar work up a plan."

"I'll get right on it," Root replied. "And due to the sensitive nature of this intelligence, I suggest we keep it among the three of us."

Paulson nodded as he rolled up the document that proved *1898* terrorists were now using United Security's *NightOwl* to hide orders for their next attack. "Sir Wilton Thatcher really is the owl himself."

Duane Root walked directly to Eduardo Juarez's office. "Give me the results from Paulson's latest cardio tests." No "please."

Juarez hid his displeasure by hovering over a sheet of formulas. His work space was surrounded by computer terminals on robotic arms. Root thought: how small Juarez looked, bent over a draftsman's desk with all those arms and screens hanging over him.

"I don't have all day," Root said. "I know the data is in."

Moving with uncharacteristic slowness, Juarez pulled a manila folder from his lone filing cabinet. "I erased all evidence of the SCOPE search. This is the only copy."

"Good." Root scanned the data before marching out.

Fifteen minutes later, Juarez heard a knock on his open door.

"May I come in?" Pilar asked.

Juarez brightened. "Sure."

She closed the door and sat, crossing her legs. The office was drab, with no sensibility—in the Jane Austin sense—no art, no color, no emotion. But she was used to ignoring the gray. "Hi, Eddie."

He studied her. "You want something, don't you?"

"What makes you think—"

"You know you can get anything from me. So what is it you want?"

"Um, you wouldn't by any chance have Jerry's latest medical results, would you?"

Juarez laughed. "Root beat you to it; he just took them."

Her face twitched, but she covered it with a plastic smile. "You kept a copy for me, didn't you?"

"I always do." He handed over a manila folder.

She reviewed it more thoroughly than Root had. After a minute, she said, "His heart is worse than last month."

"Which was worse than the month before," Juarez added.

Pilar fanned her fingers through the pages. "He's not taking care of himself, and he's taking on more stress. Did you run these through Med-Pro?"

He nodded. "Software predicts a heart attack within two years."

"And what do you think?"

"I'm no doctor."

She flicked her hair. "I'm just asking what you think."

Juarez looked into glowing, emerald eyes. "The assumptions are conservative. Maybe closer to one," he said.

There was an awkward silence. Pilar's face tightened; she knew what was coming.

Twirling a pencil, Juarez swallowed. "So, have you given any more thought to when you might start dating?"

"Oh, Eddie, you know my philosophy about dating in the work place."

"Well, yeah...I know, but I thought you said that because you were married. Now..."

More awkward silence.

"I'm sorry," he mumbled.

"I'm sticking to my rule: separation of personal relationships from work, but if I ever bend the rule, it'll be with you."

A trace of disappointment seeped onto his voice. "What about Root?"

She flustered. "Duane's married."

"He screws around."

"Jealousy doesn't become you, Eddie. But rest assured, my relationship with Duane is strictly business."

Juarez slumped. "I'm sorry, Pilar. I just hoped that—"

"Shhh." She leaned forward and spoke in a whisper. "You and I have had something special since our first day on the job. Let's not spoil it." She stood to leave. "Thanks for the reports. I'll see you tomorrow."

Pilar hadn't consciously flirted with Eddie, but after years of manipulating him, such behavior came as naturally as breathing. She would need him on her side when Paulson died, and at his present pace, Jerry would die soon.

"You're really jazzed by this Patriots thing, aren't you?" Root asked Pilar as they stood next to their cars in the parking lot after work.

"This is important—being part of the war on terror."

"Don't you think it's distracting the company at a crucial time? The current world climate's a gold mine for us."

Her eyes narrowed. "SCOPE's the real gold mine. Current product sales are peanuts compared to SCOPE's potential. Hundreds of millions—maybe billions. I'm meeting all deliverables for the rollout—and for the Patriots—so what's the problem?"

"We shouldn't be involved in you-know-what. It's illegal and unseemly."

"My husband's murder was illegal and unseemly."

Root sneered. "The patriots are Paulson's hobby, and a very expensive one at that. He should plow the money into R&D. That's how to boost profits."

"SCOPE will boost profits in less than a year—take off like a rocket." She flashed her sharp eyes. "Is money all you think about?"

"No. I think about security, too." Root's expression remained hard.

Pilar raised an eyebrow enough to get Root's attention. "SCOPE will roll out on schedule and be a huge success, even with me working on *Patriots for Freedom*. I guarantee it. Worry about your men's program instead of about me. I'd swear you're dragging your feet."

Root's forehead turned red.

She had struck a raw nerve and changed the subject. "So how do you think Jerry's health is holding up to the strain?"

"I give the old man three years tops before his ticker gives out."

Pilar chuckled. "Old man? He's only two years older than you." She straightened his perfectly tailored lapel. "Patience, Duane. His heart will fail; your time will come."

"Aren't we getting ahead of ourselves?"

"I grew up in the slums of Sao Paulo, not you, so don't lecture me about getting ahead of myself. Just get the damn men's program on schedule. The more terrorists we eliminate, the safer we make the world for obscene profits. That's how it's good for the company."

"So you think about profits, too. We understand each other."

She nodded, but as they stepped into their cars, Pilar wondered whether she understood Root at all.

* * *

SCOPE, not scantily clad neophyte assassins, was the key to power in Paulson Electronics. As head of security, Duane Root controlled the awesome tool, not the malleable man who had designed it or the exotic woman who would sell it.

SCOPE (Security Cipher Of Paulson Electronics) was a groundbreaking surveillance system scheduled for rollout later in the year. The brainchild of Eduardo Juarez, SCOPE melded state-of-the-art hardware with innovative software.

Juarez developed the SCOPE parallel processing computer in conceptual patterns of six virtual sides that fit together as perfectly as hexagons filling a two-dimensional plane. Instead of a linear stream of ons and offs, SCOPE worked with hexels, six-dimensional processing units. While the six dimensions were invisible, their structure existed virtually, each side of each hexagon connecting to six others. The processing capacity of one SCOPE hexel could do the work of six conventional central processing unit (CPU) instructions, and the gains were exponential. It took 36 CPU instructions to do the work of two hexels; 216 instructions to do the work of three hexels, and 1296 for four hexels. It was a breakthrough of staggering proportions.

SCOPE was the brain behind Paulson Electronics' ultra-sensitive laser-based surveillance equipment. SCOPE-controlled cameras and microphones could see and hear from incredible distances because of the coherent laser light that carried the signals. When Pilar had scoffed, Juarez told her, "It's a matter of precision. Our SCOPE-controlled devices are so powerful and so precise that our sensors on satellites can capture data on the ground. The software self-corrects for the tiniest vibrations, and its A.I. functions figure out any missing data using ideal observer models."

"How can SCOPE possibly do that?" Pilar had asked.

Juarez had flashed his impish grin. "When you look over a stone wall and see the roof and top story of a two-story building, your brain fills in an image of the lower floor that your eyes can't actually see. SCOPE does the same thing with data fragments that aren't read cleanly. SCOPE can't always break codes because ciphers don't follow logic, but level-four SCOPE can read a computer file from the sky with ninety-nine percent accuracy."

"But what about distance?" Pilar had asked.

"Lasers produce coherent light. When light waves are coherent, they vibrate in parallel and don't interfere with each other, the way normal light does. That difference allows laser light to travel enormous distance without spreading out or adding random noise. The signals we use are thousands of times more accurate than standard methods."

Pilar didn't understand the science, but she got the message when Juarez read her father's computer backup CDs in Brazil.

SCOPE was designed with security in mind. Each level of the product, six times more powerful than the one below, was cloaked from other SCOPE users of equal and lesser levels. Juarez had named the levels to match the SCOPE initials: 1-Simple, 2-Complex, 3-Official,

4-Private, and 5-Executive.

Pilar used this structure to prepare a sales plan for three basic markets. Individuals would be sold level-1 systems (Simple), for making personal and internet applications faster. Businesses would buy level-2 (Complex), using it for everything from managing employees' web usage to better satellite communications. Level-3 (Official) would enable law enforcement to be more effective because SCOPE-controlled components were more sensitive than conventional surveillance devices and because AI functions would allow more powerful inference algorithms to be used. Paulson Electronics used level-4 (Private) to ensure their product was not abused. As an internal safeguard, level-5 (Executive) was reserved for Paulson and Security Chief Root. This monitored Juarez, who had created the powerful tool but was given only level-4 access. Level-5 could monitor users at its own level, giving Paulson and Root audit control over each other.

There was one aspect of the high-tech security business that SCOPE had not mastered. United Security of England had recently perfected an encryption tool called *NightOwl*, which cloaked security codes behind perpetually evolving firewalls. Even root algorithms in *NightOwl* were altered so that the fastest super-computers could not break the code.

Sabah Al Khair (a.k.a. *1898*) was one of the terrorist organizations that employed *NightOwl*, so the product was underground. Wilton Thatcher and United Securities denied its existence. Only SCOPE could even detect (if not solve) *NightOwl*, and SCOPE was not on the market yet, so it was Jerry Paulson's word against Wilton Thatcher's. Thatcher was beyond reproach ever since the Queen knighted him.

* * *

Jerry Paulson considered himself a man of action but not of the physical variety. He wheedled and cajoled with intensity, but he *did* few things more strenuous than walking to and from his Mercedes. Reclining on a Lay-Z-Boy in his den, he called Duane Root on the telephone one Sunday evening in April.

"Exercising?"

"Yes," Root said, breathing hard. "Just finished some interval training."

That was all the small talk Paulson could endure. "I'm calling for a status report on the women assassins."

Root cleared his throat. "As you recall, we decided that Pilar would manage them."

"I know what we *said*, but you've always kept your hands on everything, so I thought…" Paulson picked up on Root's hesitation. "You still don't think the women will succeed, do you?"

"Frankly, no. *Charlie's Angels* is pure fantasy. I think it's a bad idea that tickles the prurient fancy of people who don't understand the difficulties of covert operations."

Paulson huffed. "People like me? Am I Charlie or Bosley?"

"By 'people,' I was speaking generally."

"*Right*. So you're going to let Pilar hang out to dry on this?"

"I wouldn't say that. I think it's important to have leaders who believe in their projects. Pilar believes in the women, so she should be in charge."

Huffing again, Paulson said, "I've known you too long to be fooled by your spin. Say what you will, but you're distancing yourself from a loser. Go back to running. I'll call Pilar to get my status."

Twenty miles away, Pilar was walking on a treadmill in her basement. When the phone rang, she looked at the caller-ID display—Jerry Paulson. She turned off the treadmill and put down a SCOPE marketing plan.

"Pilar, it's Jerry." Paulson's voice was jocular. "It seems that Duane has lost so much confidence in the Aities that he's willing to give you rope to hang yourself. Since my neck is out there, too, I hope you have a good report."

"I'll show it to you first thing tomorrow."

"You should know by now that I can't wait."

* * *

Jimmy Taylor was a good detective who made a bad first impression. Fifty-two, overweight, and balding, he looked rumpled even when his clothes were fresh from the cleaners. Plastic glasses slid down the bridge of his nose, prompting Taylor to repeatedly nudge them back in place.

On subsequent impressions, Taylor's positives outweighed his appearance. He was businesslike without being rude, smart but not pompous. He wanted results, not credit, which made him popular at work. Determination gave him both the reputation and appearance of a bulldog, but he was so likeable that friends called him Jimmy and so respected that colleagues called him Boss.

The Alexander Gates case was never far from Taylor's mind. Gates had disappeared from the steamboat *Louisiana Lady* on the last night of a Civil War theme cruise that ended in Chattanooga. Gates collected rare artillery ammunition and was a hedge fund manager. He might have been murdered or might have sneaked away to avoid prosecution for securities fraud, but there was no hard evidence supporting either theory. None of Gates's off-shore bank accounts had been touched, and his body hadn't been found. At the time, Gates's brother, Thomas, had been the prime suspect because of an ongoing family feud, but Taylor was now convinced Cynthia James was involved because her mother had died in Alex Gates's cabin on an earlier cruise. Cynthia had motive and opportunity. Most interesting of all, two of Gates's rare cannon balls were missing along with him.

Baffled by Cynthia James, Taylor couldn't sleep. Instead, he brooded at the cluttered desk in his Chattanooga den, clenching a green Pentel pen in his teeth as if it was a cigar. He thought better that way. Where had Ms. James gone? He had traced her from Stanhope to Boonton, but then she had disappeared—moved out of her apartment without taking anything, not even her truck. No new address or accounts were showing up under her name.

The clock on his computer tormented him: 3:42 a.m. Taylor took a draw on his Pentel and tried to make sense of notes scribbled on a piece of yellow-lined paper. The apartment owner and postman had been cooperative over the phone. Cynthia's rent was being paid by money orders with a Manhattan postmark. The place was being cleaned by Maids-In-America, also paid by money orders. Her mail was not forwarded or held. Taylor imagined the maid being greeted by an ascending pile of junk mail inside the door each month.

Taylor looked up. 3:43. He wondered if Cynthia James might be dead. No, she was alive; he was sure—alive and tormenting him. "Damn," he muttered. "Damn, damn, damn."

9
ANWAR

Diego Madera remembered a happy childhood, not because of wealth, but because of family. And not just because of parents and siblings—grandparents, aunts, uncles, and cousins, too. His family was close-knit and resourceful.

The happiness literally had to be beaten out of him. His first whipping had come when he was eight.

"It takes more strength to hate your enemies than to love your family," his father had said between swipes of the cane.

"I don't want to hate, Papa," Diego had whimpered.

"Trust me, my son, you do, but you need to be strong."

By the time he was nine, he took it like a man. But had the beatings been worth it?

Actions speak louder than words, his father had said, and Diego agreed. He would beat his children, too—when he had them—enduring pain would make them stronger. He was a Madera. And he was the strongest Madera. Occasionally, he thought about being happy, but happiness was a luxury to a Madera, particularly the leader of *1898*.

His father had died five years ago while trying to blow up an oil well in Texas, an explosion that left a nasty u-shaped mark on Diego's cheek. His father had been dedicated. His father had also been a fool. When Diego took over, he made changes in the organization. He expanded the vision of *1898* from pinpricks to mighty blows. He brainwashed and trained outsiders to do the dangerous jobs—like blowing up highway interchanges. Most importantly, he killed off *1898*—officially. All Maderas assumed Arab names. All terrorist work was done in the name of Sabah Al Khair…and Allah, of course.

He was now Anwar, and it was interesting how he had changed since assuming the new moniker. His brothers thought he looked taller, probably because he stood a bit straighter. His sisters thought he looked darker, probably because he grew a beard that came in black as coal. His cousins thought he looked hungrier, probably because he could taste the foul decadency of the United States. The women who were brought to him as prospective wives thought he looked more dangerous, probably because he enjoyed killing.

Women. Even the strongest of those presented to him were too weak to be his partner. He got no satisfaction from sexual relations with inferiors. One pretender hadn't cried when he cut her, but she had been too passive—a mate would have to stand up to him. Two of his sisters would have been acceptable, but he wasn't into perversions.

Late at night, walking the beach, Anwar wished he could be more like his cousin, Roberto Garcia, who got pleasure from fucking American women at the same time he used them for the cause.

The cause of his organization was noble. Spain had been decrepit in the year 1898, Anwar admitted, but all the more reason to hate the imperialistic country that had picked a fight and raped her.

Anwar sat on a piece of driftwood, feeling the waves run over his toes. He looked south and thought about his legacy. *1898* had been little more than a pathetic cult that talked tough until the Spanish Civil War. The Maderas had run drugs and used the money to support the Fascists. The taste of blood money revived dormant hatred in Diego's grandfather, who began to beat it into Diego's father and uncles. A new defiance infected the family. Talk was replaced by action.

Diego was sixteen on his first mission. He was working as a longshoreman in Cadiz where he and his father sneaked explosives into a shipping container being loaded into the hold of an American freighter. The colors had been brighter that day—the smells more pungent. Feeling cool water surging over his ankles, Anwar relived the excitement he had felt anticipating his father's detonation of the charge. Diego had been sweating, but his father was cool as an Artic breeze. "Patience," his father kept saying. Only when the ship had cleared the harbor did he radio the signal.

The rumble was like distant thunder—music to Diego's ears. Alas, the ship did not sink, and the shipping company did not suffer because it was insured. The lost goods weren't even a blip to the U.S. economy. The job was a flop—aimed at the wrong target—the work of angry dreamers. Anwar was a doer.

He stood and walked through the surf, feeling the draw of each receding wave pulling sand from under the arches of his feet. It humbled him to compare his strength to that of the sea. That's what he thought about when he became discouraged at the task of bringing down America—as great as its strength, it was nothing to the power of the ocean. Of course, this war, like all wars, was a contest of men, not oceans. Anwar drew confidence from this truth, because his will was greater than any American leader. Had the President of the United States been lashed until he could accept the blows without a whimper?

He took off his shirt and flung it on the beach. Diving into the water, he plunged out through the waves, pushing off the bottom to get himself clear of the breakers he jack-knifed over. The water washed the weight of the family from his shoulders, allowing him to be a normal man under the stars for a few minutes. There was no United States, no history of the Spanish-American War, no revenge to plan, no drug and racketeering organization to manage, no Sabah Al Khair, no futile search for a life partner.

Sometimes, he thought about a woman, or travel, or relaxation as he swam. Such thoughts never lasted more than several minutes—any longer would be a sign of weakness. In penance, he would slice his lower back with a sharp fingernail and revel in the sting from salt water.

Now, diving through the ocean as if he were a dolphin, Anwar weakened to become Diego. He pictured a woman better than any whom Roberto Garcia bragged about screwing in his massage parlor. Swelled with inspiration, he pitted his human desire against the power of nature—the chill of the ocean in late April, the pull of the ebbing tide.

Tomorrow, he would plan Operation Aqua, organize the next class of recruits, and move money from one shore to another. Family squabbles would be brought before him for arbitration. A blindfolded woman would be presented to him as a possible wife. She would be rejected, of course, and sent back down the mountain without ever knowing where she had been. If she were worthy, she would already be diving through the water with him and basking in the power of the ocean.

He liked his poetic side, which emerged during night swims. That's what gave him the vision that his father and grandfather lacked. That's what kept his mind fresh. That's what gave his strength the flexibility to withstand any force, any blow.

The next morning, a truck brought two blindfolded visitors up the hillside that he had climbed in the dark. Despite his cynicism, Anwar saw the woman first. She was led into a private study, where she stood, back arched and head high. She wore a white blouse and black pants that matched his white shirt and black trousers, the uniform of *1898*. "What is your name?" he asked in Spanish after uncovering her eyes.

"Sonia."

He eyed her critically. Her figure was firm, her facial features sharp, the way he liked. Her hair was lighter than his, again, as he preferred. She was as pretty as a woman with steely eyes could be. She looked barely twenty-two. "Do you know why you are here?"

"Yes. To be tested as a possible mate—to carry the seed of the next leader of *Eighteen Ninety-Eight*."

"What do you think about that?"

"It would be an honor."

He liked that she didn't fawn over him by saying it would be a *great* honor. She had been well-schooled. He stroked her hair—thick. "When did you pledge allegiance?" He already knew the answer, but he liked to test the women. Many lied, adding time to their service record.

"Nine years ago."

He nodded. She was truthful, but a pang nipped at his stomach. They were into the next year's class. Soon they would be bringing him teenagers. He paced around her and pushed up the back of her blouse to examine the welts. He nodded—she had more than women with twelve years.

He kissed her, feeling little pleasure because there was no challenge, but she was reasonably sensual—he could learn to love her. "Are you ready?" he asked.

She gulped and nodded.

Grabbing her wrist with one hand, he dug his nails into her skin until he drew blood. She winced, but did not make a sound. His hand and fingers were like a vice, driving the nails deeper into her flesh. She gritted her teeth, chest heaving, but didn't cry out. He twisted his nails so they gouged. Blood spurted out of her but no sound.

His eyes glimmered—she might be worthy. "Are you ready for the final test?"

She nodded, holding the clench of her jaw.

His heart drummed. He wanted her, not just because he was aroused, but because he was tired of waiting.

He raised his free hand and drove the fist onto his knuckles just above the wound, hammering his sharp nails into her nerves.

Sonia sniveled in pain…and shame. Not loudly, but audibly.

He released his grip and wrapped a towel around her wrist.

Sinking to her knees, she bowed her head. "I am not worthy."

He raised her chin with his fingers. No tears. She was strong—she had come very close. So close that he felt sorry for himself. It was the first time he questioned the standards of leadership.

He took her hands and gently pulled. She rose to her feet.

"Sonia, I have two favors to ask," he said.

"Anything," she said through a closed jaw.

"I want you to marry my brother Miguel," he said, making it sound like a command. "You would live here."

She blinked three times. "I am honored if he will have me," she said. "What is the second favor?"

"Stay until this afternoon," he whispered. "You can meet Miguel after lunch. And maybe we will go swimming."

Anwar's conversation with his second visitor took place in his library. They spoke in Spanish. "I apologize for the blindfold, Gatan," Anwar said. "Did you bring the latest formula?"

"Yes. Here it—"

Anwar waved him off. "I am not a scientist, so I do not care to see—only to know that it works. Give it to my brother, Miguel. If he agrees, then we will use it. What about the dilution problem?"

"We solved it with a coagulant that keeps the poison from dissolving into harmless grains. One hundred million lethal doses per reservoir is the specification. This coagulant allows us to meet the goal."

"How many fatalities?"

"So much American water goes for long showers and watering grass. Their wasteful habits work against us."

"How many *deaths*, Gatan?"

"I estimate one one-thousanth of one percent of the doses."

Anwar did the math—100 reservoirs, 100,000 total deaths—and smiled. "You are sure the poison will be lethal after boiling?"

"Positive."

"How heavy will the poison be for each site?"

Gatan checked his notes. "Three hundred kilos, so I recommend one hundred three-kilo bags per reservoir. They will be easy to handle and dissipate quickly. It will be packaged in flour bags." Gatan added in English, "Gold Medal."

Anwar calculated quickly. "How will we distribute thirty thousand kilos of poison to one hundred sites?"

Gatan grinned. "We won't have to. All the ingredients can be obtained locally in American stores. All we have to do is get the formula and money to the cells so they can purchase ingredients. But can we do that safely?"

Anwar tapped the device on his hip, and his eyes glowed. "That will not be a problem."

10

MARIA

Carole encouraged Cynthia to go to the main house on Saturday nights to socialize with her colleagues. The Aities' bonding sessions gave Carole time to catch up on paperwork.

"Who has guard duty?" Cynthia asked as she joined the others around the kitchen table.

"Greg," answered Joanie. "Here's a glass of wine, Bond. You've got some catching up to do." Cynthia took a swallow, losing a few drops from the corner of her mouth. She glanced out the window toward the garage, above which the four men lived. Greg, Dumont, Larry, and Juan were bodyguards, training partners, cooks, gophers, and housekeepers whom Joanie had christened "the Boys." Joanie followed Cynthia's eyes. "Hey, Cyn, what do you think those poor guys are thinking about right now?"

"You mean, besides your breasts?"

Joanie arched her back and stuck out her tongue.

"Those boys are just there to torment us," Charisse sassed. "One for each of us, right down to the Latin Lover for Chita-Rita-Maria."

"Not for me," Maria protested. "I wouldn't sleep with Juan if he were the last guy on earth. He's not smart enough."

"Proves my point," Charisse said. "We're thinkin' about it…they're thinkin' about it…"

"Know what they're really thinking over there?" Joanie mused. "They're wishing they could watch us in a girl-on-girl four-way."

"You got that right," laughed Charisse.

Cynthia felt herself blush, and she glanced at Maria. As the others joked, she thought about the seed Maria had planted. *Why hadn't Cynthia experimented with women during her lost decade?*

It was an interesting question. Before she met Thomas, thoughts of intimacy with a man disgusted her, so why not turn to a woman?

Another woman would understand her sensitivities better than a man…a female would be the patient partner that her damaged psyche needed…and on the practical side, no birth control.

The Aities' training program had sucked the last vestige of romance out of sex with a man. Was that why she was thinking about the alternative? Had training to kill men knocked her fragile instincts out of kilter? Cynthia dared to imagine what it would feel like to kiss Maria. The notion seemed deviant, but when she thought about it, deviant didn't mean bad. After all, they were training to be assassins. The line between good and bad grew blurrier by the sip.

The party moved into the living room and didn't break up until the wine ran out. Stretching, Joanie rose. "Ah gots to git some shut-eye."

"Sleep?" Charisse responded, uncoiling from her chair. "Shit! You'll be sneaking your wide white butt out to the garage in twenty minutes."

"Ha! And tripping over your bony black ass in the driveway."

Joanie and Charisse razzed each other going up the stairs.

Cynthia and Maria sat side-by-side on the couch. With half-glasses remaining, Maria suggested, "Stay up 'til we finish?"

Cynthia nodded.

"I never thanked you enough after my mishap at Bubbles," Maria whispered. *"Thank you."*

"You're welcome." They clinked glasses. A faint voice in the back of Cynthia's mind said: you're glad it's only the two of you; it's the opportunity you just thought about; she's beautiful, sensitive, and totally uninhibited. Maybe she's thinking the same thing.

Cynthia felt vulnerable, like the first time she wanted to kiss a boy. She licked her lip—just a flit of her tongue—and stopped breathing.

Maria set her hand on Cynthia's knee. "You're curious but uncomfortable."

Cynthia shook her head.

"Yes. I can tell. You've never been with a woman. That's okay."

Cynthia was speechless, lightheaded.

Maria squeezed Cynthia's hand. "Let's hold that thought and see if you feel as curious when you're sober. Tomorrow, and every day after, remember—whatever happens, we're friends."

Later, lying in bed, Cynthia's inebriated brain heard voices. Homophobic ministers droned into one ear while Maria's words echoed in the other. "You're curious and uncomfortable…. Yes. I can tell." As usual, Maria had Cynthia pegged dead-on. Thomas appeared in her mind's eye, then Maria. It was Maria's image that lingered. Cynthia clenched her fists. "Shit," she muttered. "I don't need this now."

* * *

A week later, Cynthia and Maria sat side-by-side on the bungalow's wicker couch, looking as if they had been called into the principal's office. Carole stopped pacing. "Relax. This isn't about breaking curfew. We just got word that one of the I-Eighty bombers will be in Bermuda next week. He's spent years establishing himself in Manhattan. He doesn't know we've made him, so he should be easy to hit. You two have been chosen to take him out."

Cynthia's eyes widened. "Why *two* of us?"

"This man, Dante Salmanda, likes to watch two girls get it on with each other before joining in, and he goes for your type, Cyn." Reading Cynthia's confusion, Carole added, "Maria's on this job because she's bisexual."

Cynthia colored, coughing out the first words that floated into her head. "So you're our secret *double*-agent?"

Maria looked away.

Carole eyed Maria then Cynthia. "We only have a week to get ready, ladies. You two need to be comfortable. The mark has to believe you really like each other and that you'd welcome him in a three-way. If you're convincing, ya'll'll poison him when his guard's down."

Cynthia's mind wandered—recalling last week.

"Did you hear me, Cyn? You won't have any problem with this, will you?"

Cynthia shook her spinning head. "No. No problem."

"Good," Carole said.

Cynthia's pulse quickened. "Will Maria and I have to…rehearse?"

Carole laughed. "No kissing, if that's what you mean. Only dancing with each other. You'll kill the mark before it gets physical."

Over the next hour, Carole laid out the plan, and Cynthia's pulse returned to normal.

Afterwards, Maria said to Cynthia, "Walk me back to the house?"

Cynthia nodded.

Outside, Maria said, "We need to talk."

"I'll say. Last week, I had no idea that you were…You let me believe you were as curious as I was."

"I'm sorry. I didn't want to freak you out, and I was drunk."

"When were you planning on telling me?"

"I guess I was waiting for the right time."

"Whatever." Cynthia kicked at pebbles in the driveway. "What about you and Joe getting married?"

"Bisexuals get married all the time. I want kids and a husband—a normal family."

"Bisexuality is *normal*? Did you tell Joe?"

"Wasn't an issue. It's not something I need, but it's nice in the right situation."

"Am I the *right situation*, Ree?"

Maria touched Cynthia's forearm. "Yes and no. You're the yes part, but the timing's bad."

Cynthia shook off Maria's hand. "What about the timing of this three-way thing? Jeez. Did you set this up?"

"No. And please don't be mad at me. I didn't know anything about this until you did."

Cynthia frowned. "I have two jobs coming up. I have to focus on work."

"I know.... 'Night, Cyn."

Cynthia stalked into the bungalow without saying goodnight.

A week later, they were in a Philadelphia Airport hotel, meeting their support team. Cynthia asked Mindy Spinks, the team leader, about the plan. "After all the meticulous training for other missions, why are we being rushed into this one?"

Mindy regurgitated the party line. "Salmanda is one of the bombers, and we just ID'd him. He's easy to get to in Bermuda; and we found out when he'd be going. If he dies outside the U.S., it diverts attention."

"Not good enough. Why me?"

Mindy buckled under Cynthia's glare. "Well, it's my opinion that the mucky-mucks are getting cold feet about your Spanish job—because you're untested. They ordered a simple mission to get your feet wet—in a place where they speak English. They also want to see if the medical examiners think it's a heart attack.

"One more thing, Cynthia," Mindy said. "Salmanda was one of the *Parsippany* truck bombers."

* * *

The trendy Bermuda crowd was shoulder-to-shoulder in the Moongate Lounge, Hamilton's newest dance club on Front Street. Rotating glitter balls hung from the ceiling, reflecting flashes of silver light that made the purple-gray lounge look like a Las Vegas stage. The noise reminded Cynthia of Bubbles. She sniffed expensive scents while squeezing between eager men and teasing women. Make that boys and girls—the clientele looked to average about eighteen. Cynthia felt old, and she sucked in a gut already flat. Attired in skimpy dresses, Cynthia and Maria anchored themselves at a cocktail table, sipping soft drinks until Dante Salmanda arrived.

When he sat at the bar, the Aities pressed their way onto the tiny dance floor. Cynthia wondered if Salmanda would notice them among the jail bait. Within seconds, he focused on two *women* gyrating together to a driving beat. Maria pressed her mouth to Cynthia's ear. "Don't worry. Just keep doing things like we rehearsed. He'll notice. He'll want you." Cynthia, her ear tingling to Maria's breath, was flushed without building a sweat.

They glanced toward Salmanda. He wasn't handsome, but he had the body language of self-confidence. Both women smiled at him and then at each other. When the song ended, they pushed to the bar near Salmanda's stool.

"Two Vodka Collinses, please," Cynthia called to the bartender.

Maria turned to Salmanda. "You were watching us. Do you like to dance?"

"Yeah."

Maria brightened. "I'm Julia. This is Amy."

Cynthia smiled.

"My name is Dante." Salmanda motioned to the bartender. "Put those on my tab."

"Thanks," Maria said. Salmanda was staring at Cynthia. In Spanish, Maria asked him, "Want to join us at our table?"

Salmanda nodded then followed them in a snaking path through the throng. Once they sat, the loud music kept them from talking, but Salmanda communicated with his eyes. Cynthia felt her dress melting under his gaze.

After a few minutes, Cynthia shouted, "Wanna dance with us?" Salmanda nodded, and the three danced, cautiously during the first song, but then suggestively, touching each other's hands and hips as the crowd shoved them together.

After three songs, Maria said to Salmanda in Spanish, "Too crowded, Dante. Do you want to party with us in our hotel?"

Salmanda nodded. "Where?"

"Elbow Beach. Take a taxi and meet us in room three-oh-four."

"Why not share the taxi?"

"We came together on a scooter." For Salmanda's benefit, the women exchanged smiles, giving him a chance to picture them straddling a revving bike in short dresses. "We're in room three-oh-four. Pick up a few bottles of red wine, okay?"

Outside, Salmanda watched the women put on leather jackets, gloves, and helmets and roar into the night with Cynthia driving. They raced to a parking lot on the edge of Hamilton, the chilly air numbing their legs.

Cynthia stopped the bike next to a van. Inside, Mindy had hot tea and warm blankets. With team member Alan Rider at the wheel, the van sped toward South Road and the Elbow Beach Hotel. As Cynthia and Maria warmed up, Mindy helped them don disguises—wigs, glasses, baggy pants, tennis shoes, gloves, and raincoats.

Rider parked the van in the Elbow Beach lot. Carrying a cell phone and high heels under her coat, Cynthia ducked into a side entrance and went up to Room 304 via the staircase. Maria followed two minutes later.

Once inside the room, both women removed their disguises and stuffed them into a garment bag in the closet. After straightening their dresses and hair, they checked in with Mindy by phone before settling in to wait. The décor was lost on Cynthia, who stared at her reflection in the mirror, seeing a stranger. She wiped beads of perspiration from her brow, sure her heart was audible.

"He's not coming," Cynthia said.

"I saw the look he gave you. He'll be here. He had to get the wine, remember."

Eyeing Maria's black leather driving gloves, Cynthia said, "If he's into the dominatrix look, he'll lean your way."

Ten minutes later, Mindy called to say Salmanda was on his way up. Maria turned on a portable CD player; Cynthia reminded herself to breathe.

Salmanda knocked.

Maria gave Cynthia a thumbs-up. "We'll be fine," she whispered.

They opened the door, hip-to-hip. Salmanda admired Cynthia.

"I'll take those," Maria said, accepting two bottles of wine. While Maria went to the bathroom sink, Cynthia turned the other way, strutting toward the drawn window curtains in time with the music. Salmanda followed. She could feel his eyes caressing her rear. Maria opened a bottle while Cynthia engaged Salmanda in conversation.

"We've never seen you before. First time in Bermuda?"

"No.... You two dance good."

She flashed a smile. "We dance better in private."

Maria brought over three plastic cups of wine. "A toast! To people who appreciate dancing," Maria said. They all tipped back their cups, but Cynthia didn't drink on the chance Maria had mixed up the glasses. Maria cooed, "Have a seat, drink up, and let us entertain you." She handed the open bottle to Salmanda.

While he sat on the bed holding a cup in one hand and the bottle in the other, Maria removed her gloves to the music, then she and Cynthia danced. Separated, they moved easily, but as Salmanda sipped wine, the women drew close enough to stroke each other. Then they kissed each other's fingers. In spite of the deadly game, Cynthia felt a tinge of pleasure when they touched.

Salmanda drained his cup, poured another, and kept staring. "Kiss—on lips," he encouraged. Sweat dripped off his chin.

Cynthia thought: what was taking so long? Had he drunk the poison or not? She gulped, and her throat scratched like sandpaper.

Maria spoke in Spanish. "We'd rather kiss *you*. Come on and dance with us—get our blood pumping."

Salmanda rose off the bed and put the cup and bottle on a dresser. "Great body, Amy," he said in English. His hand slid around her rear as he sucked on her mouth, erasing the sensation of Maria's finger.

"What do you like, Dante?" Maria asked.

He separated his lips from Cynthia long enough to say in Spanish, "I like to talk dirty. I want to fuck your friend while you two eat each other."

Maria pretended to think about the offer. "I'm good with that."

"Tell Amy what I said."

Cynthia had understood, so there was no surprise when Maria explained, "He wants to screw you while we sixty-nine."

Cynthia nodded and forced a smile. *What was taking so long?* She blocked out revulsion when he kissed her. "Get started," he whispered. She allowed him to take her hand and place it on Maria's breast. Cynthia felt her shoulder straps slide off—Salmanda's or Maria's hand? It didn't matter. It was all she could do to keep her spinning head from taking off like a helicopter. There was a hand on her ass. Maria was smiling; Cynthia tried. He gave them licking, leering nods of encouragement. Maria's lips were inches away...and coming closer.

Salmanda coughed. He grimaced and stumbled into Cynthia. She forced her arms between their torsos. Salmanda staggered. "Oh! H-help me," he muttered, grabbing Cynthia's shoulders. She shoved him away, watching him flail for something to hold.

"You okay, big guy?" Maria said.

"Ah—" Bug-eyed, Salmanda dropped to his knees. His face changed color before their eyes. The women stood and watched Salmanda die, groaning and clutching his chest with both hands. After a quiver, he slumped forward, motionless, head and knees on the floor as if bowing toward Mecca.

Cynthia stared at the body, enjoying a tingle. Goosebumps popped out on her arms. She sucked in a huge lungful of air and remembered her stepfather. The feeling was sweet. Dark but exceedingly sweet.

Maria tugged Cynthia's hand. "Let's go."

No response.

Maria shoved Cynthia. "What's the matter with you?"

Cynthia shook herself into action. The women put on their disguises and thin gloves before Maria felt Salmanda's wrist and neck for a pulse. "He's dead."

Cynthia called Mindy on the cell. "The dance is over and our partner dropped out. We're going home. Right, I almost forgot." Cynthia put hers and Maria's plastic cups into her coat pocket. Turning to Maria, she said, "I didn't touch anything else. How about you?"

Maria shook her head.

They slipped out of the room, taking the CD player and empty garment bag.

"What the hell got into you back there?" Maria asked after they exited into the parking lot. "You were in a daze."

"I don't know. A rush—like I was high."

"You scare me sometimes, Cyn." Maria opened her eyes wide. "Yes, definitely scary."

Patriots for Freedom had assassinated its first *I-80* conspirator.

The Bermuda medical examiner's report listed "heart attack" as the cause of death.

* * *

While Cynthia and Maria were in Bermuda, Anwar met with his most effective fundraiser, Roberto Garcia, in the study of his hacienda. Speaking in Spanish, Anwar said, "I trust the trip was enjoyable."

"You and your blindfolds—even for your cousin! Why did you bring me here ahead of schedule?"

"To give you a letter for Valeriano. The drug shipment will be early, and the date of our project has been delayed. It has become more expensive. We need more money—if you can manage not to get distracted by your whores."

"You are jealous, Anwar."

Anwar smirked at his cocky relative. "You're sick, addicted to the evils of the flesh. If you didn't raise so much with your harem, I would have nothing to do with you."

Garcia laughed. "You hypocrite."

"A woman is like fine wine—worth savoring. But you have no

standards."

"You should approve of the way I degrade Americans."

Anwar waved Garcia away. "Enough. Be prepared for the drugs a week early so you can ship them to the U.S. as soon as possible. We need the money."

Garcia balked. "What are we funding this time?"

Turning to face Garcia, Anwar glowered. "Every person need only know his own job, and your job is moving drugs. Do that, and let others worry about how the money gets spent. Now go. And do not open the letter. If the seal is broken, Valeriano will know you cannot be trusted."

Watching his brothers blindfold Garcia, Anwar thought ahead, calculating the price of vehicles, apartments, food, clothing, and ingredients.

Once Garcia departed, Anwar got down to the business of preparing orders. Sometime in the early morning, *NightOwl* would scramble the floating encryption algorithms. Shortly thereafter, Anwar's coded orders would instruct 100 cells in the United States about Operation Aqua. Each cell would purchase specified ingredients and mix and pack 100 three-kilo Gold Medal flour bags with concentrated poison. Then, on August 31st, all 100 cells would throw the bags into designated reservoirs. Access locations were being chosen where bags could be tossed near the confluence of water and outgoing pipes. The August date would fall in the summer, when American security would be lightest and water consumption the highest.

At 4:15 a.m. local time, Anwar's *NightOwl* receiver beeped. He fine-tuned the GPS signal. The origin was Sir Wilton Thatcher's second-floor study in Crestmont Manor outside London. The root algorithm was legitimate. Anwar transmitted his orders to the U.S.

There would be one more set of commands in August.

Anwar could see it all play out in his mind. The first evidence of a problem would be when people started dying, but deaths were a secondary objective to the terror that would spread. Eyes glowing with anticipation, he turned to his brother, Miguel. "Fear of water is just short of fear of air as the ultimate terror."

In southern New Jersey, a bearded man sat at a desk inside a log cabin. Using a cell-phone, he down-loaded an encrypted file from a satellite to his laptop. He spoke in Spanish. "Julio, run the translator."

An owl hooted while two computers churned for fifteen minutes.

"It's done. We have the formula." Julio pointed to a spot on the map spread over a card table. "And we have our reservoir, Rey. Here."

Rey's grin was camouflaged by his beard. "For Stone Harbor."

11

JIMMY TAYLOR

In Chattanooga, Jimmy Taylor gulped a drink of water before his appointment with the Chief of Police. Taylor would be discussing the missing person case of Alexander Gates, the managing trustee of the Gates Collection, the largest privately owned artillery ammunition collection in the world. Taylor's gut told him that Gates was dead. There was no physical evidence of a crime, but Cynthia James had motive, opportunity, and the allure to distract a known womanizer like Alex Gates.

"Re-open the Alexander Gates case, Chief. Remember, the James woman ran from me when I went to her home. Now, she's disappeared. At best, she's hiding something; at worst, she's guilty of murder."

Chief of Police Greg Haskell shook his head. "Jimmy, that's not evidence we can use to get a warrant."

"Don't you think it's more than coincidence that none of Gates's accounts have been touched since he disappeared?"

Haskell, formerly the Chief of Detectives, examined his immaculate fingernails. "None of his *known* accounts."

Taylor started to object, but Haskell put up his hand. "What else have you been up to? You haven't been using department resources on this case, have you, Jimmy?"

"No. But the Feds have a watch on his assets, and I've been checking with the FBI on my own time. Even Gates's overseas accounts have been dormant."

Haskell straightened his tie. "There's a big downside to reopening this case. It'll put unwanted scrutiny on the tourism industry. It's no secret, Jimmy, that I have a shot at being named interim D.A. I'd have to be mighty sure of success before I re-open a high-profile case. Do you have any *new* evidence?"

Taylor shook his head.

"I didn't think so. Is there any physical evidence that Alex Gates was kidnapped, harmed, or murdered?"

Taylor shook his head again.

"Jimmy, we need something that'll stand up in court."

"I've told you about the bartender's mother dying the year before when two of Gates's cannon balls rolled off a shelf. She died of complications from a fractured skull—ruled an accident. I know that's not evidence in our case, but it gives the James woman solid motive. And remember, there were two cannon balls missing from Gates's crate on the *Louisiana Lady*. So we have a missing man, two missing cannon balls, and an entire river for a vengeful daughter to dump them into. And the daughter, exercising thirty feet from Gates's cabin, has twenty minutes between security watches."

"So prove it."

"You've tied my hands. Re-open the case."

Haskell winked. "You seem to be making progress with the case closed. I'll continue to look the other way and make sure the Chief of Detectives does the same. The dormant accounts are significant and so's her flight. Get something concrete, and I'll see what I can do. Political realities are always changing. Now get out of here and catch us some criminals."

Taylor left Haskell's office with slouched shoulders. Plopping himself onto a chair in front of Bob Jefferson's desk, Taylor said to his partner, "Hey, Bob. Remember the Alex Gates missing person case from a year ago?"

"Sure, Boss." Jefferson was tall and lanky with a deep voice.

"I think I'm going crazy. Tell me again why we didn't go harder after the female bartender."

Jefferson pulled a pack of papers from a folder marked "Loose Ends."

"Let's see…" He thumbed through a few pages. "I assume you don't need me to tell you that the pols wanted to close the case." Taylor rolled his eyes and slid his pen into his mouth. Jefferson looked at his papers. "No body. No physical evidence. No witnesses placed her with Gates that night. The crew said she'd been exercising in the early a.m. every night for weeks. There were statements from Gates's friends that he was ready to go underground because of shady business—maybe flee the country. We thought he might have used a disguise to leave the boat, or he might have smuggled an inflatable raft on board in the cannon ball crate. That would account for the extra space. And we liked the brother more until his alibi checked out—his roommate and the woman next door verified Thomas was tossing and turning all night."

"And the reasons we liked Cynthia James?"

"Opportunity. A triangle between her and the Gates brothers. Nobody saw Alex Gates get off the boat. No activity on his offshore accounts. The ammo dealer swears there was a full crate of four cannon balls." Jefferson looked up. "And what you found out later about James's mother dying in Gates's cabin on a prior cruise. That gives her motive, and the missing cannon balls are quite a coincidence."

Taylor talked through the pen in his mouth. "And last time I was in Jersey, she bolted before I got to the door—ran into the woods and then raced away in her car." He rolled the pen between his fingers. "So which side of Cynthia James's scale is heavier, innocence or guilt?"

"With or without Haskell's finger pressing down on the innocent side?"

Taylor harrumphed. "Without."

"Guilt. But we can't prove it with what we have."

"How *can* we prove it?"

Jefferson thought. "It would help to have a body. A confession would be nice."

"And?"

"And, I think we're more likely to find a body than get a confession from that ice maiden. And if the body's in the water, it's a grain of silt in the river."

Taylor shuffled to his cluttered desk where he reviewed notes from numerous interviews with passengers and crew on the *Louisiana Lady*. As much as he wanted to find something new, he came up empty. A woman in the adjacent room had heard a female voice in Alex's cabin—when Cynthia was still working in the bar—and later, running water between 3:00 and 4:00 a.m., but there was nobody who admitted seeing him after he said goodnight to friends in the bar around midnight. His bags were outside his door, ready to be taken ashore, when the neighboring woman put hers out at 5:00 a.m. No matter how Taylor fit the pieces together, there was no evidence to support his instincts.

Jimmy Taylor's guess was based on more than the fact that Cynthia had fled from him in New Jersey. It was based on more than the way her mother died. There was the interview a year ago, full of subtleties. Taylor leaned back in his chair, slid a Pentel into his mouth, and recalled his interrogation of Cynthia James, picturing everything.

He had set up in stateroom 120 on the *Louisiana Lady* to interview crew members about Alexander Gates. It was late evening on the day of Gates's early morning disappearance. When Cynthia entered the cabin, Taylor thought she moved like a cat. Her shapely physique was that of an athlete. She wore her bartender's uniform—white shirt, black pants, gold vest, with western tie—and neither sought nor avoided eye contact. She was as cool as any of the crew.

Once Cynthia sat on a folding chair, she seemed less attractive. Taylor sat on the end of one twin bed. The quarters were cramped—smaller than a cheap hotel room. A tape recorder hummed. Taylor had the recording memorized, so there was no need to play it again. The conversation came to him—word for word.

"Ms. James, tell me of your whereabouts from Monday evening around eleven p.m. until the passengers disembarked this morning."

"I was working in the Louisiana Lounge." She pronounced it *Loosiana*, as did all the crew. "I was there until about two-forty or two-forty-five."

"Did you see or speak to Alex Gates in the lounge last night?"

"Yes."

"Please elaborate."

"He ordered drinks. I served them. We chatted. He flirted."

"Did you flirt back?"

"Yes. He's very handsome and a *very* good tipper."

"What did he talk about?"

"Nothing that he didn't think would help him get inside my pants."

Taylor raised his eyebrows. "Did you have any reason to suspect that he wanted to...ah, have a romantic relationship?"

"Yes. He told me."

"Were you interested?"

"There's a rule against fraternization with passengers."

"But were you interested?"

She shifted position on the chair. "No."

Taylor spoke while jotting notes. "How much did Alex Gates drink last night?"

"I served him three glasses of wine. I don't know what he drank earlier...or later."

"Was Mr. Gates intoxicated?"

She hesitated.

"You're an experienced bartender, right? Did you think he was drunk?"

"No. He was loose—buzzed—but not drunk."

"You say you left the lounge at two-forty."

"Or two-forty-five. I went straight down to my quarters and changed for my workout."

"Why did you choose that night to exercise so late?"

"I always exercise when I get off from the late shift."

"Go on."

She squinted.

"About the exercising?" Taylor prompted.

"I work out on the exercise bike on the stern of the boat every morning from about three to four."

"How long did you work out that night?"

"Sixty-five minutes."

"Did anyone see you?"

"Yes. The night watchman comes by three times an hour. I checked my watch each time."

"What time zone was your watch set to? Chattanooga's in the Eastern Time Zone, while the night before the boat was in Central."

"Central. I never changed to Eastern time."

"Then what?"

"I finished exercising. A little after four. I walked two cool-down laps around the deck, checked the bulletin board for changes in the schedule, went down to my quarters, showered, and went to bed."

"Hmm. Most people's recall doesn't sound so…rehearsed."

She frowned. "Would you rather I stumble over words and keep changing my story?"

He waved it off. "Sorry if I sounded harsh. Did you see anyone after exercising and before bed?"

"No."

"Not even roommates?"

"All three were asleep—or at least their eyes were shut."

"They didn't wake up when you showered?"

"The crew bathroom is right next to the engine room—nobody can hear the shower over the rumble."

Taylor made a note. "Did you see Alex Gates?"

"No. Not after he left the bar."

"When was that again?"

"I don't think I said. I believe he left around midnight."

"Did you know his room is right at the back of the deck where you were exercising?"

"Yes. He told me his room number."

Taylor leaned forward. "Why would he tell you that?"

She matched his lean. "For bar charges—every night, all week."

Taylor sat back and put his pen into his mouth. "You know, we've had a lab team going over Alex Gates's cabin with a fine-toothed comb." Taylor paused for effect. "Were you ever in his cabin?"

"No," she said.

Though it was a lie, Taylor said, "Witnesses say they saw you near his cabin door sometime after three."

Cynthia was decisive. "They must be mistaken. Whoever they saw wasn't me. I ducked into the door by the Purser's office to check the bulletin board before I went to bed, but not back by his cabin."

Taylor flipped through his notebook. "You said you flirted with Alex Gates. Did you *like* him?"

"No."

"Would you have been interested if there wasn't a rule against it?"

She hesitated. "No."

"Really?"

"He liked me. I flirted back. That's it."

"But you said you didn't like him."

"I didn't. Flirting is good for tips."

"Was Alex Gates a good tipper?"

"As I already said: very good."

"But nothing was going on between you two?"

"No. But my boss noticed the flirting. She warned me about getting involved."

"But didn't you get involved anyway?"

"No. I follow orders."

Taylor tapped the notebook on his thigh. "I've heard passengers and crew talk about a competition for points between the Gates brothers, and that you were keeping score."

Her look implied, "Is there a question?"

"Were you aware of a contest involving points, and if so, what was it about?"

Cynthia smiled for the first time. "It was a tipping contest. They each claimed to be the bigger tipper. I kept track, that's all."

"Is that normal?"

"No, sir. But the Gateses weren't normal passengers."

"How so?"

"They drank a lot, tipped a lot, and were into outdoing the other. We don't get a lot of sibling rivalries like that."

"So which one was the bigger tipper?"

"Alex."

"Back to that night. While you were exercising, did you see Alex Gates, or anyone else, around his cabin?"

"No. Except for the night watchman."

"What about the next morning?"

"No."

Taylor's look begged an explanation.

"I was still in bed when the passengers disembarked. When I got up, I went about my normal turnover duties until the new passengers began boarding this afternoon." She coughed.

Taylor gestured. "Water?"

She nodded. He poured.

"Ms. James, do you know whether Mr. Alex Gates collected anything unusual?"

"Yes. He said he collected artillery ammunition. He was very proud of his collection—some family foundation started by his grandfather. He mentioned the Smithsonian and other museums where his pieces had been shown."

"Did you see any of his cannon balls?"

"No."

"Did you know he had some on board?"

She hesitated. "Yes. He talked about them in the lounge on Sunday night—the day he said he bought them in Florence."

"Did he say how many he had on board?"

She pursed her lips and shook her head. "No, but he used the plural—*balls*—so it must have been more than one."

"Ms. James, do you know why there would be crumpled newspapers jammed into half his cannon ball crate."

Beads of sweat seeped onto her brow. "N-no."

"Give me a theory, Ms. James. Any guesses?"

She bit her lip. "Maybe the crate was too big—so newspapers were used to fill up extra space."

"Then how could Monday's paper get into the crate?"

Cynthia's eyes darted toward the door.

"He brought the crate on board Sunday morning, right? So why would *Monday's* paper be crumpled inside…unless somebody removed something?"

She focused clear and cool on Taylor. "I don't know. I'm not a detective."

"Ms. James…don't leave the boat."

She rolled her eyes. "Am I dismissed?"

"Yeah." Taylor sucked on his pen. "For now."

In his mind, Taylor admired the way she had stood and walked out of the cabin. Had it been a year? Seemed like only days ago.

* * *

That night, Taylor sat in his den, thinking about Cynthia James. The day after the interrogation, Taylor had checked her name on the

Internet, finding nothing. With a few minutes to kill before Leno, Taylor brought up Google and typed, "Cynthia James."

On the 41st item, he saw something new. A Cynthia James showed up as a surviving sister in a profile about an *I-80* victim. There were no living parents, so it could be her. Taylor Googled "Samuel K. James," finding fifty hits. He started reading articles, printing those that looked promising.

"Jimmy! Leno's on," his wife called from the bedroom.

"In a minute."

One article reported Sam's family had moved from Cooperstown, New York, after an incident with Sam's stepfather. Taylor Googled local newspapers in the Cooperstown area and printed a list before turning off the computer.

At 8:00 a.m. the next morning, Taylor was on the phone. After three extension switches, he heard, "Bill Wooster, *Cooperstown Gazette*."

"My name's Taylor from the *Chattanooga Sentinel*. I'm looking for someone who can tell me anything about a Sam James living in Cooperstown in the early nineties. He would have been around fourteen then."

"Sure. I remember him. How can I help?"

Taylor swallowed hard. "I'm following up on human interest stories about I-Eighty victims and their families."

"Did Sam's mother die on Route Eighty?" Wooster asked.

"Sam's mother?"

"Yes. Karen Smith. She moved from Cooperstown after her daughter killed her husband—second husband. Moved to take a job in New York."

Taylor's heart accelerated. "Um, no. It was *Sam* who died."

"Shit! I hadn't heard. I followed the family for a while because the story here was such a big deal. We don't get many killings in town."

Taylor crossed his fingers. "The daughter was named Cynthia, right?"

"Yeah. Cynthia and Sam James. The stepfather was named Frank Smith. A real charmer, but what an asshole. An alcoholic. I'll bet your paper wants the inside story on the whole sordid mess."

"What can you tell me?"

"You got shut out by the police, right?"

"Ah, yeah, right."

"Figures. They sealed the files 'cause of the girl being only seventeen and raped like that."

"You sound like you reported the story."

"Yup." Wooster's pride came through in his voice. "I remember like it was yesterday."

Taylor squinted, as if straining to see Wooster's eyes from a thousand miles away. "We're most interested in Cynthia. What was there about her story that will resonate with readers today?"

"Ah, Cynthia. She was a sweet girl. Not flashy, but pretty. It shouldn't have happened to her."

"What shouldn't have happened?"

"The violence. She was all beat up—lip cut, bruised ribs. When the stepfather was done with her and went for the mother again, Cynthia nailed him in the head with a softball bat. Smith died from swelling of the brain." Wooster paused, but Taylor was too savvy to interrupt him. "I saw the girl. Hair cut short after it happened. Eyes didn't focus, like a zombie. She didn't talk or smile or anything. She got off without doing time, of course. Everyone in town felt for her. Due to the circumstances and her age, the case was sealed. I wanted to do a touchy-feely follow-up a month later, but her mother told me they were leaving town—that Cynthia couldn't stay in the house. The mother wouldn't let me talk to her. She couldn't go to school. Very sad."

"Uh-huh," Taylor said.

"Then the mother got a job in New York and the family moved. I heard there was a hotshot shrink in Manhattan." Wooster paused. "What a damn shame about Sam. He was a good kid. I always wondered… You must know what happened to Cynthia and her mother."

Taylor swallowed. "No. I'm just starting on the story. That's why I'm calling around. By the way, where was Sam during the rape?"

Wooster choked on his answer. "Baseball practice."

Taylor said goodbye and hung up. He was intrigued. Cynthia's trauma in Cooperstown was significant. Pondering the case, Taylor wondered: did Alexander Gates try to rape Cynthia James?

12

BON VOYAGE

The final weeks of Cynthia's training prepared for ways the plan could go wrong. When Cynthia complained about misplaced priorities, Carole said, "Job one is bringing you home alive. Anything that makes that more likely is worth practicing, and I don't care how much you bitch about it."

Cynthia shut up.

Every afternoon, she faced a series of improv scenarios: Cabrera having a bodyguard; the poison not working; witnesses in the killing zone; Cabrera being injured and unable to go running. The only times Cynthia failed were when Carole added multiple twists.

At a going-away barbecue the night before her departure, Cynthia asked Carole, "Why not Maria for this hit? She's a good runner and speaks the best Spanish."

Carole threw back her head and laughed. "It's important to the program that the first mission in Spain be a screaming success. We want the best, and you're the best. There, Cyn, you fished the compliment right out of me."

Later, Maria found Cynthia facing the ocean at the foot of the stairs to the beach. Maria stopped on the last step and massaged Cynthia's shoulders. "Any second thoughts?"

Cynthia stretched her neck and gazed at the surf. "Sure. I think about it every day—the morality and mortality—trying to talk myself out of it, but each night the answer's the same. I'm going because we're doing right. My brother, your fiancé and father, and all the others who died deserve my best effort."

"What about Thomas?"

Cynthia raised a hand and covered Maria's, where it soothed a shoulder. "Thomas might always be a maybe. What if I can never love him? But this mission is real, and it's where my focus is. I'm nervous, but it's a good nervous."

Maria gave Cynthia's shoulders a baby-bear hug from behind—not too hard, not too soft. "Good luck, Cyn."

"I wish you were going with me." She leaned her head back on Maria's shoulder. "I really want to nail this bastard."

Cynthia would be traveling to Spain as Cynthia Moss of Garden City, Long Island. Her strike team was booked on a "Spain Fiesta" bus tour, starting in Madrid and going to Cordoba, Seville, Gibraltar, and Costa del Sol. After the hit in Seville, they would stay on the tour unless a problem developed. The most likely problem? Being wanted for murder.

That night, at the Newark Airport Hilton, Cynthia met the other members of her expedition. Gabriella Sanchez, the team leader, would be Cynthia's roommate on the tour. Gabriella, 38, was a former Secret Service bodyguard who spoke fluent Spanish. With dark hair and coloring, Gabriella could pass as a Spaniard but could also act totally American. Superficially, the team leader was Carole Burns's opposite. Where Carole was tall and lean, Gabriella was short and buxom. As professionals, however, they were alike—thorough and demanding.

The two men on the team were David Smathers and Sergio Guardado. Sergio, the son of a Russian mother and Spanish father, spoke in Cynthia's presence only when addressed. He was hulking, quiet, and kind to others, particularly Gabriella. Having grown up in Madrid, Serg was the team's local expert.

David Smathers, like Cynthia, had never been to Spain, but he spoke passable Spanish. He was a career bodyguard who looked the part, though he joked that he'd rather disarm you with quips than brute strength. While not exactly handsome, he had an endearing grin, and Cynthia was glad to have a relationship with Thomas Gates. Otherwise, David might have been a distraction.

Gabriella snapped her fingers. "The plan's pretty simple. Serg and I just got back from a week in Spain where we shadowed Cabrera. He runs every morning—early—but there's no pattern of time and place that we can be sure of, so I'd rather make a running date than try to choreograph a chance meeting on the fly. The good news is: he goes to Carmen's Café every night to pick up girls. He likes 'em lean and athletic. Cynthia, you'll meet him there the first night. If he makes a play for you, you'll make a running date for the next morning—get him to Parque de Maria Luisa. That's plan A, so we can isolate him before most people hit the streets. If he doesn't take the bait, we'll go back to Carmen's the next night and take him out there. That's plan B."

Cynthia tapped her false fingernails on the table. "Why the poison under long nails?"

"Liquid or pills won't fly when you're out running, plus the nails'll work in the bar, too. He drinks beer out of long neck bottles—hard to get anything into the mouth without being obvious."

"Why did you two come back to the U.S.?" Cynthia asked. "Why didn't David and I simply meet you in Spain?"

Gabriella's flashing eyes made Cynthia feel naïve. "It's important that we travel the same as anyone taking a vacation tour. And frankly, your Spanish isn't good enough to deal with every eventuality on your own. Traveling with fake IDs can be tricky."

Gabriella looked at David. "Remember, don't shave until the job's done." David nodded.

After Gabriella had reviewed maps of the city and the layout of the nightclub twice, she said, "It's late. We have a long day of travel tomorrow. You guys'll sleep in shifts. I don't expect any trouble here, but you have to get used to it."

The men said goodnight and went to their room.

Gabriella shut the door and glared. "You're not impressing me, Cynthia. This is dangerous shit. No exercise with protective pads."

"I know."

"Cocky 'cause you've killed a man? I've seen your file. You won't have a freakin' baseball bat, and it won't be two against one."

Cynthia measured her response. "First of all, I can't afford to lose my cool. Second, Carole said you'd be hard on me."

"Oh she did, did she? And did Carole say why?"

Cynthia sat on Gabriella's bed. "She said you wanted to be one of the assassins. She said they rejected you—probably because you're too old—and you're bitter about it. And Carole said that your second choice was the training job that she got."

Gabriella's eyes narrowed, but she said nothing.

"Look, you're my boss," Cynthia said, "but I have to tell you—we need to get along, or we'll fail. And if we fail, I'm the one likely to die. But if we all do our jobs, I'm gonna nail the bastard, whether you believe in me or not."

From that moment on, things were fine between them.

In the same hotel, a woman Cynthia had never met prepared for a flight to Central America. The trim woman's passport identified her as Cynthia James. She would be managing food and beverage services for rallies sponsored by *Patriots for Freedom*. She would keep a journal to be passed to the real Cynthia James when they both returned to the States. Only then would Cynthia learn what Cynthia James had been doing while Cynthia Moss was striking a blow for freedom.

13

SPANISH MOSS

Cynthia enjoyed Madrid, a vibrant mix of old and new. In the Plaza Mayor, Cynthia was mesmerized by intricate carvings adorning the building facades. The balconies reminded her of the French Quarter in New Orleans. The tourist map of center city was missing a few streets, but Gabriella prevented them from getting lost in a maze of alleys. Cynthia's first meal in Spain was lunch at a quaint bar just off the plaza. All the food was displayed on counters, in cases, or hung from hooks; Cynthia wondered if they refrigerated anything in Spain.

"Don't speak any Spanish," Gabriella lectured while they traversed a modern section of the city. "You ordered lunch in Spanish. Don't do it again. In Seville, it'll be important that people think you can't speak the language. So what are the only things you should say?"

Cynthia answered in the sing-song rhythm of a schoolgirl. "*Buenos días, por favor,* and *no hablos español, Señorita Sanchez.*"

Gabriella patted Cynthia on the head. "*Muy bueno.* Tonight we'll practice switching the middle fingernails—by Tuesday we should do it in fifteen minutes. Ah, there's the Prado. And when you see the security, you'll be glad we're clean. You are clean, aren't you? No nasty stick pins in your hair?"

"No, *Señorita Sanchez.* I good student."

The Prado was more art museum than a person should tackle while jet-lagged. The endless rooms became indistinguishable from each other, and Cynthia, dragging feet that felt like marble sculptures, got lost several times. When Gabriella took her to see Goya's work, Cynthia's bones felt the hatred in his illustrations of the Spanish war with Napoleon. There was a darkness in the drawings to which she could relate.

Before turning in, Cynthia practiced replacing regular fake nails with the special hinged ones. She had trouble spreading the glue. It took eighteen minutes. "Not bad for someone who can't keep her eyes open," Gabriella said.

On Saturday morning, the team went for a stroll in Parque de Ritero. Sergio walked twenty yards ahead of the ladies, with David thirty behind. As they passed the Crystal Palace, its windows glistening like diamonds in the morning sun, Cynthia asked Gabriella, "Do we really need protection? We haven't done anything."

"Their job now is to see that you're kept safe so you *can* do something."

Cynthia thought for a moment. "What are the guys looking for?"

"Anything unusual. Like a man wearing an overcoat in warm weather, or people who look out of place. Sergio's spent a lot of time in Spain, so he knows the customs. David is ready to react to trouble ahead and watch our backs. I'm doing the same thing. While talking with you, my eyes are darting around behind these shades."

During a leisurely circle around a large pond and the street performers who lined one side, Cynthia said, "Why does Cabrera like to screw Americans if he hates us so much?"

Gabriella cocked an eyebrow until Cynthia said, "Oh."

Gabriella nodded. "He gets off on degrading us. It's men like him that make the f-word a profanity instead of a pleasure. Which is it for you?"

Cynthia's raised eyebrows and lowered chin conveyed an emphatic, "Excuse me?" She hoped that would be the end of it.

"Just curious. It seems to me that if you'll kill a man for money when he wants to screw you...Well, maybe the f-word is profane."

Cynthia didn't want to get into her prudish Protestant upbringing or past traumas. "Let's drop it, okay?"

Gabriella let it go, but only for an hour. After lunch, while sitting on the grass near a pond in front of the Crystal Palace, she used the presence of two swans to reopen the dialog. "The white swan and the black swan make me think about the good versus evil of sex. How about you?"

Cynthia rolled her eyes. "Jeez. Why won't you let it go?"

Gabriella lowered her voice. "Because you're selling sex. I need to know your attitude about what you're selling. Is it beautiful or profane? It makes a difference in how we should prepare—make-up, clothes. Like I said, this won't be anything like the drills. Am I getting through?"

Cynthia pulled at some grass. "It's profane, mostly. Petting when I was a teenager was scary; I felt guilty because of religion. Then I was raped. After that, I stayed away from men to the point that people thought I was a lesbian. Since then, arousal seems wrong. The negative association is so strong that evil excites me, so there's a bit of a turn-on in this job." When Gabriella said nothing, Cynthia said, "Does this mean I'm fired?"

"No." Gabriella smiled. "What you feel isn't that unusual. It'll help us get ready with the right look for your body language."

Cynthia's eyes twinkled. "So, you're gonna take over Carole's wardrobe-advisor job."

"We can't completely trust the taste of a cowgirl, can we?"

Cynthia looked around, making sure nobody was close enough to hear. "What about you? Have you ever killed a man you had...you know?"

"Yes," Gabriella said. "Both directly and indirectly. I've slept with informants—spies and double-agents—who were killed by others, and I've killed sexual partners myself."

"Did you like it?" Cynthia asked.

"The sex or the killing?"

Cynthia chuckled. "The killing."

"Yes. The men I eliminated were enemies. It feels good to kill enemies. And it felt good to do a job for my country. I'd do it again."

Cynthia wasn't sure if Gabriella was telling the truth. After a moment, Cynthia squinted. "So how'd you get on the team if you're not a new face?"

"Plastic surgery, longer hair, and fifteen extra pounds. I used to be thinner."

"Will *I* need plastic surgery? Marco neglected to mention that in his recruiting speech."

Gabriella smiled. "Well, only if you plan on being a career professional."

That was something she hadn't thought about.

On the way to the hotel, Gabriella reviewed their cover. "One more time. What's our history?"

Like a well-prepared student, Cynthia rattled off their cover story. "You're my aunt's friend. When she got sick, you stepped in and took her place on the tour because you love Spain. We've been acquainted with each other, but not too well, so we shouldn't be expected to know every detail. I'm from Garden City; you're from Manhattan. We met the guys at the airport while waiting for the flight. They've been hitting on us, and we've been encouraging them. You and Serg are one item in the making; me and David another."

"Good. Now, you have time for a nap."

The afternoon was spent on a bus tour of Madrid. The guide was Lucia, a jovial middle-aged woman whose English was little better than Cynthia's Spanish. The tour was bilingual, with the guide talking for a few minutes in Spanish then repeating what she had said in English.

At the stop by Palacio Real, Cynthia and Gabriella bought ice cream: one Italian gelato and one Spanish helado. Finishing off the gelato, Cynthia asked, "Why'd they send us on the bilingual tour? There's a lot of wasted time."

"Two reasons," Gabriella said. "This company uses a hotel in Seville that's two blocks from Carmen's Café. For that convenience, you'll put up with the Spanish and like it."

"What's the other reason?"

"It's a good tutorial for you. Listen to the Spanish, and then check your comprehension with the guide's translation."

Before re-boarding the bus, Cynthia engaged the guide in English. "Lucia, you know a lot about Spanish history. What can you tell me about the Spanish-American War—from Spain's point of view?"

Lucia frowned. "A dark time."

"What did the Spanish people think at the time?"

"Then, there was a...backlash among intellectuals against the Spanish government that brought on humiliation. As years passed..." She hesitated.

"Tell me the truth," Cynthia said.

"Spanish people realized that United States...bullied a sick country and stole our empire—Cuba, Guam, the Philippines. The sinking of battleship *Maine* was a convenient excuse to promote international theft and destruction of Spanish Pacific fleet."

"What about today?"

"Old news, best forgotten. Everyone involved is dead long time."

"But are there any Spaniards who still hold a grudge?"

"Hold a grudge?"

Cynthia thought. "Are there any still mad at America for the war?"

Lucia's eyes darkened. "One hears crazy rumors, but there are crazy rumors about everything, yes? We should be going."

The team got together at a stop outside the Plaza del Torro bullfighting stadium. "Nobody's acting suspicious," Serg said.

David smiled. "Except for the way the men look at you two."

Cynthia tried not to smile, but the job's emphasis on appearance had given her a touch of vanity.

"So the four of us can start hanging around together," Gabriella said. "Two single guys. Two single gals. David, you and Cynthia sit together on the next leg, okay?" David nodded.

That night, they dined in the hotel restaurant. David entertained them with coin tricks—not what Cynthia expected from a bodyguard. The day ended with fingernail practice—fifteen minutes on the dot—and a decent night's sleep.

Sunday would be a long day. After traveling from Madrid to Seville—with a stop in Cordoba—the team would make contact with the mark that night. As on all travel days, they had to be packed by 7:00 a.m. and finished with breakfast for departure at 8:00. Aside from testing her Spanish comprehension, Cynthia's time on the bus was useless for preparation because the strike team had to play at being tourists.

The mosque/cathedral in Cordoba fascinated Cynthia. It was a mix of Roman, Moorish, and Castilian cultures in one massive building. The guide explained that over the past 1500 years, Southern Spain had been controlled by three different cultures in 500-year reigns: first the Romans, then the Islamic Moors, and finally the Catholic Castilians. Cynthia learned that when the Moors built the mosque in the tenth century, they reused arches from Roman buildings to support their giant structure. Five centuries later, after the Castilians drove the Moors out of Spain, they destroyed all the Mosques except the one in Cordoba. Here, they built a Cathedral inside the Mosque, resulting in a building that combines all three of the major influences in present day Castile.

Strolling inside with David, Cynthia gaped at the walls and ceiling. "Incredible! This is the most amazing structure I've ever seen. It makes you think about yourself."

"What do you mean?"

She hesitated. "Well, things that seem like they'll last forever are only temporary. They don't disappear; they're changed to become part of something else."

"Mumbo-jumbo," David laughed.

She was trusting her life to this man, but that's not why she opened up. "Did you know I was raped?"

He looked down. "I'm sorry."

"It's like those Roman arches; the rape isn't in me the same way it was ten years ago. But it's part of who I've become—part of what I'm doing here."

David started to reply, but changed his mind. A few minutes later, he took her fingers the way a shy boy takes the hand of a girl. Cynthia knew it was appropriate within their cover.

"Hope you're over it," David said.

"Over what?"

"The rape. That was a gutsy thing to tell a man."

Her throat closed down. This guy looked the same as men who had annoyed her for ten years, but he didn't act the same, and he sure didn't talk the same.

When they boarded the bus, Gabriella and Sergio were already sitting together, so Cynthia slid in next to David, giving herself the next few hours to think about not thinking about him. She found her eyes coming back to his jaw, covered with stubble.

On the highway to Seville, Cynthia's heart rate accelerated when a police car pulled the bus over to the side of the road. "We weren't speeding," she whispered across the aisle to Gabriella. "Should we be worried?"

"Relax. This is routine. The police will read the computer log to verify that the bus hasn't been speeding and that the driver hasn't exceeded his allotted driving hours."

Cynthia strained to hear the policeman and driver.

The stop proved to be exactly what Gabriella said it was. Once the bus was on the road again, Cynthia said, "That's a pretty good idea. If we did that in the U.S., the roads would be safer."

"No way it'll happen," Gabriella said. "We Americans think we have a God-given right to break the law." After a short pause, both women looked at each other and exchanged twisted smiles.

* * *

The bus was late arriving in Seville, eliminating a planned daylight reconnaissance of the Parque de Maria Luisa. The team ate dinner at a restaurant close to the hotel before attempting to make contact with Cabrera. Serg and David hurried to the Carmen's Café, settling in at the bar. When Cynthia stepped out of the bathroom, towel wrapped around her, a black outfit was lying on her bed.

"I watched him for a week," Gabriella said. "Based on the women he picked up, these clothes should get his attention."

"Did he try to pick *you* up?" Cynthia asked.

"Oh, no," Gabriella said as she brushed Cynthia's hair. "I was in a gray wig, and Don Juan Cabrera likes his women young and lean."

Cynthia reached for her nail kit, noticing a slight tremor in her fingers.

"No," Gabriella said with a pat on Cynthia's knuckles. "No poison tonight."

"I forgot. I'm a little nervous."

"Goes with the job sometimes."

"So he likes black. Why not the zippered V-neck?"

"This one better matches your attitude and body-language for a first contact. You'll use that Protestant hard-to-get act—because if he likes you, he'll want to take you home tonight. When you don't let him, he'll want you even more."

"If he wants to take me home, why not just do it at his place?"

Gabriella brushed Cynthia's hair with long even strokes. "Too many risks—too little control. We might resort to that if there was no other way, or if a mark had bodyguards, but not for Cabrera."

"I still don't get the clothes. If not the V-neck, why not a short skirt and spiked heels? I thought that's what—"

"These heels are low—what a runner would wear. The pants are thin and tight enough for him to tell you're athletic. He doesn't go for the cheap hooker look. This neckline will give a glimpse of cleavage. Don't forget to lean down a few times to show it off."

Doing her make-up the way Maria had taught her, Cynthia was applying mascara when Gabriella touched her wrist. "That's enough. You look fine."

"But—"

Gabriella took the mascara. "Look, Cyn, this guy'll decide if you're worth his while in two seconds. He won't notice how much mascara you have on. After that, it's your sex appeal that'll make him want you. That comes from inside—self confidence."

Cynthia nodded. She pinned up her hair with the stiletto, got dressed, and put on round orange earrings that resembled tiny fruit—one microphone and one transmitter.

Gabriella's cell phone vibrated. "Yes.... Okay." She clicked off. "That was Serg. Cabrera just walked in. It's show time. Break a leg."

Cynthia's hands jittered on the short walk to Carmen's. She wished Maria were there. She slapped her forearm. "Stop shaking," she mumbled. "Be an actress. Be Carmen...da-*dump*-da-dump. Keep moving." After a pause at the café door, she pushed it open.

A row of Purple Fuchsia plants hung inside the front windows. The crowd was young, and the place hummed, less oppressive and brighter than she expected. Carole had told her from the first day of training that there was always a chance Cynthia would have to flee the United States. Cynthia loved Seville and liked Carmen's. She could hang out here.

It took less than ten seconds to identify Alejandro Cabrera, who looked like his pictures. He leaned his lanky frame against the bar rail as if he were a model for *GQ*, hair gelled and T-shirt sleeves rolled over his shoulders. He was talking to a blonde with too much make-up and not enough clothes. The blonde was staring at his stubble—scruffy and dangerous. Cynthia wondered how guys could keep the perpetual three-day-old beard look. Serg, who had been saving a barstool next to Cabrera, shuffled away so Cynthia could move in. She sat and stared straight ahead, hoping the irregular thu-*thump*-thump-thump of her heart wasn't making her bounce on the stool. She felt plain—thirsty and plain. *Keep moving.* She rotated her seat and motioned to the bartender. "Vodka, por favor."

The bartender asked her in Spanish what kind of vodka she wanted.

"*No hablos español.*"

"Stoli," came a resonant voice from her right—Cabrera. "Ask for Stoli." His smile was that of a man who thought women fantasized about him. The blonde at his side shook her shimmering hair, looking jealous. Cynthia tried to smile, but her jaw tightened.

"I speak English. I am Al Cabrera." His English was good. The blonde frowned.

"Cynthia Moss." Her voice was dry.

She extended a hand, expecting him to kiss it with continental flair, but he shook it—with an encouraging squeeze. "Come here often?"

That wasn't the suave line she was expecting. Nothing came out of her mouth but air. *Keep moving. Be Carmen.* She rocked on the stool and crossed her legs. "No. It's my first time in Seville. You?"

He laughed. "This is my place—my *Cheers*—where everyone knows my name." He waved at a chunky man at the corner stool, as if to prove his point.

"Oh, yes. *Cheers*. TV." She smiled at him, feeling less terrified. The blonde was gone.

"How long will you be in Seville?"

Cynthia's drink arrived, and she picked it up. "Just two days. I'm on a tour. Do you know any good places to run in Seville?" That had slipped out too quickly. Oh, well...

"Ah, you are a runner?"

She nodded. "I like parks and run every morning." She leaned down to smooth the calf of one pant leg.

He sat on the stool next to hers. "So do I. Perhaps we can run together."

"Maybe." Her jaw relaxed enough to smile. "Where would we run?"

"The Paseo de Colon along the river and the Parque de Maria Luisa by the exposition grounds. Where is your hotel?"

"Near here." She re-crossed her legs, feeling the heat. "We could meet outside my hotel."

"Or..."

"Or what?" she asked, leaning over to flick an imaginary spec from the toe of her shoe.

"I'll have to study your...face and think about a worthy spot."

"You flatter me."

Cynthia nursed her vodka, but it disappeared during a discussion of *Don Quixote*. They chatted through a second drink, which Cynthia poured into a used glass when Cabrera went to the toilet. He came back cracking jokes that weren't funny, but she laughed. Cabrera smirked, pleased with himself. "It is a beautiful night. Would you like to go for a walk?"

Cynthia hesitated. A walk was allowed within the guidelines, and it would keep her moving. "Okay. Where to?"

"Follow me."

Cynthia unveiled her best smile. "I think I should be careful where I follow you."

Cabrera paid for her drinks and put his palm on the small of her back, guiding her toward the door. His heat penetrated her skin. Along the way he waved, winked, and pointed at everyone along the bar. Her insides contracted. She was tonight's notch on Cabrera's belt.

They strolled three blocks down the sidewalk and around the corner, talking about nothing. After they walked even more slowly for two more blocks, Cabrera complimented her figure and ran his hand around her waist. There were few pedestrians, so Cynthia stopped. She knew David was shadowing her, but she was still nervous. "We should be getting back. My hotel's the other way, and I want to run early."

"I will walk you to your hotel," he said. "What time should we meet tomorrow?"

She pretended to think. "Oh...how about six?"

"Six, at your hotel," he agreed.

Two blocks later, his hand had slid below her waist.

"And here we are," she said, stopping outside the entrance. "I'll see you right here tomorrow."

He leaned to kiss her; she turned so his lips landed on her cheek. His beard was more ticklish than scratchy.

"Thank you for the drinks and walk, Al. I look forward to our run. Wear a black muscle shirt. I like black."

With a persistent twist of his neck, he slid his lips over hers. There was no pleasure, but she allowed him to kiss her. He tasted like her stepfather.

14

SUNRISE IN SEVILLE

There was no sleep for Cynthia James. She stared at the ceiling, waiting for the sun so she could assassinate a terrorist. Was this really the same thing as a soldier killing for his country, or was it murder? At the compound, she had been a model student, allowing everyone to believe that her mind was as trained as her body, but a shadow of doubt always lurked—lurked because Cynthia refused to surrender free will. Free will. Freedom. That's what this was about.

Whenever her resolve weakened, she thought of Sam, his freedom gone, his remains confined to a buried urn. Was that a cheap mental trick? Maybe, but Sam, with his insight and empathy, might have changed the world. Now that weight was on her shoulders.

The team was up at 4:45 a.m. Cynthia glued on her lethal nails in fifteen minutes. Serg and Gabriella left the hotel at 5:15—outfitted with binoculars and portable tape players—on the way to Parque de Maria Luisa. Cynthia had suggested a night reconnaissance of the park, but Gabriella had said no. "Too dangerous. The park is closed until dawn and seeing things in the dark won't help. Go over the maps and pictures again while you wait."

Cynthia dressed in black—bicycle shorts, sports bra, and Reeboks. She clipped her hair with the stiletto, laid out the map and pictures of the park on her bed, trying to memorize them until 5:55.

Outside, she stretched against a lamppost at a spot that could be seen from David's room. She knew he was dressed in black running clothes—with twenty back-up outfits laid on his bed.

Cabrera arrived two minutes late, wearing his favorite black muscle shirt and running shorts. David wouldn't have to change.

"Good morning," Cabrera said.

Cynthia's mouth was full of cotton. She nodded.

Cabrera set the course and pace of the run—winding through city streets to the Paseo de Colon along the river, then toward Parque de Maria Luisa. After they had run a mile, the sun peeked over the horizon, bathing the city in soft gold that glistened off the dew on the leaves of orange trees, but Cynthia was blind to the beauty. She was as jittery as a thoroughbred before a race and had to restrain herself from sprinting ahead. She reminded herself to breathe through the nose to calm down.

The rhythm of the run settled Cynthia's nerves. Her strides were like the beat of a metronome. There was little conversation—she doubted her ability to string together two sentences, and Cabrera was content to stare at her body. When the path narrowed, he always allowed her to run ahead. There was nothing subtle about him. She thought about Sam and ran on.

As they entered Parque de Maria Luisa, Cynthia listened. She heard the call of the Spanish Timbrada Canary—sector "A" was clear of people. She started to clench her fists—to squeeze out tension—but stopped the moment she felt her fingernail tips touch her palms. She spread her fingers, a motion that drew his attention.

"Nice nails," he said.

"Thanks." She was relieved that she could talk. She accelerated for three strides, pulling ahead in an effort to distract him. Her fingers curled into their usual running position. When he pulled abreast of her, his eyes were on her sports bra. She relaxed enough to notice things besides his eyes.

This section of the park was immaculate, with grass mown, flowers blooming, and a canopy of palms, elms, and Mediterranean Pines. And orange trees, of course, which added a citrus scent to the cool air. They ran single file down a narrow stretch of macadam. At the next fork, Cynthia bore left—on the less traveled dirt path. Cabrera followed. Descending a gentle grade into what Gabriella had defined as sector "A," Cynthia saw Serg, looking through binoculars. Everything was a go. Ten seconds later, she and Cabrera were alone. Where the path was most sheltered by hedges, Cynthia halted.

Cabrera stopped at her side. "Something wrong?"

"No. Just right. I want to rest with you—where it's beautiful and quiet." She flashed him a smoldering smile she had been practicing in the mirror for months—available but discerning, sexy not slutty. He drank in her eyes. His hands caressed her waist, their touch causing her stomach to clench. Looking up into his face, her jaw muscles contracted the way they did when a dentist's drill whirred in her mouth. She ran her thumbnails into the cuticles of her middle nails until they clicked.

His kiss was aggressive. Bitter. His tongue darted between her teeth like a python. He pulled her close—she felt him stiffen against her abdomen.

Cynthia's gut churned. She stopped breathing, fighting an urge to throw up. In the background, she heard a birdcall that meant something, but she had to focus on the task at hand. She ran her hands under the back of his shirt. He thrust his tongue farther into her mouth. The taste of her stepfather made her bite his tongue. She jerked her fingers, injecting the poison—too abruptly. She thought: shit, did I fuck up?

He grunted and glared into her eyes. "So, sadistic bitch, play hard to get but like it rough." He dug his nails into her lower back.

"Ouch! It was an accident—my nails. Sorry."

He clutched her buttocks with both hands and yanked her tight. "You like *this*." He sucked hard on her ear, his beard scraping her neck.

She wanted to jerk her knee into his crotch, but she was trained to endure the disgust. No blows—nothing that would contradict evidence of a heart attack. He tried to grind himself against her pelvis, but she slipped away from his weakening grasp. He grabbed for one of the three images that swirled before him. Then, with his eyes glazing into a fog, he slumped to the ground, gasping for air, hands on his chest.

Cynthia smiled. A warm wave surged from her insides out. So much adrenaline, but only one man to kill. She quivered, not wanting to move, not trying to move. Dark music resonated in the back of her mind, drowning out something else. What? She jerked herself alert. *The birdcall*. She knelt, cupped her hand over Cabrera's mouth to stifle his last gasps, and listened. It sounded like a hundred Goddamn birds, but she had to pick out the rare one—the one unlikely to be heard in a city park—Bethalot's Pipet. That meant Serg was blocking someone on the entry path. Serg could delay anyone with one of his many ploys—from curious bumpkin to pompous braggart—so there was no need to panic. She would follow the plan and continue out the exit path where Gabriella was watching.

Cabrera gurgled and shook like an epileptic. After three twitches, he jerked once—as if he'd been charged with electric paddles—then was still. Cynthia felt his pulse—nothing, but it was hard to be sure with her own racing.

Cynthia stood and stared, wiping his spittle from her palms onto her shorts. She was still high, smiling at a corpse, but at least she was thinking—thinking that this was even better than killing Salmanda in Bermuda, and thinking… *Shit, don't just stand there.* She started jogging slowly. After ten dizzy strides, it hit her: she heard the call of the Northern Wheatear. Someone had come down Gabriella's path, too. David would hear the call, so she should meet him at the fallback rendezvous, but was it through the hedges to the left or right? They had been over this a hundred times. Left, she thought, go left, toward the Plaza de España.

She scurried to the hedge and squeezed through dense branches that scratched her arms and legs like tiny razor blades. This place looked nothing like the photos. The sun wasn't visible through the canopy, so she oriented on sounds, figuring any noises she heard were coming from the Plaza. She wouldn't have heard the Blue Chaffinch if she hadn't been listening for it—David's signal. She pushed through what seemed like the hundredth hedge, never so happy to see a grin.

"Come on," he said. She fell in beside him, running without thinking—through a parking lot roofed by tree branches and into the large plaza facing a semi-circle of ornate, stone buildings.

"How'd it go?"

"I got him... I'm pretty sure."

"Serg'll hang around to confirm."

They jogged around the plaza, saying *"Buenos días"* to as many early risers as they could. They stopped twice to ask directions. People would remember the athletic couple in black running clothes. They ran back to the hotel on busy streets, waving to everyone. She noted that with his three-day beard, David looked remarkably like Cabrera. She thought it ironic that two people who looked so much alike could be so different.

After debriefing and packing, Gabriella and Cynthia waited for a taxi that would take them to the airport.

"It's *my* aunt who's on her death bed, right?" Cynthia asked.

"Yes. That's our ticket home.... You look nervous."

Cynthia shrugged, her heel tapping nonstop. "I'll feel safer when we're out of Spain."

"You'd be fine, even if you stayed. The M.E.'s report will say: heart attack. Any witnesses that saw you with a male runner in black will swear it was David."

"But you're still pulling me out early."

"Just to be safe. And it'll give us a believable reason to take the same tour in the future."

Cynthia squinted. "What does that mean?"

"There's another target along the same route. It's great cover. The guys will continue and do some surveillance on a mark in Costa del Sol."

"Who? What do you know?"

Gabriella laughed. "You sound eager."

Cynthia looked at her shoes.

"So...was it like training?" Gabriella asked.

"No. You were right. I've never been so nervous in my life—worse than in Bermuda."

"No partner this time. That's a big difference. It's hard to kill someone by yourself, even if the mark's scum. Don't worry, it'll be easier next time."

That's what Cynthia was afraid of. A chill stiffened the back of her neck

* * *

At the same moment Cynthia James was thinking about the morality of her job, Jimmy Taylor was putting the finishing touches on a material witness warrant. None of Alexander Gates's off-shore accounts had been touched since he disappeared in May of the previous year, making the theory of voluntary disappearance less likely every day. With the trail of physical evidence growing cold, Taylor had convinced his boss that their best bet was to lean on Cynthia James. For political reasons, the material witness warrant was related to a missing person case, not murder. The main problem would be finding Ms. James. Taylor still didn't know where she had gone. But he was getting closer—he'd found her name on the catering roster of a new charity.

15

PILAR IBANEZ

Pilar Ibanez called Jerry Paulson as soon as she saw the internal security alert: *WCT0074/PFF-080-0025-01*. The Chattanooga Police Department had issued a material witness warrant for Cynthia James—a problem that Pilar was confident she could handle. She had known Chattanooga Chief of Police Greg Haskell at Boston University—a lucky break. She hadn't risen from the slums of Sao Paulo to the upper echelon of the fastest growing surveillance company in the world by missing out on opportunities.

"Come in," Paulson said.

"What happened?" Pilar asked. "We promised Cynthia James we could protect her."

"An oversight. When we hired Ms. James, there was no outstanding warrant, so legal didn't push for amnesty. Then it slipped through the cracks when the program got rolling. Some detective located her name on our catering staff; we can only stall him so long. You said you had an idea about how to clear this up."

"Well, Jerry," she said, "the Chief of Police in Chattanooga is an acquaintance of mine from BU."

He raised an eyebrow.

"We dated a few times."

"Serious?"

"We never slept together, if that's what you mean. He was just like every other big man on campus, wanting a shot at the exotic foreigner. The important thing is: we've stayed in touch, and I understand him. Haskell's very ambitious. Chief of Police is just a rung on the ladder for him, so he won't roll over. And he'll only go for something that's his idea. But knowing that's an advantage. If you'll let me trade municipal SCOPE for his department, I'm confident he'll back off on the warrant. He'll see the potential, and it would be a good test site for us."

"What would it take?" Paulson asked.

"Well, I'll offer SCOPE for a year."

"Make it six months." Paulson shifted his bulk. "What level?"

"Level three is the municipal program," she said.

Paulson nodded and thought for a moment. "You know, legal will see this negotiation as in their sphere."

"Not if they don't know about it," she said. "Do you want *official* negotiations about a matter that could be interpreted as obstruction of justice? Haskell will keep my offer confidential. I'm positive."

He scratched his chin. "Then fly to Chattanooga and meet with your friend. Convince him to lay off Ms. James. You can offer up to level-three for six months. Go tomorrow."

* * *

Three officers competed to fetch Pilar a cup of coffee during her wait by the sergeant's desk. Finally, the Chattanooga Chief of Police came out to greet her. After exchanging pleasantries, they walked to his office where a rumpled detective fidgeting as if he wanted to be somewhere else. Jimmy Taylor rose and shook Pilar's hand.

Gregory Haskell hung up his Armani suit jacket and sat behind an oak desk too large for the office. "I've asked Detective Taylor to sit in because he was the lead investigator on the case. Any problem with that?" Pilar shook her head. "Good. So what's so important about Cynthia James that a New York marketing vice president needs to come all the way to Tennessee?"

Pilar crossed her legs and smiled. "It's really the business of my country."

Haskell chuckled. "I assume you mean the USA?" She nodded. "I'm glad to know that our little missing person case is so important to the *country*, but I'm just a simple Tennessee cop. You'll have to explain it to me."

She pursed her lips. "Ms. James is employed in sensitive work that is of the utmost importance to the nation."

"*What* sensitive work?" Taylor blurted. "She's a bartender, for crying out loud."

"Easy Jimmy. I'm sure Ms. Ibanez was about to explain, weren't you, Pilar?"

"Yes. As you know, the nation is at war against terror. The president is correct when he describes it as a long struggle on many fronts. Ms. James is involved on one of those fronts."

"What exactly does she do?" Taylor asked. "Water their drinks?"

Pilar looked at Haskell, but the Chief shrugged. She glanced at the walls and asked, "Is this room secure?" Haskell nodded. "Here's the deal. Ms. James performs classified activities to help remove terrorist threats. She's a patriot."

Haskell put up his hand. "Whoa. Are you telling us she's an *assassin*?"

"I didn't say that."

The chief snapped his fingers. "What does your company have to do with this?"

She uncrossed her legs. "Off the record, we've provided certain surveillance equipment and technical expertise."

Haskell flexed his fingertips and gazed at the ceiling, as if for divine guidance. "Despite your statements about *the country*, I take it that Ms. James is not employed by the government?"

"The government is an unofficial supporter of her activities."

"Very unofficial, I would imagine. Can I also assume that you won't tell us the names of unofficial supporters?"

Pilar stared at a point three inches above Haskell's shoulder.

He continued. "And assuming you have the unofficial backing you claim…"

"That's right," Pilar finished. "I can't discuss the players with you. It's not important, anyway."

Haskell passed the ball. "Jimmy?"

Taylor rolled his pen between his fingers. "Are you telling us to back off because the Feds want to prosecute her…or so she can keep killing?"

Pilar flinched, but she covered it by crossing her legs. "You make it sound like killing terrorists is wrong. Do I have to remind you what happened on Route Eighty? Terrorists don't play by the rules, so neither does Ms. James's organization. Every source of funding or communication they disrupt could save us from the next attack. You want names? I can't give you names, but rest assured that they are patriots, courageous enough to support what has to be done to protect the American way of life, even when they have to get their hands dirty."

When she was done, Haskell smiled as if there was fife and drum music in the background.

"What's your involvement in all this?" Taylor asked.

Chief Haskell waved his hand to get their attention. "Hold on. We're making this adversarial…and too complicated. Pilar, Paulson Electronics is indirectly involved in these assassinations, isn't it?"

She stared again at the point three inches above his shoulder.

"I'll take that as a covert yes. Now let's get back on track. What do you want us to do about our investigation of Ms. James?"

"Drop it," she said.

Haskell cut off Taylor's objection by asking, "And what's in it for us?"

"Pride in doing the patriotic thing."

"Not good enough."

"Then what do you want?" she asked.

"Jimmy?"

As soon as Taylor opened his mouth, Pilar knew the Chattanooga Police Department had been prepared for her visit. "You called us less than an hour after the James warrant went into the system. That's pretty impressive. We've heard of your company's SCOPE product. We want to know more about it."

"I'm not in security," she said, glancing down at her nails.

Taylor unfurrowed his brow. "Nothing technical then. Just give us the layman's version."

"Well, we have sophisticated new surveillance systems. They use satellites, lasers, and revolutionary software to read almost anything encoded anywhere." She hoped her explanation was vague enough.

Taylor huffed. "Sounds like a search engine."

"Ah, but search engines only find what's indexed to be found. SCOPE finds information people *don't* want found. SCOPE can read computer disks remotely without anyone knowing."

Haskell cleared his throat. "A police department could really use something like that."

She feigned surprise. "That's blackmail."

A mischievous smile escaped Haskell's lips. "Maybe. But I see it as being *patriotic*. If Paulson Electronics gives us access to these systems, then Cynthia James gets to do *whatever* for her country. If you say no, we'll have to haul her assassinating ass in for questioning."

Haskell softened his tone. "We go back a long way, Pilar, and I have no doubt we're on the same team. So let's work something out that saves you from having to block our warrant in a court of law—in public."

Pilar caught Haskell's gaze and swung her eyes sideways at Taylor. The Chief picked up her message. "Jimmy, would you mind waiting outside?"

"No problem." Taylor looked happy to escape.

Once Taylor closed the door, Pilar fluttered her eyelashes. "For old time's sake, I've persuaded Mr. Paulson to give the city of

Chattanooga level-two SCOPE for three months in exchange for withdrawing the warrant. That's a hundred thousand dollar value."

Haskell chuckled. "We may be hicks, but we're not dumb. Level-two is what you'll be selling to corporations. We want level-three for nine months."

Now it was Pilar's turn to smile. "You sly horse-trader. I should have known you'd have done your homework...Let's see. I said three months; you said nine. Do you see common ground in between?"

They shook hands on six months of free level-3 SCOPE in exchange for a six-month amnesty for Cynthia James.

"So, Greg, how about I buy you a drink? Maybe we can work out an extension of Ms. James's amnesty."

He gazed into her eyes and hesitated. "Sorry. No can do."

* * *

Shortly after 5:00 a.m. London time, a high-frequency signal emanated from Sir Wilton Thatcher's private study in Crestmont Manor. The signal bounced off a satellite and altered the *NightOwl* root algorithms, effectively protecting hundreds of ciphers as if they were unbreakable one-time-pads. The team of code-breakers from Paulson Electronics would have to start from scratch.

16

THREE MISSIONS

A cult requires charismatic leaders. In Southern Spain, the most charismatic personality within *1898* was an Islamic cleric who called himself Valeriano and was known to followers as the Wise One. Valeriano—born Juan Madera—dressed in flowing robes and recruited youths for an Islamic school, but behind the scenes, he recruited for another school, one that converted weak minds to the cause. SCOPE had traced several of the Wise One's recruits to the Route 80 attacks.

Valeriano—old and frail—had no weakness for women. He thought moral weakness had been the ruin of Spain, poisoning the country until the embarrassment of the Spanish-American War. There was no apparent way he could be a target for a seductive assassin. But *Patriots for Freedom* thought otherwise. The key was his aide, Enrique Pascual.

Pascual, 35, had been serving Valeriano for almost ten years. Pascual admired women—when he was out of Valeriano's sight. Such an opportunity presented itself in the form of a newly-hired maid at the hotel where Valeriano and Pascual stayed when recruiting in Madrid.

Manuela Cortez, a.k.a. Maria Lopez, was backed up by Gabriella Sanchez's support team. Gabriella set up a command post in a hotel room on the same floor as the mark. She used cell phones and walkie-talkies to communicate with Maria as well as David Smathers and Serg Guardado, both disguised as janitors. The team's risks were modest. Valeriano was feeble and his aide unarmed. The challenge was to make Valeriano's death look natural, because an assassination of the Wise One would spark retaliation from Islamic extremists.

Pascual was predictably punctual, but Maria's housekeeping cart blocked his doorway. Again. The second day's conversation built on that of the first.

"*Buenos días*," she said, moving the cart to the left. Pascual's eyes widened as he faced the pretty chambermaid. Self-conscious, he bumped into the cart as she moved it back to the right. Speaking in Spanish, she said, "I am so clumsy. I seem to be in the way. Can I do anything to make your stay more comfortable?"

Pascual was tongue-tied, looking at the hall carpet.

Smiling, she said, "I suppose I should move the cart."

She stepped back and to one side, so he could exit his room, but he faced her again in the hall to the side of the cart. He passed by close enough to smell her citrus scent.

"How is your mother?" Pascual asked.

Maria's shoulders sagged. "My mother is no better this morning. Thank you for asking, but..."

"But what?"

Maria stepped closer. "*Señor*," she whispered, touching his arm. "There's something I'd like very much to talk about with you this afternoon. I get off at four."

"What is it?" he asked.

"Yesterday, your words of wisdom about my mother's illness gave me strength. Islamic teachings seem more helpful than stale Catholic tenets. I was hoping you could give me more spiritual advice."

Pascual shrugged. "If I can be of help, then..."

She batted her eyelashes. "Will you meet me here at four?"

Pascual's eyes brightened. "If I can get away."

The door adjacent to Pascual's opened, and Valeriano stepped into the hall. "Come along, Enrique," the Wise One said with a scowl.

Enrique Pascual followed only after he winked at Maria. He was already plotting how he could be back at 4:00 p.m.

Pascual's getaway proved easy. He feigned dizziness and said he needed to lie down for a few hours before dinner. Valeriano, engaged in a meeting with cult recruiters, waved Pascual away.

At 3:55, Pascual found Manuela's cart outside Valeriano's room. He found Manuela inside, irresistible. She gazed up and down his body before saying in Spanish, "Help me with the bed."

"What? I thought you were off at four."

"This is my last room, but..." Admiring him, she walked backwards to the hall and pulled her cart inside before shutting the door.

"What are you doing?"

"We are going to have to make the bed anyway, so..."

"What about your mother?"

Maria licked her lips. "She is much better this afternoon."

"But don't you keep the cart…"

"Outside in the hall? I don't want anyone to know we are in here. Do you? We may be a while."

Pascual shook his head. "We have to be out in an hour."

"Then we should get started."

Maria unbuttoned the front of her uniform. "I've never done anything like this," she said, making it sound like a lie.

It was easy for Maria to get Pascual to drink a glass of drugged water. They kissed, and she allowed him to touch her until he grew drowsy. Once he was unconscious, Maria positioned her cart to the side of the bed closest to the door, which was where she waited, her uniform partly-unbuttoned, hair disheveled. Pascual lay half-naked on the far side of the bed.

Lying in silence, Maria thought about Cynthia.

When Maria heard the lock disengage, she slapped Pascual's leg.

"Wake up!" she shouted in Spanish. "We must have fallen asleep."

Valeriano took in the sordid disarray of tangled sheets and exposed skin, while Pascual blinked vacant eyes. Maria couldn't tell which man was more surprised. Valeriano spread his arms so that his robe took on the shape of a bird of prey. "What are you doing, Enrique?" Valeriano bellowed in Spanish. He averted his eyes from Maria as she buttoned up. "What is the meaning of this outrage?"

Pascual tried to shake his head clear. "What time is it?" was all he could say.

"Time to pay the price for your sin, Enrique!"

Valeriano's eyes were fiery coals. Blood vessels bulged on his forehead. "My own aide, whom I've treated as a son! This is how you repay me?" Turning his wrath toward Maria, he shouted, "Get out of my sight, you worthless whore!" Valeriano was hyperventilating.

Maria stood and wobbled, grabbing the cart for balance. Her lunge shoved the cart forward, ramming a sharp corner into Valeriano's thigh.

He cried out in pain. Reaching one hand to his leg and the other into a shaking fist, the Wise One battled for self-control. "You're not worth the effort to smite," Valeriano hissed. "Be gone, before I extract my revenge on your filth."

Maria stumbled out the door, pushing the cart ahead of her.

Halfway down the hall, David Smathers overtook her from behind, taking the cart and shoving it into a housekeeping closet where he pulled off syringes attached to all four corners and hid them in his jacket. Serg watched the hall as Maria and David scurried down the stairs to the basement. Serg followed a few moments later.

In the hotel room, Valeriano was violently shaking Pascual's shoulders. Enraged, blood pressure rising, Valeriano's heart was failing, but he was too frantic to know. Until the moment he crashed to the floor, the Wise One berated Pascual with self-righteous shouts.

In the backseat of a rental car, Manuela turned into Mura Winterdeer, a Native American flying from Madrid to Denver via New York. The hotel never received notice from Manuela Cortez, but her abrupt departure made sense when Enrique Pascual described the fury that had preceded his mentor's fatal heart attack.

* * *

Joanie Lee, a.k.a. Joan Archer, entered Spain disguised as a plump brunette, but for the evening, she removed the padding and wig. She oozed sex appeal in a skin-tight dress when she strutted into a Madrid strip club named Zorra's to audition for a dancer's job. As planned, Joanie danced poorly, and although the manager was interested in her body, he didn't hire her. Joanie lingered with a pout and two double-Scotches.

When Ramon Benitez arrived at Zorra's, he noticed Joanie sitting at the bar, her blonde hair catching light from the strobes. A pair of strippers danced on a raised stage in the center of a large oval bar. The barmaids walked between hooting admirers and the dancers, in what served as a moat. Joanie saw Benitez, and had she not been engaged in deadly business, she would have laughed at the inept disguise of his middle-aged appearance. He wore a shirt unbuttoned to his navel, displaying three heavy gold chains and sparse white chest hairs. His comb-over and moustache were dyed an absurd black.

They made eye contact.

"*Buenas noches, señorita,*" Benitez said over the noise as he slid onto the stool next to hers.

Joanie shook her head. "I only speak English."

"That is good. I speak a little English. What is your name?"

"Amber."

"Ramon," he said, eyes locked like heat-seeking missiles on her cleavage. "Not many girls like you here. Except dancers."

"Yeah, well, that's my problem," Joanie slurred.

"Problem?"

For Benitez's benefit, she straightened her shoulders. "I came in to audition for a job. I was nervous, so I had a drink first. Maybe two. Well, I didn't get the job. I don't think the manager liked my dancing, and he wanted me to speak Spanish." As Joanie spoke, she breathed deeply, and Benitez nodded sympathetically in time with her expanding lungs. "I was disappointed, so I had another drink. Maybe three." She rolled her eyes, and he looked away from her breasts long enough to acknowledge her plight.

"I am sorry," Benitez said, but he looked far from sorrowful. "How can Ramon help?"

"Well, I could use another drink. Vodka."

Holding up two fingers, Benitez called, "*Camarera! Vodka. Dos.*"

After they were served, he said, "I sure you great dancer."

She brightened. "Do you really think so?" He nodded, the same way he nodded to everything she said.

Joanie gave him a head to toe. "I like men who keep themselves in good shape, and I really love to dance. How about you?"

"I am fine," he replied.

She nodded toward the strippers. "Which dancer do you like best?"

"I like you dance."

"No. Which of those?" she said, pointing.

Benitez swiveled around to face the strippers. Joanie emptied poison from a ring into Benitez's vodka with a slick move she had been practicing for months.

"Which one?" she asked, teasing his lips with a vodka-flavored finger.

He faced her. "I...like...you," he said between sucks.

"Then let's drink to you and me."

Benitez sipped, but Joanie downed her entire drink. Licking her lips, she said, "I like a man who can handle his liquor."

He nodded.

"Drink up," she said, making a tipping motion with her hand.

Benitez made a show of chugging his drink then put his hand on her thigh. After ogling her chest and squeezing her leg, Benitez said, "Does Amber want go my hotel?"

"Where's your hotel?"

Benitez smiled as if on his way to heaven. "Two minutes," he said, holding up a pair of fingers.

"I have to go to the ladies' room first. But when I get back, we'll go, okay?" His nod was emphatic. Arching her back, she held up five fingers. "Don't go away. Five minutes. Can you wait five minutes?"

Benitez didn't want to wait five seconds, but he nodded again.

"I'll be right back." Joanie pushed both empty glasses toward the barmaid. "Check please." She turned the corner into the foyer and headed for the door, not the ladies' room.

Her two backups followed, one whispering, "The glasses went into the tub. We're good to go."

When Benitez staggered off his stool a few minutes later, the patrons, mesmerized by erotic dance, didn't notice the gasping man. It wouldn't have been the first time a customer feigned a heart attack to the gyrations of a Zorra's stripper. Only after Benitez was on the floor did a lone man make a tentative move to help, but it was too late for Ramon Benitez.

By the time the rental car arrived at the Madrid airport, Joanie was the same plump brunette who had entered the country. The getaway was as clean as the kill.

* * *

When Joanie arrived home at the compound, the Aities were reunited for the first time since Cynthia had left for Spain. They stayed up until after midnight in the living room of Odessa, listening to Joanie recount her adventure.

"...and he died with a smile on his face," Joanie said. "But enough about me. What about your mission, Charisse? In all the excitement, I don't even know the details."

"Piece o' cake," Charisse said.

"So give me a slice."

Charisse settled into her chair, waiting until the others were quiet. "The mark liked to shoot up with his bitches before fucking them. I hooked up with him in Casablanca at a place that was the opposite of Rick's Café—a real dive. He heard me drop a few buzz words and was all over me like mud on a pig. Three drinks, and he was flyin'. From then on, it was easy.

"I brought him to the room the team had rented. He got a hard-on watching me shoot up. I switched syringes during a kiss. I really wanted to strangle the scumbag with the elastic, but I stuck to the plan. He injected enough heroin to kill an ox. As he's dying, he's watching me wipe down everything I might have touched, and he's got a shit-eating grin on his face. He's mumbling, 'Take it off and fuck me, babe.' So I tell him, 'Done. Consider yourself fucked.' Nobody ever saw a happier stiff."

Cynthia laughed along with the others, but there wasn't anything funny about it. So why did she laugh? Human nature, she rationalized—probably the same reason soldiers at war laughed at gallows humor. Her throat felt like dry gravel. She thought about Thomas, but that didn't help. A swig of water did, but not much.

17

RECOGNITION

The *Patriots for Freedom* recognition banquet was held in New York City in July. Prior to the gala dinner for members of legitimate programs, Jerry Paulson held a covert reception in a suite at the Plaza booked under a false name. The banquet was part of an elaborate smokescreen; Paulson's highly secure gathering was for the real VIPs: the Aities, their training staff, and strike teams.

Entering the suite, Cynthia felt like a crasher. The decorating budget couldn't have dealt in amounts less than thousands—not even for ashtrays, which glittered as if made of diamonds. Too many staffers hovered, offering champagne and caviar like beer and pretzels. Too much food adorned a sideboard covered in satin. Too much everything. Too much money.

Paulson shook hands with each of the guests, introducing himself and the Aities' Director, Pilar Ibanez. At the sight of Pilar, Cynthia did a double-take. Pilar's hair was darker and shorter, her figure fuller, but around the eyes and nose her facial features were similar to Cynthia's.

Pilar, who had downed one too many Amaretto Sours while waiting for the bus from Stone Harbor, responded to Cynthia's stare with a frown. "Do I have broccoli stuck in my teeth?"

"No. Your teeth are fine," Cynthia said. "Perfect, as a matter of fact. I was just…admiring your dress."

Pilar ran her hand over a gold chain belt and down the hip of the long-sleeved black dress. "Oh, it's from the spring line at Saks."

"Really? It's stunning."

They chatted amiably until they heard someone tapping his glass with a spoon. A few conversation groups chattered on, but at Jerry Paulson's first words, "Good evening, ladies and gentlemen," the room fell silent. It was Paulson's bearing, not volume, that commanded attention.

Paulson's body language engaged his audience. "Welcome. *Patriots for Freedom* are working around the world." He paced as he spoke. "Where healthcare is needed, patriots are healing. Where technology is lacking, patriots are providing. Where education is desired, patriots are teaching. Where enthusiasm is waning, patriots are rallying.

"Hundreds of patriots have traveled to South America, Europe, Africa, and Asia, spreading the gospel of freedom. At tonight's banquet, we will honor many people for their contributions.

"This private gathering is to recognize you for your particular efforts in the cause of freedom. I think you know what I mean." He winked, and most everyone chuckled. "For those of you who don't know, I'm one of many benefactors of *Patriots for Freedom*. On behalf of myself and fellow patriots, I want to extend heartfelt thanks for jobs well done. Your success has exceeded our goals."

His guests applauded, and Paulson beamed like a proud father.

After a few seconds, he lowered his chin an inch and held up a silencing finger, a theatrical gesture that was his trademark. When he spoke, his voice was somber. "As you know, our company is one of many touched by tragedy. Please join me in a moment of silence for all victims of terrorism."

Cynthia lowered her head. She remembered a similar moment at the memorial service for her father. She had been distraught, and her little brother had squeezed her hand—given her the strength to make it through that awful day. She clenched her fist, wishing Sam was watching over her. No, she didn't believe in that—he was gone. But what if he had left her condo a few seconds earlier? Or later? Where would he be today? What would he be doing?

She pictured his impish nine-year-old smile the evening he sloshed a whole can of lighter fluid onto the charcoal and almost burned down the garage. Years later—after the rape—when their mother had the flu, Sam cut school so Cynthia would have a swimming partner. She remembered the poem he had written for her: "Reach for the Stars."

If she had just held their good-bye hug for five seconds instead of one…

She thought about the men she had killed to avenge Sam's death. She was glad they were dead, but if she were to kill a thousand terrorists, their deaths wouldn't make up for Sam's.

Her eyes were drawn to Paulson, his head bowed, fists clenched. Blood vessels pulsed on his forehead. Was revenge enough? Would assassinations balance *his* loss? Before she could make a guess, Paulson raised his head. "Amen."

During the next half-hour, Cynthia watched who socialized with whom. Maria engaged a quiet Latino, who blossomed in her presence. Eduardo Juarez was easy to overlook, yet Maria detected worth.

Joanie Lee ignored the executives and gravitated to the most powerfully-built men, David Smathers and a blonde Adonis who photographed various groupings of Paulson and his guests. He was Bruce Swenson, personal assistant to Duane Root—in layman's terms, an executive bodyguard.

After charming the musclemen for a few minutes, Joanie sidled over to Cynthia. "Why didn't you tell me one of your support team was such a hunk? None of my guys were built like Dave."

Cynthia shrugged. "He's a great teammate and bodyguard."

Joanie flicked an imaginary cigar in a Groucho imitation. "He can guard my body any time."

"You'd be very safe."

"What can you tell me about him?" Joanie asked in her normal voice,

"You mean besides what you can see for yourself? Let's see. He's trustworthy, loyal—"

"Ha! Sounds like a freakin' Boy Scout."

Cynthia smiled. "You're a piece of work, Joanie."

"I know all about *me*. Tell me about *Dave*, down and dirty."

"There isn't anything to tell. And even if there was, he's a friend."

"But not a *boy*-friend?"

Cynthia chose her words carefully. "No. I'm still with Thomas."

Joanie excused herself and approached Bruce Swenson and David Smathers with a predatory swivel. Cynthia wondered whether Joanie would entice David. The very thought made Cynthia crave alcohol. She started toward the bar, but Jerry Paulson's long arm steered her toward Pilar Ibanez.

"I want some pictures of you two," Paulson said. "Bruce, take a few shots over here." Cynthia's heart skipped a beat because the photo-op put Joanie alone with David. The blip in her chest felt like jealousy.

While Swenson's Nikon whirred, Cynthia and Pilar heard a muffled cell phone. "Is that yours?" Cynthia said through a ventriloquist's smile.

"No. I don't carry one away from work."

Once Swenson had his shots, Pilar elaborated. "I work long hours and treasure my privacy."

Cynthia chuckled. "I don't like them either, but I thought I was the only holdout."

Pilar lost her balance and grabbed Cynthia's arm. "I want you to know how proud I am of your work in the field. Whatever Paulson is paying you, you're worth more. I'd hold out for a raise, if I were you."

"I'll tell him you said that."

Pilar laughed. "I envy you, Cynthia."

"Why?"

"You're on the front lines—taking revenge against the murdering scumbags. If I were younger, I'd be right there with you."

Cynthia wasn't sure whether that was alcohol talking. Even drunk, Pilar was a captivating creature with dangerous eyes. Pilar would make a good Aitie.

When the party broke up at eight, Cynthia watched Maria leave for dinner with Eduardo Juarez. Sparks were visible. Having heard how smart Juarez was, Cynthia deduced it was brain-lust-at-first-sight for Maria. For Juarez, it was the more common brand of lust. As usual, once Maria left a room, it seemed dimmer.

Joanie departed with Bruce Swenson. Cynthia was relieved and confused. She looked around for David, but he was gone, too. Before she could get out the door, Jerry Paulson draped an arm around her shoulder, which made her neck muscles tighten.

Paulson closed the door. He smelled of Scotch and Polo. "I'm very proud of your success, Cynthia. I'm giving you a raise of fifty thousand."

"Pilar Ibanez is clairvoyant," she said.

"What?"

"Never mind. That's very generous, Mr. Paulson."

"It's Jerry."

"Thank you...Jerry."

He lowered his voice. "My security people are gathering intelligence for your next assignment. I'm not at liberty to tell you who I've picked, but I *can* tell you that you'll be going after the terrorists' chief technology provider. You'll be briefed soon, but I wanted to give you a heads up. This one's *really* important."

Paulson tightened the arm around her shoulders. She wanted to scold him, but he spoke first. "One more thing. We've taken care of your legal problem in Chattanooga."

"What do you mean?"

"Just between you and me, we traded some cutting-edge technology to the Chattanooga Police in exchange for their dropping a material witness warrant."

Cynthia hesitated.

"You're free. So you see, we really are patriots for *freedom*. Now enjoy the dinner and then a vacation."

In the hall outside the suite, Cynthia passed an imposing man with a shaved head. His glower gave her a chill.

Duane Root had advised against Paulson's egotistical reception. No matter how secret, the gathering was a security risk, but Paulson had been adamant—and money talks. Root refused to go inside and be photographed, but he couldn't resist lurking outside the suite—for security reasons.

Paulson's one-on-one with Cynthia James hadn't gone unnoticed; little of significance escaped Root. Lately, much of his attention had been devoted to problems. He was frustrated by the delays plaguing the men's program. The military advisors were so busy covering their asses that it took forever to get the simplest procedures to the training team. Ballyhooed electronic gear failed field trials. The number of people involved caused security nightmares. Root had urged everyone to work harder, but Murphy's Law held up to all appeals.

Worse, Pilar's female squad was running smoothly—and at a fraction of the cost. Tonight's party was a tribute to her organization. She was moving up in the only eyes that mattered: Jerry Paulson's. To Duane Root, this was cause for concern but not panic.

18

NEW MISSION

"I said: I want Cynthia James on this one." Jerry Paulson sat behind his desk, drawn blinds blocking the sunshine.

"But Jerry, are you sure you want to do this?" Pilar Ibanez replied. "I mean—going after Wilton Thatcher?"

"He has to be stopped."

"But he's not a direct backer of terrorism. He's a businessman dealing in security, just like you."

"Not *just like me*. He sells to known terrorists—not just *Eighteen Ninety-Eight*, but Islamic extremists, too. His damn *NightOwl* is allowing their communication—their plans—to avoid detection, and he's personally involved in encrypting codes. By doing so, he protects terrorists. Those who harbor terrorists are our enemies."

Pilar squirmed in her chair. "Thatcher's a competitor, Jerry. You can't go around killing competitors."

Paulson turned beet red and ground his teeth. "Damn! This bastard is using *his* product, *his* technology, out of *his* study, in *his* house, on *his* estate. Case closed. Remember, Pilar, my son and your husband were murdered by people Thatcher is protecting, and it's my money that's funding the Patriots. Now get the James woman on this! She *is* the best we've got, isn't she?"

"So they say."

* * *

Cynthia James enjoyed the first 24 hours of her vacation with Thomas Gates at Skytop, a mountain resort in Pennsylvania. The place was old-fashioned—manicured lawns, stone lodge, full American plan. Thomas was old-fashioned, too. She found it endearing that he held doors for her, and she liked being told she was beautiful, even when her morning-hair looked like used straw.

It was time to test her sexuality. Thursday night, she had taken X-80 before they made love, and she had used the crutch again when he wanted a morning pick-me-up, teasing him in the shower until arousal kicked in. Feeling guilty for cheating, she resolved to do without the stimulant tonight. And she wouldn't fake it, either.

"A penny for your thoughts," Thomas said as they approached Indian Ladder Falls late Friday afternoon. They had walked the last few minutes in silence on a forest trail cushioned with pine needles, and they were the only human souls taking in the thundering waterfall.

They sat on a flat boulder, hypnotized by the endless stream of falling water that drowned out other sounds in the forest.

She kissed his cheek. "The penny first." He laughed, fishing a coin out of his pocket. She said, "I love the mountain air. It may be better than the seashore." She inhaled. "Mmm. The pine scent is wonderful."

"I think you're enjoying life, so everything seems wonderful." He gave her a squeeze. "You didn't say much about your job in Spain, other than it went well. Does that mean they promoted you to assassin?" He was joking, but Cynthia flinched. Thomas frowned. "Cynthia?"

Turning away from his gaze, Cynthia wondered if she looked as guilty as she felt.

"What's going on, Cynthia?"

Her voice was barely audible over the falls. "I didn't tell you what really happened in Spain. I'm not supposed to tell anyone...." Cynthia nestled into his arms so that her shoulder blades pressed into his torso.

"I'm..." She stared into the waterfall, wondering if the truth would scare him off—and whether she wanted to tell him. If she loved him, she should tell him, but would anything be gained?

"You're what?"

"I'm not sure. The truth is..."

He kissed her neck. "Are you sure you're ready to share?"

"Mmmm. No."

"Then...maybe you should wait."

After a long pause, she murmured, "Thank you. I'll wait."

By the time they returned to the stone lodge, the dining room was closed, so they went downstairs to the pub. The manager found Cynthia there, sitting with Thomas at a corner booth, mahogany black as iron. She had a phone call. Leaving Thomas to order, she ran up one flight to the main desk, taking the steps two at a time.

"It's Marco. Don't you have your cell phone on?"

Cynthia slumped. "And hello to you, too. I'm on vacation,

remember?"

"Not for long. The organization has assigned you to a new project. Time is of the essence. You report to the training center Sunday evening, ready to start first thing Monday."

"So soon?"

"'Fraid so. This one's hot, Cynthia."

"Can I ask what the job is?"

"Just be there."

Cynthia trudged downstairs but perked up before Thomas saw her. It would do no good to tell him now. Better to break the news tomorrow.

When he fondled her that night, Cynthia was tense, sexual fulfillment riding on hope. An orgasm will happen because it's meant to happen, she thought.

But it didn't happen—not even close.

Frustrated, she flopped face down on the bed before Thomas was satisfied. Neither of them knew how to talk about the problem, so they lay next to each other, miles apart.

The following morning, they were hiking in the woods—pretending things were fine—when she told him.

"What?" Thomas snapped.

"I said I have to go back to work Sunday night."

"More traveling?" he asked.

She nodded. "I'm making a difference on this job."

"How?"

She looked over his shoulder, focusing on a pine tree.

"What about us?" he asked.

"Is there an us?"

He slumped. "After last night, maybe not."

"So I'm just a sex object to you. Someone to get your rocks off."

He could have said any number of things that would have tempered her anger, but he stood silent. She folded her arms and waited for him to say something, every second making his recovery more difficult.

The next minute was interminable, but she stared him down.

"Well, Cynthia, look at it from my perspective. You won't talk to me about what happened to my brother. You won't reveal the big secret of your job. Then you give up on me in the middle of making love. Now you're going off to who-the-hell knows where. What am I supposed to think?"

"Don't ask *me*," she huffed.

"What do you mean by that?"

"What do I mean?" she said, turning crimson. "I mean: don't ask me what you should think—tell me what you *do* think."

He looked at her as if snakes slithered out her eyes. "I-I think…"

"Fuck you," she said. "You don't even know *what* you think!" She turned and stomped toward the lodge, unaware that songbirds sang as if nothing were wrong in their forest.

Thomas, clueless as a bird, was too dumbfounded to go after her.

On the drive home, Cynthia waited for the apology that never came. She might have allowed him to grovel back into her good graces, but she didn't open that door. Three times she almost offered an olive branch, but each time she wavered. The silence grew heavier and heavier as they drove. The invisible weight came from Cynthia's doubt—doubt as deadly as the poison she used on her marks.

Cynthia thought back to the day they had met—she an insecure bartender, he a quiet passenger with soulful eyes. Thomas had drank too many beers, then over-tipped her—awkward flirting—but at 2:00 a.m., when it had been just the two of them in the lounge, he sat at the piano and played *The Ashokan Farewell* so beautifully that Cynthia's eyes moistened. He was sensitive—the kind of man who was meant to help her find herself. How different he was from his brother, a shameless womanizer.

Alexander Gates was three years older than Thomas but looked younger. It was their eyes. While Thomas's eyes reflected the sentiment of *The Ashokan Farewell*, Alex's danced to a rock 'n roll beat edged with jazz. Alex was dangerous, the kind of man who haunted her—and the specific man she stalked.

Each Gates brother tried to dazzle her with broad smiles and big tips, and she enjoyed the flirtations. At first, she assumed her pleasure was due to attention from Thomas, but as the week rolled along, it was Alex who caused her pulse to quicken—he made her feel alive. And he made her laugh—sometimes with his radio announcer's voice, and sometimes with wry observations that connected to her dark side. Alex had invited her to run away with him to the Cayman Islands. As big a mistake as that would have been, she had fantasized about joining him.

That week on the *Louisiana Lady* had been the genesis of her life as an Aitie. She had been a butterfly, breaking out of a ten-year cocoon, using sexuality to manipulate men. Now, she was riding in a car with the good Gates—the one who loved her—with an insurmountable barrier between them. Preoccupied with silence, she missed the Route 53 and 202 cut-offs that would have avoided construction delays at the I-80/I-287 interchange. The temporary bypass bridge was only two lanes each way, and they crept for an hour in bumper-to-bumper traffic. Grief for her brother was so profound that Cynthia, barely able to swallow, was grateful for the silence.

When the car stopped at the train station, Thomas avoided her eyes. "Cynthia, you never loved me, did you?"

She clutched the steering wheel, irked that he wanted to talk about her void—now that it was too late.

"Why did you sleep with me?" Thomas asked, his voice barely audible.

Cynthia bit her lip. Her eyes were dry.

"Why was it so important?"

No answer.

Thomas's forced smile cracked. "Funny, but I thought you were fond of me." He exaggerated his cynicism. "When you kept sleeping with me—even though you didn't like it much—I thought you just needed time to fall in love. That you wanted to fall in love."

Cynthia remained silent.

"So, why, Cynthia?" His voice was sharp. "Why seduce me the night I confronted you about Alex?... You wanted to keep me quiet, didn't you?... You never gave a damn about me—"

"That's not true," she said.

He was sucking wind as if he had sprinted a hundred yards. "Tell me something that *is* true."

"You're a good man. You deserve better than me." That was from the heart, cold as it was.

Thomas got out of the car and pulled his bag from the backseat. They looked at each other through a half-opened car window for five seconds that felt like thirty.

"Go, Cynthia." He turned and walked toward the train platform.

She pulled away from the station without looking back.

Cynthia didn't drive home. Instead, she made a call from a payphone, speaking with manufactured confidence. "Hi! It's Cynthia. "I'd like to see you tonight. Are you alone?"

"Um...yes...."

"Good. I'm in Westfield. I need directions—away from the Route Eighty construction."

She jotted notes. "Thanks. I'll be there in about an hour."

Fifteen minutes away from Sparta, Cynthia pulled onto the shoulder and washed down an X-80 pill with bottled water. In his parking lot, she popped two cinnamon Certs, recoiled her hair, and touched up her face. On the stoop of a brick townhouse, she patted cheeks already colored and straightened jeans too tight to wrinkle.

19

DAVID

David Smathers opened his door shortly after 11:00 p.m. He wore a black, Jack Daniels T-shirt a size too small. No, after an appreciative look at the definition of his chest and arms, Cynthia concluded the shirt was just right. She placed a lingering kiss on his cheek then walked inside.

"Sorry for the short notice."

"That's okay…. Can I get you something to drink?"

"A beer's fine." She followed him into the kitchen.

Her mother had told her that you can learn a lot about a man from his living space. Cynthia expected to see a typical bachelor kitchen—empty pizza boxes on the counter—but there were utensils in the drainer, cookbooks with fingerprints on the bindings, and a spice rack with half-empty bottles.

"Where's the bathroom?"

He pointed. "First door on the left." He flipped a switch that brightened the living room with recessed lighting. Without moving her neck, she scanned the condo; she was impressed by what she *didn't* see—the three Ds: dirt, dust, and darkness. No clutter, either. She smelled pine cleaner, so he'd probably tidied up. She wouldn't risk bursting the bubble by opening a closet. Instead, she looked at the walls. No posters of rock bands or athletes. No "Three Stooges Golfing." Those really were Ansel Adams prints—Bridal Veil Falls and Half Dome. There was a Bermuda watercolor, a print of a stuffy college campus, and a marquee poster for *Casablanca*, all framed. His furniture was solid—This End Up tables, couch, and loveseat with green-gray striped cushions. Plus one leather recliner—aimed at the TV—that looked like it was the only seat he ever used. The candle on his coffee table had never been lit, but it was there.

The powder room smelled of too much Lysol—he'd definitely

given it the twice-over. The toilet seat was down and clean. He had a magazine rack stocked with *Sports Illustrated, Newsweek,* and *Field and Stream.* The *SI* swimsuit issue was hiding in the back. She thumbed through a few pages while sitting on his throne. The so-called swimwear doubled as porn props—not much any woman could wear.

After she was done peeing, she poked her head into the bedroom and flicked on the light. The walls showcased a mix of framed prints: Harley-Davidson, Monet, trout fishing, an artsy phoenix, and a poster for a French film staring Capucine—in *French.* David's place wasn't the Louvre, but at least the Coors Light Twins had been packed away. A clothes tree collected what otherwise would have been strewn on the floor. In the center of it all was a king size bed...made...soon to be unmade. Clean sheets might be too much to ask on short notice. She set her pocketbook on the bed in case she'd need an excuse to come back.

"Nice place," she called down the hall.

David was waiting in the living room with two Amstel Lights and a grin. He handed a beer to Cynthia.

She blushed as if she'd been caught doing something naughty. "I gave myself a quick tour."

He held out his palm. "That'll be five bucks."

She laughed because his timing was good. "Put it on my tab," she said, sliding her fingertips across his palm—cool from holding the beer. Two dark magnets lured her eyes. Was it wrong to want a man because he was unpredictable? She'd worry about the answer later.

She figured minimal small talk was in order. "This isn't what I expected from a bodyguard. More like a grad student, naturalist, or maybe photographer...swimsuit photographer."

It was his turn to blush. "I was pre-law, if you can believe it. My dad pushed me from the time I was fifteen, but law school wasn't for me. Actually, I hated it."

She was hot—over eager. Take it easy, she told herself—stay cool, more chit-chat. "Was your father pissed?"

"You could say that. He threatened to disinherit me. I went off on my own—body-building, body-guarding, and body-lusting. Hey, I was shallow, but at least I know my limitations."

"Do you have more depth now?"

"Maybe you'll test the waters—decide for yourself." He leaned in for a kiss. Very nice.

That was all the encouragement she needed. Sweat moistened her brow and underarms. Her furnace was stoked. She sucked on her beer bottle as if it were something else. He noticed. Cynthia took his free hand—warmer now—and led him to the bedroom. When she reached up to let down her hair, he touched her wrist. "Leave it—less to get in the way. We only get one first time."

It should have been perfect.

After they made love too quickly, she lay on her stomach, waiting for David to fall asleep. Cynthia inhaled through her nose, enjoying the sensation of her sweat evaporating in the night air. His bedroom smelled of Ben-Gay, making her wonder if he were injured. He had seemed fit enough, although the sex hadn't empowered her the way she had expected. They had been out of sync—like the sound-track of a movie one sprocket off. Perhaps rebounding to David had been a mistake, she thought. She wanted to slip away, leaving a note, but he wasn't cooperating. Instead of falling asleep, he was feathering his index finger over her backside as if finger painting.

"I've loved you since the day we met," he said.

The remark caught her unprepared. "Is that the same line you feed all your women?" She regretted the catty words before they slipped out of her mouth.

He chuckled. "No. I tell them I've wanted to *sleep* with them since the day we met, which isn't the same thing."

A devilish tingle rolled up her spine just behind his finger.

His next erection brushed her hip. She smiled and draped an arm over the side of the bed, probing the floor until she felt her pocketbook. She fumbled inside for the pills...then on the table for her warm, half-full bottle of beer.

During breakfast, he said, "Cyn, how about a road trip?"
She laughed to cover her surprise. "When?"
"This morning."
"You don't give much warning."
"I'm not very good at planning."

She studied his beard. She wanted to slide her fingers over the stubble then wanted to shave him and watch it grow back. *Where did that idea come from?*

She controlled her wandering mind. "Where would we go?"
"There's a place I want to show you."
She hesitated. "Okay."

He opened the hall closet and tossed her a helmet and black leather jacket. "You already have tight jeans. You'll make a good biker chick."

A half-hour later, she was straddling the back of his Harley, arms wrapped around his torso. The vibrations of the engine were like a double-dose of X-80 on the ride across the Delaware River into Pennsylvania.

After an hour leaning into mountain curves, they arrived at a security gate where he punched-in four numbers to gain entry. Ten minutes later, he eased the bike to a stop in a shale driveway of a house surrounded by forest. "So what do you think?" he asked after turning off the engine.

"Terrific."

"It needs a paint job, but I'm glad you like it."

"Right." She smiled at the misunderstanding and dismounted.

He did the same. "It was my dad's. When he died a few years ago, he left it to me. It's part of a hunting and fishing club my ancestors helped found over a hundred years ago."

"A bodyguard biker who hunts and fishes, huh?" She took off the helmet and straightened her ponytail, then pirouetted, gazing high in the trees. "I already know you're a bird-watcher. Give me a bird call."

He took off his helmet, puckered his lips, and twittered a pathetic chirp.

"What's that supposed to be?"

He leaned closer, bringing their lips within an inch. "The Black-Winged Biker."

After the kiss, she expected him to sweep her into the house and make passionate love, but he said, "Let's go for a hike. I want to show you the property. The club has thousands of acres, two trout streams, and four lakes."

"I have to be back in Stone Harbor tonight."

"Ever heard of the telephone? I think they'll cut their superstar a little slack."

Cynthia had heard Joanie describe orgasmathons with Bruce Swenson, and she had read imagery about flight, fire, and jellied legs. Tonight was to be Cynthia's turn, yet she was skeptical even as David slipped off her clothes and the X-80 kicked in. The usual creepiness was missing but not the *fear* of creepiness, and the fear made her tentative. Every move was awkward, her head in smoke, not clouds. She experienced reality not nirvana.

After nerves played out her anxiety, Cynthia lay alone with a patient man who loved her. She didn't have to fake it. No bells, but the clinical product of blood, hormones, drugs, and emotions qualified as a climax. It wasn't perfect—wasn't even pretty—but it was a start.

They cuddled on a blanket in front of a massive fireplace, observed by a gallery of mounted wildlife. Nestling into David's warmth, Cynthia reveled in the sense that the next time would be better.

"I've loved you since the day we met," he whispered.

He was very convincing.

20

STONE HARBOR

On Monday evening, Cynthia returned to Stone Harbor. She sought out Maria, finding her on a stationary bike in the gym, strengthening an injured knee.

Maria bounced off the bike; they embraced. "Where have you been? I was worried, and Carole is *really pissed*."

"I'm fine, and she'll get over it."

"I hear you have a hot new mission."

Cynthia sniffled.

"Are you okay, Cyn?"

"Yeah. I broke up with Thomas, but then I…"

"I'm sorry." Maria patted Cynthia's shoulder. "What happened?"

Cynthia took a step back, wiping moisture from her cheeks. "I'm okay."

"Tell me about it while I finish up."

They mounted adjacent bikes and talked while peddling.

"Good news and bad news. I broke up with Thomas. Then I slept with David Smathers." Two cheek wipes and a sigh followed. "I could never open up to Thomas about the job, you know? Lay it all out there."

Maria nodded.

"But David knows and accepts what I do. He understands."

"What about the rules against dating—"

"It was just one weekend."

Maria turned her head sideways until Cynthia looked over. "It wasn't *just* a weekend, *was* it, Cyn?"

Cynthia shrugged. "If it blossoms, we'll see each other on the sly."

"Will he be on your support team this time?"

"I don't know. If he is…well, we'll focus on the mission."

Maria looked skeptical. "What are you looking for with David?"

"I just want to have some fun, you know? He makes me laugh and…"

"So how was he?" Maria raised an eyebrow. "*Fun?*"

Cynthia smiled. "With Thomas, sex was like solving a math equation, but with David, it's closer to an art seminar on a wrestling mat."

"That sounds like fun," Maria said.

"I'm using X-eighty as a crutch…. Ree, how did you get over the date rape? Allow yourself to relax?"

"If I tell, you'll think I'm—"

"I really want to know. How did you get over it?"

"A woman," Maria said.

Cynthia should have known.

Maria stopped pedaling. "She was ten years older—the costume designer for a movie. I was doing make-up. The director—a brilliant artist—had jilted me. She was sensitive to my vulnerability. She taught me things about myself that I never knew. She taught me that loving myself was the first step. Her gentleness allowed me to accept affection from a new direction, in my own time." Maria waited until they made eye contact. "I told you because you asked. You'll heal in your own way."

Cynthia smiled, happy and frightened that two people loved her. "Carole's waiting for me."

There was no time for reminiscing when Carole welcomed Cynthia to the bungalow. They started to work, even as Cynthia picked at oriental salad with chopsticks.

"You lost a day, so listen up. You're going to London. The target's named Sir Wilton Thatcher. Here's his picture. He's an English nobleman, sixty-four, rich, and connected. His wife's some sort of duchess. Thatcher runs a hi-tech British security company that happens to be a competitor of Paulson Electronics. The company, United Security, specializes in counter-surveillance gadgets."

"Where do I come in?"

"As you've probably guessed, Sir Wilton has a weakness for the ladies, especially beautiful Americans young enough to be his daughter." Cynthia recalled her stepfather and pushed the plate away. "Thatcher's M.O. is to invite single executives—all male—to quarterly house parties where he picks one of their dates as his conquest for the weekend. Understand?"

Cynthia shook her head.

"Thatcher's company's developed a state-of-the-art encryption system called *NightOwl*. It has a device that transmits signals via satellite to perpetually scramble keys—so secret they deny they have it. Code-breaking software has to keep starting from square one. *Eighteen Ninety-Eight* is using *NightOwl* to shield satellite communications. It's like a Star Trek cloaking device for information."

"How will killing Thatcher help de-code *NightOwl*?"

"Funny you should ask, 'cause your assignment isn't just to kill Thatcher, but to steal the transmitter. Based on the type of signals the device puts out, the Paulson people have built a detector the size of a cell phone. Don't have a clue how it works, but they say it can find the *NightOwl*, on or off.

"If we can get our hands on the *NightOwl*, the experts'll be able to break the code. This operation's very big. The rumor is that Mr. Paulson himself is taking an active role."

"Why does he want me?"

"The bosses were impressed with how you handled your last mission. We expect this Thatcher business to be thorny."

"What makes it thorny?"

"No backup and a risky escape from what may be the most secure private residence in the world."

Cynthia thought a moment, a smile flickering. "What happened to the rules about backups and escape routes?"

Carole shrugged. "When people want something bad enough, they make exceptions."

Cynthia sat back in her chair.

"You'll do okay. The main problem is access to the device. We could knock off Thatcher a number of places, but to get the transmitter, it has to be done at his estate." Carole waited for questions, but Cynthia nodded for more information. "The *NightOwl*'s only used every few months, and only from Sir Wilton's second-floor private study. That much the Paulson people can be sure of through SCOPE signal homing. If we can get you inside for one of his house parties, we're sure the device will be in that study. The good news is Sir Wilton has his naughty fun late at night in the same room, so..." Seeing that Cynthia had something on her mind, Carole asked, "What?"

"This is a two-tiered seduction, right? I'm gonna have to get one of these executives to invite me as his date for the weekend, and then I have to entice Thatcher to pick me for his one-night stand."

"Yup. That about sums it up."

"No—not quite. Then I still have to kill him, steal the device, and get out of *the most secure private residence in the world* without being suspected."

Carole chuckled. "Well, *that* about sums it up."

"Is Thatcher's duchess wife present for these parties?"

"Sure. Lady Thatcher's the hostess. She doesn't trust her husband, so she watches him like a hawk. She scrutinizes in-house security tapes more than her husband does. Every hallway is monitored. Lady Thatcher wants to know if her husband is cheating. So far, he's fooled her."

"What's the primary weapon?" Cynthia asked.

"Poison, of course."

"Not those damn nails again."

"Nope. Since Thatcher serves champagne in his study, you'll use the poison Joanie used—out of a ring."

"Have you selected which executive I'll bewitch?"

"Nope. But it doesn't matter who you get in with—just that you get in." After a pause, Carole asked, "Any questions?"

"How do we know Thatcher invites one of the dates to his study?"

"Gabriella Sanchez interviewed one of his conquests who said Thatcher met her in the study at three in the morning. She also heard from her date that it was a regular thing. The executives know about it and try to bring girls that Thatcher'll favor—and he likes Americans. It's a competition. The guy who brings the chosen one gets a bonus."

"Sounds sick," Cynthia said. "That makes him our kind of guy. When did Thatcher make his play for our source?"

"At the dance after Saturday night dinner."

Cynthia closed her eyes for a few seconds then opened them wide. "How does the woman—or should I say, how do I—get to the study without showing up on the hallway cameras?"

"Our source says she went through a door that connects a closet off her guest suite to a closet in Thatcher's study—a secret passage. The study connects on the other side to his bedroom. The Thatchers have separate bedrooms."

"Then it's a done deal in advance," Cynthia said.

"What do you mean?"

"It always has to be from the same room. Thatcher has to know who he wants when the bedrooms are assigned—or else, he settles for whoever gets assigned to that room. Who makes the room assignments, Mr. or Mrs. Thatcher?"

"Don't rightly know," Carole admitted.

"I need to talk to that source."

"I'll have Gabriella set something up."

Cynthia's pulse quickened. "That's the second time you mentioned her name. Don't we have a London team?"

"No. You'll use Gabriella's team—same roster as before."

Cynthia rubbed her brow. "How much time before the next house party?"

"Eight weeks. You'll all go over A.S.A.P. so you have time to get invited."

Cynthia swallowed then pulled out her notebook. "We better get busy."

Cynthia had deluded herself that the physical ordeal was past—that she had graduated—but Carole burst that bubble. "You never graduate. Once an Aitie, always an Aitie." They ran on the beach and swam in the ocean each morning before breakfast. Carole drilled hand-to-hand combat and self-defense over and over.

New lessons taught Cynthia to deliver poison from finger rings. The poison was stored in the hollow gem setting. She used her thumb to spin the gem to the palm-side of her finger, flicking the safety off in the process. Then, holding a champagne glass from above with all five fingers, she pressed the ring's release button against the rim so poison dropped into the glass. Cynthia practiced the maneuver until her fingers ached...then practiced more.

Killing Thatcher would be the easy part. Then she had to locate and remove the *NightOwl* device. Joanie Lee, electronics expert, taught Cynthia how to operate the pocket-size detector.

"A monkey—or a man—could use this thing, Cyn. Turn it on here. Follow the lighted arrow. The brightness of the color indicates how close you are."

"If it's so easy, why did they make such a big deal out of having you teach me?"

"Finding the *NightOwl*'ll be easy. Extracting it could be hard. The actual transmitter will be the size of a cell phone, but it could be bolted inside a desk drawer or built into a big screen TV. You'll need to remove the right part. That's where this comes in." Joanie held up a plastic casing the shape of a large banana. "This is the All-in-One. You can see why I like this tool, huh? Technology—ain't it wonderful? You'll be able to crack a Brown Super Fortress safe or make a key in sixty seconds. Take it."

Joanie handed the All-in-One to Cynthia, who pressed a button that started a grinding noise. She dropped the tool as if it were radioactive. Joanie bent down and turned it off.

Giving her best "Q" impression, Joanie shook her head. "Don't press that button, double-oh-seven—unless you want to start World War Three. I said, 'take it,' not 'try out the vibrator function.'"

* * *

The evening before the flight to Heathrow, Cynthia reunited with Gabriella's strike team in the airport Hilton. David offered a bland handshake greeting, which left Cynthia hungry. As before the Spanish mission, there were maps to review—maps of London, the grounds of Thatcher's estate, and the house itself.

Gabriella explained the plan.

David attacked every point. "I don't like leaving Cynthia by herself."

"It's the only way to get her inside," Gabriella replied.

"What if you and Serg can't get her out?"

"We'll have a month of training. We'll get her out."

"The escape's too dangerous, and we could be followed."

"We know it's risky, but war requires risks."

"What if we think it's too dangerous and say we won't do it?"

Gabriella looked at Cynthia. "If the assassin accepts the risks, then I think we can, too. Remember, all bonuses have been tripled."

David gave Cynthia a glance of respect. She made her first comment. "David, if I can't get a date to the house party, you won't have to worry about a risky getaway."

He grinned. "You'll get a date. That's the one part of the plan I'm *not* worried about."

21

ENGLAND SWINGS

The first night in London, Gabriella introduced Cynthia to their inside source at a bustling pub near Piccadilly Circus. Dot Barski was a sleek Polish-American with lush hair. After introductions, Gabriella sat back while Cynthia took the lead.

"You know why we want to talk with you, right, Dot?"

"I was told it has to do with Edward Smythe, the house party at Crestmont Manor, and Sir Wilton's…late-night appetites."

"That's right. So for starters, where did you meet Edward Smythe?"

"At a reception at the American Embassy, where I'm an admin."

"What were you wearing?"

Dot cocked her head. "Probably a skirt and sweater."

"Be sure. Think harder," Cynthia said. "Was the skirt short? The sweater tight? Low cut?"

"Definitely not low-cut. That's frowned on at work. I remember now. It was my mauve sweater. Not too tight. The skirt wasn't short—sort of like this one, but dressier."

"How long before Smythe asked you to the house party?"

"After three dates."

"Did you sleep with him before the party?"

Dot raised an eyebrow.

"That's okay," Cynthia said. "Let me ask it this way. Did he say or imply he *wanted* to sleep with you?"

"Yeah. On the third date." Dot's smirk was that of a promiscuous school girl who took pleasure in shocking prim friends. "And I'm not embarrassed. I wish he hadn't waited so long."

"Anything unusual about the sex that might have made Smythe select you for the house party? Positions? Props?"

Dot shook her head. "No props. We were good together. He was more thoughtful than most guys. He made a point of asking what I liked."

"And what did you tell him?"

"That I was versatile."

After another minute, Cynthia had exhausted her questions about Smythe's preferences in bed. "I'm interested in how the guests arrived and who assigned rooms."

Dot reflected for a moment. "We came in a van. All eight of us—the four executives and dates. I'd never met any of the others. The van pulled into the driveway outside a stone wall. The mansion belonged on *Masterpiece Theatre*, a massive stone manor house. Sir Wilton greeted us in the driveway then took us on a tour of the grounds and stables."

"Did Smythe tell you in advance what Sir Wilton might have in mind?"

"Oh, yes. I was insulted," Dot said as if she weren't. "But Edward said it was a harmless game that could earn him a bonus—he promised to share. He doubted I'd have to do more than…you know." Dot made a yanking motion with her fist. "Edward had told me that I should flirt with Sir Wilton, so I did. All the girls did. Sir Wilton and I hit it off from the start. He's got charisma."

Cynthia made some notes while a waiter delivered three fish and chip dinners. As the ladies ate, Cynthia continued, between bites. "Gabriella tells me there are exterior steps to the main entrance of the house. Do you recall where Sir Wilton was when you and the others walked up the steps?"

"He was at the bottom. He definitely waved us ahead of him."

"And who made the room assignments?" Cynthia pressed. "This is important."

"Thatcher was the one who suggested the rooms. He said something to his wife like, 'Why don't we put Edward in the Blue Room?'"

"You're sure it was Sir Wilton?"

"Yes."

"What did Lady Thatcher say?"

"She said that would be fine."

Cynthia looked Dot in the eyes. "Do you think Lady Thatcher liked you more or less than the other three women?"

Dot laughed. "Oh, definitely *less*. In the foyer, Edward goaded me into making a snide comment about Her Ladyship's figure—sort of chunky. Either she has great hearing or the acoustics of the foyer are like a whispering arch. If looks could kill…"

"What were you wearing when you arrived?"

"Edward suggested something hot, so I wore tight clothes: a red sweater—not low-cut, it was last fall—and black dress pants."

"Anything else about clothes we should know?"

Dot rubbed her chin. "Not clothes, necessarily, but when Sir Wilton asked me at the dance to meet him in his study, he suggested I wear something kinky."

"Did you?" Gabriella asked.

"Stockings and garters. That's as kinky as I had with me."

Cynthia followed up. "Anything kinky about Sir Wilton's sexual preferences?"

"No. I think he just got off on the look. Anyway, Edward was right about the...you know."

"Did Smythe share his bonus?"

"Yeah. He gave me three hundred pounds, so I guess I'm a high-priced whore."

Cynthia asked about the Blue Room.

After a series of questions concerning the layout of the house and the closet connection, Gabriella took over. "What did you wear to the dinner-dance?"

"A black gown—with a slit up one side."

"Low cut?"

"Definitely."

"How was your hair?"

"I wore it up."

"Jewelry?"

"Pearl necklace and earrings."

"What about Lady Thatcher that night? Where was she?"

Dot laughed. "Her Ladyship got bombed and flirted with the executives. She passed out long before midnight. I got the impression that was par for the course."

Gabriella and Cynthia exchanged nods. "Anything else?" Gabriella asked.

"No," Dot said.

"Then we're done." Gabriella stood. "Thanks for coming."

Dot glanced at both women. "Aren't you forgetting something?"

"Right." Gabriella handed over an envelope.

After they'd seen Dot to the Tube, Gabriella asked, "So, what do you think about shopping for a black gown instead of the blue one?"

"Truthfully? A waste of time. I have a few weeks to make an impression on prospective dates, but I'll only have a few minutes to make an impression on Thatcher before he assigns rooms.

"You're right," Gabriella said. "What you wear to the dance is irrelevant."

They sat on stone steps that gave them a view of Piccadilly Circus. "I say we go after Smythe," Cynthia said. "Don't even bother with the others unless I crap out with him."

"Why not pursue all four from the start? Hedge our bets?"

"It might send up a red flag. These four guys work together. Anyway, we know specifics about Smythe. Can we confirm he hasn't asked anyone to the party?"

"David's contact assures us he's still unattached."

"Then it's about time I meet Edward Smythe."

Just when Gabriella thought her assassin was getting a swelled head, Cynthia floated back to earth. "So how should I go about meeting him, and what should I wear?"

The two women discussed Cynthia's seduction of Smythe while taking a leisurely walk to Covent Gardens. Cynthia let Gabriella do most of the talking.

"I think we should set the trap at Wimbledon. Smythe is a member and plays there two or three times a week. How's your tennis?"

Cynthia shrugged. "I don't play much, so—"

Gabriella laughed. "I only care about how you look in your tennis outfit. You won't have to be any good...at tennis." Gabriella became more animated. "We'll get you and David onto Smythe's regular court, right before his time. You'll be frustrated, you'll linger, you'll flirt. I'm sure you can get him to give you a lesson, since he prides himself on his abilities. He's always on the lookout for new talent. None of them take the same date twice. I think he'll check you out *very* closely. We'll shop for tennis outfits at Harrods tomorrow."

Cynthia looked worried. Gabriella said, "You've seen the file and his picture. You don't have a problem dating a black man, do you?"

Cynthia shook her head. "I'm fine with that, really. I was just worrying about playing horrible tennis at Wimbledon, of all places. Any chance I can get a few lessons before I meet Smythe?"

Gabriella laughed again. "David is good. I'm sure he'll be happy to give you a few pointers. Have you ever played on grass?"

* * *

From the corner of her eye, Cynthia saw two men approaching the court. They were ten minutes early. She figured she could stall for five minutes past the 6:00 p.m. court change. That gave her fifteen minutes to get Smythe's attention.

It took less than one.

David feathered a drop shot to her backhand, requiring that she race toward where Smythe was unpacking his gear. A futile dash ended with Cynthia bracing her hand against the low fence separating the court from his bench. Exaggerating her need for oxygen, she leaned on the fence for a moment to catch her breath. The smell of grass reminded her of helping her father with yard work. There was eye contact, and she treated Smythe to a smile.

"Hello there," he said. "Nice try. Can't get them all."

Cynthia had assumed Smythe would "sound black," but his accent was so British that she couldn't stifle a smile.

"I guess you're right. I *can't* get them all."

"Hey, Cynthia," David shouted. "Hurry up! We're running out of time, and I want to finish the set."

She gave Smythe a sideways glance. "He's killing me and it torques me off. I should be better than this."

"Follow through more on your backhand," Smythe suggested.

During the next few minutes, David orchestrated every rally, maneuvering Cynthia near Smythe time and again.

"He's *really* torquing me off," Cynthia whispered to Smythe when she got within a few feet. Her soft voice drew him closer. "I have to get some lessons."

On the pretense of finishing the set, David and Cynthia kept the court two minutes past six, the set ending with Cynthia—chest heaving in front of Smythe—cursing one last drop shot.

"Don't fret, it's a nice day," Smythe said. "My name is Edward Smythe." He held out his hand.

She shook it. His hand was firm. "Cynthia Johnson."

"Are you serious about wanting lessons, Cynthia?"

Still breathing heavily, she motioned for Smythe to hand her a towel. "Thanks. Yeah, I'm serious," she said, shooting a nasty glance at David, who slid tennis balls into their plastic cylinder on the far side of the court.

"I'd love to give you a few pointers," Smythe offered as he walked onto the court. "When are you free?"

"Is tomorrow too soon?"

Smythe smiled. "I could meet you here at six tomorrow on this very court. I have it reserved. You'll be my guest."

"Six would be great."

"Perhaps we could share a bite to eat afterward?"

She pretended to think. "That would be nice."

"Until tomorrow at six then," Smythe said with a formal nod.

Cynthia lingered to watch her tennis instructor warm up.

"Coming, Cyn?" David called. Smythe's sympathetic glance was the last thing she saw before turning to join her playing companion.

"You were great," she said to David, "the way you maneuvered me close to him was a work of art."

"No better than you, Lady Temptress. From what I saw, he'll want to *stay* close."

"You don't sound very jealous."

"The job comes first. Him liking you is part of the job."

Cynthia shrugged to cover a vacuum in her gut.

Cynthia was on time for her lesson, dressed in white—stretch shorts and a top that revealed her tapered midriff. When she arrived, Smythe was waiting with a remote-control ball machine set up behind the baseline on the far side of the net. Assessing her tennis togs, he said, "The elders might object, but they'll be watching. So let's get started and give them something to watch."

After adjusting her grip and spending a few minutes on footwork, he began sending balls her way. Cynthia took well to his instructions. She was a natural athlete, and he was a good teacher, using a hand on her arm or hip as needed to get her into proper position. He removed the machine at 6:45, and they spent the last few minutes rallying. She improved noticeably during the hour.

As they approached the clubhouse, Smythe pointed out the lounge where they would meet after showering. Thirty minutes later, she was sipping a white wine. She questioned him about London. He countered about New York. Over dinner, they talked about politics, hobbies, and amusements.

"I like to dance," Cynthia said, "but haven't found a good place in London yet."

"I know a few clubs. What kind of music do you like?"

"Anything with good rhythm that's not too loud."

"Well, the volume may be a problem, but I think I know a place."

"Really? Could you tell me where it is?"

"Better than that, I can take you there, if you like."

"Smashing! Isn't that what you Brits would say?"

"Smashing it is. By the way, Cynthia, how long will you be in London?"

"A month and a half. Why?"

"Oh, there may be a chance we can get out to the country in a few weeks. Do you like the country?"

"I love the country! Woods, lakes, streams," she said.

"Do you ride?" he asked.

"I love the country. Woods, lakes, streams."

They laughed.

After Smythe paid the check, he said, "We have some time before the dance club opens. Until then, how would you like an insider's tour of London?"

It was quite an outing. He knew more anecdotes about the Tower of London than the Beefeater who had shown Cynthia around the day before. He knew the security guard at Parliament, so they got an after-hours tour. He walked her through the most vibrant street life in the city—straight to a private club's front door, and he knew the password.

The nightclub was classy but loud. It had once been a bank, and the paneled walls and marble floor echoed the latest sounds. Unable to talk over the reverberating bass, Cynthia and Smythe communicated with body language. To Cynthia's surprise, they were on the same frequency. When a slow number began, he leaned close, saying "Do you think your tennis friend would mind?"

Her throat contracted. "You're none of his business, and he hasn't been much of a friend lately."

They nestled together, swaying to the music.

"I don't think I properly thanked you for the lesson. Thank you so much."

"Would you like another lesson?" he asked.

Her mind flashed back to the parking lot in Wildwood where a similar discussion had taken place with a different man. "A lesson in what?"

"Why, tennis of course. We've just scratched the surface, as you Americans would say." He scratched her back. She rebuked herself for enjoying his touch, but that couldn't stop the goose-bumps on her arms. She began to think of him as Edward instead of Smythe.

A week later, Edward came to watch her return match with David, who had to extend himself to fend off her improved game, 6-3, 6-4. That night, Edward asked Cynthia to the house party at Crestmont Manor.

During the fortnight before the weekend affair, Edward squired Cynthia around London. Their cruise to Greenwich was on United Security's private yacht. For a Shakespeare experience, he treated Cynthia to *Romeo and Juliet* from a private box at the new Globe Theatre. They received a VIP tour of Buckingham Palace. But Cynthia had the most fun when Edward took her on a pub crawl. The wetter his whistle, the dryer his sense of humor. Using tricks Carole had taught her, Cynthia avoided drinking much of her ale, but despite temperance measures, she had consumed too much by the time they left the last of six pubs. She didn't have to act dizzy—she really needed to hold Edward's arm during the zigzag walk to her hotel.

"What does your friend Gabriella do when you're out on the town with me?"

"She does okay," Cynthia slurred. "She met a guy she likes."

Edward squeezed her hand. "If she's out tonight perhaps we can…?"

"That's pretty presum…presumptuous of you," she teased.

"I just want to extend our date as long as I can, but if you think I'm being presumptuous…"

"No, Edward. I don't mind presume…presum… Oh, just gimme that British not-so-stiff upper lip."

It was torture to get up for the dawn run, but Cynthia forced herself to go at the appointed hour, hangover and all.

"You're a very lucky girl," Gabriella said as they emerged from a pedestrian underpass by Apsley House on the edge of Hyde Park.

"Yeah. Edward is a nice fringe benefit," Cynthia replied.

"You're a stupid girl, too," Gabriella said as they started to jog through the morning fog.

"What?"

Gabriella picked up the pace as she lectured. "You're so full of yourself that you're making sloppy mistakes. Never get drunk on the job! Smythe is business, and don't forget it. You can sleep with him once you get to the manor. You can even like it, but don't drink and don't get hung up on him, even if he's innocent in the *NightOwl* thing."

* * *

Saint James Park was Cynthia's favorite place in London. It was where she and David walked and admired flowers whenever they had the chance. This afternoon was their last Saint James stroll before the house party. She wanted to take his hand, but couldn't risk it in public.

"It's been hard for me to stay away," she said.

"Me, too." He paused. "I don't want you to sleep with him."

A warm surge enveloped her heart. "What about the job coming first?"

He touched her hand. "It still does. I just said…well, I know what you have to do, but I said it, and I meant it."

Cynthia grabbed his hand. "I'd rather not talk about him this afternoon. I just want to enjoy the flowers, the ducks, the colors, the children. Everything."

They gazed across a pond toward Buckingham Palace. He stood behind her, looking over her shoulder. "Changing of the guard," he said. "It's overrated, but tourists flock like pigeons."

Face flushed, she imagined his strong arms wrapped around her midsection. "I don't want the guard to change."

The evening before the house party, Edward Smythe and Cynthia admired the same flowers in Saint James Park. "Are you sure I don't need a lot of fancy clothes for the weekend?" she asked.

"Tomorrow's dinner-dance is semi-formal, but I assure you that everything else is casual."

Cynthia studied his solid profile. Why was she attracted to Edward, even though she liked David? Did she possess some disloyalty gene?

Edward turned, caught her eyeing him, and smiled. "Cynthia, my dear, I think I should tell you more particulars about tomorrow's house party at Sir Wilton's."

She was happy to be diverted back to the job. "You've told me it's important that Sir Wilton like me and that I should flirt with him. What else is there to know?"

"Ah, I say, if he likes you the most of all the ladies, he very well may ask you to meet him alone late at night."

"To do what?"

"To do the same thing that any man would want to do with you late at night." Coming from Edward, it sounded like a compliment.

"And if Sir Wilton comes on to me, how should I respond?"

"Why, meet him as he wishes, of course."

Cynthia stretched open her eyes. "No."

"But yes, Cynthia. I'll get a jolly fat bonus if he selects you, and even more if he likes you. I'll cut you in, as you Americans would say."

"I'm not sure I could do that."

"Not even if I ask sweetly?" Edward cooed.

"Why would you encourage me?"

Edward laughed. "Sir Wilton is a bit of an odd duck. He lusts after young women, yet he doesn't want to be perceived as a dirty old man. Being filthy rich, he chooses to have his executives compete by offering their dates to him in the privacy of his home. He likes the naughty thrill, and I think he enjoys putting one over on her Ladyship."

Cynthia pouted. "Why would you offer me to someone else so casually?"

Edward grinned, appreciating her show. "Look at it this way. I'm sure you've been with other men, but neither the quantity of your lovers nor the intensity of your passion for any of them interests me in the slightest. I only care that you and I have wonderful chemistry. Whether you go to Sir Wilton or not, I will admire you just as much as I do right now."

His pompous speech made her think less of him, and anything that lowered her opinion of Edward Smythe was good.

Edward's smile widened. "I also happen to know that Sir Wilton has the control of a schoolboy. With just a wee bit of encouragement from you, the old bloke will shoot his wad before he gets inside your panties. So you see, neither of us will be risking very much. Plus I'll be waiting for you, and I have no such problems."

Although Edward's offer to share her with Sir Wilton was expected, it nauseated her. What kind of man would be party to such a scheme?

Edward met Cynthia in her hotel dining room for an early breakfast. Over muffins and tea, she asked, "What will be the sleeping arrangements?"

He laughed. "I wondered when you'd ask. We'll be sharing a room. Is that a problem?"

She smiled. "No problem, but will Sir Wilton and Lady Thatcher approve?"

"The Thatchers are quite liberal. All the couples sleep together."

"Do you always get the same room?" Cynthia asked

He slid his hand over hers. "No, but I prefer the Blue Room, and I get it over half the time for house parties and...oh, never mind."

Keeping her smile reserved, she followed up. "What is it about the Blue Room that you like?"

"It's lucky for me. I seem to get a bigger bonus after I stay in the Blue Room."

"Is it lucky in any other way?" she teased.

"Other sorts of luck I keep to myself."

"Well then," she replied, "I hope we get the Blue Room, and I have a feeling that we'll both be very lucky."

22

CRESTMONT MANOR

Edward and Cynthia were the last couple picked up by the United Security van. Expecting a rivalry among the women, Cynthia was pleased that tension dissolved during the ninety-minute ride to Crestmont Manor. The four men regaled the ladies with anecdotes from prior house parties—mostly stories about Lady Thatcher treating her dogs better than the servants. Edward allowed his colleagues to tell most of the tales, but he laughed hard, and Cynthia liked the sound.

She studied her competition. All three women were attractive Americans, one blonde and two brunettes. Cynthia thought she might be the chosen one based on looks alone, but she was leaving nothing to chance. From the interview with Dot Barski, Cynthia and Gabriella concluded that a tight backside was needed when Sir Wilton would be looking up the steps—and a sliver of midriff wouldn't hurt. Cynthia wore a pair of snug designer jeans and a short top. Appealing to Sir Wilton's kinky side, she wore a belt studded with small metal spikes.

When the van rolled through the outer gate, she sat up and stared. The property was immaculate, the entry drive winding through a sprawling garden of trees and shrubs that reminded Cynthia of Winterthur, where every plant was sited and pruned to give the impression that nature had enjoyed a good century. Coming out of the last curve, she saw the three-story stone mansion, dominating a formal garden on one side and stables on the other. Dot was right: the scene was straight out of *Masterpiece Theatre*.

Thatcher met them inside a second gate. He was tall and more distinguished than in his photographs. She brushed her hip against Sir Wilton's as he helped her out of the van. Her smile was taunting, and judging from his grin, it provoked the desired effect.

"I'm Wilton Thatcher," he said. "And what might your name be?"

"Cynthia Johnson."

Her Ladyship's playful Corgis accompanied the tour of the gardens and stables. Noticing that Sir Wilton was cool to the dogs, Cynthia resisted her inclination to pet them as they frolicked amid shrubbery. In the stables, it was clear that the horses were Sir Wilton's babies, so Cynthia fawned over them, accepting sloppy kisses from a filly named Sophie.

When Sir Wilton bade his guests to enter the house, Cynthia made sure she walked up last, right in front of him. Half-way up the steps, she stopped. Sir Wilton grabbed her waist to keep from bumping.

"Sorry," she said, "I was admiring the architecture."

"By Jove, so was I," he whispered.

In the foyer, the guests were met by Lady Thatcher. During the pleasantries, Cynthia played her insult. "Lady Thatcher, I hope you put the dogs outside at night."

Her Ladyship's look was as icy as a Siberian winter. Cynthia caught Sir Wilton's eye with a bemused shrug.

"Dear, what say we give Edward and Cynthia the Blue Room?" Sir Wilton suggested.

"Whatever you say," Lady Thatcher responded. "You do like the Blue Room, don't you Edward?" Cynthia noted cold stares from two of the executives, but she caught one of the brunettes breathing a sigh of relief.

Sir Wilton took the ladies on a house tour that omitted his private study. The mansion's interior was tastefully ostentatious. Cynthia couldn't understand why anyone bragged about ugly, uncomfortable furniture, no matter how old it was. The tour ended on the rear veranda for a lobster salad luncheon. The conversation was more subdued than in the van, the four executives ceding the floor to their hosts. The result was tedious, so Cynthia amused herself by playing footsie with Edward and making eye contact with Sir Wilton.

There was a choice of afternoon activities: boating, swimming, fishing, hiking, tennis, or riding. Having never been on a horse, Cynthia didn't want to risk injury or embarrassment. When Edward asked her preference, she replied, "Hiking," which would enable her to explore the grounds.

"That's right," Edward recalled, "you love the woods, lakes, and streams, don't you?"

Edward and Cynthia were late returning from their hike, drawing a scowl from Lady Thatcher at tea. The conversation was not nearly as good as the scones and clotted cream. After tea, the men adjourned for a business meeting, leaving the ladies to amuse themselves. Cynthia read a legal thriller in the garden until it was time to change for dinner.

The cocktail hour was festive. Expecting a long night, Cynthia stuck to cranberry juice. Sir Wilton complimented all four dates. Edward complimented only Cynthia.

Dinner was a drawn out, multi-course affair that would have been boring without Edward. The Thatchers sat at the far end of the table—Mrs. Thatcher wanting dog-haters as far away as possible—so Edward was free to be himself. While entertaining his end of the table, he periodically whispered into Cynthia's ear.

During the after-dinner ball, the mistress of the house drank her way to being the life of the party. The executives danced with her, and she relished the attention from younger men. With his giddy wife occupied, Sir Wilton danced with each of the Americans.

He waltzed with Cynthia. "You're quite lovely, my dear."

"Thank you."

"I have a tradition at my house parties of sharing champagne at three a.m. with the most beautiful woman present. Would you care to join me tonight?"

"I don't know what to say, Sir Wilton."

"Please, call me Wilton. And hasn't Edward told you that it would be all right?"

"Well, yes, but…"

"I can always ask one of the others—"

"No. I mean, yes," Cynthia whispered. "I'd like to have champagne with you."

"Then at three?"

She smiled. "At three."

Sir Wilton danced Cynthia into a corner and, with his back to the room, slipped a key into the cleavage of her blue gown. "This will open a door in the back of the closet in your dressing room. The door will take you into a closet of my study where I shall be waiting. Wear something kinky—perhaps that studded belt you had on earlier."

And so it was settled. She and the dirty old man had a 3:00 a.m. rendezvous.

Cynthia danced the rest of the numbers with Edward. Shortly after midnight, he escorted her upstairs, unable to keep his hands off her. She pushed the Blue Room's door closed and accepted Edward's kiss. As he lowered her zipper, a chill shot up her spine.

"Good show," Edward whispered when the key clattered onto the floor. His tongue was wet and warm, sliding inside her ear. She placed her hand on his chest, feeling the thumping that matched her own, although for different reasons. She would need a pill.

Cynthia rose carefully from her side of the bed, taking a moment to watch Edward sleep. She had been confused—repulsed at the same time she warmed to his touch. Had it just been the X-80, or had she really responded to him? Sex with Edward had been unavoidable—part of her cover—but had she truly wanted to avoid it? During intercourse, she had tried to think about David, but her mind kept slipping back to reality, pulled by her senses.

It was 2:45 a.m. She entered the suite's bath area, closed the door softly, and prepared for Sir Wilton. She pulled out a small travel bag from a secret compartment in her suitcase.

First things first—she put a ring on each hand, making sure the one marked "L" went on her left. Next, she twirled her hair and fastened it behind her head with the stiletto hairpin. She dressed quickly in an all-black outfit—midriff-baring zippered top, fishnet thigh-high stockings, and tight shorts. Remembering Sir Wilton's request for the spiked belt, she tried it on, but it was too wide for the loops, so she left the belt hanging on the doorknob. Surveying her reflection in the mirror, she unsnapped the waist of her shorts and lowered the zipper two inches—that was kinky enough.

For footwear, she pulled on high-heeled boots that hid a knife in the left calf. Cynthia checked that the knife's release was working. After spending a few minutes applying make-up the way Maria had taught her, she was almost ready. She removed the *NightOwl* detector and All-in-One tool from the travel bag and slipped them into her purse, then finished with a dab of perfume and gargle of mouthwash. She gave herself a final check in the mirror, where she saw a comic-strip hooker staring back at her.

After a deep breath, she entered the walk-in closet and inserted Thatcher's key into the lock of a door on the back wall. Just as Thatcher had said, her closet led to a second. She cracked open the door to the study and saw Sir Wilton smiling from an easy chair. He waved her in.

A fire crackled, making the large room cozy. Cynthia doubted that anyone had read most of the leather-bound books that filled the bookcases on two walls.

Sir Wilton, looking like Hugh Hefner a few years past his prime, rose to admire her. "I expected the spiked belt, but this is just as bloody wicked." Sir Wilton's gaze was focused right where she wanted it.

Cynthia saw the champagne chilling. "I used to be a bartender. May I pour?"

He indicated with an outstretched arm that she was welcome to serve.

Poof! The cork came out with her accomplished twist. She poured two glasses then picked them up with her fingers, palms above the rims. Licking her lips, she walked toward him and pushed her left ring against the rim of his glass, releasing poison into the bubbles. She gave his glass a swirl, and they clinked. "To weekends in the country," he toasted. She smiled and brought her glass to her lips, as did Sir Wilton.

Cynthia sipped during a few minutes of small talk, while he showed off photos of royalty. "It's not everyday a girl is alone with a handsome nobleman who knows so many famous people. I'll pour us more champagne." Cynthia put extra panache into her walk to the chilling bottle. He followed, placing one hand on her waist as she cradled the bottle in her fingers.

Her resolve was stiffened by his leer. "Drink up," she said, "so I can pour us each another." Sir Wilton complied, and Cynthia topped off both glasses.

Thatcher took her hand and led her to the couch where they sat. After a bit more sipping, he brought his mouth to something sweeter. The old boy was eager, pushing his tongue between her teeth. His breathing was labored, which Cynthia took as a sign of excitement, the poison, or both. She counted the seconds while he fondled her. Impatient for the poison to take effect, she reminded herself to stay cool—the same poison had taken a few minutes in Bermuda. She focused on a picture of Lady Di and kept counting.

At 100, he inched down the zipper of her top, looking like a boy trying to open a present without ripping the wrapping paper. His skin was clammy. She knew he was dying, but he didn't.

Thatcher fumbled with her bra. When he coughed, she clamped her hand over his mouth. For a few seconds, she stared into his eyes while he writhed in agony. Then Sir Wilton, clutching his chest, slumped into her arms. She held him quiet until he stopped twitching. No pulse.

No remorse, either, but her killer high was short-lived—maybe because the mark was pathetic instead of a sexy stud. There wasn't time to wonder.

Cynthia rolled his body onto the rug and zipped her top before going to her purse and activating the locator. Lights on the face of the device indicated the direction and proximity of the *NightOwl*. The beacon was fainter than in any practice. The signal pointed to the closet through which she had entered, so she went inside. She was closer, but still not within ten feet. She followed the signal to her dressing area. As the light brightened, a knot tightened in her stomach.

Cynthia was dazed as the pulsing light guided her to the pedestal sink. The locator shone bright red, indicating two inches when she held it next to Edward's toilet kit. She knew exactly what this meant, at the same time she was clueless. None of her training had prepared her for *this* event. Cynthia's hands trembled as she examined the toilet kit in which she found a zippered compartment. Switching on a nightlight by the sink, she removed what was in the pouch. The truth was impossible, although there it was in her quivering fingers. She tried to rationalize her fears. Maybe it was planted to implicate Edward. Her mind attempted to direct her body to do something. But what?

Eyes down, Cynthia was unaware of movement behind her, but the soft click of a closing door snapped her to attention. She saw Smythe's face over her shoulder in the mirror. Her heart skipped two beats. Maybe her body had shielded his view.

She fought back panic. "Did I wake you, darling?" Keeping her back to him, she added, "You were right about Sir Wilton. I hope you're ready to demonstrate better control." Cynthia's fingers fumbled the *NightOwl*, trying to get it back into the toilet kit while she looked at Smythe's approaching reflection. Thus occupied, she was defenseless when his hands came over her head from behind. There was only time to gulp in a half-breath before Smythe had her belt cinched around her neck, the studs puncturing her skin. As he yanked the choke tight, Smythe slammed her forward, pinning her thighs against the pedestal. Constrained by his body, her legs were powerless to counter him.

"Bloody bitch," he spat into her ear.

Pain tore through her throat, not from the individual gouges, but as if her neck were a ring of fire, a fire that melted her ability to think. Reflex. That's what made her hand move, for there would be no memory of intent. She reached her right hand for the hairpin, extracting the stiletto from its clip by squeezing the handle. With all her strength, she swung the weapon behind her back and drove it into Smythe's side. He groaned and released a hand to swat at the blade, which allowed Cynthia to suck in a gulp of air. She forced two fingers of her right hand under the belt and turned to face him. Smythe's hand was back on the belt and the choke resumed, but a knee to his crotch loosened his hold for another split-second.

Tightening the strangling grip, Smythe attacked like a wounded animal. He lunged forward, lifting her into a sitting position in the sink, ripping her throat. From the pain, she thought her neck was severed.

She had one chance. Cynthia raised her knee and clutched at the release on her left boot, which kicked up and down as she pawed. Listless and fading, she felt darkness descend. She stretched for a last grab.

Click. The knife handle released into her trembling fingers. With her bottom resting in the sink, there was enough space between their torsos for her to plunge the blade under his breastbone and into his heart. With all her dwindling strength, she shoved the blade upward. And then again. Three, four, five, six times she stabbed, trying to drain his heart before she was strangled.

Cynthia felt as if she were dying, but so was Smythe, and he was dying faster. She clawed the belt from her neck and let his body fall. She sat in the bloody sink, gasping. Although the belt was loose, she still clutched at her throat. Blood seeped from multiple gouges.

She tried to think—what to do?

The plan! What was the fucking plan? She had to escape with the *NightOwl*. Careful to avoid stepping in blood, she eased herself off the pedestal and looked in the mirror. There was blood smeared over her throat and stomach, as well as splattered on her clothes. She plugged the bleeding holes in her neck with her fingers and sat on the toilet, rocking while her blood clotted. Pain made it difficult to think. *Concentrate, James.* The neck wounds would have to be covered, and she had to change clothes. Thank God Gabriella had insisted she bring a turtleneck for the cool country nights.

Before changing, she removed the two weapons protruding from Smythe's body. She wiped both clean and replaced them in her hair clip and boot. She cleaned her neck and torso, but blood still leaked from her wounds, so she stuffed tissue scraps into the holes and wrapped her throat with paper towels. She wrestled off her top and shorts, replacing them with a turtleneck and loose pants that fit over her boots. The stockings stayed—too much trouble to get them off. Rest. She needed rest, so she sat on the toilet.

Cold and exhausted, she craved oxygen like a mountain climber above 8,000 meters. Wheezing, sucking sounds indicated she was breathing—sort of—but where was the air going? She thought of her mother reading *Annapurna* to a fascinated little girl. Move your feet, girl, or you'll freeze to death in the crevasse. Stand up…Okay…Left foot first….Good. Now the right.

Watching where she stepped, Cynthia dragged Smythe's corpse into the shower, then she wiped up the mess from the sink and tiled floor. She tossed the bloody towels and clothes next to the body before closing the stall door. Collapsing on the toilet seat, she rested and wiped blood off her boots. Her throat felt as if the air going down her windpipe was saturated with thumbtacks.

Don't die here. Move.

Cynthia stuffed both transmitter and locator into her purse before staggering back through the closets. She put her key into Sir Wilton's robe pocket and rolled him closer to the fire. Then she poured champagne for herself, emptied her dose of poison into the glass, and swallowed. Her throat burned as if she were gargling acid. She emptied the rest of the poison into the champagne bottle then flipped both rings into the fire. Just as she had planned before the detour, Cynthia picked up Thatcher's telephone and dialed Gabriella's number.

In a scratchy voice, Cynthia whimpered through the pain. "Help. Emergency at Crestmont Manor…Send an ambulance. Please hurry!" After she hung up the telephone, Cynthia tied the purse strap to her wrist. Her insides somersaulted, and she squeezed her eyes closed.

The jostle of being lifted onto a stretcher woke Cynthia, and she recognized Gabriella's face. Other people milled about the room, including Serg and Lady Thatcher. If Cynthia hadn't felt so violently ill, she would have been glad to see her teammates carrying out the paramedic rescue they had been practicing for the last month. Gabriella injected the antidote into Cynthia's arm. Cynthia felt instant relief. *Maybe it was heroin.*

While being wheeled out, Cynthia pulled Gabriella's head down to where Cynthia could whisper. "Not Thatcher. Smythe." To Gabriella it sounded like "Nut-hatch swine."

By the time both stretchers were secured in the back of the ambulance, Cynthia was regaining her faculties. She was aware of her throbbing neck.

"Killed the wrong man."

Gabriella's eyes bugged.

Cynthia coughed. "Thatcher wasn't the owl. It was Smythe."

"What? Who did you kill?" asked Gabriella, trying to make sense out of chaos.

"Both."

"What happened?"

Cynthia's voice was barely a whisper. "We gotta get away…. They'll find Smythe's body…. I'll be a suspect."

"Shit, Cyn, what did you do?"

Cynthia's raspy voice sputtered between laborious inhalations. "Intel was wrong. It wasn't Thatcher. Smythe was the owl. He surprised me, but I got the knife into his heart. The *NightOwl*'s in my purse."

"Yeah. I got it. Saw that you tied it to your wrist. Good thinking."

Serg's voice came from the driver's seat. "We're almost to the van. Still no one following."

"Good," Gabriella said. "We have to change to Plan C."

Serg flashed the high-beams three times. The ambulance pulled over and stopped behind a copse of trees. "Plan C," Serg shouted to David before shutting off the lights. Gabriella and Sergio carried Cynthia to the waiting van. From the rear seat, she watched David start the ambulance rolling down a slope. The ambulance disappeared into a ravine with Thatcher's body inside.

While the getaway van sped through the night, David held Cynthia's hand. Gabriella was on the cell phone, scheduling emergency travel. Then she reported in. "Yes. Eight ball pocketed, but cue ball scratched—requires re-spotting immediately."

When Gabriella signed off, Cynthia whispered, "You didn't tell them about Smythe."

Gabriella massaged her own forehead. "Something's wrong. We may have been set up."

Gabriella sifted through some papers. "I got us on Continental with Plan C identities. We have seats on the first flight out this morning. We also have three sets of false reservations to muddy the waters. David has a bag of luggage for each of us in the back." Looking down, Gabriella said, "She'll need to lose the boots and hairpin. David, get the beige shoes out of Cynthia's bag. And the C-identity wig." As Gabriella tightened Cynthia's coiled hair, she murmured, "There's blood on her ear. David, get the first aid kit."

"My neck," Cynthia rasped.

David coughed. "Ah, I left all the first aid stuff in the ambulance."

"Shit," Gabriella said.

Gabriella looked under the turtleneck. Her next "SHIT!!!" was a head-turner. "My God! Why didn't you say something?"

"I don't…" Cynthia was too sick to know what to worry about, but she was glad David was holding her hand—squeezing her hand.

"We have to get you to a hos—" Gabriella cut herself off. Cynthia had just killed two Englishmen on their home soil. The U.S. government might shield them from extradition, but Uncle Sam couldn't help in England.

"I have a bottle of Scotch in my bag," Serg said from the driver's seat. "At least it's alcohol."

"David, get it out," Gabriella commanded. "And do you have a cotton undershirt?"

"Yeah," David replied.

"Cut a bandage two inches wide. We'll use the alcohol to sterilize it. I'll use the rest as a swab."

While Serg drove as if he were racing at Le Mans, David caressed

Cynthia's head. Gabriella removed the blood-soaked paper towels and cleaned the wounds. Once she had wrapped the makeshift bandage in place and rolled up the turtleneck, she shrugged.

"It looks okay." But she wasn't so sure.

Gabriella gave instructions for their emergency identities while David handed out Plan C passports and papers.

In the terminal, they behaved as if nothing was amiss, hoping to get off the ground before the authorities looked for Cynthia Johnson at Heathrow.

The minute hand moved more slowly than a sun dial for Cynthia—now traveling as auburn-haired Cheryl Walston from Fairfield, Iowa. She was in terrible pain, still shaking off the poison. Boarding at the gate, Cynthia was scrutinized by a male attendant who looked like W.C. Fields. He blinked into her pale face. "Miss Walston, are you any relation to Fred Walston? I met him when I visited Des Moines." Cynthia, having trouble standing, gripped the attendant's podium.

She shook her head. The gate attendant said, "Oh, well," and handed Cynthia her papers. Two steps into the boarding tunnel, Cynthia wobbled, but David held her upright. Inside the fuselage, she braced on seatbacks until reaching their row. She had trouble breathing, and her scalp itched as if a thousand ants were digging out her roots underneath the wig. She opened the overhead air valve and pointed it at her face.

Every second seemed like a minute, every minute like an hour. Would they ever pull away from the gate? Cynthia swallowed her fifth and sixth ibuprofens.

It was a somber flight for row 32. The four collaborators talked little. David held Cynthia's hand across the aisle whenever possible. Gabriella pampered her for a few hours before falling asleep. Cynthia tried to think about what had happened, and why, but was unable to concentrate. Finally, she slept.

When the jet was within an hour of landing, Cynthia woke Gabriella. "I'm sure you'll find that Smythe was using the *NightOwl* to set up Thatcher. What should we say or not say about all this?"

"You could be damned if you talk, and damned if you don't," Gabriella said.

"I think the safest thing is to say nothing, but I need a way to make 'nothing' believable. I was thinking I might fake amnesia. I've read how trauma can cause memory loss."

23

HOME

By the time the authorities discovered bodies, questioned witnesses, and searched for Cynthia Johnson at the airports, the team had landed in Newark. With luck, the U.S. government would block extradition if the British managed to figure out who Cynthia Johnson really was. She hoped her fingerprint records really had been altered, as she had been promised.

A half-hour later, their limo driver couldn't understand what the holdup was. All the bags had arrived on the carousel, but his four passengers remained huddled in a corner of Baggage Claim.

"We have to stick together," Gabriella said more slowly than usual. "If the glitch was intentional, I don't have to tell you the ramifications if any of us come forward or the equally dangerous possibilities if we don't. I expect the four of us to share with each other and nobody else until we know who can be trusted. Is that understood?"

The men nodded. Cynthia was more worried about when the latest ibuprofens would dull the pain.

"Our line is that the mission was a success, and this is important—Sir Wilton was the Owl. As it stands now, Cynthia's going to fake amnesia, so don't tell anyone she found the device with Smythe.

"The driver will drop Cynthia and me at the hospital. David, you and Serg will take the device to Eduardo Juarez at Paulson Electronics, then go home and follow your usual routines. Remember. Thatcher was the owl."

Eduardo Juarez was waiting when David and Serg got off the elevator on the third floor of the Paulson Building. "Let's see it."

David handed over the package.

Caressing the *NightOwl* the way a mother holds a child, Juarez took it to his lab and began twelve hours of analysis. After running the diagnostics through SCOPE, he reviewed the reports. "Bingo!" he said, snapping his fingers. "Brilliant."

He dialed Paulson. "Jerry. It's Eddie. We broke the code. We'll have a Trojan Horse release ready by midnight. I'll be able to alter the source coordinates to match the study in Crestmont Manor."

"It's about time," Paulson said. "I'll alert the Feds that we'll pass on receiver locations." His face glowed.

* * *

Two days later, inside a cabin in the New Jersey Pinelands, Rey awoke to the hoots of an owl. He was tired after circling a reservoir seven times, mapping the drop points so he could find them in the dark. He poked the cot next to his, whispering in Spanish. "Julio, I heard something—maybe an owl, maybe not. Check it out." Julio grumbled, eased off his cot, and crept across the floorboards.

Before he reached the door, it shattered in his face, foot-long splinters flying through the room. Stunned, he cringed behind his forearms. A battering ram delivered a second blow, ripping the door off its hinges. Searchlights cast moving shadows across the log walls as ten members of an assault team, crouching behind body shields, stormed through the door. Five sleepy men scrambled in confusion.

"Take them alive," barked a deep voice. One man climbed out a rear window but held up his hands when three lights blinded him. Inside, body shields knocked down two men. Julio surrendered without a fight. Rey dove toward a tarp-covered pile in the corner, but three automatic weapons riddled him with bullets.

"Shit!" muttered the deep voice. "Stupid bastard."

Within fifteen seconds, the attack was over.

A captain shined his spotlight into the corner. Rey's body lay two feet short of a shadowy mound. "This guy doesn't look like an Arab." The captain pulled away the tarp, revealing stacks of *Gold Medal* flour bags and a homemade bomb.

Across the country, scores of similar raids captured hundreds of terrorists on the same night. Within a week, ninety cells had been raided—the rest disbanded and fled. Operation Aqua was thwarted, but like most victories in the war on terror, it wasn't publicized. In the back rooms of the national security network, however, the *Patriots for Freedom* were heroes.

* * *

Anwar and his brothers gathered for the annual *1898* Mission Banquet around a large oak dining table. After consuming mountains of paella and liters of wine, the family was in high spirits, despite the moving boxes strewn about the hacienda. Anwar stood and spoke in Spanish, his words echoing off bare stucco.

"My brothers, welcome to our new home. I appreciate your dedication during the last two days. Forced evacuations are never pleasant, but this island was not compromised by the security breach that led to the postponement of Operation Aqua. From now on, we will trust only blood members as we plan retaliation."

He raised his glass. "We allow ourselves this holiday as patriots—men who love our country enough to sacrifice personal wealth for a greater good: justice for an international crime committed against our country. Our family was impoverished by Americans conducting a war of imperialism, but we have kept faith, waiting—from generation to generation—until the moment when the fates aligned. Despite this week's setback, that moment is here to be grasped, and we shall grasp it! To Sabah Al Khair!"

The men cheered their leader, who smiled inwardly at the irony of the current project. Two cousins had just closed the purchase of a Garden State Spring Water Company bottling plant. The Americans had a cliché: blood is thicker than water. When the Madera family implemented an improved Operation Aqua, the truth of that tenant would be upheld—not that anyone outside the family organization would ever know. The Arabs would be blamed. Again.

To temper the celebration, Anwar ended the holiday as he did every year. Before bed, he went to his library, poured a glass of Roija wine, and looked for his most prized book. He had marked the box and found it easily. The worn volume fell open to page 235. It was the biography of Don Diego Madera, Anwar's great-great-great grandfather, Governor of the Philippines in 1898. Anwar sank into a leather chair and read the summary of the final chapter. "The explosion that sunk the *U.S.S. Maine* in Havana Harbor shook the crumbling Spanish Empire all the way to the Philippines. Admiral Dewey's annihilation of the Spanish fleet in Manila Bay meant disgrace for Madera. His fortune in rubber plantations was lost, along with the governorship. After he committed suicide and was laid to rest in a Manila pauper's grave, his wife and three sons returned to Spain, more ruined than their native country."

Anwar snapped the book shut and sat motionless. His frown turned into a trance. The United States, showing cracks of decay in the new millennium, was primed for a fall, and *1898* was chipping away—

first highways, then water. The sky was the limit.

Anwar reclined in his chair, the back-cushion caressing his shoulders. An embryonic smile curled his lips. The Madera family had recovered and persevered before—they would do so again. More than 100 years after the crime, vengeance would be served.

* * *

Cynthia wore her insecurity like a teenager. Blood pulsed erratically—the same way it had the night Paul "Pookie" Davis got to second base. In the mirror of David's powder room, she watched her mesh sweater flex with every breath, her bra's pattern discernable through stretching cotton. She fingered her choker—six penny-sized scars seemed to burn through the leather. Her hands quivered as she drew a glass of water and opened a bottle from her purse. She tapped one pill into her palm, popped it into her mouth, and washed it down with three swallows. She was a trained killer, yet this man had her quaking in her high heels.

She needed a few sips of wine before her hand was steady enough to light the strawberry candle on his coffee table. As warm as her skin was, she felt *his* heat when he sat next to her.

"Did you hear about all the attacks?" she squeaked. Small talk, but she could think of nothing else.

He rattled off anecdotes from several raids, as if he knew her throat was too dry to support conversation. "You don't have to say anything," he whispered to prove his devotion.

They kissed. David's lips were luscious, but Cynthia's anxiety dulled her nerves—what should have been a tingle was hardly a ting. In her mind, the choker was transparent, the scars ugly and immense. David had seen the wounds, but not with passion on the line. His desire would evaporate when he saw the purple blotches—she knew it. Self-confidence ebbed with every exhalation, so she held her breath.

"You're beautiful," he said.

Did she hear that right? She licked her lips without moisture.

"I've loved you since the day we met."

She was too anxious to speak.

David's touch soothed her ego more than it caressed her body. His kisses drew her heart into her throat. By the time he pulled the sweater over her head, Cynthia ached for him to prove she was still desirable.

"Let me take this off," she murmured, reaching for the bra clasp.

"No. Let me take *this* off." He unfastened the choker as if he were removing a splinter. When his tongue feathered across her throat, Cynthia couldn't get enough air to satisfy the erotic reactions bubbling inside her. She wished she hadn't taken X-80.

* * *

Two mornings later, she was energized, running with long strides along a trail in Tourne Park. It was early morning, when the songbirds were most vocal and the odors of the forest most pungent. The scent of decaying matter coated the inside of her nostrils. It was great to be alive.

Marco was on time, settling in alongside her brisk gait. "Good work in London," he said, glancing at her scarred neck.

"I guess."

"Anything you want to say outside the report?"

"No."

"So you really can't remember?"

"That's right."

"You know you took care of Wilton Thatcher, so you must remember something else." Marco was fishing.

"Everything went according to plan—through Thatcher's death. Then someone came at me from behind. After that, I don't remember anything until the plane. The doctors say I was traumatized."

"You'd be dead if you hadn't defended yourself. Do you remember how you did it?"

"No. Gabriella said I reacted—survival instinct. Or maybe I fainted, and the person left me for dead."

"What happened to your attacker?" Marco asked, frustration giving an edge to his voice.

"Don't know."

"What—" Marco changed to a softer tack. "What do you think *might* have happened?" Cynthia said nothing as they jogged across a small wooden bridge, their feet thumping in unison for six strides. Exasperated, Marco said, "Help me out here."

"A covert bodyguard? Someone else who wanted to steal the device? I just don't know."

"But how'd you kill him?"

"I don't know that I did. The rescue crew didn't see another body. And I don't know if it was a *him*. It could have been one of the other dates. Jealousy. *Or maybe Lady Thatcher?*"

"Cut it out. How tall was… the person?"

Cynthia pondered the question. "I felt someone behind me for a split-second. I think at least as tall as me."

"Now we're getting somewhere. Would you say the person was

strong?"

"Strong enough to choke the memory out of me...but not the pain."

Marco stumbled on a root. "Oh, how's the pain?"

"Manageable. Thanks for asking."

"What else do you remember about that night?"

"I remember being screwed by my date. Do you want to know how many times and what positions?"

Marco switched to a patronizing tone. "Please understand we're just trying to find out what went wrong. One of our operatives—*you*—nearly died, and the whole team could have been killed."

Marco ran a few steps in silence. "You mentioned your date. Did you know he was found dead in your shower?"

Cynthia swallowed, pain stinging as if a briar bush snapped into her neck. "No, I hadn't heard. What happened?"

"I was hoping *you* could tell me. Do you think he could have been the one who strangled you?"

Cynthia took her time answering. Marco had held back this information for a reason—maybe to trap her in a lie. She said, "Probably not. Whoever choked me did it in Thatcher's study. If it was Smythe, somebody else moved him back to our shower."

"It didn't happen like that, Cynthia. Scotland Yard's sure that he was stabbed by his sink, not in the study."

She shrugged. "Like I said, it probably wasn't him."

"Who else would have been strangling you and stabbing Smythe?"

Her nostrils flared. "How many times can I say I don't know?"

"Can you explain why Smythe's stab wounds were consistent with your issued weapons? Or why bloody clothes that match your measurements were found with his body?"

She rolled her eyes. "Whatever. If I killed him, I don't remember."

They came to the beach by the lake where a boy and dog were playing. Cynthia used the break to think. They ran to the end of the beach and turned around. If Marco was shooting straight, she should tell him the truth so that such mistakes didn't happen again. But if it was known she knew Thatcher wasn't the owl, Cynthia might be marked by whoever set her up.

Once they were back on the wooded path, she reiterated, "I don't remember anything else."

"Okay," he said. "In that case, you need to see someone. The trauma has you blocked. We need you to remember."

"Can I choose my own shrink?"

Marco hesitated. "I don't see why not."

"Okay."

"You'll be relieved to know that powerful friends have convinced Scotland Yard to call off the dogs. Cynthia Johnson's in the clear."

"Just like that?"

Marco slowed to a walk. "A very important man worked through his contacts at State to convince the Brits of *NightOwl*'s global threat. Our cipher guys helped big-time. I happen to know that a major attack on reservoirs was disrupted shortly after we broke the code. Sabah Al Khair called the operation 'Clean Water.' That's why I said, 'good work.' Maybe I should have said, 'great work.' Poison could have killed thousands."

Cynthia thought that her neck was a small price to pay. "I guess I should have said thank you instead of whining."

"Anything else you'd care to add?" Marco asked after they stopped near the turn-off to his car.

She smiled, appreciating the kindness in his eyes. After a long pause, she shook her head. "No."

"Then this is where we say goodbye. You take care, Cynthia."

Marco walked toward his car; Cynthia took the long way home, thinking as she jogged. If Marco knew that Thatcher wasn't the owl, he hadn't tipped his hand. It was possible that Paulson Electronics had known without informing him. Or he could be a good liar.

There was one rational explanation for the London mix-up. Paulson hated Thatcher so much that he interpreted surveillance data the way he wanted. If so, he had made a poor judgment call, but he had paid Cynthia $300,000 for her troubles and gotten Scotland Yard off her tail. It was hard to believe that such a man had set her up. The *NightOwl* debacle had to be a one-time mistake.

24

PAULA CONSOLASIO

The sign on the mahogany door read, "Paula Consolasio, M.F.T. Suite 101." Cynthia straightened and walked into an empty waiting room. Ten minutes early, she sat down in one of several comfortable chairs. Wanting to look casual—but not too casual—she had worn a maroon turtleneck and beige slacks. When a tall, slim woman wearing a stylish maroon sweater of her own walked out of the inner office, Cynthia assumed the woman was a patient. The woman, who had exceptionally large eyes, held out her hand. "Hello. My name is Paula Consolasio. Are you Cynthia?"

"Yes."

"I'm pleased to meet you, and I would prefer that you call me Paula." Her diction was precise and lyrical. Paula held open the inner door. The office was brighter than those Cynthia had suffered in her teens. The usual array of framed diplomas and certificates decorated the walls, and there were family pictures on the desk, from which Cynthia deduced Paula was married with two daughters and a cat. An oriental water pitcher sat on a glass coffee table. Paula filled two glasses; Cynthia's eyes were drawn to elegant fingers curling around the pitcher's handle.

As she sat down in one of two burgundy armchairs, Cynthia replayed why she had agreed to do what she had sworn she would never do—see another shrink. The fiasco in England had convinced Cynthia that she could use help with multiple problems, even if amnesia wasn't one of them. With the *Patriots for Freedom's* medical insurance footing the bill, she had decided to give therapy another try. No, that wasn't quite true. She had decided to show up for one session.

Donning oversized wire-rimmed glasses, Paula sat in the other chair and folded long arms in her lap. "Can you tell me what brings you here at this point in your life?"

Just like a shrink, Cynthia thought. From her prior experience on the couch, she recognized the M.O.—used when a therapist didn't have a clue how to help a patient. Cynthia played along, trying to decide whether to trust Paula.

After BS-ing around the bush for fifty minutes, Cynthia's time was up. On the way out, she asked, "What's MFT stand for?"

"Marriage Family Therapist."

Cynthia half-smiled. "I'm single with no family. Where do I fit in?"

"That would be the therapy part."

"You can disregard everything I said last week," Cynthia said as she sat down for her second session the following week. "All lies. I was trying to decide if I would trust you with my real problems."

Cynthia expected Paula to tear up her notes and ceremoniously throw the pieces into the wastebasket, but Paula tapped a pencil on the pad in her lap. "How were you feeling last week?"

Cynthia flushed.

"Beginnings are important. Why tell lies to see if I'm trustworthy? Trust is a two-way street."

"You're right. I'm sorry. I guess I got in the habit of holding back in therapy—in my teens. I just looked at my shoes and mumbled. I'm ready to start over, okay?"

"Alright."

Cynthia spoke tentatively, giving Paula time to take notes.

"I was raped by my stepfather when I was seventeen. I'd been a virgin. When he was done with me, he turned on my mother. While he was on top of her, I smashed him in the head with a bat, and he died."

Cynthia looked at Paula for a reaction, but the therapist's head was down.

"Part of my...not really sentencing, but treatment, was to see shrinks, none of whom helped. They just asked me how I felt about things. Jeez, I was a kid who felt like damaged goods. I thought it was my fault."

"Did you tell your therapists how you felt?"

"No. I was too ashamed. I was afraid if I let my shame out, I'd be damned."

"Damned, how?"

Cynthia shrugged. "Maybe lost is a better word."

"Give me an example of being lost."

"Alone. Drifting. It was ten years before I slept with a man, but at least I had my mother...and brother." Cynthia paused. "I was afraid they'd stop loving me. If I'd lost them..."

"You said 'stepfather.' Was your mother divorced from your biological father?"

"No. My real father died a few years before."

Cynthia watched Paula weigh "dead father" vs. "rape." Paula said, "I'm sorry. We'll come back to your father. What do you remember about the rape? What were your emotions while it was happening?" Paula's tone was calm, as if she were asking about the weather.

Cynthia wondered if this therapist was going to be the same as the rest. "Do you want me to relive it for you?"

"I want you to relive it for yourself. Take your time. What comes to your mind may be significant. Tell me whatever images you see, what you smelled, and what you felt."

Cynthia searched her memory for pictures in the *Like to Forget but Can't* file. "I came home from school and found him beating my mom unconscious. So much for restraining orders. I jumped on his back, but he threw me off like a rag doll."

She paused to sip water. "He hit me, and kicked me, and dragged me by the hair—like a caveman. I remember tasting my own blood. That's the taste—blood—that I associated with sex."

Cynthia looked at Paula, who nodded encouragement.

"When he, you know, entered me, it was horrible—he was an ogre with a rolling pin strapped to his crotch. I was dry and tense, and I fought, which made it worse. It felt abrasive, like unfinished wood with splinters."

"How did you feel, emotionally?"

Cynthia felt seventeen. She took another sip of water and licked her lips. "He was an arsonist, sloshing gasoline and then lighting a fire that burned everything inside me—my identity.

"He left me passed out in a heap. When I woke up, I heard moaning from Mom's room. My mom kept my dad's trophy softball bat on the bedroom wall. The bastard was grunting so loud that he didn't hear me. In a rage, I grabbed the bat and smashed him in the head. I remember just watching him lie there."

"How did that make you feel?"

Cynthia closed her eyes. "Good. Great, really—like I was on drugs. Maybe I needed that to block out the shock of what I did."

Cynthia seemed to be resting. She opened her eyes and continued. "The way he had leered at me turned my stomach. Afterward, whenever a man looked at me with desire, I saw my stepfather's lust and...I didn't respond well. Even after I had a boyfriend, for a long time I faked it. There was a man named Thomas who was gentle. I knew he was good and that he loved me, but I didn't have an orgasm with a man until I came back from Spain."

Paula hesitated. "Spain?"

"Oh, I'm getting ahead of myself. I have to give you more background before dropping Spain on you."

Cynthia laid out her story. "After the rape, I didn't eat, didn't sleep, didn't talk. I gave up on everyone, including my mom, who I blamed because of her drinking. But she didn't give up on me. I gotta give her credit. She got off the booze and, day by day, coaxed me back to life. First with sports—we'd swim and run together. I lived at home until I was twenty-three. I didn't go to college—never even graduated high school, though I got an equivalency diploma—but we read books to each other, and we talked about everything. I found out Mom was smart as well as pretty.

"I had a younger brother, Sam, and he got short-changed because of me but never complained. He knew I needed more attention. Sam was a good brother."

Before Paula could phrase a question about Sam, Cynthia continued. "I started working out so that no man could ever do that to me again. I got waitress and bartender jobs. I was pretty good at it. I would think of every customer as a character in a novel. It was easier that way, especially with men who came on to me. I'd compare my characters to those in the books that Mom and I read to each other."

"What was your favorite book?"

"*Pride and Prejudice*. I admire Elizabeth Bennett."

Paula nodded. "Did your mother work?"

"Yes. She had a job as a clerk for the SEC in Manhattan. She moved us from Cooperstown, where the rape happened, to give me a change of scene and take me to fancy shrinks. Mom put her personal life on hold for eight years. A few months after I got settled in my own apartment, she and a friend took a cruise on the St. Lawrence River."

"Go on."

"She called me from Montreal to say that she was in love with an incredible man. The next day, she was dead, her head cracked by cannon balls that fell from an overhead shelf in the cabin of her lover…a man who collected antique cannon balls."

Paula wanted to ask dozens of questions but let Cynthia keep rolling.

"The authorities said it was an accident—that she had been snooping in the cabin, stealing a locket. But she had told me the night before that the man had given her the locket. He was a liar, so I had to…"

"So you had to what?"

"I had to get away. It was a tough time for me. I took a bartending job on the *Louisiana Lady* steamboat. For a while, it was good. Then came Route Eighty. My brother was crushed by a piece of the highway while he was driving home from my house."

Paula slumped. "I'm so sorry. How old was he?"

"Twenty-four when he died, three years younger than me. We were close. He'd been a big help to me when I was depressed."

Cynthia finished her water, and Paula refilled the glass.

"Then I got a strange job offer…" Cynthia bit her lip.

"What's the matter?"

"Just give me a sec." Cynthia took a slow breath. And then another. "I'm okay. A man recruited me to assassinate terrorists who pulled off the Route Eighty attacks. I was skeptical at first, but I took the job. Based on what I've told you, I think you can figure out why."

Paula frowned, shifting in her seat as if there were a frog under the cushion.

"My first job was with…" Cynthia paused. "My first solo job was in Spain. I used poison to kill a man who planned the I-Eighty attacks. I stuck poison needles in his back, and it felt great to kill a man who had—"

"Cynthia," Paula interrupted, coughing as if the frog had leapt into her throat. "Before you go on, you should know that the laws for patient-therapist privilege in New Jersey are tricky concerning premeditated murder. If I think you are a danger to a particular person or society in general, I have a legal obligation to break confidentiality. If there are extenuating circumstances, however, I may remain silent. Your revelation puts me in a difficult situation. The more you tell me, the greater my dilemma. I heard you say, *First* job.'"

"I'm not a danger to society, but I'll let you be the judge of that." Cynthia looked squarely at Paula. "I want you to help me, but feel free to cut me off if you're uncomfortable."

Paula rubbed her chin.

"There's something you should see," Cynthia said. She lowered the collar of her turtleneck, allowing Paula to examine six scars spaced at two-inch intervals as if they were pink studs on an invisible necklace.

Paula leaned close but did not touch. "How did this happen?"

"They're souvenirs from the job I may not be able to tell you about."

"In Spain?"

"No. This happened in England. Later."

Paula pursed her lips and pondered. "We may need to talk about your work."

"I think it'll help me."

Paula looked at her watch. "Alright, Cynthia. I'm going to need some time to digest everything you've told me. We should talk about your father, brother, and mother, and love life. I think we should consider meeting more frequently."

Cynthia agreed to twice-a-week appointments, Tuesdays and Thursdays. The next session was personal from the first question. "Would you rather talk about your father, brother, mother, or sex?"

Cynthia, who had been leaning forward, pulled back. "I don't think I'm ready to talk about my family."

"Alright. Because of what you said about the nature of your unusual job, is it alright if we talk about sex, or lack of it?"

"Um...Okay."

"Last time, you said that your first orgasm *with a man* was after returning from Spain. That implies you had had an orgasm without a man."

"Not much gets by you, does it?"

Paula didn't respond. Cynthia leaned farther back in her chair. "After my stepfather, the memory was eating me alive—particularly at night—so I devised a way to make it bearable. I would think about saving others from...my fate. I'd drown a child-molester or strangle a rapist. While I fantasized about punishing them, I'd...well, sometimes I'd get aroused.

"One night, I, you know, masturbated during a fantasy where I killed off a pedophile. I was eighteen."

Paula asked, "How did you feel about that?"

"Guilty. But I continued to do it. It felt good and freed me from... It made me feel less dead."

After a few seconds of silence, Paula said, "Did you ever masturbate while you thought about making love with a man?"

Cynthia blushed. "This is hard for me."

"I know. You're doing fine. Have some water."

Cynthia sipped.

"Did you think about making love to men?"

"I tried."

"Men you knew?"

"Yes. I'd have a date then fantasize about him."

"And what would happen?"

Cynthia grimaced. "I'd see my stepfather's face in the man's eyes, and I'd have to turn him into a sex-offender. After a while, I stopped thinking about men that way."

"What way?"

"Sexually."

"Cynthia, during the ten years before meeting..." Paula checked her notes. "...Thomas, did you ever think sexually about women?"

"No."

"And now?"

Cynthia hesitated. "No." Covering, she added, "I sort of dreamt about it once."

Paula appeared puzzled, as if deciding what to say next. "Tell me about it."

Cynthia's mouth dried out. While she had never dreamt about sex with women, she had been having a recurrent dream for more than a year. In it, she is kneeling on a river bank, leaning out to look at her reflection when a skeleton reaches out of the water and grabs her wrists. She struggles as the skeleton pulls her under. When her face goes below water, she wakes up in a sweat.

"Let's see..." Cynthia knew exactly why she had the recurring dream, but it related to Alexander Gates, a subject she didn't think she could or should discuss with Paula. She manufactured a story. "I dreamt that a blonde woman was on a giant round bed beckoning me, but I couldn't get there. I slogged through swamps, deserts, and quicksand, but I never got close enough to... When I finally woke up, I was relieved it wasn't real."

Paula mumbled, "Interesting," as if it weren't. Cynthia sat still, unsure whether Paula was fooled.

For their fourth session, Paula greeted Cynthia dressed in a violet blouse and designer blue jeans. It dawned on Cynthia that Paula always wore colors in the purple family. "May I ask why you always wear the same colors: purple, violet, and lavender?"

Cynthia saw Paula tense for a moment. Cynthia knew from experience what her therapist was thinking: did she know Cynthia well enough for self-disclosure?

Paula motioned Cynthia to enter the office. "People say purples suit my coloring."

"But there's more to it, isn't there?"

Paula sat, her eyes rolling out of focus for a split second. She exhaled as if blowing out a candle. "My mother says that when I was a child, I used only purple crayons. I insisted they even smelled better." Paula's eyes twinkled. "My crayon people must have had strange skin. Anyway, purples have always made me feel good, so I wear them."

Cynthia took her seat and stared at her purple therapist. "Paula, I'd like to talk about my childhood." Paula's expression reflected approval as she gestured for Cynthia to proceed. "Did you know I would say that? The other shrinks always asked me about my childhood in the first session. You waited for me to bring it up. Why?"

"I've always found my patients to be more forthcoming when talking about things they want to talk about."

"What if I'd never brought it up? Don't you think my childhood relates to my problems?"

"I don't know whether it does or doesn't until I hear about it." The room was quiet for a moment. "Would you care to start, Cynthia, or would you prefer that I ask a few *therapist* questions?"

"I was a happy child until thirteen. Then, my dad died and..."

"Go on. How did your father die?"

Cynthia gulped water. "In a plane crash on business somewhere in the Pacific. I was devastated. I don't know what else to say, so please don't ask how I felt. At least not now."

Paula thought a moment. "Alright. You said you were a happy child. Would you explain what that was like for you?"

"I just liked to play, and there were a lot of kids in the neighborhood. Mostly boys, which was okay. We climbed trees a lot. Played guns and sports—touch football and wiffleball. You could say I was a tomboy."

"Guns?"

"You know, wars, battles. We'd use squirt guns or cap guns—sometimes just sticks. One team would go out and hide, and the other would count to a hundred and come after them. We'd stalk each other in the woods, trying to get the drop on each other."

"Like paint ball?" Paula asked.

"Sort of, but with imaginary paint. If you had a clear shot at less than thirty yards, the other guy was dead. I liked running through the woods on long flanking movements. The sitting and waiting part was tedious, though. I like sports because there's more running—more constant motion." Cynthia paused, but Paula was content to wait. After a few moments of reflection, Cynthia continued. "My dad was still alive then. He was cool..."

"Did your father play games with you?"

"All the time. Every kid in the neighborhood looked forward to Mr. James coming home from work. He'd play in our backyard or on the street with all the kids. He'd be steady quarterback or steady pitcher, you know, so everyone got an equal chance. He'd announce like a sportscaster while we played."

"What game was your favorite?"

Cynthia smiled. "Touch football. It wasn't that I was a star—the guys were all stronger—but I was pretty fast and I loved running; it was cool—cooling, actually. I've always run hot. Ninety-nine point eight is normal for me, and I had this cut-off gray sweatshirt. Well, I loved to play football in that sweatshirt because the air on my belly felt so good. I actually thought I could run faster that way. My mom hated it; she thought it made me look boyish. I wore that sweatshirt all the time."

"What happened when you were thirteen?"

"Aside from my dad dying and my mom throwing out my lucky sweatshirt?"

"Tell me whatever happened."

Cynthia turned pensive. "I grew boobs, and everything changed. B-B—before boobs—I was one of the boys. A-B, they looked at me different. Not quite with lust—I wasn't stacked then or anything—but like I was another species, one that the boys were afraid of. I couldn't be trusted anymore. It was troubling. And my mom changed, too. She was young and pretty, and when I hit puberty, she acted like my big sister, giving advice about boys and clothes, but I just wanted to play.

"Well, Mom couldn't handle it when Dad died. She was lonely and started drinking—way too much. I needed her to be strong for me, but she wasn't. She lost her self-esteem, married an alcoholic asshole. And you know the rest."

"How old were you when your mother remarried?"

"Fifteen. By then I wasn't happy. I wanted to be twelve forever."

Paula talked while she scribbled. "Can you give me three or four words that best describe how playing touch football made you feel?"

Cynthia stretched her neck. "Happy. Cool. Free. Alive. Belonging. Five, whatever."

"That's fine. Did you have any boyfriends before the incident with your stepfather?"

"A few. My mom tried to mold me into a feminine girl—I had a nice figure; boys liked me, even when I wouldn't give them the time of day. I wasn't that interested in dating, and most guys were so predictable. But there was this one boy, Pookie. What a nickname, huh? He was sweet, and we fooled around a little. Second base was heavy stuff for me. Neither of us knew what we were doing. Then…well, we've been through that. After the trauma, my life fell apart.

"I was a basket case for years. I didn't do much and lost my friends. Do you remember how I said my life had been burned out of me?" Paula nodded. "Well, it was like trying to live someone else's life. I was physically there, but I was empty, trying to stumble through life without a soul to guide me."

"Go on."

"The only good to come out of it was that it snapped Mom out of her funk. She got herself straight and helped me turn into a person again. In time, I relearned how to smile and make friends—how to be almost happy. I even let my hair grow back. But sometimes I long for how it was when I was twelve. When my friends didn't care if I was a boy or girl—only if I could come out and play."

"Earlier," Paula said, "you alluded to dating a little between the rape and Thomas."

"I tried, but the guys all wanted the same thing. Mutual affection broke down when they fondled me. *They* got more pleasure out of touching me than I did. I thought that made them creeps who should have touched themselves and saved me the trouble. I dreaded physical…intimacy."

Paula took a few moments to think about her next question. "What is your happiest memory from childhood?"

"That's easy." Cynthia closed her eyes and smiled. "I was twelve and my dad was still alive. We were playing touch football with the gang in Tommy Gilbert's backyard. Of course, I had on my lucky sweatshirt. It was fourth down by our own end zone, and Mom had called us to dinner. Dad had me run a down-out-down pattern. Mike Jones bit at the pump-fake, and my dad hit me in perfect stride, long down the sidelines. I outran two boys with my Dad calling, 'James is at the twenty…the ten…five…*touchdown!*' I felt like I was flying when I crossed the goal line. My dad ran down the field, gave me a big hug, and carried me to dinner on his shoulders."

"Do you remember how you felt when he did that?"

"I flew like a bird, touching branches ten feet off the ground."

Paula smiled. "This is good. I learned some things about you that will be helpful, and I think you learned something, too."

"Help me out. What did I learn?"

"You told me last session about a stolen past. Just now, you remembered being happy playing football, so your past is *not* lost. I saw you smile." Paula set her pen on her pad. "In addition to the darkness of your late teen and early adult years, there are thirteen years of happiness. Much of what makes you tick comes from the girl who wanted to play games when her developing body was pulling her away. Don't forget about that girl, because *she* is part of who you are. If you were happy then, that girl can help you be happy again."

"Sort of like finding colors that make me feel good," Cynthia said.

Paula gave Cynthia a smiling nod. "My husband thinks I look

good in lavender, but I wear it because it makes *me* feel good."

"Maybe I need a ratty, cut-off sweatshirt so my belly can breathe."

"Maybe you do." Paula dropped her eyes to jot some notes. When she did, Cynthia studied her therapist. Cynthia had never thought about Paula's personal life, but a brief image of Paula, in lavender lingerie, seducing her husband, was worth a smile.

Cynthia needed a new sweatshirt. And she needed to go to work. Marco, who couldn't ask Paula directly, believed Cynthia's self-serving progress reports. He had called that morning to tell her it was time to get back on the horse—she had another job.

25

BACK TO SPAIN

During a drive to the mall, Carole lectured. "The mark's name's Roberto Garcia. He raised a shit-load of money for I-Eighty by smuggling drugs through a gift shop and export business. For recreation, he likes to screw good-looking Americans who become unsuspecting drug mules."

Cynthia frowned. "So I'll be a drug mule?"

"Almost. Garcia has a massage parlor upstairs from the gift shop. When a customer turns him on, he takes her to his private room for a *full-service massage.* Sex. One of our agents—call her Sabrina—got the full treatment…and the inside info."

"I don't get it. How does drug smuggling fit with a massage parlor?"

"Garcia uses the gift shop to get legitimate receipts for Lladros. You know what Lladros are, right?" Cynthia nodded. "He's perfected a glazing process that seals cocaine inside a plastic cast so even dogs can't smell it. Every time he gets a Lladro order, he duplicates the paperwork for a second address. He sends the real figurine to the proper recipient, plus a drug-filled one to a contact in the States. His contacts keep moving from city to city and P.O. box to P.O. box. The return addresses on the fakes are for other gift shops, so if a piece is discovered, it never points to him. The duplicate packaging looks like the real thing."

"So why not have the authorities bust him?" Cynthia asked.

"Even if SCOPE evidence was admissible, we can't isolate his stuffed pieces, and the Spanish won't disrupt the export of Lladros."

"The drug operation is spread over a variety of secure locations, but Garcia comes to the shop daily to pick up the paperwork and keep his eyes out for the best talent. If he likes a woman, he'll give her a massage that turns into sex. On the rough side, according to our source.

He takes women from behind on his table. That's the only time he's ever alone, so that's when you'll kill him—when he's full of himself conquering you."

With a touch of sarcasm, Cynthia asked, "What are the two weapons that I'll have while I'm naked on a massage table and he's mounting me from behind?"

"First, you'll get on your back. Then you'll use poison—the long nails."

"Shit, I hate those damn things. And I hate having to...you know."

Carole shrugged. "I know, but it's the only way to get alone with him."

"One question," Cynthia said. "If he's doing me from behind, how do I get my fingernails into him, or use the hairclip stiletto, for that matter? How do I turn over?"

Carole smiled. "We'll go over how you'll get front-to-front, but don't worry about turning around..." After a beat, she added, "...'cause your main problem'll be getting out alive. Did I tell you that he'll have bodyguards watching it all on video?"

Cynthia frowned, but Carole smiled. "Cheer up, Cyn. You'll be fine."

Cynthia was glad her mentor was confident, but Carole wasn't going to be the one lying naked on a massage table with a sex-crazed drug dealer doing her while thugs watched on TV.

Cynthia gulped. "This seems like a huge escalation—having to actually have sex with the guy—right?"

Carole shrugged. "The easy marks are all dead.... And don't forget about Smythe."

One week later, Cynthia reunited with her team at the Newark Airport Hilton. She and David stole a few kisses before the first session.

Gabriella explained the plan then asked, "Questions?"

"How should I act when he dies?" Cynthia said.

"Frantic. Upset. But don't scream. We hope his bodyguards'll let you go, but they could do anything. They could kill you on the spot."

"Don't sugarcoat it," Cynthia deadpanned.

Gabriella smiled. "More likely, they'll let you go—to get you out of their hair—or hold you for questioning that could include *torture*." Glancing at Cynthia, she added, "Happy?"

Smiling, Cynthia bobbed her head. "Will I be bugged or tagged with any homing device in case they take me somewhere?"

Gabriella shook her head. "Garcia's electronic security is very good. We can't risk them detecting anything like that. You'll have a cell phone in your purse, of course, with one button dialing to all three of us."

Cynthia knew the phone would be useless if she were abducted.

* * *

The team took the same bus tour they had used for the Alejandro Cabrera hit—only this time they would all continue to Costa del Sol. The first few days of the repeat tour would have been boring, if not for the romantic tension stalking Cynthia's every thought. She and David had to act professionally while pretending to pretend to be an item. It wasn't easy.

Monday in Seville was their last day of relaxation. On Tuesday, they would travel from Seville, to Gibraltar, to Benalmadena, and attempt to kill Roberto Garcia, all before dinner. Seville was the perfect place for a respite. They began with a panoramic bus tour of the city (all the tours were billed as "panoramic"), followed by a walking tour of the old Santa Cruz section.

Gabriella insisted they see the Alcazar. The Islamic palace was huge, with countless rooms and courtyards, but Cynthia gravitated to the expansive gardens, where she would have stayed all afternoon, except for the luncheon. Gabriella repeatedly told them it was important that they do everything that was part of the tour, so Cynthia pulled herself away for a paella feast. While at the restaurant, Gabriella reminded Cynthia to call Garcia's massage parlor to confirm her reservation for 6:15 p.m. tomorrow—which she did, speaking English.

They walked home via Parque de Maria Luisa, which reminded Cynthia of the first time she had used the long nails. She shivered when she saw the spot where it had happened. Warmth returned when they strolled into the Plaza de España, built for the 1929 Latin America Exposition. She had jogged past these buildings with David, but nothing looked familiar. The ornate architecture made Cynthia think she was at EPCOT. Cynthia and Gabriella walked together for a time before Gabriella said, "Tomorrow's the big day. How are you feeling?"

"Like a caged tiger. It would have been easier for me to sweep in and just do it. The tour may be good cover, but it's driving me crazy."

"Being antsy is good. It means you're on edge, and we want you on edge."

"Do you want me nervous?"

"Some things go with the territory, Cynthia. A touch of nerves is one of them. If you weren't nervous, you wouldn't be human. Just remember to fall back on the training. You'll be fine. Go over it one more time."

Cynthia recited the plan.

When Cynthia was finished, Gabriella nodded. "We'll go over it again tomorrow. But I think you've got it."

"I know I've got it. I'm *ready*."

At dinner, Gabriella announced there would be free time before curfew. When the team returned to the hotel, Cynthia told Gabriella, "I want a first-hand look at the nightlights of Seville." Gabriella nodded, and Cynthia thought she might have time to herself. But hardly had she left the hotel when David called, "Mind if I tag along?" He trotted to her side. "Got to give the biddies something to gossip about, don't we?"

"Gabriella sent you, didn't she?"

"Yeah. Are you sorry about that?"

Cynthia blushed. "No." She smelled oranges. They set off for Rio Qualaquiver.

The park between the river and street was abandoned. David and Cynthia leaned on a railing at the tour-boat quay, gazing up the river. Seville was even more charming by night, the lights flickering on the water, weaving the river into the tapestry of the city.

David's hip brushed Cynthia's. Her face flushed. In less than 24 hours, she might be dead. She let her leg be drawn to David's, even as her words contradicted body language. "You know we shouldn't do this."

"Do what?"

She smiled. "Give the gossips something to talk about." When she turned to face him, he gazed into her eyes as if he could see her soul. She managed a slight shake and turned to walk a few feet away, hiding uneven breathing. "If I kiss you now…here…I don't think I'll be able to stay in control."

David touched her shoulder. "It's not like anyone will care. If it gets back to Gabby, it'll look like our cover."

"I don't want to relax for a second, so we shouldn't—"

David kissed her anyway—not like a man she had slept with, but like a boy on a first date. Delicious. Then he held her for the longest time.

Cynthia sniffled. "We probably shouldn't work together after this."

She felt David's nod on her shoulder. "Maybe we should be getting back," he said.

They strolled in silence for a few blocks.

"Why did you become a bodyguard?" When David just grinned, she added, "Behind the Harley and muscles, you don't have the personality of a tough guy."

"So you don't think I'm tough?"

"No. I said your personality isn't tough."

David scratched his stubble. "I'm strong, which helps, and not smart enough to worry about the danger." He smiled. "I'm also good at it, and Mother always told me I should find something I'm good at and stick with it. And I like to protect people I admire."

"So you sleep with all your clients," she teased.

He chuckled. "No. I believe in *Patriots for Freedom*. I protect you because I admire what you're doing. You're one of the good guys."

Cynthia turned her head so he couldn't see her tears. The stroll back to the hotel took twice as long as the walk to the river. Cynthia didn't want it to end.

"It's your last night before the hit," David offered outside the hotel, "so if there's anything I can do?"

"I know what you can do, and I'm looking forward to your doing it after we finish the job."

"Whatever you—"

She shushed him, going up on tiptoes to kiss his cheek. "Thank you, but I'm fine. Goodnight." Cynthia went inside for fingernail practice.

She breezed through the session in twelve minutes.

"Ready for bed?" Gabriella asked. Cynthia's shrug indicated that it didn't matter; she wouldn't be sleeping much. "You really should try to sleep on your last night."

Cynthia narrowed her eyes. "This isn't any *last night*, at least not for me. For Garcia, yes. I'm gonna nail the bastard, and then I'll have a lifetime of nights to figure out what I should be doing with my life."

"You've earned it," Gabriella said.

"No. *After* tomorrow I'll have earned it." She sighed, adding, "This'll probably be my last job."

Gabriella nodded, as if expecting Cynthia's retirement. "Just don't get sloppy looking ahead."

That night, Cynthia rehearsed everything in her mind, including how she would think about David when Garcia was touching her. She imagined Garcia's hands chilling her, so she pictured softer hands—knowing, loving hands that gently massaged her with warmth. Wonderful hands. Maria's hands.

Maria?

Sleep came in fits.

* * *

Gibraltar proved enjoyable enough to distract Cynthia from what would come later in the day. Her first question about the British protectorate was answered when the bus didn't move to the left upon passing the security gate. "Driving on the wrong side only works when you're on an island," Gabriella pointed out. "Just think of the gridlock possibilities." Cynthia felt silly for wondering.

Gabriella shopped in Gibraltar, but Cynthia only went through the motions. She focused on passersby, wondering if women besides Maria could interest her. She felt foolish and put on sunglasses, but she looked. A leggy blonde in red caught her eye but did nothing for Cynthia. A cyclist with glasses was more interesting, but after eye contact, she pedaled away as if she had seen a ghost. Maybe these subjects were too remote. Cynthia critically eyed Gabriella—smart, nice smile, good sense of fashion, well-endowed, and...Cynthia's boss. Not a chance. After fifteen minutes, Cynthia concluded that girl-watching was a waste of time.

The four teammates hired a guide named Joseph to drive them to the top of the Rock. The guide flirted with Gabriella, who flirted back, and with Cynthia, who pretended to have more interest in the Gibraltar monkeys. During a stop at the highest point of the road, the monkeys leapt on cars and tourists, begging for food.

A fearless monkey that Joseph identified as Mitzi recognized the guide as a regular source of food. Mitzi scampered off the rocks that lined the narrow, twisting road, settling on Joseph's shoulder with a high-pitched squawk. Joseph explained how each monkey had its own begging style.

A larger monkey, Don, latched onto Gabriella and pawed at her blouse. After shooing off the grabby monkey, Joseph joked, "Do you have any ripe fruit hidden in there? Don Juan seems to think so."

Cynthia was surprised at how open people in Spain were with sexual innuendo, but Gabriella had no such qualms. "My fruit's ripe, but it isn't for monkeys."

Joseph grinned. Men in Spain liked women who flirted, the more shameless the better.

Cynthia walked up a few stone steps to an observation parapet that revealed a sheer drop hundreds of feet to the sea. Looking down, she felt mortal. It cleared her head. She thought of herself as already dead. *Que sera, sera.* She would just do her job. Coming down from the parapet, she was more relaxed.

When the tour was over, Gabriella rewarded Joseph with a generous tip, making a playful date to meet him at the top of the Rock on New Year's Eve. Cynthia questioned Gabriella on the wisdom of familiarity with a stranger. "Knowing what we're up to, I'm wary of everyone, particularly cute guides. What if he was flirting to set us up?"

"In another circumstance, he might have been dangerous, but there's no way this guide is a threat."

"You sound sure of yourself," Cynthia said.

"It's my job to be sure. If Garcia or anybody else in Spain wanted to eliminate us, they wouldn't do it with a guide that we selected at random on an optional tour. If we had made advance reservations, I'd be more careful. And even then, I might try to out-flirt an enemy, just to keep him off balance."

"Joseph didn't look like the one off balance."

Gabriella blushed. "At least I know my weaknesses. Do you know yours?"

Cynthia thought, and two people came to mind.

26

THE HIT

The first order of business in Benalmadena was a much-needed shower. Next, Gabriella brushed Cynthia's hair while Cynthia snapped off two regular false nails, which were held on by weak glue. An application of stronger glue was followed by the spring nails with attached vials of poison. A Velcro band held the nails in place while the glue dried. Cynthia made sure the hinges were locked, tested the cuticle release, then relocked and tested them again. When the hinges opened, the needles extended a mere quarter-inch past her finger tips, but to her they looked like porcupine quills. Rotating her hands and staring at the needles, she thought of herself as Edwina Needle-Hands. She locked them for the last time. Twelve minutes.

Gabriella laid out Cynthia's clothes: white shorts and a midriff-baring zippered peach top. "You want to project the image of a good girl going bad. Moderate skin, suggestive zipper, but soft colors. This'll flaunt that major-league abdomen and a little cleavage. Wear this choker to cover the scars."

"What shoes should I wear?"

"Your Reeboks. Garcia won't see your feet on the monitor, and you'll take them off for the massage, anyway. But if you need to run..."

Cynthia dressed carefully, fumbling with her shoelaces. Her fingers were shaking. "Tie my shoes? I'm a little nervous about..."

"Sure." Gabriella tied Cynthia's shoes then twirled and pinned her long silky hair with the backup weapon. "Lower the zipper a little...a little more...you have a nice shape. Remember, you're selling subtle profanity...that's it. Perfect." Gabriella perched a pair of lethal sunglasses—stiletto in the left temple—on Cynthia's brow. "For insurance."

While Cynthia was primping, Serg dressed in a policeman's

uniform underneath work clothes. He was first out of the hotel, hustling to his assigned post near the back of the gift shop. There, Sergio saw Garcia's car and called to say that the operation was on. Within seconds of Sergio's call, a *beep-beep-beep* startled Cynthia. It was Gabriella's watch alarm—time for an X-80 pill. As she washed it down with bottled water, Cynthia was grateful her boss was meticulous about details.

Gabriella dressed in the native fashion of stretch black pants and a burgundy top, accessorizing with the same hairpin and sunglasses Cynthia wore. Gabriella talked as she dressed. "Remember, massage room number one is Garcia's. The window faces the alley, and if you have to get out that way, there's a narrow roof."

Cynthia gazed out the window toward the ocean.

"Remember what we've gone over!" Gabriella barked.

Cynthia blinked as if waking up. "Sorry."

"He uses lots of oil, and his fingers are long and strong. After loosening up all your muscles, he'll work deep into your shoulders then gradually move down your back and sides. When he switches to your thighs, his touch will become less therapeutic, more suggestive."

It clicked. Cynthia was surprised that she hadn't figured it out sooner. "You're Sabrina, aren't you? The contact who got Garcia's full service massage."

Gabriella colored. "I'll admit that, at first, I wanted to be the one to kill the scumbag, but you're the best woman for the job. I recognize that now."

Cynthia looked at the lines of her nails, long and dangerous. "If something happens to me, you're gonna try it tomorrow, aren't you?"

Gabriella turned and looked straight at Cynthia. "Nothing's going to happen to you. Ready?"

They tapped knuckles.

"One more thing, Cynthia. Remember to sign the charge slip as *Moss*."

Cynthia had practiced signing "Cynthia Moss" with the deadly nails a hundred times, but she felt a tremor and wondered how smoothly she could do it today. The added danger had gotten to her. So had the realization that Roberto Garcia would fuck her.

At 5:45 p.m., Cynthia pushed through the hotel's door for the short walk to the gift shop. David followed at shadowing distance. Gabriella trailed them both to the intersection. There, chewing gum, she sat on a bench and opened a book. Assorted cell phones and monitoring gear were stuffed into her oversized shoulder bag. With an earpiece and bouncing head, she appeared to be listening to a portable CD player while reading a trashy novel.

After window browsing, Cynthia strolled into the gift shop, which was spacious and bright. Her senses tuned, she concentrated, less jumpy. Half the floor space was devoted to Lladros, many of which were displayed on shelves that could be seen from the sidewalk, as well as the inside of the store. Cynthia hoped she didn't look as thin and gray as the delicate figurines.

A salesman approached. "May I help you?" he said in accented English.

Cynthia's heartbeat was rapid but under control. "Yes," she squeaked. *Lower.* "Ah, yes. I'm looking for something for my aunt." Each word came easier—sounding more normal. "These are all so beautiful. I don't know how to decide."

"I have a good one—very popular." He pointed to an elegant woman with a flowing dress and windblown tresses.

"Um...Okay. I'll take it."

While filling out the order form, she leaned her elbows on the counter. "I have an appointment for a massage at six-fifteen. My name is Cynthia Moss. Sabrina sent me."

The salesman admired her pose. "Ah, for friends of Sabrina, if you buy second Lladro, we upgrade to full-service massage. No extra charge."

"Yes. That's what Sabrina said I should do. I'll take a second for my best friend."

"Fill out second address here. Let me find masseur."

"Sabrina said I should ask for Roberto," she said, trying not to sound anxious.

After the salesman returned with two figures shrink-wrapped in Lladro boxes, she grabbed a pen and scribbled a signature on the credit card slip—Cynthia Moss. The salesman disappeared into the back. Once more, she leaned on the counter, tapping her long nails on the glass, examining jewelry in the case. Her rolling fingernails clicked out the beat of the finale of the *William Tell Overture*. Garcia was surely examining her on a video monitor in the back room; she stopped tapping and angled her cleavage toward the camera.

When the salesman returned, he was smiling. "Ah, *Señorita* Moss, today is lucky. Roberto free. Room number one. Top of stairs, to the right," he said pointing to the stairway. You undress, lie on table. There is towel. Roberto come soon."

The stairway was narrow and dark; every step creaked as she ascended. She felt as if she were in a cheesy horror movie, but room number one was brighter than she expected—the window wide open.

Undressing, she wasn't self-conscious about being watched. She was too busy concentrating on not sticking herself. The choker came off last. She rubbed the faint scars as if washing away the vestige of her last kill. After a deep breath, Cynthia lay face down on the padded massage table. She spread a towel over her buttocks. Using yoga discipline, she tried to lower her heart rate. At the same time, the X-80 began to warm her pelvis.

The evening sun angled through the window, highlighting the grain of the hardwood floor. She smelled salt air. A bird chirped outside the window—she recognized the call—a Spanish Timbrada Canary. Goose-bumps formed on her forearms, perspiration under her armpits.

When the door opened, it was not Garcia who entered, but a masseuse who pulled a curtain between the massage table and alcove where Cynthia had left her belongings.

"I-I thought I had Roberto."

The woman's English was choppy. "Roberto come soon."

Cynthia closed her eyes while the woman conducted a search. There was nothing to find except the sunglasses, which were difficult to activate unless one knew the trick. Cynthia's primary weapon was under her nails, and the backup was stuck in her hair. She heard a few electronic beeps and the sound of static. She held her breath.

The woman opened the door to leave. "Enjoy."

Cynthia exhaled...then heard a man say, "Wait for me—"

The closing door cut off the voice. She waited, each inhalation stretching her ribcage. Evening street traffic tapered off. The bird stopped chirping or flew away. Cynthia was alone.

When she heard the door open again, she didn't have to look over her shoulder to know it was Garcia. Cynthia sensed his danger—the room darkened as if the window curtain had closed. She reminded herself to keep breathing—in through the nose. She felt the air rush in, vibrating hairs in her nostrils. Was she scared? Absolutely, but beyond scared, she felt incredibly alive.

He sauntered around the table until she could see him. Moving gracefully, he appeared younger than in the photographs; it was no wonder the dark Spaniard had a harem of willing conquests. She gave him a smoldering look.

Cynthia felt three motors revving. The X-80 had her genitals agitated, but she was used to that. Her heart was thumping—that, too, was expected. But turmoil in her brain surprised her. She had thought it would get easier. *Think about Sam!*

Her breaths sounded like ocean waves. Her sweaty thighs stuck to the pad. Her towel shrunk to a washcloth. Her tongue tasted like sawdust.

His voice brought her back to the job. "*Buenas días, señorita. Cual es un nombre?*"

Think. *Nombre* is name, isn't it. Yes. He's asking my name. She wet her lips. "Cynthia."

"Seen-thee-ah." She could hear his smile. In Spanish, he asked if she was ready for the best massage of her life.

"*No hablos español*," she said.

"Eh," he muttered as he spread oil over her back. Under his breath, he added, "*Le ensenare español.*"

She felt his hands and flinched.

"Seen-thee-ah tense."

The cool oil tingled. His strong fingers loosened her muscles, and her response was a mixture of relaxation and disgust. For five minutes, he worked on her shoulders and back while she tried to think of David and Maria. When Garcia switched to her thighs, his oily hands sent icicles up her spine.

This was final. Real poison, real victim. Like in Seville, only scarier because she was naked and he would... She couldn't believe she had agreed to do this. *Had they given her mind-numbing drugs in Stone Harbor?*

When Garcia worked his fingers under the edge of the towel, kneading her buttocks, she fought the urge to stiffen. Underneath her chin, Cynthia ran her thumbs along the cuticles of her middle nails until she heard two faint clicks.

Garcia whispered, "Seen-thee-ah has nice body." His fingers were probing high on her inner thighs—then higher still—and when she did nothing to stop him, even higher. He pulled the towel away. A sigh escaped her lips, followed by the purr she had been rehearsing.

"This is full service part," he said, fondling her buttocks. "Seen-thee-ah like?"

She forced her dry mouth to respond. "I like. If you don't have a condom, I have some in—"

"You mean rubbers? I use rubbers. You see."

The sound of a zipper spiked her heart-rate. For agonizing seconds, she heard nothing but th-thump, th-thump from her chest. Now was the time to turn over, but she froze. This was different because he would penetrate her. Her insides lurched and rolled, even as her body remained still.

Then his knee grazed her inner ankle, and she twitched into motion. Before he had gotten both knees onto the table, she rolled to her back, pulling up her legs. A glance revealed that he had been truthful about the condom. His pants were off, his shirt unbuttoned.

Months of training flashed through her mind—countless hours of practicing with oranges and male trainers, perfecting the art of injecting liquid from the needles beneath her middle nails.

With manufactured passion, she whispered, "I like to get physical. Do you understand? Physical?" She licked her dry lips as her nails slipped inside his shirt, making faint etchings on his back.

As Garcia entered her, he muttered, "Yeah, rough." She moaned and dug her fingernails into his back, just as she had practiced over and over. The poison was delivered. She was sure of it. Pushing harder in response to the tiny stabbings, Garcia grunted a profanity in Spanish that she didn't understand. She tried to respond convincingly and ride it out…for the longest thirty seconds of her life. Between grunts, he said something in Spanish about begging. His contorted face was hideous, so she squeezed her eyelids shut, but she "saw" her stepfather. The pleasure of X-80 was overpowered by disgust. Wrapping her legs around him, she squeezed hard, as if pressure could accelerate the poison. All the while he kept thrusting like a pile-driver. She thought he must be immune to the poison, and wondered if he would ever stop.

Then he slowed, and she opened her eyes. Her breaths came quickly.

Garcia gasped. His gaze was vacant, fogged. He shuddered twice and grabbed his chest. With a sucking sound, he slumped onto her torso and quivered. Five seconds later his body went limp.

She did her best to look panicked. "Don't stop! What's wrong? What's wrong?"

She wriggled sideways from under his weight then climbed off the table. She wrapped a towel around herself, fastening it with a tuck under the armpit. With a grunt, she turned the body onto its back before hopping onto the table to do CPR. "Come on; come on, breathe!" She pressed on his chest too lightly to compress the heart; her nose-pinch was loose. *Where were the bodyguards?* She called faintly for help.

After a half minute, one of the bodyguards burst in and gaped at her.

Unaware that her towel had popped open, she shrugged. *"No hablos español."*

His voice sounded like a bassoon. "What happen?"

"Do you speak English?" she asked.

"Yes. Good English."

"Well, he was full of energy. We were…" Cynthia realized she was naked and covered her breasts. "You know. Then he grabbed his chest and collapsed." She refastened the towel.

"What you do?" he asked, shoving her off Garcia so he could take a look.

"He was doing plenty for both of us."

"Get clothes on," the man ordered as he felt for a pulse. "Shit! He's dead!"

Cynthia dressed quickly—underwear and shorts first. After zipping her top, she said, "He can't be dead. He was so strong. Let me try more CPR." The bodyguard watched until a second man rushed in, asking what happened in expletive-laced Spanish. It was the voice Cynthia had heard outside the room earlier.

While Cynthia gave Garcia useless CPR, the two bodyguards conversed in Spanish.

"He's dead. Where were you?"

The second voice was high-pitched. "I was...I was watching the monitor. How could I know he would die?"

"But what did you see?"

"He was as healthy as ever, then he stopped and flopped. Like a heart attack."

Cynthia could have dashed from the room while the bodyguards bickered, but she kept up her charade.

"This isn't getting us anywhere," said the deep voice. "What should we do? What should we tell The Man?"

"I don't know."

"What should we do with her?"

They both looked at Cynthia. And then in English, the deep voice said, "Get off, crazy broad! He's dead! Shoes get on!"

He switched to Spanish. "She can corroborate the heart attack."

"For the police?"

"No. Not until we tell Anwar. And we don't need her story. It's all on the tape, right?"

"Yeah. So *what*? Do we just let her go?"

"She will just get in the way."

"And we may not want Anwar asking her too many questions. Maybe we should destroy the tape."

"No. That will make us look guilty. But what about the girl?"

"She's just a tourist."

The deep voice went lower. "One *fine* tourist."

They both leered at Cynthia. When she glared back, they smiled innocently. She slipped on her second shoe, making no effort to tie them. "Oh God, I think I'm gonna puke!" she said, bringing her hands near her mouth.

"Not here! Get the hell out of here," the deep voice said.

Cynthia picked up her choker and purse, stumbled to the door, and ran down the stairs, holding one hand over her mouth. Her shoelaces made a faint tapping as they tickled the hardwood steps. The last thing she heard was arguing in Spanish.

"So what are you going to do?"

"Why is it my problem?"

"Weren't you supposed to have the door?"

Cynthia saw David and winked. She raised her hand a few inches, wanting to touch him, but resisted. He scratched his right ear. Cynthia smiled politely at the salesman on her way out.

"What was problem? Noise," he said, pointing upstairs.

Cynthia shrugged. "Ask the other men. They told me to go."

Bursting into the heat of the evening, Cynthia almost punched a fist in the air. Flushed, she flew down the steps. David followed seconds later. Walking down the street, she had to stop herself from running.

Gabriella held open the door to their third-floor hotel room as Cynthia bounded up the last few steps. "Congratulations," Gabriella said. "You must have ice-water in your veins."

"God no. I *have* to take a shower."

"We'll debrief after we get the nails off."

Gabriella donned surgical gloves, dissolved the epoxy and removed the nails and vials. Then she scrubbed Cynthia's fingers with alcohol.

After Cynthia's steaming shower, they sat on her bed with the radio drowning their whispers.

When the debriefing was complete, Gabriella said, "It couldn't have gone better—no need to change plans. We'll finish out the tour, as scheduled, so as not to attract attention. Two days from now, we'll be home."

"They were worried about someone named Anwar," Cynthia said. They called him 'The Man.'"

"He's Garcia's cousin—the leader of *Eighteen Ninety-Eight*—but we don't know his real name or where he lives. We don't know what he looks like or what his voice sounds like. Anwar operates in secret somewhere in the northwestern Mediterranean. I hear one man tried to infiltrate Anwar's network. He was found in the Mediterranean with a harpoon reaming his guts. Or so they say."

Cynthia swallowed. "Is Anwar on our hit list?"

"No. We don't know enough about him to know his whereabouts, much less his weaknesses. Even after breaking the *NightOwl* code, we couldn't find him."

"We should be worried about him," Cynthia said. "His people have me on tape."

"We'll guard you more closely than ever tonight, but being on the tour is our best protection."

"What about the police?" Cynthia asked.

"If they come, then you'll answer their questions, just like we rehearsed. Nothing happened that would make you have to change your story, right?"

Cynthia nodded.

Gabriella brightened. "Now let's celebrate with a nice dinner."

They found a quiet Italian restaurant a few blocks from the hotel. The place was small with large windows overlooking a marina. The men watched the door, so Cynthia faced the water, which had a settling effect on her nerves. The first sip of wine warmed her like hot chocolate on a cold snowy morning. After half a glass, the jitters were gone. Garlic and basil wafted through the air. The table talk focused on the allure of Spain. The sunset, more orange than pink, was soothing. As the last light faded from the horizon, Cynthia took her first bite of pasta at the same time David's foot stroked her leg. It was the best meal of her life.

The subdued celebration carried over to the hotel's lounge. Dancing was part of the charade, and David played his part well, holding Cynthia close. She made no effort to disguise the pleasure she felt. The married couples would be talking tomorrow morning about David and Cynthia.

Cynthia put on a drunken act as she and David staggered up the stairs. Under the guise of lovers pairing off, David would stay most of the night in Cynthia's room. She could sleep or not, but David would remain on watch, as would Gabriella, who monitored the hall with a tiny camera that was taped to the outside of Cynthia's doorknob. David and Gabriella were in communication via lapel microphones and ear pieces. Sergio slept, to be fresh in the morning.

Cynthia had worried about spending the night in the same room with David, but when the door closed, she didn't lose control—she didn't throw herself into his arms. If she hadn't been so high from the hit, she would have, but sex couldn't have made her feel any better.

He saw the radiance in her eyes. "We have to keep on our toes tonight," he whispered.

"I know. I'm fine. I'm better than fine."

His eyes cringed; she wished she had used different words. He knew that another man had been inside her. There was something between her and David that she hadn't expected—like a faint smell. Was it Garcia's scent? She wondered if things would ever be the same, a thought that made her insides plummet.

Although it was a warm night, she donned pajamas. When Cynthia left the bathroom, David went out of his way to avoid eye contact. She turned off the bedside light and had nothing to do but relive the hit and think about what she would do if David came to her.

After a sleepless night, she was disappointed that he had ignored her but thought better of him for being professional.

David kissed her forehead before switching rooms shortly before 5:00 a.m. She pretended to be asleep.

Floorboards creaked under Gabriella's tiptoeing.

"Good morning," Cynthia said. "Any reason why we can't go for a run before breakfast? I'm dying to move. We're supposed to keep things normal, right?"

Gabriella shook her head. "No run this morning. If anyone wants to get to you, a dawn run plays into their hands. When we go out, we need to stay around people. With people, we're safe." Gabriella patted Cynthia's shoulder. "Try to get some sleep."

Exhaustion overwhelmed Cynthia, and she slept until Gabriella woke her for breakfast.

27

THE DAY AFTER

On Wednesday, Gabriella signed up the team for a bus trip to Puerto Banus and Mijas. Puerto Banus was an over-priced marina that could have been in California, but Mijas, a hilltop village, was so authentically Spanish that Cynthia didn't mind that it was a tourist trap. The Mediterranean vista was awesome. She and David toured the hilly streets on burros, and he bought her gelato and a pink rose. By midday, Cynthia's high had worn off. She slept on the winding trip down the mountain, her head on David's shoulder.

There was time for a late afternoon outing to the beach. The Mediterranean beckoned her and she pestered Gabriella to let them go. After three couples agreed to join them, Gabriella consented. Jabbering about Mijas, the group walked around the corner of the hotel and crossed a road adjacent to the beach, which was less than 100 yards away.

Cynthia listened to the surf, smelled the salt air, and thought of Stone Harbor. Preoccupied with sound and scent, she almost tripped over a woman lying on a yellow towel. Cynthia's eyes popped. The woman was topless. And so was another, this one sitting in a beach chair. With all that had been going on, Cynthia had forgotten that Costa del Sol's beaches were "top optional."

Cynthia dropped her tote-bag on the sand and ran for the water. Gabriella followed, and the two women dove into the surf, followed by David. Serg scanned the beach for suspicious characters.

"Don't go too far…" Gabriella called, head bobbing above the swells, "…unless you want to tangle with sharks."

"Sharks! Are there really sharks?"

Gabriella laughed. "The Mediterranean has ten different species, but the big ones like deeper water."

"Then we'll stay close to shore."

During the swim, Cynthia thought about going topless. A year ago, she wouldn't have considered it, but now, after baring everything to kill Garcia, why not?

Back on shore, while Cynthia dried off, Gabriella removed the top of her bikini as casually as if she were alone in a locked bathroom. Cynthia reached to unfasten her top, but balked when she noticed David's furtive glance. Gabriella saw the hesitation and the reason. She laughed. "It's no big deal over here. No woman with a body like yours keeps it under wraps."

Cynthia sat in a beach chair. "Then here goes." She removed her top. The earth kept right on spinning.

The natives were easy to identify—they either paid no mind or gaped blatantly. The foreigners were comically covert. She found herself glancing up from her book, looking for David. Once he waved to her, prompting Cynthia to spread the book over her chest—a silly reaction since he had often seen her naked. She waved back, confused that David made her self-conscious.

Why did David stare? Culture and advertising defined her body as "great," but to Cynthia, it made no sense that men paid so much attention to women's bodies. Some attention was understandable—after all, she could appreciate a nice male physique such as David's—but not the adulation men heaped upon her. For Cynthia, a man's body was only part of the equation. Sculpted abs might pique her interest, but if the guy was a jerk, muscles didn't matter. She glanced over at Gabriella, who possessed the bountiful look of someone holding a perpetual deep breath. In men's lexicon, Gabriella was stacked, but Cynthia would never understand what made that sexy to men. She shook her head and asked Gabriella, "Ready for another swim?"

In early evening, Gabriella and Cynthia left the still-hot beach, chatting with three couples from the tour. All beachgoers exited through a single opening in the beach wall, up a wooden staircase to the sidewalk and street. The hotel was a half-block beyond the traffic signal at the crosswalk. Sergio paced twenty yards ahead—crossing the street—and David twenty behind. As the pack waited for the "Walk" signal, three men in suits burst out of a parked car, the tallest one flashing a badge.

"*Señorita* Moss, we are police," he said rapidly in Spanish. "Yesterday you witnessed a death. You must come with us to answer questions."

The other two men seized Cynthia's arms and shoved her into the car. She dropped her beach bag and kicked one of the assailants, but her struggle was brief, ended by a gun barrel jammed into her throat. David and Sergio looked at Gabriella for the signal to pull their weapons, but she hesitated. It was too dangerous. Gabriella shook her head, stepping forward. "I'm going with her."

"No," said the tall man, holding Gabriella back with an outstretched arm. "You can meet at station." He pulled back his sports coat so his shoulder holster was obvious. "Accidents happen in Spain."

The doors slammed shut twenty seconds after they had opened. The car sped away. Serg held David from charging the car. Gabriella stood dumbfounded.

"I got the license," David shouted.

"What the hell happened?" Sergio said.

"Anwar," Gabriella said. Separating far enough from the three dazed couples to talk freely, she told the bodyguards, "They said they were the police, but if those guys were cops, I'm J. Edgar Hoover. Serg, have your contact check the police station, but she won't be there.

"What do we know about Anwar?"

The men looked at each other. David's eyes were red. "Not enough."

* * *

The three abductors said nothing during a drive that could have been two hours—or four. Blindfolded, Cynthia listened for clues, but the humming air conditioner drowned out exterior sounds. After the car stopped near lapping water, whispering men transferred her to a motor launch.

Following a twenty-minute, high-speed boat ride, two men shoved her into an open, off-road vehicle. The only sounds were the engine and barking dogs. Three minutes later, she was guided up brick steps (she counted eight) and into a building that smelled of leather, roses, and salt. A tall man removed her blindfold. She was standing in a hallway. On the wall was a large painting of the Nina, Pinta, and Santa Maria sailing into the sunset.

An armed guard motioned her ahead with an Uzi. "This way, *señorita*." She followed the tall guard through an open courtyard into a comfortable sitting room. There, the tall guard frisked her more thoroughly than necessary, considering she was wearing a bikini, unbuttoned blouse, and sandals.

"Look for weapons," he muttered after groping her.

She bristled.

The tall man yanked out the pin of her hair clip and squinted as he examined it. The clip portion clattered on the tile.

Her lungs deflated and her heart sputtered. Her skin was hotter than sunburn. She covered her nerves by combing fingers through her hair, kinky from the salt water.

The tall guard mumbled something while tapping the pin in his palm. Then he picked up the clip, rolled it in his fingers, and stuffed both pieces into his jacket pocket. The tall guard departed through mahogany double-doors. The shorter guard pointed to a chair where she sat, breathing for the first time in twenty seconds. She studied the room, which was lined with portraits of men who resembled the guards.

The double-doors opened. "Anwa— I mean *Señor* Madera will see you now," the taller guard said, pushing her into a paneled library that featured French doors open to a patio. It was pitch black outside. She looked for a clock, but saw none. Seated behind an oversized desk was a dark, rugged man in his early forties. He wore a white shirt, open at the neck. A beard partially covered a scar at his left cheekbone. A younger man sat in the corner, holding a notebook. All the men's eyes looked alike. The doors closed behind her, leaving the guards on the other side.

"Have a seat, *Señorita* Moss. Welcome to my island," the man said in a Spanish accent. "My name is Diego Madera. This is my secretary, Miguel. I have brought you here to ask some questions about the death of my cousin, Roberto Garcia."

Cynthia said nothing. She rotated as if in the center of a museum gallery. Three walls were lined with bookcases partly filled with hardcovers. Ten or twelve moving boxes were piled in stacks behind her chair. The volumes in the bookcase closest to her were histories of the Spanish American War.

"Excuse the mess. I recently moved," Madera said. "Please sit."

She sat in a leather armchair that swallowed her. The chair faced the desk, Madera, and the wall of windows. There was a second armchair and a card table with four chairs by the left-hand wall.

Eyeing her attire, Madera raised an eyebrow. "Are you cold?"

Cynthia crossed her legs. "No. I'm hot. But I'm hungry...and thirsty."

Madera turned to the secretary. "Some food and wine." Miguel left the room, closing the doors behind him. Madera rose, walked to the front of the desk, and leaned his rump on the edge. "What happened during your massage yesterday? It was *full-service*, I believe?"

Clearing her throat, Cynthia looked up at Madera, re-crossed her legs, and replied, "I guess he wasn't man enough to handle me."

Madera smiled insincerely. "Let me see your hands." She

extended her fingers. "These long nails left some ugly scratches on Roberto's back," he remarked, shifting his eyes from her fingers to her bust.

"When two people like it rough, it gets rough. I've got some bruises of my own."

Looking at her thighs, he said, "And where might those be?"

Cynthia raised her jaw. "I'm not familiar with Spanish customs concerning blindfolds. Am I your prisoner or your guest?"

He laughed. "My guest.

"I'm upset about Roberto, and I will make it my business to ensure that anyone who was responsible for his death shall be punished. For example, the men protecting him yesterday are no longer... employable."

Cynthia held eye contact. "Roberto wasn't the man he thought he was. Does that make me responsible?"

He cocked his head. "When Roberto collapsed, did anyone try to revive him?"

She formed her hair into a ponytail in front of one shoulder. "Yes. I did—with CPR."

"Did you cry out for help?"

"No. Not really. Not very loud. I didn't want to get in trouble."

"Trouble?"

"If I could have revived him, nobody would have known what..."

"Was anyone else there?"

"Yes. Two men came in a little later."

Madera picked up a remote and turned on a TV and VCR. "I have something for you to see."

Cynthia watched the video of her session with Roberto, starting from when he slid his hands under the towel, and ending when she left the room. It looked like a porn movie. *Had she really been that encouraging?* From the corner of her eye, Cynthia saw that Madera was watching her, not the video.

After turning off the TV, Madera licked his lips. "You were truthful," he said as if he were proud of her.

Furrowing her eyebrows, she asked, "Why did you go to the trouble of bringing me here? You saw the video, so you know what happened."

Madera smiled. "Oh, I wanted to hear it from someone who was there—and from someone who has nothing to hide." His eyes scanned her body. "And also... Well, Roberto had many conquests. I wanted to meet the one who was, as you say, *too much woman for him to handle*."

She stood. "And is meeting me enough?" She walked about the

room, running her index finger down the spine of several books, waiting for an answer that didn't come. She pulled out a large volume and opened it at random. "After meeting *you*, I know you're a dangerous man, *Señor* Madera." She replaced the book and walked to the center of the room.

Cynthia ran her hands over the back of her chair as if it were a man's shoulders. "Danger is my biggest turn-on. Roberto was dangerous, but I was cheated when he had a heart attack." She faced the open patio doors. "I love the sound of the surf. It sparks primal—"

Three knocks shattered the mood. At Madera's command, Miguel entered with a tray of food and wine. After setting up a meal of fish, cheese, and fruit, Miguel excused himself.

"Sit. Eat," Madera said as he poured two glasses of red wine from a carafe. He looked at Cynthia as if he owned her.

"May I have some water, please?"

He fetched a pitcher from the corner of his desk.

While she forced food down her dry throat, Madera watched her swallow. "What happened to your neck?"

"An accident."

He raised one eyebrow. "Was it painful?"

"A little." She drank some water.

His eyes darkened. "Did you cry?"

"No."

She poured another glass of water then wiped her mouth with a napkin. "Your guards are watching us on monitors, aren't they?"

Chewing, he nodded.

"And if we were to make mad, passionate love on your Persian rug, they would be watching, yes?"

Again, he nodded, this time with a glint.

"Too bad," Cynthia said. "If I'd known I was being watched yesterday, I wouldn't have been able to let myself go."

"Why do you say that?"

Cynthia swallowed. "Because I think you're wondering what it would be like to be with the woman Roberto couldn't handle." A smile appeared as she licked wine from her lips.

"You are direct, *señorita*." He watched her chew and poured more wine. Cynthia alternated between wine and water while encouraging him to drink wine. She wanted to get him buzzed, and she would need every drop of liquid she could get.

"I am experiencing much bad luck," he said. "Very troubling."

"What sort of bad luck?"

"Associates of mine have been dying of heart attacks—all healthy men."

She hesitated. "That *does* sound like bad luck."

"Roberto. He was the youngest and healthiest—no history of heart trouble. I suspect that blood and tissue tests might reveal foul play." He frowned. "What do you think?"

She swallowed another bite, and gazed into his eyes. "Heart attacks can afflict anyone of any age. I'm sorry for your loss."

"Are you a heart expert, *Señorita* Moss?"

"In heart*ache* perhaps…. May I have more wine?... And water?"

When she was done eating, Cynthia asked, "Is your beach covered by security cameras?"

He chuckled. "You *are* an aggressive one, aren't you? No. No cameras on the beach. My men have orders to know exactly where I am, of course, but…"

She raised her eyebrows. "But…?"

He whispered, "But they don't have to be close enough to see everything."

Standing, she said, "I feel like a walk on the beach."

Madera nodded, but it was the face of Anwar that interested her. His eyes were brooding…troubled.

Internal heat, not the warm air, caused the perspiration covering her body. They walked toward the sound of water. Cynthia glanced left and right, guessing he had lied about outdoor cameras. Halfway across the sloping beach, she kicked off her sandals and squished sand between her toes. At the same time, his hand took hold of hers. Playfully, she bumped hips.

Stars sparkled in the sky, but there was no moon. The ocean was black, but she was not afraid of the water. She welcomed its support. Swimming had helped Cynthia battle depression. From age nineteen to twenty-six, she had swum laps with her mother three times a week. In the water, she was comforted by buoyancy—safe from the frightening world of land, air, and people. Water had helped her survive.

She was violating every training rule. She had no weapons. There was no getaway route. She hadn't been briefed on the target, island, or villa, and she had no backup. Adrenaline, sex appeal, and guts would have to do.

Anwar broke the silence as they neared the water. Squeezing her wrist, he said, "You started to say that the sea sparked something primal."

She felt his fingernails bite into her skin. "Yes. They say all life originated from the sea. I feel the power of the ocean; it inspires my basic urges to… Most men don't perform well in the water. They say it's too cold."

When he tightened the grip on her wrist, she rotated her arm toward his thumb, pulling free. They stared, each sensing the tension as the last vestige of a wave washed away from their toes.

"Do you really like it rough?" he asked.

"Are you man enough to handle me *and* the water?" In the faint light, she could see a spark in his eyes. At least he thought he was man enough, which was all she cared about. The next wave rolled around their ankles, and she kicked water onto his pants. "Take those off."

Cynthia slid the blouse off her shoulders, letting it fall onto the wet sand where another wave lapped over it. Anwar admired her from head to toe. He took a step toward her then stopped. His body language was conflicted, as if he sensed danger in her. She parted her lips to speak.... Let your sex appeal emerge, she thought. *Move.*

She realized she wasn't breathing. *Inhale through the nose...* She heard a steady inhalation fill her entire body, not just her lungs. Anwar and she faced off in the starlight.

She pivoted and skipped into the surf, diving when the water was up to her knees. Twenty feet out, she looked over her shoulder and saw him undressing. Again, she dove away from shore, electrified by the water sliding over her skin. The next time she looked, he was closer.

Kneeling so that only her head was above the surface, Cynthia waited until Anwar was a few feet away. Then she stood in the thigh-high water, back arched and bikini top held in front of her chest. There was enough starlight to see that he was aroused.

She pouted. "I took off the top. Can you get the bottom?"

When Anwar knelt and touched her hips, she drove her left knee into the point of his chin, the impact numbing her leg. Before his head snapped back, she wrapped the bikini top around his neck, yanking his head under water as she rotated behind him.

"Oh, yeah," she moaned. "That's it!" He was thrashing without leverage, dazed and clawing at her wrists. As she choked him, she held his head under for insurance.

He struggled and momentarily got his head above water, although he could neither inhale nor cry. He could grab, however, and his nails cut into her wrists.

She cinched the bathing suit tighter. "Ahhh! Harder! Yeah!" she grunted amid her exertion. "Don't stop!" The pain from her wrists brought tears to her eyes; she clenched her jaw and muttered, "Yes, yes, yes," in time with labored breathing. Her muscles burned for oxygen as she wrenched harder.

He arced as if electrocuted...then dug his nails deeper, but her hands were too strong for a strangled man. His grip relaxed, his flailing ceased.

Her vocal charade continued after he stopped twitching. "Oh God! Faster! Harder!" She hauled him deeper into the ocean, making splashing sounds for both of them. When the undertow made it difficult to hold her ground, she unwrapped his neck, and the tide dragged his corpse away.

Her dizzying rush was cut short by shouts from the hacienda: "Diego! Where are you?"

28

THE SEA

"Diego!"

Cynthia dropped to her knees and gazed at the heavens while refastening her bikini. She knew one thing about astronomy—above the equator, the North Star was always to the north—and she knew enough Mediterranean geography to know that if she swam north from an island off Costa del Sol, she would get to the mainland, eventually. She sighted the Big Dipper and followed its handle to Polaris, the North Star.

Damn! She was on the south side of the island. She had no idea which direction would be faster, or how far it was to the mainland. It was going to be an exhausting swim. If clouds rolled in, she would be lost.

"Diego!" The shout was closer. A flashlight panned the waves to her right.

Cynthia swam underwater away from the beach for thirty yards before surfacing to listen.... Barking dogs.

Using breaststroke to keep her ears above water, she swam out far enough to escape the power of waves and the reach of searchlights. Then she chose to swim west around the island—because the tide pulled her that way—keeping the shoreline in range by listening to breaking waves. The North Star would keep her from veering out to sea. As Cynthia swam, she listened for activity from the hacienda. She could have moved more quickly on land, but that's where they'd look for her first—with the dogs.

Searchlights skimmed across the water 200 yards behind her. Cynthia hoped that if Anwar's body were found, his men would think both lovers had drowned. No, they would see ligature marks on his neck. She kicked on, hunted in the darkness of shark-infested waters, yet feeling as if she could swim around the world.

When she heard no breakers, Cynthia turned toward the North Star. She was losing track of time, and without the sound of waves, she required more concentration to stay on course. The barking faded away. She was alone against the sea, her adrenaline rush over, a helpless fly on an endless surface. Now, time was her enemy. Even though the ocean wasn't frigid, she only had a few hours before the sea would claim her, so she had to cover distance without exhausting herself.

Cynthia was a strong swimmer and settled into a rhythmic crawl, breathing every fourth stroke. After counting twenty breaths, she raised her head to reorient on the North Star. She had stayed on line. By counting strokes, she gauged time and distance, swimming for ten minutes—less than a quarter of a mile—then switching to breaststroke for a five minute rest. After two such rotations, her arms were lead pipes, forcing her to drop her ratio to five minutes crawl, ten minutes breast. Twice, she rolled over and swam backstroke to rest and loosen up.

After an hour, she couldn't get her arms out of the water. She wasn't swimming, she was trying not to drown. Her knee ached, her wrist burned, and her strokes got shorter, her kicks weaker. If not for the buoyancy of salt water, she would have slipped under.

Needing help, she searched for motivation. She tried thinking about her family, but their ghosts beckoned her to join them. No. She didn't want to die. Chilled and desperate, she felt a presence next to her. Two people, David and Maria, were urging her on. Cynthia swam with renewed strength, sensing that wherever David and Maria were at that moment, they were each thinking of Cynthia. Fatigue washed everything out of her mind except life-sustaining thoughts. She pictured Maria's eyes and David's grin...and she struggled on.

After twenty minutes of breaststroke, her pathetic frog kick was barely treading water.

Based on her progress, fatigue, and a guess at the distance, she wasn't going to make it to the mainland.

The North Star was growing fainter.

A cramp knotted her calf as if it were caught in a vise. The irony—all this water, and she was dehydrated. She dipped her head below water while kneading her muscle long enough to loosen the vise. She changed to sidestroke with a scissor kick to torture different muscles—then to elementary backstroke to conserve energy and make sure she was following the right pinprick in the sky.

She was still alive, but confused. She knew why her left knee ached, but why did her right wrist burn? She remembered Anwar's nails gouging her. Had she been cut? Was she still bleeding? The sharks! She stopped swimming and squinted at her wrist, but the night was dark and the ocean wet. She sucked at the spot where it burned, but tasted only salt. Were the sharks circling her right now? When her head slipped under, she kicked herself up and gulped air.

She twisted her head to look for fins, but there was nothing on the surface except starlit swells. *What was that?* Was it a nip at her toe? She kicked and began to swim, trying to keep her legs closer to the surface. She hadn't been paying attention to direction. Fighting panic, she felt a pain rip through her leg. A shark? No, just another cramp. She massaged it out then drifted on her back, resting and looking up. The North Star was fading.

Cynthia rolled over and kicked. When she was sure she could go no farther, she willed herself farther still. The longer she swam, the colder and more tired she became. Cramps came more frequently.

Cynthia's fingers and toes went numb. She was unable to cup her fingers, making her strokes less efficient with every pull. But she kept swimming, or more accurately, she kept from drowning.

Cynthia thought about Maria. Their friendship demanded everything of Cynthia to keep it alive. An exaggeration? Perhaps, but desperate times require desperate motivation. She vowed that she would not die on Maria. "Whatever happens, friends forever. Whatever happens, friends forever," she chanted until a mouthful of saltwater threw her into a coughing fit. She sighted the North Star—at least she hoped it was the North Star—and labored forward.

Cynthia, her saturated skin folding like clothes a size too large, was in survival mode, lucky to have lasted this long. If it had been winter, she would have died from hypothermia. If she hadn't been in excellent condition, she would have drowned from exhaustion. And if not for David and Maria, she would have given up.

It was the longest few hours of her life.

A rain shower passed, and she turned up her head and opened her mouth, stretching for each drop the way a baby bird begs for food. She heard a wave, a reassuring sound of the seashore. Delirium must have set in, but it was a pleasant hallucination.

Or was it? She kicked, pushing her head up like a periscope, turning, squinting. There was nothing to see, but the sound was from the right, so she paddled in that direction, praying for land. Breakers?

Breakers. Definitely breakers, and they were louder. She floundered toward the sound.

She felt bottom, but when she got close to shore, her legs couldn't support her weight, so she crawled on hands and knees. Once she was clear of the water, she collapsed, shivering, into a fetal position on a patch of sand no bigger than a blanket.

She slept.

Later—could it have been hours?—she awoke to rays of light. Dawn. The rain had stopped. Rested but shivering and sore, she struggled to her feet and stretched. She scanned the beach. There wasn't much. It was a tiny island, no more than two acres. No trees or food. She crawled around, lapping rainwater—from depressions in rocks—as if she were a dog. There was more good news. She could see hills, golden brown, growing clearer as the sun came up. The mainland. She guessed she was a mile or two out. Could she make it? With the tide—maybe.

She had seen the tide tables in the newspaper on Tuesday night. When was high tide? Wednesday—yesterday—it had been mid-morning. When? What time was it now? How long would the swim take? If she missed the tide...

Easing into the water, Cynthia locked on the tallest mountain and started swimming again. Even with rest, her arms were too tired for the crawl stroke. She would either make it or drown with breaststroke. The only way she could tell if she was making progress was to look back at her haven. It was getting smaller. She swam with a second wind. Daylight meant less fear.

There were a few boats about, but she didn't dare call for help—the boats might have been Anwar's. Then she panicked again, fearing that what she saw was his island, but the shoreline ran as far as she could see. It had to be the mainland. Frog-kicking and waving her hands back and forth a foot under the surface, she stayed afloat.

The sun inched higher, but she was still a few hundred yards away from land. Her spirits rose when she felt the swell of a wave pull her gently toward shore. Now, the closer she got, the more the waves pushed her toward the beach. Another shower passed overhead, but she didn't waste energy trying to catch the raindrops. She was so close.

Her toe felt something like sandpaper.

When her foot confirmed the bottom, she cried for joy, her lips splitting. She staggered to where she could crawl, then she crawled to where she could lie. Water lapped at her legs and sides. The tide was coming in, so she crawled until she was safe. Then she collapsed, shivering against the sand.

Water! She needed water more than rest, so she forced herself to crawl until she reached a rock jetty. Halfway up the beach, there were tiny puddles on the tops of three concave rocks. She hoped it was rainwater, not seawater. She tasted. No salt, so she licked the moisture before rolling back onto the sand. She'd just rest a minute, she told herself, but when she woke, the sun was high in the sky.

The rest helped, yet she fell the first time she tried to stand, her legs collapsing like cooked pasta. But the second time, she stayed up and wobbled in the direction of a ramshackle building where two people sat outside, mending a net—or else knitting a giant sweater.

The two fishermen came to help her. Neither spoke a word of English, but despite her trembling, she coughed out enough Spanish to communicate. The fishermen gave her tea and bread, and wrapped her in a blanket that smelled of dead fish. And there was shade under their roof. As she regained her senses, she learned she was sixty kilometers east of Benalmadena.

"Do you have a phone?" she asked in Spanish.

One of the fishermen had a cell phone that she could use. She called the *PFF* emergency number and was told to keep the line open until they homed in on her signal. She slept with the phone pressed to her cheek.

Two hours later, Gabriella shook Cynthia awake.

Cynthia blinked several times to be sure. "I have to tell—"

"Shhh. You don't have to tell us anything right now," Gabriella soothed. "Rest."

Cynthia whispered in English, "Yes, I do. Anwar...is dead."

"What? How do you know?" Gabriella asked.

"I killed him. His men are looking for me."

Gabriella glanced at the fishermen. "Shhh. Wait 'til we're alone."

Thirty minutes later, an ambulance arrived at the fishing shack and rushed Cynthia to an emergency room in Malaga. Two hours later, she pronounced herself well enough to leave. Four hours after that, the doctors agreed she was properly hydrated, and Cynthia Moss was discharged. There was a debriefing session in the back of a rental car on the way to the airport.

"Anwar's dead?" Gabriella said. "Who is he, and what the hell happened?"

Cynthia sipped tea from a Styrofoam cup. "He introduced himself as Diego Madera, but he was Anwar. One of his men called him that. He would have killed me—"

Gabriella interrupted. "Tell me everything that happened after they abducted you."

Cynthia told her story with pride, her voice getting stronger. There was particular satisfaction when she recounted luring Anwar into the surf, then strangling him. "...and when I was sure he was dead, I let the undertow take him, and I started swimming. Then it was boredom, fatigue, and fear of drowning."

"Do you think you could find the island?"

"Maybe not, but if we can get aerial photos, I could identify it. I saw the house from the beach."

Gabriella nodded. "Then we'll take pictures of every friggin island in the Mediterranean."

Once their jet left the ground, a sense of relief overcame the strike team—Gabriella most of all. She whispered in Cynthia's ear. "I know I let you down, and I'm so sorry. They snatched you using our own police scam." Cynthia felt a shift in the boss-subordinate dynamics as she listened to Gabriella pour out guilt.

After Gabriella and the men fell asleep, Cynthia had hours to herself. She looked across the aisle at David, wanting to hold him, yet David could not keep her from replaying her adventure. *Anwar had been the best kill yet.* Such a thought made her shudder, but she put negativity out of her mind. Cynthia had assassinated Anwar with nothing but her guile and bare hands. With every breath she felt energized by the fatal power she exerted over dangerous men.

Cynthia didn't come down from her high until the jetliner began its descent to Newark Airport.

* * *

David and Cynthia scheduled a weekend rendezvous at a surfside motel in Ocean City. She waited for him on Friday night, hair down, wearing the red bikini from Spain. Sweat glistened on her forehead. She avoided the air-conditioned room and sat smoldering on the steps so she could listen to the surf and see David the moment he drove into the lot. She hadn't taken X-80—there would be no need for it.

Anticipating David's arrival, she smiled. It occurred to her that every dangerous man who had touched her intimately was dead—and that *she* had killed them. Thomas hadn't been dangerous, but David was. A jolt shot up her spine.

Patriot or serial killer? David or Maria? A familiar engine was getting louder. She stood and saw David on his Harley.

When he got off the bike, she embraced him, sucking his tongue between her lips.

"Whoa! Hot stuff," he panted, pretending to catch his breath.

She took his hand. "Come on."

"What about—"

"We'll get your stuff later. Follow me." Her head was clouded with a storm more powerful than drugs. She was possessed by a craving she couldn't control.

They sauntered toward the ocean hand-in-hand. "Listen," she said rubbing his forearm. "Do you feel it? The power?"

David listened to the waves. "I think so."

The water was warm on Cynthia's toes. "Leave your clothes and follow me." Before he could say anything, she skipped into the surf. When knee-deep, she dove out into the water, enjoying the tingle on her feverish skin. David watched her frolic in the moonlight while he stripped to his briefs. When he waded out to where she had crouched, she stood and held her bikini top in front of her chest.

"I got the top, now you get the bottom."

As he lowered before her, she pulled her wet hair into a ponytail and tied the bikini top around it. The knot would keep her hair out of the way, and she didn't want to lose her lucky bathing suit.

29

CHARISSE

Abdul Mommari was from either Morocco or Cadiz, depending on the source. To his family and friends, he was a Moroccan college professor. To SCOPE intelligence, he was an *1898* operative—born Julio Madera—who had been in Salt Lake City the day of the I-80 attacks. To the *Patriots for Freedom*, he was the man they would assassinate while he attended a cognitive science conference in Barcelona. The bearded 45-year-old professor had a weakness for tall dark American women. Since Charisse White was the only such woman at the conference, it was inevitable they would connect.

"Professor Mommari!" Charisse called from across the hotel lobby.

Mommari, who was returning from dinner with colleagues, looked pleased as Charisse glided across the marble floor on sculpted legs.

"As I explained this morning," she said, "I've read all your papers on visual perception. I appreciate your agreeing to talk with me about your work."

Mommari waved off his dinner companions. "You are prompt," he said to Charisse in thickly accented English. "Where would you like to talk? The lobby? Or the bar—it is very quiet there."

"Walk with me," Charisse said. "It's such a beautiful night. I want to show you my favorite place in Barcelona. Have you been to the park around the corner?" The desk clerk and Mommari's colleagues witnessed their departure with prurient interest.

At the entrance to the park, Charisse did not acknowledge Alan Rider, who masqueraded as a drunk under a blanket of newspapers. Charisse encouraged Mommari to talk about his research while they strolled along tree-lined paths. She encouraged him to do more than talk when she stopped near a secluded fountain and rubbed his abdomen. They kissed in a moonbeam that shone through the canopy.

Mommari was enjoying the kiss so much that he never felt the sharp blow to the back of his head. Once he slumped to the ground, two masked figures bludgeoned him to death with lead pipes. Then they turned on Charisse with artfully placed blows, before robbing her and Mommari of all valuables.

As Charisse moaned on the gravel walk, she struggled to keep her wits. The pain-killer helped, but she hurt enough to be reminded of the main reason why she had been against the change from poison to a robbery/beating. She heard Carole Burns's country drawl: "SCOPE read the results of Mommari's check-up. His ticker's in perfect shape, so the bosses say, 'No heart attack.' They want us to mix it up." Charisse heard Cynthia recounting how Anwar had been suspicious of all the heart attacks. If Cynthia hadn't been so convincing about the London glitch being due to Paulson's vendetta against Thatcher, Charisse would have refused to do this job. She moved her throbbing arms and legs—they worked—then rolled onto her stomach, which was a less painful position. At least Mindy and Joe hadn't broken any bones. Her head pounded, and she wished she could give her sister Aities a few sympathy punches.

Cynthia would get a few extra shots because she had insisted on Gabriella's support team for the Roberto Garcia job, and Cynthia was the *prima donna* who got whatever she wanted. The schedule had jammed up with Cynthia's job going off a week earlier, so Charisse lost Gabriella's team. Charisse remembered Cynthia's saying, "Mindy's team is no second string. Their record is spotless; it was Gabriella and me who had the glitch in England."

Although it might take until morning, Charisse knew she would be discovered. The police would investigate, but there would be no doubt she was a victim, too. When interviewed by the police, she would describe two thugs. It was painful for Charisse, but it was the plan the *Patriots for Freedom* had implemented. It would look like a robbery that turned tragic for a professor who happened to be in the wrong place at the wrong time. Joe Martin and Mindy Spinks would never be caught. Once Charisse had been questioned, she would be on her way to America.

She heard a dull throb—like an electric bass. No, it was something else—footsteps. Charisse eased open her eyes, expecting to see the shoes of a romantic couple through her swollen slits. But there were no women's shoes, rather two pairs of men's boots. There were stripes on the side of the pant-legs—two men in uniform. The police must have found her and Mommari's body on a random patrol. Things were moving along more quickly than planned. Perhaps Alan Rider had directed the officers her way.

The feet came closer.

The last thing Charisse saw was one of the boots accelerating into her face. It was the first of a series of vicious kicks that killed her. The same fate had befallen Alan Rider minutes earlier.

A mile away, two men in uniform approached a van parked on a poorly lit dead-end street. The people inside the van were monitoring the police-band radio, which had broadcast nothing about a crime in the park. The men in uniform pounded on the van's windows.

"*Policia! Abra la puerta!*"

The two occupants exchanged glances, Mindy Spinks pushing her palm down in a calming motion. Joe Martin laid his coat over the police-scanning equipment and his 9-mm Beretta. More knocks at the window.

"*Policia! Abra la puerta!*"

Mindy nodded to Martin, who turned the key until the power window on the driver-side engaged. The window slid down six inches.

"What is it, officer—"

Phut-phut... Phut-phut-phut. The man outside fired two bullets into Martin's temple before putting three rounds into Mindy's head. Then the shooter alternated—a shot into one slumped body, then the other, until the clip was empty. The two men in uniform marched away.

One said to the other, "Terrible accident, Hammer. Perhaps they should have been wearing seat belts."

* * *

"Damn it, Duane. What the hell happened?" Pilar Ibanez's Brazilian temper boiled. After a long day analyzing the tragedy with the war cabinet, they were alone in Pilar's parked BMW.

Duane Root was unemotional. "I don't know."

"How can *you* not know how or why my whole team got whacked? You know everything, for Christ's sake!"

"Calm down, Pilar. I'm sure I'll find out, and when I do, I'll help you recover from this setback."

Root put his arm around Pilar and gave her a comforting squeeze, but she nudged him away. "What do you mean?"

"I mean, this fiasco is bad for you. You'll need damage control, or you'll lose everything you've worked for."

"But I'm insulated. How can they trace anything back to me?"

He patted her hand. "Your trouble isn't with the law. You can't be connected to the dead team. Neither money nor orders can be traced to anyone at the company. I've taken care of that. No, your problem will be with Paulson. He'll be looking for a scapegoat, but I can insulate you from the fallout."

"How?"

"Luckily, you're on record as having opposed the switch from poison to the beating."

"What do you mean, *on record*?"

"You told me in my office, and I use level-five SCOPE to record all conversations. I can edit the recording to your best advantage."

Pilar tried to comprehend this news, wondering what else she might have said in his office.

Root lowered his voice. "I can guess what you're thinking, but I wouldn't release anything that compromises you—now that our partnership will be moving to the next level."

"What do you mean: the next level?"

Root peered into Pilar's eyes. "The tragedy in Barcelona has changed the balance of power in the company. You're less useful. But if you were to become useful in a personal way...Well, I'd be happy to help you."

Pilar swallowed hard. "How exactly would you help me?"

"Oh, perhaps I could fabricate evidence that Paulson himself ordered the hit on Charisse White. CIA level-three could discover it after we close the government contract."

"Who would believe that?"

"These days, an accusation is enough to ruin someone. While he's under suspicion, you and I could take what we've worked so hard for." He pushed her chin up with his fingers. "As you know, Pilar, I go to Boston every week on business. You have lots of friends in the area, right?" She nodded. "Why don't you start coming up to have dinner with me on Wednesday nights? I'm sure I could make it worth your while."

Pilar shivered. Her mother's voice recited a list of reasons *not* to sleep with Root. She reminded her mother's spirit that for now, she needed the bastard. He had power, and she needed his support to survive. She recalled the night she had come within one jerk of a wrist from swallowing a bottle of sleeping pills. If she didn't have her job, she would revisit that bottle. To keep her job—her power—she would do anything, but did anything mean *that*? Her father's voice told her: don't do it. Her dead husband told her: be a survivor. The voices were evidence of insanity. She knew that, but if she knew, then she wasn't really insane, was she?

After she allowed him to kiss her, Pilar said, "I'd like that, Duane, but first, tell me everything you know about the murders."

"Someone must have broken a code, or one of your people got sloppy. They had to have a good source to be able to take out all four."

"But why would they wait until after Mommari was killed?"

Root looked at her as if she were a child. "Maybe they thought Mommari was expendable. Everyone is expendable."

* * *

Gabriella Sanchez spoke faster than usual when Cynthia picked up the phone. "We have to meet tonight. We can't talk on the phone. Remember the nine-one-one contact location?"

Cynthia met Gabriella at a noisy Applebee's. When Gabriella sat at Cynthia's booth, she wasted no time with small talk. "I've got bad news from Spain. Sergio's contact confirmed that Charisse White and all three members of her team were killed last night in Barcelona. I'm sorry. It was a set-up. After what happened to you in London, there has to be a traitor in *Patriots for Freedom*."

Cynthia turned white.

Gabriella said, "I know, it's terrible news. I've already told Serg and David. We're scheduled to do the next job with Joanie Lee in Malaga—"

"No. You can't," Cynthia said.

"I know. Do you want to talk to Joanie, or should I?"

"I'll do it," Cynthia muttered. "And Maria, too, though they've probably heard." That was all she could say before sobbing. Grief was nothing new to her, but this was the first time she felt responsible.

"I'm a fucking idiot," Cynthia said. "I told Charisse to go when the evidence that she shouldn't was stamped on my own damn neck."

Cynthia, wearing jeans and a gray sweatshirt, heard pebbles grind under her Reeboks. The driveway seemed narrower, Odessa less imposing. The whole compound was smaller—the way a school looks after graduation. As she circled the outside of the house, she wondered how soon the training compound would be closed.

Maria and Joanie waited at the bench—by the bottom of the steps leading to the beach—where the Aities met for privacy. It was a cool late August evening; they both wore jackets. Cynthia approached in the darkness, and the trio embraced with the intensity of shared loss.

"You've heard about Charisse?" Cynthia said.

Maria nodded. Joanie answered, "Yeah. From Carole. My job's

canceled. Carole says we're gonna be shut down within two days."

"That may be for the best," murmured Cynthia. "What else did Carole say?"

Impersonating Carole, Joanie said, "Ah ain't lettin' mah girls walk into any more cotton-pickin' ambushes 'til there's an *in*vestigation."

Nobody laughed.

They sat on the bench and stared at Charisse's empty space.

"What's next?" Maria said to no one in particular.

"You know," Joanie said, "I wanted to stick around this time to actually finish something."

"I have two extra rooms in my condo," Cynthia said. "Why don't you stay with me until you figure out what you want to do?"

Non-committal mumbling.

"Well, think about it." Cynthia did some thinking of her own. Should she go through with her plan? She coughed. "Maria, are things good enough between you and Eddie for you to ask him to help us? You know, to use his SCOPE expertise to find what really happened?"

"I already asked. He said he's willing, but anything he does through the company can be traced back to him by Root and Paulson. Eddie doesn't want them to know he's suspicious. He doesn't want to blow his career."

"But would he help us if it could be done outside the company's security?"

"Probably. Root and Paulson couldn't know he was involved with an outside user. But SCOPE hasn't been released, so nobody else has it."

Cynthia stood and faced them. "That's not entirely true. Jerry Paulson told me he'd traded technology to the Chattanooga police for my amnesty. I'll bet he traded SCOPE. If we can get the police there to work with Eddie, maybe they can find out what happened without exposing him."

"Why would the Chattanooga police help us?" Maria asked.

"Because I can offer them something they want...me. There's this detective who's been tracking me. He wants to question me about a... missing person."

They stared at Cynthia, who looked down and paced back-and-forth as if seeking answers in the sand. When she looked up, her eyes were ice. "Maria? Joanie? If we find out who the traitor is, would you two be willing to avenge Charisse?"

Joanie and Maria glanced at each other, then at Cynthia.

"We're responsible," Cynthia said. "We urged her to go."

Ten seconds seemed like sixty.

"Okay," Joanie finally said. "Anything for Charisse."

After a pause, Maria said, "Me, too."

Cynthia went back to pacing, her lips pursed. The others watched her in silence.

After a minute, Cynthia squatted facing the bench. "Okay. I'm going to Chattanooga. I want you two to learn everything you can about Root and Paulson. If SCOPE reveals the traitor, we'll need a way—a weakness—to get at him."

"What if it's neither?" Joanie asked.

"It has to be one," Maria said. "From what Eddie tells me, the traitor has to have level-five. He says Paulson doesn't believe there's a traitor—that it was just bad luck."

"There's a traitor," Joanie said. "But do you really think Eddie can identify which one? Carole said our orders came in so laundered that she never got two from the same source."

"That may be true," Cynthia said, "but Paulson told me in New York that *he* selected the mark for the London job. If orders originated from him, there are trails somewhere, and we know one of them goes through Marco. Everybody makes mistakes, and all we need is to get a whiff of one."

Nobody had anything to add. They stood and stared at the empty bench before going to bed.

30

CHATTANOOGA

Jimmy Taylor had thought the phone call was a prank. Yet the untouchable suspect was sitting in Chief Haskell's office, wearing a white peasant blouse and denim skirt, making an astonishing proposal.

"What's so hard to understand, Chief Haskell? If you get me the information I'm asking for, I'll turn myself in for questioning in the Alexander Gates matter—give Detective Taylor a one-hour shot at me outside of my amnesty. Right now, you can't even mention the subject." The man she had introduced as her lawyer, David Smathers, nodded.

Jimmy Taylor watched and listened. In the fifteen months since he had questioned Cynthia James, she had become more confident. Instead of one-word answers and evasive gestures, she was almost eloquent.

"What exactly would you want us to do?" Taylor asked.

"I'd like you to use some of the SCOPE time you received—in exchange for my amnesty—to probe for specific evidence. I want the names of people who passed certain traitorous information. You can use anything else you find for yourselves, or you can give it to the Feds. I'm sure they'll be very interested."

Haskell asked, "Jimmy, do we know how to use this SCOPE system?"

Taylor took the pen out of his mouth. "It's pretty complicated. We're barely able to do local reconnaissance. I don't see how we could program the kinds of things she's talking about."

"I'll guarantee you an expert to do the training," Cynthia replied. "What else?"

Chief Haskell looked at his rumpled detective. "Jimmy?"

Taylor studied Cynthia's eyes. "I think we have to know something of your suspicions before we consider your proposal."

Cynthia re-crossed her legs. All three men noticed. "Off the record?" she asked.

The two policemen exchanged glances. Haskell answered, "Only for matters outside our jurisdiction. Anything you say relating to crimes committed, or to be committed, in the state of Tennessee, or on its waterways, will be *on* the record."

Cynthia looked at David, who nodded. "Fair enough," she said. "I don't know what you learned when you made your deal, but I'll give you the basics. There's a private organization that covertly disrupts terrorist activities. Recently, a mission was compromised, leaving four operatives dead. I believe there's a traitor in the organization. If you find out who it is, you'll get your hour with me."

Haskell looked at Cynthia. "Why are you doing this?"

"For the memory of a good friend. Let's leave it at that."

The chief of police leaned back in his chair and stared at the ceiling. "Ms. James, it sounds as if you expect that we'll find evidence to prove what you're saying."

"I do, but we need a SCOPE user to get it."

"Then why not go to the FBI?" Haskell suggested. "They could put the whole thing out of business, including your traitor."

"Because the FBI doesn't have SCOPE yet. You do."

Haskell looked around the room. "We'll need to discuss this."

"Take your time," Cynthia said.

After escorting the visitors to a waiting room, Taylor returned and blurted, "You're thinking of doing this, aren't you? Why? We'll get a free shot at her when the deal expires."

Haskell nodded. "I know, but it sounds as if she doesn't have a clue her amnesty runs out. This way, there's something for everyone. The department gets access to a SCOPE expert so we can take advantage of the product. You get to question Ms. James, and if we break a high-profile case before the election, we both can advance our careers. Plus, we may uncover other crimes. But if she comes in, can you break her?"

"Yeah, I'll get her," Taylor said. "I don't accept unsolved felonies."

Haskell snapped his fingers. "Then let's make a deal."

The next day, another player in the Alexander Gates case contacted Detective Taylor, which was why Taylor waited on a bench outside the Chickamauga Battlefield Visitors Center at 7:00 a.m. Taylor took a deep draw of air—serenity. He thought of the irony—how places of death are often so peaceful. He sucked on his pen and wondered what he could get his wife for her birthday.

Thomas Gates jogged until he saw the Visitors Center. Slowing to a walk, he recognized Taylor, whom he had met during the missing person investigation. Taylor watched him negotiate the last few yards through a copse of trees.

Standing up, Taylor said, "Good morning, Mr. Gates."

"'Morning. I suppose you're wondering why I asked to meet," Gates said. They walked side-by-side. "The truth is, I've been withholding information about my brother's case. I was protecting someone."

"Who?"

"One of the bartenders on the boat. Cynthia James."

Taylor wanted to tap-dance. "What did you withhold?"

Gates stopped near a row of cannons and pulled a plastic snack bag from the pocket of his running shorts. Inside was a piece of paper. "When you had me look through my brother's luggage, I saw something on my brother's briefcase tag that I'd seen before—on this note. See that ink mark in the corner? It's very distinctive. I think Cynthia wrote Alex's name on the briefcase tag. Handwriting experts could confirm it's hers."

Taylor took the plastic bag and examined the handwritten note, which had an excess ink squiggle on the upper right corner.

"Thomas, The contest will be decided tonight. You are ahead. Be in your stateroom, ready to come with me. Wait for me to rap on your window sometime between 3:00 and 3:30 a.m. —Cynthia"

"Where'd you get this?" Taylor asked.

"She gave it to me the night my brother disappeared—before I left the bar."

"What time?"

"Around eleven, I guess."

"What was the contest?"

"She was awarding points if we made her laugh, showed sensitivity, or won races—stupid stuff. Alex and I thought she was hot, and our sibling rivalry sucked us in like horny teens."

"Did you win?"

"I thought so when I got the note, but…"

"So Ms. James didn't come to your cabin at three?"

"No."

"Any time that night or early morning?"

"No. I didn't see her again—on the cruise. It was the last night."

"But you saw her again after?"

"Yes. I tracked her to her apartment in New Jersey."

"And?"

"And I told her I thought she might have been involved in my brother's disappearance, but she denied it."

"Why didn't you tell me this before?"

"We became...quite involved."

"But you're here now. Has the attraction waned?"

"Yes, you could say that. I protected her for selfish reasons, but now...well, I want to do the right thing."

Taylor squinted into the rising sun. "Why the cloak and dagger meeting?"

"I don't want her to find out I turned against her."

Taylor clenched his jaw. The park was quiet except for the birds. "Are you afraid of her?"

Gates started walking again, and Taylor followed alongside, his shorter legs taking three steps for every two of Gates's. "Cynthia got herself caught up in something very dangerous—something that's made *her* dangerous, too."

"What's so dangerous?"

"It has no direct bearing on the case."

Taylor frowned. "Why not let me be the judge of that?"

Gates shook his head.

Taylor played a hunch. "I was hoping you'd tell me she was involved in assassinating terrorists—that way I'd have more faith in your story."

Gates stopped and put his hand on a tree trunk.

Taylor coaxed him back into the conversation. "Why do you think she gave you this note?"

"I thought—hoped might be a better word—that she would come to me that night. Now, I think she wanted to keep me in my room so I wouldn't be suspected of anything."

Taylor cocked his head. "Suspected of what, Mr. Gates?"

"We both know my brother disappeared and hasn't been seen since. I was feuding with him on the cruise. I was a suspect, as you recall."

"Did Cynthia have any reason to harm your brother?"

"She believes my brother killed her mother. She'd also lost her father, and she was..."

"She was what?"

"She had a traumatic experience when she was—" Gates snapped his mouth shut.

"Go on."

"No."

"Were you going to say: when she was raped?"

Gates glared.

After an awkward silence, Taylor asked, "Anything else?"

"No. I don't think so, Detective. What are you going to do?"

"We have the briefcase tag you mentioned, but it's a complicated case. Your note will be helpful, but it may not be enough to take her into custody right now."

"Then when?"

Taylor shrugged. "That's hard to say."

Gates turned red, kicking at a stone. "Detective, by coming to you, I've opened myself to some danger, so from my perspective, time is of the essence."

"I understand your position, but I need to be able to convince the D.A. and a judge to issue arrest and extradition warrants. That may not happen quickly."

"Then when?"

Taylor shrugged. "I really don't know, but I'd like to hold onto this note. I'll keep it a secret."

Thomas threw up his hands. "Always secrets. Keep the damn note. I'm out of this." He jogged away. Taylor let him go and wondered what had gone wrong between Cynthia and her lover.

31

SCOPE

The September wind had changed—blowing from the north. Cynthia thought the chill was appropriate. She looked up at the gray, three-story house backed by gray clouds. The colors were appropriate, too. There was something final about the closed window shutters on Odessa.

She laughed the false laugh one makes when the alternative is tears. "I've never seen shutters *shut*. I always thought they were just decorations. Now, the name makes sense."

Carole put her arm around Cynthia. "Batten down the shutters—protection from the winter ocean winds. But you're right—on newer houses, they don't close."

"Why are you closing up Odessa? You could rent it to a big family or you could…"

"Too late in the season. I'll rent it out next summer. I have the bungalow for myself."

"I guess. The boys are all checked out of the garage, huh?"

"Yep."

"What about…" Cynthia knew her conversation was inane, but she needed the sound of voices. She tried to think of something else to say. Tumble and Weed stretched canine necks. Cynthia scratched them.

The sound of breakers made her think of Spain. Goose-bumps popped up on her arms. "I think this…closing is good for me," Cynthia said. "I'll miss the people, but I have to get away from the…you know."

"Yeah," Carole said. "It can wear on you."

Cynthia stared at the shutters. Closed and latched. She would miss the compound, but it was time.

"We're all loaded up," Joanie called from the car. She and Maria joined Carole and Cynthia on the front walk, where they took a last look around.

Maria squeezed Cynthia's hand. "Ready?"

"I guess."

Joanie imitated Carole. "Then let's saddle the stove and ride the range."

The three-hour drive to Boonton was subdued. Cynthia kept her attention on the road, Joanie wasn't her vivacious self, and Maria had no energy to get them talking. The only conversation of substance had to do with what rooms Maria and Joanie would take in Cynthia's condo.

Maria and Joanie had no place of their own, so it was practical for them to accept Cynthia's offer, if only for the short term. But the shadow of Charisse hung over the trio. Cynthia gave Joanie two weeks, tops, before she moved on. Then Cynthia would have to deal with the David versus Maria question, which now had Eduardo Juarez in the mix. Eddie and Maria had become a regular item, and Maria was more radiant than ever in his presence.

Cynthia's cookie-cutter condo was similar to thousands of others across the country—living room, eat-in kitchen and powder room on the first floor, two bedrooms with two baths on the second, and a basement—furnished in Cynthia's case as a TV room with convertible couch. That was Joanie's room, but she was rarely home. The only signs she lived there were her clothes—hanging in the laundry area, folded in an open suitcase on the floor of a utility room, or tossed behind the couch until laundry day.

Joanie was out on a date with Duane Root's bodyguard, Bruce Swenson, when Cynthia and Maria sat in the living room discussing Eddie Juarez's trip to Chattanooga.

"We're on for next week," Maria said. "Eddie agreed to do the training session, as well as provide temporary higher security—to make it worthwhile. He was lukewarm at first and asked a lot of questions about why I wanted him to help."

"And what did you say?"

"The truth," Maria replied. "I told him I thought Paulson or Root set up Charisse and that we wanted a SCOPE user to investigate. He perked up when I mentioned Root. I gather they don't get along too well. Eddie asked me to act as his assistant. He showed me how to set up some of the SCOPE equipment."

"You really like him, don't you?"

"He's fascinating—awesome—but he doesn't talk down to me. Doesn't treat me like a pretty face. It's like Eddie sees something special in me, you know? I think he's the one. I want the whole package," Maria said, beaming. "A ring, a house, kids."

"You'll make a great mother...and wife."

They glanced at each other. Cynthia was sure Maria knew what she was thinking.

"So..." Maria paused. "What about you and David?"

"Things are good—still refreshing. He's offering what he calls 'commitment without strings.'"

Maria laughed. "What's that?"

"He was very precise," Cynthia said. "He says it's sharing fun and making each other laugh all the time, but the important part is nursing each other when we're sick, and..." She colored. "...well, great sex when we're healthy.'"

"Is that what you want?"

"I've missed out on a lot, so yeah, that's part of what I want. But not all."

"What else?" Maria asked.

"Real intimacy."

"Any chance of marriage?" Maria asked, wetting her lips.

Cynthia shook her head, "I don't think marriage is in the cards for me. Too much baggage."

* * *

A sleepy Jimmy Taylor was waiting at the Chattanooga Police Station when Eddie Juarez arrived at 7:00 a.m. to conduct the SCOPE training session. Juarez was full of energy, bouncing around as if on drugs. His assistant was a beautiful woman, the equal of Cynthia James, thought Taylor, who cleaned his glasses.

Taylor's partner, Bob Jefferson, waited in the department's SCOPE room, an over-sized janitor's closet without the mops.

Unfazed by the cramped quarters, Juarez took charge. "Get the file on your most difficult case. Give it to Maria. She'll scan the documents while I set up the satellite interface and select your software."

Taylor sent Jefferson to get the file. Maria opened a suitcase and assembled a cube-shaped labyrinth of plastic rods. Juarez explained, "What we'll go over are specific techniques for examining paper trails and computer files for cause and effect relations."

Jefferson returned with a manila folder, which he gave to Maria. Juarez continued. "I'm installing a modified level-four version of SCOPE, good for one week. You normally have level-three—useless on this project, which we'll call 'Plantation.' Level-four has a scanning sensitivity six times greater than your version. Watch this."

Without opening the folder, Maria set it inside the cube of plastic rods. She fastened the four SCOPE scanners to the rods, two on top of the stack, and two on the side, each on a sliding track. "Now, she's scanning the file," Juarez said with pride, even though little was happening. It took less than ten seconds for the horizontal and vertical laser scanners to slide the length of the rods.

"The contents of those papers were just stored in your SCOPE database. Level-four is so sensitive it can detect pencil markings, distinguishing between the sheets of stacked paper. It can also decipher almost any handwriting."

Taylor rolled his eyes.

"Okay, Jimmy, hit the home key and ask a question into the mike. Ask who conducted an interview or something."

"Bob, which file did you bring?"

"The Jackson murder."

Taylor pressed the home key. "Who interviewed Gloria Jackson about her husband's death?"

Immediately, the terminal displayed:

    01 Aug 01 16:47 R Whitworth.
    02 Aug 02 09:13 J Taylor.
    03 Aug 03 10:15 J Taylor.
    CLICK ON SELECTION FOR MORE INFORMATION

"Gotta be a parlor trick," Taylor said.

"No trick, Detective. Ask another question."

"Where did Gloria Jackson say she was when her husband died?"

The terminal displayed:

    01 Aug 01 16:47 G Jackson says she was at sister's house.
    02 Aug 02 09:13 G Jackson says she was at mother's house.
    03 Aug 03 10:22 G Jackson says she was shopping.
    CLICK ON SELECTION FOR MORE INFORMATION

Taylor's eyes widened. "That's right. Wife changed her story. How'd it do that?"

"Once the information's scanned, SCOPE does what a human mind would do, only faster and more accurately."

"But how?"

"In layman's terms, SCOPE reads and translates your file into a hexel database. That took about ten seconds, and it's the slowest part of the process. Level-four has four virtual dimensions. Think of your brain as a three-dimensional database, with neurons firing off in all directions to get information through a myriad of indexes."

Taylor sucked on his pen. "You lost me."

Eddie scratched his chin. "If I asked you for your home phone number, you'd know it right away. But if I ask you for the number of the plumber who gave you an estimate two weeks ago, you wouldn't remember the number, but you might have put his business card in your wallet. It would take you a few more seconds to open your wallet and find the number. SCOPE would have that number, as well as every number the plumber had ever called and every number his contacts had ever called, and so on—all instantaneously. That's the extra dimension."

Taylor furrowed his brow. "I don't get the dimensions. I've heard that time is the fourth dimension; so what's the fifth? A band?"

Juarez laughed. "The dimensions are virtual, so it's hard to understand. Think of it this way. A circle is two dimensional. The circle, when rotated upon itself, becomes a sphere, but the circle can't envision that because it's just a flat circle. It can't comprehend a third dimension. If you were a four-dimensional being, you could understand the concept of the sphere rotating around itself to form what I call a quartzel. But we can't picture it because we only 'know' three dimensions."

Taylor's frown deepened.

"I've locked your system into a satellite laser scanner that's passing over Chattanooga. You can ask SCOPE questions about anything on your department's computers. SCOPE can read digital data via a power booster and super-GPS locator. Ask who authorized some departmental activity. While you think of a good question, Maria will start the perp-pass, Chattanooga-oh-three, on the FBI's one hundred most wanted list. Maria, that's on the TN-seventeen file."

Taylor picked up the microphone. "Who are the prime suspects in the disappearance of Alexander Gates?"

The terminal displayed:

01 May 18 T Gates. (case inactive)
02 May 19 C James. (case inactive)
CLICK ON SELECTION FOR MORE INFORMATION

Taylor shook his head. Juarez suggested that Taylor ask why the case was inactive. Taylor asked, and the screen displayed:

01 May 26 J Taylor reclassified case.
02 May 26 G Haskell e-mails to J Taylor.
CLICK ON SELECTION FOR MORE INFORMATION

Taylor clicked on the second line and read two e-mails that Chief Haskell had sent about the case. With a shake of his head, Taylor stuck his Pentel between his teeth. "Powerful stuff."

"Excuse me, Eddie," Maria said, "I have the perp-pass." She handed a printout to Juarez.

"Take a look, Jimmy," Juarez said.

"Whoa! Are you shittin' me?"

"No shit," laughed Juarez. "Six of those guys have been in Tennessee in the past month. William Holly, number sixty-five, using an alias, bought gas with a credit card in Chattanooga an hour ago, and the same card's imprint is active for a current motel stay."

"Damned powerful stuff," Taylor said. "Bob, call in the Holly info to the desk. Ask the sergeant to page the chief."

"Detective Taylor, I suggest you open the manual. Detective Jefferson can catch up when he gets back. I want to get out of here in time to enjoy the sunset from Lookout Mountain. We'll start with the password algorithms you'll need to harvest various databases...."

The session ended at 4:00 p.m.

"According to the deal, you have one week with the modified level-four," Juarez reminded them. "Make it count. Find out who set up Charisse White, and you can question Ms. James for one hour."

Taylor nodded. "And we can use anything else we find, right?"

"That's right."

The detective couldn't hide his excitement. "This stuff is fantastic. How come it's not out in the field, catching crooks?"

"The company will be rolling out SCOPE very soon. We're negotiating with the CIA and FBI, and when they're on board, we'll release the product. Then departments like yours will be more likely to sign up."

Taylor rolled his pen. "Eddie, why are you helping us?"

"I have my reasons."

Taylor noted that Juarez looked at Maria.

That evening, Eddie Juarez and Maria Lopez relaxed over dinner. Maria wanted to talk. "You came up with the Plantation name because of *Root*, didn't you? A clever play on words?"

"Glad you caught that."

"I still don't understand how Chattanooga will get at Root's files, even with a modified level-four. The way you explained it to me, Root and Paulson have level-five."

"They wouldn't use level-five for everything. It kicks off a warning to the other level-five user as an audit function. So Root wouldn't use it to plant evidence to set up Paulson, or vice versa. Plus, Root may want some evidence to be discovered by law enforcement agencies when they get SCOPE. If so, he'd make sure it was detectible by level-three. Anything the FBI will be able to find in a few months, the Chattanooga Police will find now."

"That makes sense," Maria said. "Why didn't I think of it?"

"You didn't design the system. But you were a big help today. You picked things up quickly."

"I have another question, Eddie."

"Shoot," Juarez said. He refilled their wine glasses, emptying the bottle.

"Everything in SCOPE is virtually hexagonal, right? Powers of six, and all."

"That's right."

"Then how come there are only five levels of SCOPE. Why not six? If it was SCOPES with an S, level-six could be called 'Super.'"

He coughed then laughed. "That's good. But there already *are* six levels. The lowest level is level-zero."

"Zero?"

"In information technology, some numbers are counted at their offset, or their distance from zero, meaning that the lowest level starts with no offset. So the six levels of SCOPE are zero through five."

"What's the zero level? Why haven't I heard of it?"

"Good question. Like the base level of a house, it's a foundation on which everything else is built."

"Do you think they'll be able to find what Cyn wants?" she asked.

"They were fast learners. If the evidence is there, I think they'll find it."

"And is it there?" she asked, taking his hand.

"I wouldn't bet against it."

* * *

While Eddie and Maria were sleeping late in Chattanooga, Pilar Ibanez was in Washington, D.C., making SCOPE sales pitches to the FBI and CIA. Both agencies were impressed with SCOPE's capabilities, so these meetings were all about price. At the morning session, the FBI negotiated with intimidation, cramming a walnut-paneled conference room with fifteen lawyers and executives. Pilar was the only woman in the room.

After her presentation, FBI Deputy Director Donald Jones made no effort to mask a patronizing tone. "One hundred twenty-five million dollars a year is a lot of money, considering we'll have to upgrade our hardware to handle the software. Surely, you can do better on price. The United States has spending limits, even for the war on terror."

Fifteen pairs of eyes glared at Pilar as if she were a profiteer.

She welcomed the spotlight. She stood and removed the jacket of her pin-striped suit, draping it on the back of her chair. Her white, knit blouse was simple yet flattering. Gliding around the table, she forced heads to turn. "Mr. Jones, in the package before you, we already *have* done much better. Your own airport security analysis conservatively predicts that SCOPE will save the government one hundred thirty million dollars per year. You'd be five million ahead if that were the only savings. But I refer you to other government studies that estimate SCOPE will save the FBI over two hundred thirty million more in surveillance, counterfeit recognition, database communication, fugitive pursuit, fingerprint analysis, etcetera. The FBI is scheduled to replace outdated hardware next year, so SCOPE-compatible equipment will cost only an additional fifty million. Your own consultants have told you that the FBI would save money if our price were *two* hundred twenty-five million, so I think one-twenty-five is quite a patriotic discount, don't you?"

Pilar looked directly at the open-mouthed deputy director. "Ah, Mr. Jones, I see you're impressed that we know the results of your studies. One more reason to purchase our product. Gentlemen, I believe our offer is so patriotically fair, that you have no choice but to accept it."

With his bluff called, Jones played his last card. "In the name of cooperation, we'll agree to pay one-half the total cost, if the other agency does the same."

She smiled. "That would be fine with Paulson Electronics. One base price for one *shared* version of the product. One database equally accessible to both agencies. Why don't you call Langley right now and have them send over their top men? We can all agree to your proposal by the end of the day."

Jones's ace had been trumped. "I, ah, didn't mean one database. The files would have to be separate, of course—security issues, and all." Jones sought support, but his colleagues were all looking at Pilar.

She waited until Jones's eyes returned to her. "I'm sorry, Mr. Jones, but I don't think so. If you want sole control over your own version, the price is one hundred twenty-five million dollars a year. That's the price *today*. After your attempt to low-ball a generous offer, Mr. Paulson may be so displeased that he'll insist on an increase."

Deputy Director Jones signed the preliminary letter of intent a half-hour later. An afternoon meeting with the CIA became a formality, for word travels fast among rival spy organizations. The CIA signed to ensure the same price that the FBI had received. It was a great day for Pilar, who was rewarded by Jerry Paulson with a $50,000 bonus.

* * *

Early the next morning, Duane Root stamped his feet in leaves on the forest floor in Tourne Park. Someone was coming—running, from the sound. He peeked around a boulder. Her. *About time.* He crushed a cigarette butt on the side of the boulder and dropped the butt into a small freezer bag with two others.

"Good morning, Ms. James."

To Cynthia, the voice came out of nowhere—grating, like a piece of heavy machinery that needed oil. She stopped and glanced right. An impeccably dressed man stepped from behind the boulder.

"My name is Duane Root. We've never been formally introduced, but we saw each other outside the reception in New York."

"I remember."

He stepped onto the trail and straightened a lapel. "I'm a busy man so I'll get right to the point. You have the Chattanooga police engaging in dangerous spying. Have them stop."

"I don't know what you're talking about."

Root's eagle-like eyes bored into hers. "Don't mess with me, Ms. James. I know all about your trouble in Chattanooga. I know their department has SCOPE, and I know you went to talk with them. And now I know they're making SCOPE inquiries that will lead to no good for anyone, especially you."

"Why are you here?" Cynthia asked, pulling a hand down her ponytail.

Root scowled. "To warn you."

"What does that mean?"

Root's forehead turned pink. "For someone who's supposed to be intelligent, Ms. James, you aren't very quick. Items in the national interest are not for amateurs."

"Your boss has paid me pretty well for an amateur."

"You're an expendable slut."

"What does that make you, Mr. Root?"

He tugged his sleeve. "Unlike you, Ms. James, I've never killed anyone."

"I suppose you've never inhaled, either."

Root growled. Cynthia tensed, watching Root's hand rise from his thigh toward the opening of his coat. But he only flipped off a leaf. "Be careful..." He made a gesture toward her neck without touching it, rubbing his thumb and forefinger together as if testing the quality of silk. "The next time you might not be so fortunate."

"Is that a—"

"I think you understand me perfectly."

"Sounds like a threat."

Root almost smiled. "And one more thing. *Your* neck isn't the only one you should worry about. I know who your friends are."

After a moment of silence, Root pivoted and marched down the path. Rubbing her upper arms, Cynthia shuffled backwards, keeping him in sight until he disappeared around a bend.

* * *

Late that night, Jimmy Taylor hunched over a terminal in the cramped SCOPE room in the bowels of the Chattanooga police station. He knew he was spending too much time after-hours on the search for suspected traitors, but he couldn't keep away. SCOPE was addictive. Learning to use it was like traveling through a time warp of surveillance history—from the first telescope to satellites—in two mind-numbing days. "Incredible," he mumbled as a document popped onto his screen. This one was an e-mail from Duane Root's PC. Taylor merged the e-mail with two other suspicious documents and the transcript of a phone conversation between Root and an unknown man in Barcelona. Taylor then used SCOPE's A.I. function to request a more focused search of the Paulson Electronics security system for connections to Charisse White, Barcelona, and *Patriots for Freedom*. He started the search and waited.

The screen displayed the results. Taylor took off his glasses and leaned close so he could read without them. Taylor slapped his palm on the table. "Hot damn!" He saved and printed the document, then repeated the A.I. criteria focus.

All night he mined data. With each discovery, his awe increased. When he had everything he could find about Duane Root and the Barcelona murders, Taylor didn't stop tinkering, didn't stop learning, didn't stop asking questions.

He was still in the SCOPE room, sipping his eighth cup of coffee, when Bob Jefferson poked in his head at 7:45 a.m. "In early, Boss?"

Taylor shook his head clear. "Um, sort of." He patted the chair next to his. "You gotta see this stuff, Bob."

* * *

Two days later, Pilar Ibanez was buoyant. It was the best day of her professional life. At 10:00 a.m. on October 2nd, the FBI and CIA officially announced that each had contracted to use SCOPE software at a cost of $125 million dollars per year for a period of two years, with an option to renew. Thanks to the publicity blitz orchestrated by Pilar, the media covered the announcement like a Kennedy wedding.

Pilar's promotional rollout campaign, held back for just this day, was implemented. Jerry Paulson was pre-booked on CNN, and all the papers, wire-services, and Internet sites reported the news. She had bet that the FBI and CIA would announce before Columbus Day, and the company was rewarded. The field force of technicians was installing the system for clients who had pre-ordered. New orders came pouring into the Internet site and phone bank that had been beefed up at Pilar's direction.

And this was just the first day.

Thanks to Pilar's marketing plan, SCOPE was perceived as the must-have product in the information age. Eddie Juarez may have created SCOPE, but Pilar turned it into one of the fastest success stories in the history of capitalism.

Paulson scheduled a kick-off party at the Plaza, timed for coverage on the nightly newscasts. The major anchors interviewed Paulson, the company's phone number and website visible on the podium.

Pilar had planned on a conservative suit for the party, but Paulson persuaded her to wear a shimmering golden gown. Formidable and sexy, she was the evening's sensation. Paulson worked her into every interview, and by the end of the day, millions of male news watchers had a crush on the fiery Brazilian-American.

A few months earlier, Eddie Juarez would have been jealous to see Pilar getting so much attention while he toiled in the background, but on this night, he was happy. He had Maria Lopez clamped on his arm.

Duane Root brooded in the corner. Although he had foreseen that Pilar would be lauded for her marketing plan, he hadn't anticipated what a phenomenon she would become. He had underrated her sex appeal. For that oversight, he berated himself. The triumphant rollout exonerated Pilar for the failure in Barcelona. She didn't need Root's protection. Worse, Root knew he was no longer the unrivaled heir apparent to Paulson's empire.

* * *

The next day, Cynthia received a bulky FedEx envelope from the Chattanooga police. That night, she met with Maria and Joanie in her living room.

"It's Root," Cynthia said. "The Chattanooga SCOPE scan identified correspondence from Root that initiated the Barcelona ambush. The surprise is…Pilar Ibanez was in on it with him."

Joanie's and Maria's eyes glazed, just as Cynthia's had when she read the report. She handed them the documentation. Once the shock had worn off, Cynthia continued. "Root also withheld evidence that Edward Smythe was the owl."

"Why?" Maria asked.

"Money and power," Cynthia said. "To control Paulson Electronics and take it public. By fabricating evidence, Root used Paulson's hatred of Thatcher to get Paulson to push for the hit. My mission was designed to fail. Internally, Paulson would take the fall for fingering an innocent man. If Paulson was forced out, Root and Ibanez would take over and make a fortune. But I brought back the *NightOwl* and withheld the truth. So there was nothing to use against Paulson."

"Why did they have Charisse murdered?" Joanie asked.

Cynthia's jaw tightened. "When I didn't squeal, Ibanez and Root agreed on the need for a bigger disaster. Charisse and her team were sacrificed. I'll always have to live with what I didn't say."

Maria leaned over and stroked Cynthia's hand. "We all pushed her to go."

Joanie asked, "What is Paulson doing about the traitors?"

"Nothing. Apparently, he doesn't know what we know. He has no suspicions that anyone inside is betraying him. He's just a clueless patriot who underestimated them."

"Why doesn't Paulson know?" Maria asked. "He has the same level-five as Root, right?"

Cynthia shrugged. "He either never looks at things down at level-three, or Root doctors Paulson's reports. Or something else."

"I'm sure you're right about Root and Ibanez," Joanie said. "They've shacked up in Boston—once that I know of and maybe more. When Bruce gets drunk, he talks. Root will be going there again on Tuesday. If form holds, Pilar will join him Wednesday evening for dinner and a roll in the hay."

"So what do we do now?" Maria asked.

Cynthia stood and paced the length of the room and back. She had made her decision and was surprised she remained cool. "With your help, I'm gonna take out Duane Root."

"Whoa, Nellie!"

"Joanie's right. Isn't that a bit rash? Can't we go to the authorities?"

Cynthia shook her head. "Root paid me a visit. He knows that Chattanooga is sniffing around with SCOPE. He threatened me, telling me to butt out, or else."

"Did he say anything about Eddie?" Maria asked.

"No."

Joanie said, "Tell Paulson about the threat—or tell the police."

Cynthia shook her head. "Root's too dangerous. He wanted me dead in England, and he had Charisse and her team murdered in Spain. When this evidence comes to light—and it will now that the FBI has SCOPE—what do you think he'll do to me? Or to you? I'm not waiting for him to come after me again. Besides, if we play it straight, the SCOPE evidence probably won't hold up in court until after years of appeals. Root'll be free to extract his revenge."

After letting her remarks sink in, Cynthia added, "I'd like your help, but I'll do it alone if I have to."

"I'm not saying yes," Joanie said, "but what kind of help are you looking for?"

"I'm working out a plan that requires your expertise in supporting roles. You'll be accomplices with full exposure to murder charges."

"What about including others?" Maria asked. "David would do anything for you."

"I know, but this will be just among the Aities—for Charisse."

There was a tense pause before Joanie said, "Count me in."

With less enthusiasm, Maria said, "Okay, but I reserve the right to pull out, okay?"

"Fair enough," Cynthia said.

"So what's your plan?" Joanie asked.

"I think we can do it this Tuesday, on Root's *first* night in Boston."

32

PAYBACK

The night before Bruce Swenson was to accompany Duane Root to Boston, he had a date with Joanie Lee. Before leaving him with a smile, she spiked his beer with a drug that induced a severe case of diarrhea. His smile turned to a twenty-four hour grimace. Swenson couldn't make it out of his bathroom, much less to Boston.

After leaving Swenson, Joanie made another stop: Pilar Ibanez's home, three hours before dawn.

Dressed in black, Joanie sneaked to the breezeway connecting the house and garage. She passed a sensor around the door to the garage. No alarms—locked, but that was expected. Using a flashlight and her All-in-One tool, she picked the lock. After disconnecting Pilar's BMW car alarm, she replaced the EZPass unit. While inside the garage, she spliced a diverter into the phone line, which ran through the garage to the house. All incoming calls would return endless rings. On outgoing calls, Pilar would get busy signals. Joanie was in and out in eighteen minutes, withdrawing to sit behind a tool shed until Pilar left for work.

For more than two hours, Joanie told herself silent jokes.

When the garage door opened, a hazy pink graced the eastern sky. Five minutes later, Joanie knelt at the back door, working on the lock. *Click.* The knob turned. Before opening the door, she activated an electronic code-breaker. She would have ten seconds to find the alarm pad. Her heart was steady, calmed by confidence in electronics.

Pushing open the door, Joanie held a flashlight in one hand and the code-breaker in the other. She counted, "One-thousand one, one-thousand two..." Following the indicators, she hurried through the kitchen to the pantry. There was the security pad. Joanie watched the whirring lights as the key came up: 3625. She punched it in, and the red light went out. It had taken eight seconds.

Joanie retrieved a garment bag she had left outside the door, took off her shoes, and put on slippers. Then she searched for Pilar's bedroom. With a photograph as reference, she rifled through Pilar's closet until she found the dress, belt, purse, and shoes Pilar had worn to the New York reception. Joanie also took a pair of pantyhose. A quick alteration to Pilar's PC disabled its modem.

Joanie returned to the kitchen, put on her shoes, reset the alarm, and slipped out the back door ten minutes after entering. She drove the rented van to rendezvous with Cynthia and Maria in Mystic, Connecticut.

On Tuesday evening, Pilar Ibanez returned home to reheat Monday's casserole and try to relax, but she couldn't. She was thinking about Boston. Each Wednesday evening's routine was identical. Following a dinner at Legal Seafood, she and Root walked back to the hotel. Champagne chilled in an ice bucket by the sitting room couch.

Pilar had taken one last trip to Boston after SCOPE's coming out party so Root wouldn't suspect her impending power play. But the thought of sleeping with Root again made her shudder. She wouldn't go to Boston on Wednesday. Instead, she would call Root with some excuse. Next week she would break off their personal relationship. By then, she'd be ready to make her move.

* * *

Cynthia's makeover began in the van as soon as she and Maria left their bed and breakfast in Mystic late Tuesday afternoon. Cynthia put on thin hip and bra pads then squeezed into a body stocking that covered everything below her neck. After donning surgical gloves, Cynthia shimmied into pantyhose and the black cocktail dress Joanie had removed from Pilar's closet. Cynthia built up the inside heel of each shoe with Moleskin, adding a half-inch of height. That was close enough—any higher and she wouldn't be able to walk normally. The inside collar of the dress was lined with clear plastic to protect the fabric from makeup.

Once Maria parked the van in Boston, she went to work behind mirrored windows. She gave Cynthia green contact lenses then folded and taped Cynthia's hair tight to her scalp. Maria applied a foundation one shade darker than Cynthia's skin. Working from an enlarged photo, Maria used lip and eye liner to alter Cynthia's features—making her lips appear wider and her eyes rounder. Shadowing around the nose exaggerated its slight hook. Then Maria brushed on Cover Girl to hide the neck scars as if they were pimples. Finally, Maria forced on a short black wig so tightly it gave Cynthia an instant headache.

Cynthia glanced in a handheld mirror then asked, "How do I look?"

"Great. But don't forget the belt."

"Right." Cynthia put the gold chain around her waist then pulled on black dress gloves, straining finger-by-finger to slide them over the surgical gloves. When all ten fingers were tighter than O.J. Simpson's, she examined the contents of her purse and tote bag before stepping out of the van.

"Good luck," Maria whispered.

Cynthia nodded. She wobbled until adjusting for the heel wedges. By the end of the block, she was smooth enough to turn the heads of two men walking the other way. The autumn night was cool, but Cynthia wore no overcoat. Her hands sweated.

She breathed rhythmically, reviewing her mental checklist the way Carole had taught her. She became an actress—her part, an angel of retribution. But something was different this time. Cynthia's finger twitched.

The doorman of the Park Plaza smiled when the olive-skinned woman approached the hotel entrance. He called Ms. Ibanez by name and held the door, a gesture she acknowledged with a smile. An eager bellhop offered to carry her tote bag, but she discouraged him with a self-sufficient wave. Gliding through the lobby, she was a picture of confidence. Three clerks smiled as she passed the front desk. It was the fourth time the Latina had graced their lobby. None of the employees noticed her spastic finger. She pressed her hand against her thigh to stop the twitch.

In the elevator, she felt the walls closing in. Her throat was a clogged air filter. There was less fear than during the other hits, but more...more what? When the doors opened on the seventh floor, she thought: more guilt? No, but something close. "Think," she mouthed. "Complete the mission."

Striding down the hall, she reminded herself not to look up at the security camera. She thought about aborting. The mark was more dangerous than the terrorists she had killed, but this wasn't the same, and she had the jitters to prove it. This hit had no *Patriots for Freedom* sanction. But Root would kill her for sure. That did it. She put one foot in front of the other. With every step, she grew more resolved. At the door to Suite 708, Cynthia took out a handkerchief, knocked, and waited. The door cracked open, and a bushy eyebrow appeared behind the vertical slit.

Cynthia spoke in a scratchy whisper. "Pilar to see Duane."

"Oh," said the bodyguard. "You're a day early."

"Yes," came a raspy reply, which caught in her throat like fish bones. "I wanted to surprise him. Sorry, I have a cold."

"Mr. Root," the bodyguard called, "Ms. Ibanez is here." The voice sounded as if it came from under water.

"Well, let her in," Root commanded from the next room, but Cynthia didn't hear that. She did hear the bodyguard unchain the door. Root called, "Be there in a minute, Pilar."

Cynthia entered the suite and caught the bodyguard's thigh with her swinging pocketbook, then stuck her free hand into the tote bag.

"Ow!" he grunted.

Cynthia exhaled when she didn't see Root. She let go of the hidden pistol and looked apologetic. "Oh, the ID pin clipped on my purse popped open. There. I've fixed it. Sorry."

The bodyguard rubbed his thigh.

Root, buttoning his cuffs, strode in from the bedroom. "What a pleasant surprise, Pilar."

She held the handkerchief in front of her nose. Looking down and speaking through the cloth, she rasped, "I'm not feeling well. May I use the bathroom?"

"Of course," replied Root. "But what's wrong?"

Cynthia coughed and slipped inside the bathroom before Root could get a good look at her face. She locked the door, took off her belt, and listened. She heard her heartbeat and air rushing into her lungs. She pressed an ear to the door.

Root asked, "Why'd she come a day early?"

"Dunno."

"Do you think she's all right?"

"Dunno."

"She's not herself. Should I order champagne?"

"I dunno!"

Root turned to face the bathroom door. "Pilar, are you alright?"

"I'll be fine in a minute," she coughed.

After a few seconds, the bodyguard said, "Ohhhh...I gotta sit down. Ah, boss...I don't feel so—"

Cynthia reminded herself that she was an actress playing the sexy assassin. Her finger twitched, but just slightly. She reached into her bag then quietly opened the door. Root was facing away from the bathroom, holding up his slumping bodyguard. No more thinking. It was execution time. Cynthia took two steps and swung a short iron bar at the back of Root's head as hard as she could. *Thud.* Root crumpled. There was blood but no spurting. She dropped to her knees, straddling his back as soon as he hit the floor. She cinched her belt around his neck. Viciously, she strangled Root as his bodyguard moaned in delirium. She had no coherent thoughts, just sensations: tingles and jolts. There was an ice shaft down her spine—maybe from guilt and shame, or maybe hate. She kept cinching.

By the time she loosened the chain, both men were motionless. There was no going back, so she went forward.

A few minutes later, the desk clerks, doorman, and bellhop saw Ms. Ibanez leave alone. The other times, she had departed with Mr. Root. The doorman, who prided himself on his memory, saw that she carried a tote bag. Today was Tuesday, a day earlier than the woman's prior visits. He also noted that she wore gloves but had not worn a coat against the chill. Strange.

Cynthia hoped that he didn't notice the twitching finger.

33

ALIBIS

Maria started the van as soon as she saw Cynthia approaching. Washcloths, solvents, and a mirror waited on the backseat. While Maria drove southwest, Cynthia wriggled out of the dress and pantyhose—removing the collar lining—and put them in a garment bag along with the shoes and purse—minus the ID badge and needle. Next, she took off the body stocking, hip pads, and bra. After removing makeup and combing her hair into the same ponytail she had worn when she left the bed and breakfast, Cynthia slipped into her regular clothes and took out her contacts. She placed everything they wanted destroyed into a plastic garbage bag. During a short detour through a warehouse parking lot, Cynthia tossed the bag into a dumpster that was scheduled for incineration Wednesday morning.

A few minutes later, she hurled the iron bar into the Neponset River.

With the evidence disposed of, they relaxed from hyper to merely agitated, and Cynthia described what had happened in the hotel.

"Did you feel that killer high you talk about?" Maria asked.

"Just fumes. It wasn't the same." Cynthia's eyes turned glassy. "What's done is done, but this was a mistake…my mistake."

"We're in it together."

Cynthia didn't hear. "I couldn't escape," she murmured. "The legacy of *Patriots for Freedom*." Cynthia bowed her head.

"You mean revenge."

Cynthia nodded.

Neither woman spoke for the next half-hour.

When she saw a sign to Mystic—three-miles—Cynthia said, "Remember, when we get back, no talking out loud to Joanie. She'll have notes for us about the tapes."

Maria parked the van two blocks from the bed and breakfast. They left Pilar's clothes inside. After sneaking into the two-bedroom carriage house suite, Maria and Cynthia went to their room where Joanie sat on a bed in the middle of three portable tape players and a recording chart. Four slices of pizza lay in a box balanced on the end table; only the weight of two coffee mugs kept the box from tipping onto the floor. Cynthia flashed a thumbs-up sign, and Joanie gave them both silent hugs before handing over a log of what had transpired during their absence.

Joanie motioned toward the pizza box then patted her stomach. "I left you two slices each," she whispered.

"I'm starving," Cynthia murmured.

Joanie gave Cynthia an ear-piece connected to a listening device affixed to the wall shared by an adjacent suite. While Joanie packed up her electronic gear, Maria and Cynthia glanced at the log. One entry was underlined. During Maria's shower, Cynthia reviewed the log in detail, cross-checking descriptions of various recordings so she would know what she had "said" and to whom.

> 18:04 Baxters came back to adjoining suite
> 18:04 Started 3-way Liverpool Rummy Tape #1
> 18:30 Ordered Domino's pizza by phone using CJ's voice
> 18:59 Pizza delivered and paid for
> 19:07 Baxters left for dinner
> 20:12 Ended 3-way Liverpool Rummy Tape #1
> 20:17 Started "Thelma and Louise" on the VCR
> 20:29 Paused movie
> 20:30 Placed CJ Phone Tape #1 to aunt's machine
> 20:35 Placed ML Phone Tape #1 to sister's machine
> 20:45 Called Bruce to see how he was doing
> 21:12 <u>Live call to DS using CJ's voice</u> (David asked if CJ sick)
> 21:35 Live call to EJ using ML's voice (Eddie too rushed to talk)
> 21:45 Resumed movie
> 22:05 Baxters arrived home at their suite.
> 22:05 Started CJ/ML Tape Conversation #1
> 22:55 Baxters turned in
> 23:35 End of movie
> 23:42 Ended CJ/ML Tape Conversation #1
> 00:35 Started CJ/ML Tape Conversation #2
> 01:09 Ended CJ/ML Tape Conversation #2
> 02:12 Baxters used bathroom
> 02:14 Started CJ/ML Tape Conversation #3
> 02:35 Ended CJ/ML Tape Conversation #3

Cynthia heard Joanie on the phone in the next room talking to Bruce. "Sorry to wake you, baby. I feel so bad about you being sick. I miss you so much. I'm coming back early to take care of you. I'll leave at dawn. Luv ya."

Joanie popped her head in and waved goodbye. She would take the van.

A few minutes later, Maria emerged from the bathroom in a satin nightgown. Cynthia handed the ear-piece to Maria. Showering at three in the morning was rude, but the Aities were interested in being noticed. Joanie's impersonations and the audio tapes would establish their alibi, but they needed the guests next door to remember them.

Despite the hot shower, Cynthia couldn't settle her nerves. She dried off and pulled on a T-shirt and cotton running shorts. The butterflies in her stomach were fluttering just below barf speed. She steadied herself with breathing exercises. After two minutes, she was still agitated, but she couldn't stay in the bathroom all night. She wiped a clear circle in the foggy glass. She *looked* steady.

As soon as she felt the cooler air in the bedroom, Cynthia's calmness evaporated. She was almost as nervous as she had been entering Root's hotel room.

Maria handed over a note that read, "They're awake and bitching about our showers."

Forcing a smile, Cynthia sat on one of the twin beds and tried to brush her damp hair, but a trembling hand betrayed her. Maria turned on the radio then sat on the bed and took the brush from Cynthia's fingers. Maria whispered, "You did the right thing. He would have killed you."

Cynthia nodded.

"Here. Let me," Maria said. She pulled the brush through Cynthia's hair. It was the right gesture at the right time. Cynthia watched Maria's face behind her own in the mirror at the foot of the bed. She tried to think, but couldn't keep a train of thought. After counting fifty strokes, she gave up and enjoyed the hair massage.

One hundred strokes later, her pulse was still abnormal. Maria put the brush on the end table. "There."

Mouth parched, Cynthia wanted to say something, but the words wouldn't come. By the time Cynthia turned, Maria had walked into the bathroom. When she came back, she was sipping a glass of water. "Want some?" Maria held out the glass.

Cynthia nodded, accepting it with both hands. Maria's fingers slid along the palm of one hand during the exchange. A shiver tingled

Cynthia's spine. She looked at Maria's face, seeing concern.

"Thanks." Cynthia held the moisture on her lips before swallowing.

"Drink some more," Maria said. "You don't want to get dehydrated."

"You're right. I'm not thinking clearly," Cynthia whispered, "and our lives are on the line."

Maria popped in another video—*Airplane*—and they sat next to each other on one of the twin beds, making fun of the movie while eating cold pizza. Cynthia inserted the earpiece and picked up the rustle of covers in the next room. Despite gnawing doubt, she laughed with Maria at gags that had never been funny before. Maria nodded off before the movie ended, her head resting on Cynthia's shoulder. Cynthia stroked Maria's hair and wondered if either would be able to live with what they had done.

An amplified snort woke Cynthia. Mr. Baxter was stirring. Cynthia nudged Maria. "They're up next door."

Maria purred and squinted. She hugged Cynthia, the moment brief but intimate.

In a flurry of flailing arms and legs, they got ready.

When the Baxters left their suite for breakfast, Maria's and Cynthia's giggling exit drew glares. "Oh, good morning," Maria said. "You must be in the next suite. I hope we didn't keep you up last night. We couldn't sleep."

The Baxters bristled and hurried to breakfast before the offensive guests could join them, but their escape was short-lived. At the community dining table, the Baxters sat across from Maria Lopez and Cynthia James, the one with a scratchy voice, long hair the color of dark honey, and unsightly scars around her neck.

34

ARREST

Jerry Paulson's voice was barely audible when Pilar picked up her phone a few minutes after 10:00 a.m. Wednesday. "Come to my office right away." He sounded lost and hung up before she replied.

Within a minute, she stood in his doorway. "Yes, Jerry?" His skin was the color of onionskin paper. "What's wrong?" she asked.

Paulson choked on his words. "I received a call from the Boston Police—terrible news. Duane was murdered last night in his hotel."

Shock buffeted Pilar, followed by relief and confusion. She sat without thinking and searched her brain for something to say that would dampen sparks of happiness. "T-that's terrible," she said. If Paulson noted insincerity, he didn't show it. Pilar fine-tuned her anxiety. "But he had a bodyguard—Bruce, right?"

"Swenson called in sick yesterday, but another guard was there. Apparently, he was drugged. He's hasn't given a statement yet, but he should be coherent soon." Paulson crumpled the front page of *The New York Times* in his fist.

"So what happened?" Pilar asked, her native accent creeping into her voice.

"They say it was a woman. A woman in a black dress. She came in alone and left alone. I'm waiting for a still from the hotel's security tape to be faxed."

"How was he killed?"

"They say he was strangled and hit on the head. Won't know which killed him until the autopsy."

As the shock lessened, relief cleared Pilar's head. With Root gone, Paulson would surely turn to her. In fact, based on his call to her this morning, he already had. Perhaps she would gain control over SCOPE by the end of the month. Anything was possible. Even if Paulson avoided a heart attack, her hard work would be rewarded. She was number two now, ready for her chance.

Pilar was relieved for another reason. The only time in her career she had deviated from her formula for success had been the coerced affair with Root.

She snapped out of her reverie. Paulson was asking her something. "Did I tell you the police were coming here to talk to us? Do you have any idea who would want him dead?"

Who might want Root dead? The answer gave her a chill. But why would one of the Aities kill Root?

"No," she said. "I don't know why anyone would have done this terrible thing."

After a moment of eerie silence, Paulson's fax machine kicked on.

"This should be the killer's picture," he said. "By the way, hotel witnesses say they had seen the woman visit Root before."

This perplexed Pilar. Had Root been two-timing her while they were two-timing his wife? Pilar wanted to hover over the machine as the picture inched out, but she remained seated behind a mask of calm. A few more seconds wouldn't make a difference.

Paulson shook his head in disbelief. "What the...?" He held the paper out. "Can you explain this?"

There on the page, she saw her grainy picture in the hotel hallway—down to her black dress and chain belt. Nauseous liquid bubbled up her throat, but she held it down. "Oh! The hotel must have pulled the wrong tape. I've been up to see Duane a few times in Boston—while I was visiting friends—and I met him at his hotel before we went to dinner." She was pleased at how smoothly she had produced the explanation. "But I wasn't there last night, so it has to be the wrong tape."

"Really?" Paulson said, relieved. "Let me see." He took the picture. "What about the date-time stamp? Isn't that yesterday's date?"

"No. It can't be. I wasn't..." But there it was in the lower right corner: yesterday's date. Her jaw quivered, but only for a moment. She sat up straight. "You, better than anyone, know how these things can be doctored."

"Were you having an affair with Duane?"

"Why would you ask such a question?"

"You can have lunch with him here any time. Why go to Boston, if not to see him away from his wife? I don't blame you if you're lonely. Your husband's been gone a while."

"As I said, I have friends in Boston, and while I was there..." Her Portuguese accent had taken control. And then it hit her. She stood and grabbed the picture.

"What is it?" Paulson asked.

"The dress! I never wore that dress in Boston. I swear that can't be from the hotel last night or any other night. It can't be! I wasn't there...It's from somewhere else, or it isn't me."

"Is there anyone who can verify that you weren't in Boston last night?"

Pilar shivered. "Oh, Christ. I don't know. I was home."

"Did you make any calls? Maybe accessed the Internet?"

She couldn't control the jitters. "No. I didn't log on. I did try to phone my dad in Brazil but couldn't get through. I don't remember any incoming calls. I read marketing reports all night."

"Just stay calm, Pilar, and tell the police the truth. They'll be here in a few minutes." Putting his arm around her shoulder, he soothed, "You're staying here with me until we clear this up." It was a command from the CEO—she slumped into a chair.

Pilar's mind raced. Root's murder could have been committed by one of the Aities, but they had no motive to frame her. She had been their biggest supporter. A resourceful woman like Cynthia James could have killed Root without disguising herself as Pilar.

She was still confused when two Boston detectives arrived with an arrest warrant. There was little conversation. Her protests were met with a cynical, "Save it for the judge." They placed her under arrest for the murder of Duane Root, Mirandized her, then led her away in handcuffs. She was numb.

Paulson called after her, "I'll get the best criminal lawyer in Boston. Don't say anything. Hang in there."

Earlier that morning, before Pilar left for work, Joanie Lee had adjusted Pilar's car's odometer and returned the EZPass unit, removing the substitute. Immediately after Pilar departed, Joanie picked the lock, entered the house, and replaced the shoes, gloves, purse, dress, and belt in Pilar's closet. She left the pantyhose hanging on a bathroom towel rack next to another pair. As she worked, Joanie was encased in a body stocking—just as she had been the morning before—and after she was done, she threw her shoes and stocking into a commercial dumpster.

* * *

Pilar's stay in jail was brief, thanks to bail money put up by Jerry Paulson and persuasive arguments by her defense attorney, Carolyn Bachman, a stout, no-nonsense woman who didn't sugarcoat Pilar's predicament. With all that was at stake, Bachman was surprised Pilar thought her proclaimed innocence would carry the day.

As evidence mounted against her, Pilar lost faith in the legal system, if not her innocence. Required to stay in the jurisdiction, she lived in a Boston hotel, growing to hate the city she once loved.

"You have to trust me to defend you," Bachman argued one afternoon in her firm's large office, decorated in money. "You say you know who did it, but you won't tell me who it is. You're tying my hands!"

Pilar raised her chin. "I don't want to drag certain people—"

"Right," Bachman interrupted. "The *patriots* you keep alluding to. And your blessed career. Listen. You don't *have* a career. It's over."

Pilar returned a blank stare.

Bachman shook her head in frustration. "We have more bad news. I received copies of the transcripts and documents that the prosecution is using to support motive. Here." She plopped a stack of papers in front of Pilar. "Read them. I'll be back in an hour. We'll talk then." Leaving Pilar in the conference room, Bachman went to help more cooperative clients.

It was sober reading. A memo from her to Root saying "a major hiccup" in Spain would "undercut the big guy." A reply suggesting "a male solution could bury a female." None damning by themselves, but as Pilar worked her way through the pile, her stomach sank. Six e-mails between her and Root set up meetings in the parking lot—meetings that had allegedly been recorded. She listened to tapes while following transcripts. She was heard saying, "If we take them out, I have to have your support." Root's response was, "That's what partners do for each other." When Root was heard asking if tomorrow should be "the day when color fades," Pilar's voice said, "Do it." The next day was the day Charisse White was murdered. Now *that* was damning.

The last tape was of a vehement argument between her and Root two days before his death. Profane threats. She had never said or written the words attributed to her; the so-called evidence was all electronic magic, but the SCOPE seal of approval lent authenticity. She pulled her personal cipher card from her wallet to scan the imprints on each document. The usage code was for level-three decoding, however, the false evidence had been created above her level-four. She knew there was only one living person with the clearance. The unanswered question was: why?

Although there was no mention of Barcelona or Charisse White by name, the manufactured evidence provided a plausible reason for the Aities to think Pilar was guilty. Level-3 clearance must have picked up bogus evidence of her involvement, and Cynthia James or one of her cohorts must have discovered it and read between the lines. It was brilliant—one heinous traitor gets put away for murdering the other. In a twisted way, Pilar was proud of her assassins' efficiency.

When Carolyn Bachman returned to the conference room, she found a more cooperative client. "This changes things," Pilar said, her fingers tapping on the table.

"Darn right. Now they have the final piece of the puzzle: motive. That goes with damning eyewitness accounts by hotel employees and the bodyguard that put you at the scene—"

"No," Pilar interrupted, her green eyes flashing. "That put someone who *looks* like me at the scene. Is there any physical evidence recovered at the crime scene that places me there?"

Bachman shook her head. It could be the start of a defense. "The forensics report should be in later today."

Pilar gave her lawyer more. "The woman who killed Root is Cynthia James; she looks something like me. The make-up that made her my double had to be done by Maria Lopez. They both saw me wear that black dress and chain belt at a party. They must have bought an identical outfit. Have someone check purchases at Saks. The man who faked and leaked the false evidence is my boss, Jerry Paulson." For fifteen minutes, she rattled off facts and theories, Bachman taking frantic notes. Pilar and Bachman went home that night with real hope.

The hope was short-lived. The next day, forensic evidence backed up the eyewitness testimony. Carpet fibers on Pilar's shoes and the knees of one pair of pantyhose matched that of the carpet in Root's hotel room. Flakes of Root's skin were found on her belt and the chain pattern matched the marks on the victim's neck. Traces of Root's blood was spattered on the sleeve of her dress. The only female DNA on the dress and every pair of pantyhose in Pilar's house belonged to her. There was no trace of Cynthia James, Maria Lopez, or Joanie Lee. All three Aities had alibis, corroborated by guests at the bed and breakfast in Mystic and a pizza delivery boy, as well as by telephone calls they had placed from Mystic.

Carolyn Bachman shook her head. "This DNA evidence places you at the scene."

"No," Pilar snapped. "My *clothes* were there. I wasn't."

"What about the EZpass records?"

"I used the turnpike coming home, not the Mass Pike, or whatever those fuckin' computers say."

Bachman blanched. "They double-checked your unit."

"But it's not the truth."

The lawyer leaned forward. "Whatever your so-called truth, the *legal* reality is that they've got you cold. I can attack witnesses' testimony, and I can suggest a frame-up, but as it stands now, we'll lose. All the evidence suggests that you did it. Maybe we shouldn't put all our eggs in the innocent basket; maybe we should make the most out of the legal reality."

"What's that? Life instead of lethal injection?"

"There's no death penalty in Massachusetts," Bachman replied, "and your hand is better than you think."

Pilar rolled her eyes. "Right."

"If you have to go to prison, there are variables, such as, what kind, where, for how long, and under what parole terms. You're still a young woman."

Pilar kept tapping her fingers, each tap causing a tiny wave in a glass pitcher of water on the table. "So how good is my hand?"

"You've got a few cards we can play. For example, you can threaten to implicate the government as an accomplice in some of the illegal activities of *Patriots for Freedom*. The Feds may well force the D.A. to deal in order to cover up ugly secrets. Granted, all the publicity will make it harder to get a sweetheart deal, but everything is negotiable."

Pliar grabbed her fingers to keep them from tapping. Her eyes darted from wall to wall as if there were bars on the windows. "Damn. You can't let them put me in jail."

"Look at me, Pilar.... You seem agitated. Are you all ri—"

"I'm fine. I just need a cigarette." Pilar rubbed her fingers together like a safe-cracker.

"What's wrong?"

"Those fuckin' bitches!"

Bachman leaned back, waiting for the profanity's echo to die. "You seem upset. Perhaps we should seek a psychiatric evaluation. There may be—"

"No." Pilar's face contracted into a grimace. Her Portuguese accent shaped rapid-fire words. "No insanity defense. I've been fuckin' framed. Get that through your thick skull."

"Okay. Okay. No insanity plea." Doubt seeped into Bachman's tone, and she could tell that Pilar heard it. "But we'll need something more than your wo—"

"I've got something more. Like you said: I've got stuff on the govern—" Pilar sucked for air. "Wait." Her eyes crossed and her chest heaved. "Water."

Bachman poured a glass.

Pilar waited until her breathing calmed. She sipped then held her forehead until the hyper-ventilating episode ebbed. "Listen carefully."

35

HONOR

"Ahem."

Jimmy Taylor looked up at the woman clearing her throat. A green Pentel slid out of his mouth and clattered onto the desk. The woman was Cynthia James, striking in a white sweater and black skirt.

"Good afternoon, Detective," she said. "Cat got your tongue?"

"Ah, well, no lawyer this time?"

"It's just you and me. Your SCOPE information was helpful, so I'm here to honor my part of the bargain. You have one hour of my time—to question me."

Taylor had expected notice. He called the chief and listened to a short one-sided conversation, adding a few uh-huhs. Placing a hand on his forehead, Taylor calmed himself. When the hand came down, his scowl was replaced by a strained smile. Looking around the bustling squad room, he said, "Let's go somewhere quiet to do this, okay?"

He took the Alexander Gates file out of his drawer then motioned her to follow. After finding an empty interrogation room, he ushered her inside.

"Now you have me where you want me, Detective," she said with an anxious smile.

"Didn't think I'd ever see you again. Especially after I heard Duane Root had been murdered in Boston. He was a man you had us investigate, and now he's dead. Quite a coincidence, no? I suppose you don't think you'll get caught for that one either." He focused his eyes through thick glasses upon her scars.

"I didn't come here about Mr. Root," Cynthia said. "I'm fulfilling my end of our bargain. You provided me with the information I requested, so I've come forward to answer your questions about Alexander Gates. The clock is ticking." She looked at her watch. "Fifty-seven minutes to go."

Taylor opened the folder labeled, "Cynthia James." He read out loud. "Karen Smith. Died in an accident when cannon balls belonging to Alexander Gates cracked her skull on a St. Lawrence cruise boat. Karen Smith was your mother.

"Alexander Gates. Missing along with two cannon balls he bought in Florence, Alabama—missing from his stateroom, a cabin that was just a few feet from where you exercised on the stern at three a.m. A jury will be very interested in the cannon ball connection to your mother." Taylor glared at Cynthia.

"Is there a question, Detective?"

"Yeah. You had motive and no real alibi. The night watchman's schedule left you a twenty minute window of opportunity. So how did you do it?"

"Do what?"

"Murder Alex Gates."

She arched her eyebrows. "Oh, I came here thinking it was a missing person case. If you're questioning me about murder, then you must have found the body, in which case you would have done an autopsy, and you would know the cause of death. Since you would already know *how* it was done, I don't see what I could add."

Taylor stuck the Pentel in his mouth and growled before softening. "Look, Ms. James, I also found out that you were raped by your stepfather and that you killed him to stop him from raping your mother." He paused as if expecting a comment, but she remained silent. Taylor pushed on. "That's quite a trauma to go through as a teenager. The court is always sympathetic in those cases."

The fish didn't bite.

"Ms. James, you said you would cooperate."

"Ask me questions about Alex Gates, and I'll answer, but don't expect a response when you dredge up my stepfather."

After a few moments of frowning, he tried a different form of coercion. "We picked up some interesting things in our SCOPE surveillance. It seems that certain women were stalking victims in Europe. Perhaps you and I could make another deal. I'll not divulge what I've learned about deaths in Spain and England, if you'll tell me what I want to know about Alex Gates."

She covered her surprise by looking Taylor in the eye. "Whether or not your source is reliable and whether or not the so-called evidence will hold up in court, you won't use that."

"And why not?"

"Washington, the press, and the American people would make those women heroines."

Taylor removed his glasses and rubbed his face. She was right. Anyone who eliminated terrorists was a hero. Taylor shook his head. Part of him felt the same way—in matters of national security, sometimes the end justified the means, but he still wanted murderers punished.

"Why did you run when I came to your place in Stanhope?" When Cynthia didn't answer right away, Taylor added, "Don't say you *decided to go for a run*. You saw me through the blinds and jumped off your rear balcony."

"Yes, I recognized you. I was startled...and frightened by a policeman from another state coming to my home. I've read stories of planted evidence. I panicked. I shouldn't have. I'm sorry about that."

"People run when they have something to hide."

Cynthia felt beads of perspiration on her forehead, but she didn't wipe them off. She was glad that Taylor wasn't monitoring her pulse.

Taylor smiled as if he enjoyed watching her sweat. "Perhaps you'd like to take a polygraph test?"

She tried to chuckle. "As you know, a lie detector test is not part of the agreement. I could call my lawyer—"

"That won't be necessary. We have other things to discuss."

After forty minutes, he was still bombarding her with questions.

"What about your mother's death?"

"What about it?"

"Didn't you accuse Mr. Gates of killing your mother?"

"If you'll check my statements to the Canadian police, you'll see that what I said was, Alexander Gates wasn't telling the truth about his romance with my mother, so maybe he wasn't telling the truth about how his cannon balls crushed her skull."

"So you hated him?"

"I distrusted him."

"So you murdered him for revenge?"

She paused. "No. I didn't murder him."

Taylor removed a piece of paper from his folder. "Let me show you something to refresh your memory about that night." He handed Cynthia a copy of the note she had given to Thomas Gates.

Cynthia blinked several times as she read. A cold vise squeezed her chest. She had deceived Thomas, but she still had trouble accepting that he had turned over the note—turned her in.

"So?" she said, handing it back—wishing she had never written it.

"Did you write this?"

"Yes."

"Didn't you give this to Thomas Gates so he would stay in his room while you killed his brother?"

"No."

"Then explain why you would have written such a note and then *not* gone to Thomas's cabin?"

"I changed my mind. I was attracted to Thomas, but when I thought about breaking the company's rule against a relationship with a passenger, I came to my senses."

"Didn't you go to Alex Gates's room instead?"

"No. I was exercising."

Taylor produced a tag clipped to a sheet of paper. "What about this ink swirl on the corner of Alex's bag tag? It matches the one on the note you wrote to Thomas."

Cynthia looked at them, her heart pumping double-time. "They're *similar*."

Taylor slammed down his pen...then counted to ten. "I'm sorry. I could use a glass of water. How about you, Ms. James?"

She looked at her watch. "That would be nice. Thank you."

Taylor left her alone for two minutes, during which she controlled her breathing to settle her heart rate. Knowing she was being watched through a two-way mirror, she moved only to re-cross her legs. Glancing at her watch again, Cynthia did the math—two minutes. Unless he wouldn't let her go.

After Taylor returned with a pitcher of water and poured two plastic cups, he resumed the interrogation. "The dealer in Florence, Alabama, told us that he sold Gates *four* cannon balls, but only *two* were found in the crate. What happened to the other two?"

Cynthia took a sip of water. "I have no idea."

"Come on, Ms. James. Your mother was killed by Alexander Gates's cannon balls, and you just happen to be on a cruise with him where he and two of his cannon balls disappear. That's more than coincidence."

"Is that a question?"

Taylor ground the pen between his teeth, making his next question angry. "Why hasn't there been a single sign of Mr. Gates and his money?"

"I don't know."

"I think you do. I think you murdered him and dumped him in the river."

She tugged at the hem of her skirt. "Your theory is wrong."

Taylor huffed in frustration. "Your denials don't wash. Nobody else but you could have committed this crime."

"What crime?"

"The murder of Alex Gates."

"Are you charging me with murder, Detective?"

Taylor waited until she blinked. "It isn't murder if he tried to rape you." They stared at each other for five seconds before he said, "If Gates…you know. I can see where you might snap. That wouldn't be murder. So, did Alex Gates try to rape you that night?"

"No."

"Did he come on too strong?"

Cynthia hesitated before answering, "No. I didn't see him after he left the bar."

"I know how broken up you were by what happened in Cooperstown. I'm sure your doctors would testify on your behalf concerning the trauma at such a young age. So if—"

"I didn't murder him, Detective."

Taylor sucked on his pen and smiled. "I could make your life miserable."

Cynthia looked him in the eye. "It already is."

After a silent stand-off, she asked, "Are we done here?"

"Yeah. I'm afraid so."

"Then my part of our deal is complete?"

Taylor nodded. The meeting had lasted an hour and three minutes.

Cynthia stood and extended her hand. Before retracting her fingers, she left a folded piece of paper in Taylor's palm. "Goodbye, Detective. I know the way out."

"Goodbye," Taylor said. There was a lingering moment of eye contact before Cynthia exited the interrogation room.

Taylor read the note.

Detective Taylor, Chattanooga has a temporary resident named Abdul Hasan Said, aka Abe Sacks, who currently resides at 1120 Bailey Avenue, Apt. #2B. Since his apartment is filled with explosives, he is a danger to society. —An Anonymous Patriot

Jimmy Taylor smiled as he rolled his Pentel between his lips. He had no doubt that this not-so-anonymous tip would be productive.

36

THE LAW

The country was mesmerized by the Pilar Ibanez case—corporate intrigue, sex, money, power, infidelity, betrayal, murder, and an exotic defendant. Cynthia stayed home to watch the preliminary hearings on Court TV. At the end of the second day, the defense leaked word that there might be a "major development tomorrow." The announcement made Cynthia sweat.

At night, she lay awake, listening for the doorbell or the phone—maybe the authorities would just break down the door. If they came, she wouldn't run this time. She'd play the hand she dealt herself, keeping her hole card covered until the last bluff. Cynthia felt a noose tighten around her neck.

The next morning broke crisp and clear, with autumn leaves floating in the breeze—one of the 25 "ten best days of the year." After an early run, Cynthia cleaned her condo with both TVs blaring so she could listen from every room. There was no word of any new evidence, but the commentators predicted something big was about to break. Sure enough, a press conference was announced for 6:00 p.m. Cynthia vacuumed the carpet over and over, killing time.

At 6:02, the district attorney stepped to a podium covered with microphones on the courthouse steps in Boston. Defense attorney Carolyn Bachman stood with an associate, to the D.A.'s right, two steps behind. Next to the associate was Jerry Paulson.

Paulson's bulk added stability to Pilar's claim of innocence. The press had reported he was paying for the defense, and it appeared to Cynthia as if he were paying with more than money. His face was pale, his eyes recessed and baggy.

The D.A., who looked like a D.A., cleared his throat; the crowd of reporters hushed. "Ladies and gentlemen, due to the late hour, I will make this brief." He glanced at the defense team. "We are pleased to announce that the case of the Commonwealth of Massachusetts versus Pilar Ibanez has been resolved. This afternoon in closed chambers, Ms. Ibanez gave a sworn allocution to Judge O'Brien, admitting to reckless endangerment in the death of Duane Root."

Gasps from the crowd interrupted the statement.

"The Commonwealth is satisfied with her veracity, as well as her remorse. An agreement was reached on sentencing. Ms. Ibanez has received a suspended sentence of three years in—"

Shouts from the press drowned out the D.A.

He held up his hands until there was silence. "This concludes the joint statement. Questions?"

The roar from the press made it impossible for the D.A. to respond. He held up his hands again, then pointed. "Mr. Wood."

A skinny reporter in an ill-fitting sports coat lowered his hand. "In view of the nature of the crime and charges filed, why agree to the lesser felony and suspended sentence?"

The D.A glanced left. "There are extenuating circumstances that we can't go into in public."

"Did Ms. Ibanez agree to testify against others?"

"I can't get into specifics." The D.A. tugged at his tie. "Rest assured that the Commonwealth is satisfied that justice has been served." There was a flurry of follow-up questions, but the D.A. turned to the defense team. "Carolyn, do you want to field a few?"

Looking relieved, the D.A. slipped out of the picture as Bachman stepped forward, her face blocked by a bouquet of microphones. "The defense agrees with the Commonwealth that justice has been served." As soon as she took a breath, the rush of questions resumed. Cynthia saw that Paulson, on the left edge of the picture, swayed, his weight transferring from one foot to the other.

Finally, one voice was heard above the others. "What about all those 'not guilty' statements?"

Bachman waited until Cynthia felt tension in the silence. "The law concerning legal guilt and innocence can be gray. My client's mental state at the time of the incident in question was complicated. All 'not guilty' statements by my client were related to murder charges and are truthful as I interpreted the law with the facts at hand."

"What's the deal?"

Bachman looked to her left. "The law and courts apply the scales of justice to many cases. In conference with other parties about the complex inter-relations between multiple cases, the defense became convinced that a guilty plea on reckless endangerment would serve justice, using a strict interpretation of the law."

"Where's Pilar?"

"My client is hoping the press doesn't reveal where she is, so you'll understand why I won't answer that one."

The skinny reporter shouted above the buzz. "Hey, Jerry! Any comments from the company?"

Bachman looked over her shoulder at Paulson, who stepped forward. Squinting into the TV lights, he displaced Bachman behind the microphones as easily as an NBA center gets rebounding position against a point-guard. "Yes, I'd like to make a statement on behalf of Paulson Electronics."

A voice came from the back of the crowd. "Finally, a straight-shooter." The reporters laughed.

Paulson didn't crack a smile; his jowls drooped like a basset hound's. "Paulson Electronics is saddened by everything about this case. Pilar Ibanez has been a gifted, valued employee for many years. She played an integral part in getting needed products into the market at fair prices. Her legacy at the company will be based on business accomplishments that have benefited the people of this great country in ways they will never know."

Several voices shouted, "What don't we know?"

Bachman tugged at Paulson's elbow, but he shook her off, almost stumbling. He wiped sweat from his brow with a handkerchief. "No, Carolyn, I want to answer."

"Watch it, Jerry." Bachman's whisper was picked up by the microphones.

Paulson steadied himself with both hands on the podium, blinking several times in an attempt to focus. "Pilar Ibanez is a patriot. She—" His eyes glazed, and he couldn't wipe the perspiration off as fast as it seeped onto his forehead.

Cynthia stood and stepped closer to the TV. She knew that look. She'd seen it on the twisted faces of her marks. Jerry Paulson was having a heart attack.

Paulson staggered, knocking over the podium. Bachman and two reporters in the front row tried to catch him, but his bulk was such that the tangle of four people tumbled to the pavement.

The microphones, now on the ground, picked up shuffling and screams. A woman's voice cried, "Somebody call nine-one-one!"

In her living room, Cynthia watched bailiffs rush to Paulson's aid. They pulled him off the two reporters and rolled him onto his back, unbuttoned his shirt, and started CPR. Cynthia's own heart was racing, but it was to her neck that she raised her hand.

* * *

Two days later, Cynthia James opened an envelope that Carolyn Bachman had forwarded.

Dear Cynthia, Congratulations on a flawless frame-up. You were lucky that nobody called me at home that night, but those are the breaks. You should know that the SCOPE evidence implicating me in Root's scheme was fabricated above my level-4 clearance. That's Root or Paulson, so it must have been Paulson, although I wouldn't have thought he could stoop so low. You had no way to know the evidence was planted, so I will try to forgive you.

I had nothing to do with Root's Barcelona betrayal. I'll always regret having tried to handle him myself, to save my career and get control of the company. For ambition, I lay down with garbage, so it's not surprising that I came up smelling like garbage.

Tell Maria she did a great job on your make-up, and I'll bet Joanie was involved, too. Do me one last favor. If Paulson survives, kill him. —Pilar

Upon reading the note, Cynthia's insides churned. After vomiting, she called Maria then Joanie.

They met in a corner booth of Molly Malone's on Route 10.

"So what do you think about the note?" Cynthia asked.

"Pilar had no motive to kill Charisse," Maria said. "Everything we knew about her was positive before the SCOPE stuff."

Joanie asked, "So what do we do?"

"Find out the truth," Cynthia said.

"Then what if she's innocent?" Joanie asked. "What if it's Paulson?"

Cynthia shrugged.

"We can ask Eddie," Maria said. "He's level-four. If Pilar is right about Paulson, Eddie can help."

Cynthia shook her head. "No. Nobody but us. It's for Eddie's own protection. Maria, you have to promise not to tell him anything about this. I know it's hard, but it has to be just us." Cynthia slumped back in her seat, shaking her head. "I've been an idiot. I didn't see that by going after Root, I made everything worse. I thought *my* revenge was sanctioned because I was a fucking patriot."

That night, Cynthia dreamt her usual dream where the skeleton pulls her into the river. She woke in a panic, afraid to go back to sleep.

Sweating, she promised herself that she would find out if Pilar had been set up—and by whom. She also vowed to stop rationalizing evil in service of good.

* * *

"I wondered when I would see you again," Paula Consolasio said to Cynthia as they faced each other in the therapist's office the following morning. After Cynthia shrugged, Paula continued. "Should I ask what your illness was, or would that be wasting my time?"

Cynthia shook her head. "I wasn't sick. But I couldn't talk to you. Now I can."

Paula jotted notes. She said, "I see that you are *not* wearing a turtleneck."

"Can't slip anything past you, can I?"

"Since I know you don't like me to ask, 'How do you feel?' I'll let *you* start, alright?"

Cynthia repositioned herself on the leather chair. "Well, I may be in love with both a man and a woman…. Does that bother you?"

Paula adjusted her sleeve. "Are you concerned about my reactions to what you tell me?"

"What do you thi—" Cynthia shook her head. "Sorry."

"This is about *you*, Cynthia."

"I know. Help me figure this out."

"Alright. But help me understand how you feel. Tell me more about the man and woman…Is the man Thomas?"

"No. His name is David, a former associate from *Patriots for Freedom*. He was there when I needed him, and he sparked intensity that had been missing before the woman…well, it's hard to put into words what she did for me."

"Who is the woman?"

"Maria. She's another associate—even closer…my best friend."

"What did she do for you?"

"I knew I had to love myself before I could love someone else, but I thought self-love and romantic love were totally different. Caring for Maria, I saw how loving myself and loving another were alike. That opened my eyes."

"How are self-love and romantic love alike?"

Cynthia smiled. "We trained together. She was always there when I needed anything. My self-esteem rose to where I respected myself. Self-respect melded into self-admiration. I saw similarities between her and me, and I wanted the same fulfillment for her that I did for myself. That's when I knew I loved her."

"You mentioned intensity."

"Of emotion. I'd do *anything* for her, and that's a good feeling. Very emotional. But not physical...yet."

"Yet?"

"I'm curious."

"About what?"

"Sex, of course. If the emotions are this intense now..."

"Are you seeking intensity?"

"I do keep using the word..." Cynthia blushed. "The sex with David is very intense. More so than with Thomas."

Paula nodded. "So...what about Thomas?"

"We broke up.... Actually, *I* broke up with him over my job. I don't blame him. I just have to learn from it. And before you ask, yes, I got together with David on the rebound, but I've always been fond of him, so there's a good foundation. I think we're much better suited."

"Better suited than you and Maria?"

"Ah, the million-dollar question."

Paula's jaw tightened for a moment. "More intense?"

Cynthia nodded. "I see where you're going. You think I should seek the relationship with more fire—so I won't crave violence."

"No. But it sounds as if maybe *you* think you should try the more intense relationship, and *that's* more important than what I think."

Leaning back in her chair, Cynthia looked up, eyes unfocused.

"Are you bisexual?" Paula asked after Cynthia reestablished eye contact.

Cynthia shook her head slowly. "I'm not sure. Does fantasizing about one woman make me bisexual?"

"Fantasizing about something doesn't make you anything; it's only a fantasy. It's what the fantasy means."

Cynthia shrugged. "So what does it mean?"

"You tell me. Tell me about the fantasy."

Cynthia swallowed. She was a teenager again, facing a therapist who was trying to peel away the scab protecting her scars. She hadn't trusted therapists then, but now...

"I fantasized about kissing Maria—and touching her, and being touched. It was erotic, but once I was aroused, I thought of David pleasing me. Then Maria. Then David. Back-and-forth, like I was cheating on both of them. I forced my mind back to Maria—I wanted to feel what it would be like. In the fantasy, she whispered, "Invite him to join us," and she opened a door. David was standing there—more than willing. We did wicked, erotic, *ménage à trois* things together, and...I did..."

"What did you do?"

Cynthia slouched in her chair. "When I used to masturbate, I would just lie on my back and imagine things. This time, I positioned my body to fit the fantasy. On my back, then on my stomach... kneeling... you know."

Cynthia fanned her flushed face and took a sip of water. Not enough. She took a full drink.

Paula did the same. "You were saying...about positions."

"Play-acting like that seems perverted."

"You say it *seems* perverted. Did it *feel* perverted?"

"I don't know. My whole life may be a perversion."

Paula pursed her lips. "Forget about perversions for a minute. Did the fantasy feel good?"

"Yes."

"How?"

Cynthia smiled. "Let's just say it was all about me. Not like making love for real."

Paula paused, as if her next question was significant. "Why do you think you fantasized about David and Maria together?"

Cynthia scowled.

"Look, Cynthia, whether I say the words or not, my job is to help you answer the tough questions. If it were easy, you wouldn't need my help. I think you've thought about this.... Why do you think you fantasized about them together?"

Cynthia sat forward. "I think it's about healing...and my search for love or maybe intimacy. David and Maria are each like a drug that heals me, so I want to find out if they're more potent when taken together. Yet I'm afraid the combination might be lethal." She brightened. "But also because sometimes it's fun to think about things that'll never happen, and this will *never* happen. Never should." Cynthia shook her head. "I'm really screwed up, aren't I?"

Paula made a noncommittal gesture with her pencil. "Why do you say that?"

"I think about the best people in my life doing something like this—it's like I want to see who wins."

"And who wins?"

"You tell me," Cynthia said.

Paula smiled. "There are no quick solutions. It's like a tangle of bras in the dryer. If you try to separate them with one pull, you only make it worse. You have to start with one end of one bra and see how it twists and turns amid the others—then you trace it out slowly, untying the knots, one at a time."

Cynthia's eyes relaxed. "Some of my bras have been tumbling in that dryer for a long time."

"You're sounding like the therapist. Let's stop the dryer and sort laundry." Paula jotted some notes. "Cynthia, do you ever picture another woman in your fantasies?"

"No. No other woman has ever interested me."

"Interested you, how?"

"Made me curious about lesbian sex."

"What do you think it would be like?"

Cynthia paused. "Maria told me it was like high tide."

Paula nodded. "What do *you* think?"

Cynthia's closed her eyes in a slow-motion blink. "I think it would be smoother than with a man—not as intense as with David. I'd enjoy feeling the exact same things as my partner—real sharing."

"Don't you share with David?"

"We share, but during sex, we experience different sensations. I like that, too."

"Do you think you have to choose Maria or David as a lover?"

Cynthia rocked for a few moments. "Yes.... Yes, I think I do."

"Why?"

"I think I'll have trouble with the complications...you know, like in any triangle. One lover's difficult enough, and I think I can only handle one if I want to be saner."

Paula's praying mantis eyes grew larger. "And do you want to be saner?"

"Yes. That's why I came back to see you." Cynthia peered at Paula as if expecting instant wisdom.

"If you had to choose either David or Maria—today—who would it be?"

Cynthia hesitated. "David. I think."

"Why?"

"Well, it'll be easier, but that's not the real reason. Maria and I will be close no matter what, so I'll never lose her. The thing with David may not work—long term—but I should find out."

Paula made a note then put down her pencil. "You've experienced a lot in your life, some of which has been traumatic. Our work together is going to involve understanding the traumas and finding healthier ways to deal with all them so you can experience happiness and love."

Cynthia forced a smile. "Untangling the bras, right?"

37

SEEDS

An ivy-covered brick wall surrounded the mansion. Cynthia pictured Wrigley Field and thought of her father, a Cub fan who had promised to take her and Sam there when Sam was a little older. An accident had broken that promise, but Cynthia faced this brick wall because she had made a vow to herself.

An armed man buzzed her through the outer gatehouse after her car was scanned for weapons. An intercom voice ordered her out of the car, then a valet drove it away. At the gate of an inner wrought iron fence, another guard frisked her while a German Shepherd sniffed her crotch. Two more guards searched her again in the mammoth foyer of the mansion, inspecting her fingernails and confiscating her handbag, belt, and jewelry.

Paintings hung on every wall. Cynthia was no art expert, but they looked very good—and very expensive. The décor was more tasteful than pompous—a woman's touch.

Sherri Paulson gave Cynthia a cool reception in the upstairs hall, but when Cynthia approached Jerry Paulson, he smiled as he labored to sit up in bed. "You're a sight for sore eyes. You did a great service for the country. It's a damned shame *Patriots for Freedom* had to end."

Cynthia shrugged. He was either a sincere patriot or a great liar. She wondered if the bigger shame hadn't been the founding of the organization, but she wasn't here to debate the merits of her service. "I feel the same way, Mr. Paulson. Thank you for seeing me."

"It's Jerry."

"Jerry, that's really why I'm here. About the way the Aities program ended."

"Oh? I thought you came to kill me."

Cynthia's eyes widened. She spun around, expecting guards to burst through the door. Nothing.

Paulson coughed. "Relax. I know you're nosing around, trying to connect me to the quadruple murder. I still have my sources." There was a faint twinkle in his tired eyes.

"Then why agree to see me?"

"I respect you, and I like you, Cynthia. And besides, if you tried anything, you'd never get out of here alive." He gestured at a security camera in the corner.

Cynthia measured him. Paulson was a wasted shell—nothing like the man she had met in New York. She reminded herself that his current health had no bearing on guilt or innocence. "About how the program came to an end?" she said.

"Horrible business," he wheezed. "Sit down. What do you want to know?"

She pulled a chair next to his bed. "I'll be brief. At the time of her arrest, did you think Pilar Ibanez was guilty?"

Paulson adjusted his pillow. "At first, I couldn't believe it was possible, but after she pleaded out..."

"You paid her legal bills."

Paulson lowered his chin an inch. "I was protecting the interests of the company and respecting what she had done for us."

"So you think she's guilty?"

"The evidence was overwhelming. She was damn lucky she didn't go to jail for years."

Cynthia thought about her phrasing. "Assuming for a moment that Pilar was innocent, who could have planted the evidence against her?"

Paulson coughed. Cynthia feared the interview was over, but he revived after a few shallow breaths. "Since evidence was picked up by a level-three user, an alteration could only be an inside job, done by someone with level-four or five. It wasn't me. If it had been anyone using level-four, I would have known."

"Uh-huh."

"I had Eddie scan everything on every log. That means it was a legitimate level-three find. The evidence damned both Ibanez and Root, so it couldn't have been Root. That doesn't leave anyone else. The evidence had to be legitimate."

"It's hard to believe Pilar would leave memos of her involvement lying around."

"She wouldn't. Some of the evidence was audio, and on the rest...well, if anyone had shown a piece of paper to someone at the company—anyone who had a handheld level-three scanner—then the person could have scanned it as easy as passing a wand over a page."

"Is that likely?"

"It's possible."

"What if it *was* Root? What if he had fabricated evidence against Pilar—as insurance. Couldn't he have planned to release the false documentation to bring her down with him if things went south?"

"Highly unlikely."

Cynthia tapped her fingers on her knee. "What if Root had his ace-in-the-hole stashed somewhere hidden, on some kind of time-release, so that if he wasn't around to stop it, the information could appear and be discovered? Or, could someone else have released it after he died?"

Paulson's voice was agitated. "That would take level-five clearance. Root's security codes haven't been used since his death, which leaves me, and I didn't do it. The only other level-fives now are Juarez and the new security chief, and they didn't get it until later."

"Okay, Jerry. I'll admit that you had nothing to gain and everything to lose. I just want to find out what happened. This seems like something that can't be explained, so maybe there's some sort of black hole."

Paulson managed a painful laugh. "You're a smart girl, Cynthia, but you'd have to be a genius to come up with a black hole in SCOPE."

Shaking her head, she said, "I hope you recover completely and find new dragons to slay."

He tapped the side of his head. "Ah, well, there's more than one way to slay a dragon."

Sherri Paulson entered the bedroom and ended the interview, but Paulson had planted a disturbing seed.

* * *

Cynthia drove from Paulson's mansion to David's cottage in the Poconos. Pulling into the driveway at dusk, she smelled a fire and saw his motorcycle—plus Eddie Juarez's car. "So much for a romantic getaway," she said to herself, unloading groceries. She would have to go out for more food.

Inside, Cynthia spied gun cases in the mudroom—it would be a macho weekend for the boys. There were new recipes she wanted to try, so she would make the best of things.

After a sensual hello kiss, David was full of explanations. "Eddie's weekend plans fell through, so I invited him up. This is a way I can thank him for the bodyguard job. Hope you don't mind."

"Not at all," she said, her mind on ingredients. What were the odds David had capers?

"If you had a cell, I could have told you. Anyway, Maria picked up extra food."

"Maria?" Cynthia flinched. She wasn't sure if she was happy or apprehensive. When Maria entered the living room, Cynthia smiled from the inside out.

Put two couples together and the men will find a way to let the women prepare dinner. David and Eddie cleaned shotguns in front of the hearth, while Maria questioned Cynthia as they chopped vegetables in the kitchen. "So, what did Paulson say?"

Cynthia leaned over the counter to make sure the men were out of hearing range. "Not much," she whispered. "We'll talk about it later." In conversational tone, she said, "I was surprised to see you two."

The smile that spread over Maria's face was the kind that not only lit up a room, but decorated it. "Hey, when Eddie says, 'Let's go,' I say, 'Where?' He loves this club—says he wants to pump David about joining."

"You're gonna marry him, aren't you?"

Maria colored. "If he asks."

Cynthia stopped whatever her hands had been doing. Dinner seemed trivial. "He'd be crazy not to."

David interrupted the moment, getting two beers from the fridge. "You ladies want anything?"

"We're fine," they said with matching smiles.

After David returned to the couch, Maria said, "He's a keeper, you know."

"I know."

Maria brushed Cynthia's knuckles. "Whatever happens, you and I are bonded for life."

Cynthia enjoyed the goose-bumps. She cleared her throat. "I should have told you before that I lo..."

"I know you do," Maria said. "I love you, too."

They hugged. "Thanks," Cynthia said, "It's nice to know."

Later, after dinner, wine, cleanup, wine, Hearts, wine, table-talk, wine, and more wine, Cynthia and David staggered to his bedroom. Their love-making was deliciously sloppy, nakedly intimate. In the sweaty afterglow, David said, "I've loved you since the day we met."

"It's nice to know," she said, feeling doubly blessed. Twice, in a few hours, and she meant it both times.

38

LUNCH

Pilar hosted an Aities' reunion luncheon on November 18th, Charisse White's birthday. All three attended because of the date's significance—that and their curiosity about what Pilar had said during plea-bargaining. When Cynthia, Joanie, and Maria arrived at Pilar's country house in a hired van, the hostess led them to the living room. A fire burned in the stone fireplace, warming the house with the aroma of burning oak, but the atmosphere was chilly. Pilar appeared pleasant enough, but the tension was such that Cynthia had trouble breathing until a glance from Maria dissolved the stress.

The house would have made a great photo spread for *Country Living*. The dining room table was set with stoneware and a floral centerpiece. Two male Brazilians prepared a meal that looked better than it tasted. All through the lunch, Cynthia checked to make sure her watch was still working. Half-way through the entrée, Pilar's smile began to look sincere, an observation Cynthia chalked up to the wine. Joanie dominated the conversation—nothing new there—talking about her impending move to Arizona to take a job as a telephone troubleshooter. "The wind's changed," Joanie said. "Just like in *Mary Poppins*. Time to move on."

By dessert, Cynthia's anxiety had eased, but she wasn't having fun. Maria forced a polite smile; Joanie—talked out—tried not to look bored. Pilar said, "I'm sure you wondered why I *really* asked you here."

Cynthia blinked, activating her antennae.

Pilar raised an eyebrow. "I thought that would perk you up."

Cynthia held her breath.

Pillar paused, savoring the moment. "Not to worry."

Cynthia exhaled.

"I didn't say a word about the Aities—not concerning patriotic missions and not concerning the frame-up." Pilar didn't have to say what frame-up. "I didn't say a word about anyone, but I threatened to say plenty. The Feds know I know about government officials who looked the other way while *Patriots for Freedom* broke international laws. They want everything to stay nice and quiet. And they recognize what we did for the country. They slapped my wrist so I *wouldn't* talk."

The words were reassuring, but Cynthia wasn't assured. There was a coiled energy to the way Pilar moved and spoke that wasn't right for the occasion. Maria sensed it too; she touched Cynthia's watch and mouthed, "Thirty minutes." Cynthia covered her laugh.

Pilar stood and said, "Let's adjourn to the living room for dessert." Her stride was confident. Cynthia followed—she'd seen the cheesecake.

After they were settled in chairs around the fireplace, Pilar poured coffee and tea, a flushed smile on her face. "Charisse wouldn't want the long faces."

Maria and Joanie made harmless replies while Cynthia wondered where Pilar got the gall to act as if she had been Charisse's friend. Pilar may have supervised the Aities from afar, but she hadn't known Charisse. In fact, Charisse would have been entertained by the tension that poisoned the party. That thought brought a smile to Cynthia's lips. She could gut out another half-hour. In the meantime, she sipped tea and pondered what the Aities would joke about on the drive home. Probably the food, décor, and awkward atmosphere.

"Let's play Truth or Dare?" Pilar said after topping off the cups.

Cynthia kept her groan to herself, but not Joanie.

Pilar flashed her eyes. "So, tough assassins are afraid of a little personal revelation."

Joanie bit. "Aities aren't afraid of anything."

"Then truth or dare?"

Joanie fluffed her hair. "Truth."

"What's your best physical feature? No false modesty allowed. What is it for you, Joanie?"

Arching her back, Joanie said, "You have to ask?"

Joanie's bust cut the tension, and Cynthia chuckled along with the others.

"Maria?" Pilar said. "Your best feature."

Maria blushed. "My eyes, I guess."

"And Cynthia?" Pilar asked, completing the circle.

Cynthia was light-headed. With a twinkle, she said, "Everyone says it's my midriff, but I think it's my tush."

Joanie feigned shock. "Such language!"

Maria shared a smile with Cynthia before setting down her teacup. "This tea is great. May I have more, please?"

"Sure," Pilar said.

"What about you?" Joanie asked Pilar. "What's your best feature?"

Pilar stood. "Oh, I'm not in your league, but I suppose it's my legs." She leaned over to pour Maria another cup, flashing her calves in front of Cynthia. Then she tossed a few logs on the fire while her guests relaxed with their hot drinks—

—which had been drugged with Rohypnol.

Cynthia's eyelids wanted to close. She shook her head clear, but her chin drooped onto her shoulder. Joanie's eyes were closed. Where was Maria? Cynthia couldn't get her eyes to roll right. All she saw was Pilar flopped in an armchair. Where was the cheesecake?

When her guests were unconscious, Pilar stripped off the mask of fatigue. Standing, she called in Portuguese, "Doctor, it's time."

The two Brazilians came in from the kitchen wheeling stretchers that had been hidden in the catering van. After the doctor administered morphine injections to Maria and Joanie, Pilar and the second man muscled the two unconscious women onto stretchers and bound them to the side bars. The doctor moved on to Cynthia, setting up a dual syringe line, injecting a reversal agent for the Rohypnol, as well as Versed and sodium pentothal. Taking Cynthia's vital signs, the doctor adjusted the balance of drugs until Cynthia relaxed to the edge of consciousness. His job was to keep her alert enough to comprehend questions but unable to know the significance of her answers. In his skilled hands, the drug mixture was close to truth serum.

Pilar sat down and patted Cynthia's hand. "Wake up, honey."

"Ohhh. My name's Cynthia, not honey."

Glancing at the doctor, Pilar saw his nod. "Good girl. Open your eyes. Do you know who I am?"

"Pi-lar." Cynthia's eyes were vacant, her voice flat.

"Very good." Pilar spoke slowly. "Can you tell me who killed Duane Root? Concentrate, Cynthia. Did you kill Duane Root?"

"Yes."

"That's a good girl. Who helped you?"

"Maria."

"How did Maria help?"

"Make-up. She's good. Did she do yours? You look pretty."

"Thank you. But why did she do your make-up when you killed Root?"

"She made me look…like you," Cynthia slurred.

"Why did she make you look like me?" Pilar asked.

"So...so it would look like...you killed Root." The doctor made an adjustment to the drugs.

"Did anyone else help you?"

"What?"

Nothing for ten seconds. The doctor added a touch of stimulant.

Pilar nudged Cynthia. "Did Joanie help, too?"

"Yes. She stole clothes...blocked the phone...blocked..."

"What else?"

"Put clothes back. Fixed the phone. Fixed computer."

"Did anyone else help?"

"No."

"One more question, Cynthia. It's important. Do you understand? It's very important."

"Yes. Important."

"Why did you frame me for the murder?"

"Because you had Charisse killed."

"You know that's not true, don't you?"

Cynthia said nothing and looked at Pilar with glazed eyes.

"Do you know who planted the evidence that made you think I was responsible for Charisse?"

"What?"

"Who made it look like it was my fault?"

"Eddie," Cynthia said.

"You mean Jerry Paulson, don't you?"

"Eddie."

Pilar shook Cynthia's shoulders. "Are you sure it wasn't Paulson?"

"No. Eddie."

"Ah, Eddie," Pilar said, letting go of Cynthia. "Yes. Eddie. I underestimated him. I knew he had the brains, but I never thought he had the balls. You're a good girl, Cynthia." Pilar laid Cynthia down on the couch and rubbed her temple. The doctor removed the stimulant from Cynthia's line and replaced it with morphine.

Pilar spoke Portuguese to the second man. "Jorge, remove her pants and get her onto the third stretcher." Pilar splashed water onto her flushed face from a bucket that one of the men had carried in. Thinking more clearly, she commanded, "Doctor, get the branding iron ready. Start with the blonde. Remember, watch the temperature. Second-degree burns. The upper inside of her left breast."

Donning heavy cooking mittens, the doctor nodded and removed the iron from the fire. The red-hot end had a circular circumference two inches in diameter, with the branding surface one-eighth inch wide. Inside the circle was a one-inch high "80." The iron hissed like a pressure valve when dipped in the bucket. Using a thermometer, the doctor checked the temperature and re-submerged the iron until he was satisfied.

While the doctor prepared the brand, Pilar unzipped Joanie's sweater, unhooked the bra, and pointed. Jorge swabbed antiseptic on the skin.

"Ready? Jorge, hold her."

While Pilar and Jorge held Joanie, the doctor lowered the brand onto Joanie's chest. *Ssss*—the sound of a match dipped in water. Joanie's body quivered as the iron seared on the circle-80 brand.

Pilar motioned at the wound. "Jorge." Jorge placed a sterile dressing that had been dipped in antibiotic ointment and Silvadene onto the wound. The doctor and Pilar moved on to Maria. The doctor reheated and re-cooled the branding iron while Pilar injected four needles of Novocain into her own thigh.

The swabbing procedure was repeated on the right side of Maria's face.

"On the cheek, away from the eye, and miss the mouth and ear. Lower, by the jaw line. Down a bit. There. Do this one a little lighter."

Ssss. The iron burned a red circle-80 into Maria's face. Again, Jorge applied dressings to the wound with Silvadene.

The branding procedures were repeated with Cynthia. Pilar's eyes glowed as she instructed. "Make sure her burns are worse." The iron burned two brands into Cynthia's skin, one high on the side of her right buttocks, and one on the right side of her abdomen, each causing her to writhe like a worm.

While Jorge attended to Cynthia's wounds with Silvadene, Pilar removed her own pantyhose and lay down on the couch where she swabbed her lower thigh. When Jorge was done treating Cynthia's burns, Pilar directed, "Jorge, hold me. Doctor, make mine lighter, just above the knee."

Despite the Novocain, Pilar grunted when the brand singed her skin. As Jorge spread Silvadene on her burn, Pilar gritted her teeth and waited for the doctor to administer reviving shots to the other women.

Maria and Joanie regained consciousness first. Maria was lethargic, but Joanie had to be gagged to stop a stream of profanity that erupted as soon as she felt bonds on her limbs. It was another fifteen minutes before Cynthia was lucid. Pilar dismissed the doctor and Jorge before she stepped onto the raised hearth so the women could see her from their stretchers. With the fire back-lighting Pilar's red skirt, Cynthia thought she was viewing the Devil.

"Ladies," Pilar began, "When you murdered Duane Root, I took the fall to protect you. The price for my silence has been paid today. We've all been branded with an eighty to unite us."

"It is our own self-proclaimed best feature that has been branded. Joanie, you have one burned into your breast. Every time you think about wearing a low cut sweater, you'll be reminded of your part in the crime.

"Maria, I'm sorry, but for you it had to be the face—close to your eyes. I had the doctor go a little lighter on you because of the location. You'll see your punishment every time you look in the mirror to apply make-up.

"Cynthia, since you did the actual deed, you received two brands, one on your abdomen and one on your buttocks. They're both on the right side so you can lie on your left during recovery.

"My burn is on my leg, of course—my thigh."

Scanning the patients' eyes, Pilar saw fire in Joanie's, tears in Maria's, and dullness in Cynthia's.

"Your anesthetics and burns were applied by a leading anesthesiologist from Brazil. He was assisted by a registered burn nurse. Everything was done with safety and sanitation in mind, but second-degree burns are serious. You'll never have felt such pain as in the first few days. We'll leave you with a supply of dressings, Silvadene cream—to keep the burn moist—and a selection of pain-killers, and I strongly suggest that you consult a burn specialist.

"You each will need to be fitted for prescription stockings to allow the smoothest possible healing. I'm leaving you the names of top doctors at St. Barnabas Burn Center in Livingston.

"I'll be around because of my plea-bargain terms. If you care to retaliate, you'll know where to find me, but I suggest you accept the punishment I devised. Justice has been served today; all debts have been paid in full."

The three women were still groggy. Tears leaked from Maria's eyes. Cynthia remained silent, while Joanie gargled something into her gag. Stepping off the hearth, Pilar asked, "Will you behave?"

Joanie nodded. When the gag came out, Joanie spat, "You friggin' bitch! If any of us don't heal, I'll track you down and pull your intestines out your friggin' cunt!"

Pilar glowered. "Don't bait me."

"You friggin' Brazilian bitch!"

Pilar stuffed the gag back into Joanie's mouth. "I said the same thing about you, only you were the *blonde* bitch. I was bitter when you turned on me. Now, all accounts are squared.

"In your shoes, I might have done the same thing to avenge Charisse. I hated you, but I respected you. Now, I'm moving on. We all have to move on.

"I'll swear the group branding was a *Patriots for Freedom* sisterhood thing. If you say otherwise, I'll go to the authorities and finger you for those unsolved European murders—with documentation, of course.

"Doctor! It's time," she called to the other room. "One more thing, ladies. Because of Cynthia's cooperation, there was no need for torture.

"Now, the doctor will sedate you. After your vital signs are stable, we'll untie you and head for the airport in the catering van to get these men back to Brazil. We're leaving the rented van for you to drive home. The keys are on the coffee table. There's Silvadene and various pain-killers and dressings, with instructions. You should wake up in about two hours. You'll have your pocketbooks, personal possessions, and cell phones."

That was the last Cynthia heard before going under.

Joanie woke before the others. The first thing she did was inspect her breast bandage, flinching—the morphine was wearing off. She tried to stand but staggered and fell with a groan. Dizzy and swearing at the pain in her chest, Joanie crawled to Maria and kissed her forehead. When Maria squirmed at the touch, Joanie held her so that Maria wouldn't try to get up before she was ready.

"Maria?" Cynthia groaned.

"She's okay," Joanie answered. "You?"

Cynthia started to stretch, but cringed as if stabbed. "My stomach hurts like a bitch. And my ass."

"It's the brands."

"Shit. I'd hoped it was a dream." Cynthia toppled over and cried when her rear touched the couch. She was cold, wearing only panties below the waist. Looking around, she saw her pants folded on a chair. Cynthia forced herself off the couch, stood, and limped away. She returned wearing Pilar's bathrobe and carrying a glass of water. "Jeez, just going to the bathroom was a problem. If I'd had on pants, I couldn't have done it."

She and Joanie helped Maria into a chair before they all gulped from Cynthia's glass, Maria taking hers through a straw. Grimacing, Cynthia limped to the kitchen again, this time returning with a pitcher, three glasses, and cheesecake on a tray. Not even Cynthia could get down more than one bite of dessert. They drank water and struggled to get their bearings. Cynthia stood, leaning on the back of Maria's chair. Feathering her finger over Maria's good cheek, Cynthia muttered, "I screwed up. I trusted her. It's my fault."

"It's not your fault," Joanie said. "When we fried Root, we agreed it was one for all and all for Charisse. It still is. None of us saw this coming. How could we? Pilar's fuckin' crazy."

Probing around her bandage, Maria asked, "How bad is it?"

"I don't know," Cynthia said.

Maria's eyes widened. "Get a mirror and cut this off. I have to see."

Afraid of what they would find, all three were still compelled to look. Carefully, Cynthia removed the tape around the edges of the gauze…then the gauze itself. Maria winced when tiny fibers pulled at the tender wound as if glued, but she gritted through the tears. "Keep going."

When Cynthia finally separated bandage from skin, she and Joanie tried to mask their revulsion. Maria took a handheld mirror from Joanie and opened her eyes. There was a sickening liquidity to the burned skin, which resembled molten lava. Maria sat frozen.

"It'll get better," Joanie soothed. "Burns heal slowly, but they heal. My Mom burned herself with boiling water, and it got better."

"All the way better?"

Joanie sighed. "Pretty close."

"How much time?" Maria whimpered.

"After three years, you could hardly see it."

"Three years! Shit! I'm sorry. I know you got burned, too, but it's my face, for God's sake. My face!" Cynthia held Maria, who leaned her good cheek onto Cynthia's shoulder. "What'll I do?" Maria sobbed.

Joanie dabbed the tears before they reached the wound.

"First thing," Cynthia said, "you cry your guts out, Ree. Then, you get better. You rely on your friends, and you move on. But it's okay to cry first." As she spoke, tears formed in Cynthia's eyes.

"What are we going to tell the guys?" Maria said. "If they know what really happened, they'll kill her."

Joanie huffed. "And the problem with that is…?"

"No," Cynthia said. "No more revenge. We're not Aities anymore. We need to think this through."

"Cyn?" Joanie said. "What did Pilar mean when she said your cooperation saved us from torture?"

"I'm not sure," Cynthia mumbled, turning away from Maria.

39
PLOTS

Eddie Juarez closed the door to Maria's room and rubbed his forehead. "That was disgusting."

"It'll get better," Cynthia said. "The prescription-stocking will help the skin heal smoothly."

Eddie looked at his feet. "I can't take her shaved head."

Cynthia was upset with his tone and took his elbow. "Shhh. Let's go downstairs."

When they got to Cynthia's living room, she said, "The shaved head is so the stocking will fit tight. It's only for a year, and we bought her stylish wigs. You know how Maria is about her looks, so you need to be more supportive."

Eddie shivered. "I don't know if I can handle this."

"What do you mean?"

"I mean, I've got my hands full taking over. SCOPE was discredited. The company's hanging by a thread one step ahead of bankruptcy. I'm the only one who can save it."

"So, what does that have to do with Maria's recovery?"

"I have to focus on Paulson Electronics. I won't have time to nurse a maimed woman."

"Maimed woman! Is that what she is to you?"

Eddie squirmed. "You know what I mean."

"No, I don't!" She stared through him.

"I mean, that while she's getting better, I should devote my time to what I do best. I don't know anything about healing burns."

Cynthia grabbed his wrist. "The burn is the least of her problems. It's the emotional wound we have to worry about. She's very fragile. It's her face." She relaxed her grip. "Maria loves you, and she needs to know that you love her. That means standing by her."

Eddie looked away from her searing eyes. "I can't do it. Not now.

Maybe when it gets better."

Cynthia dug in her nails. "You have to do it."

He yanked his wrist free. "I can't even look at her. I need to get out of here." He raised his hands as if to push past her.

"You can't go," she said, spreading her feet to block his path.

"What?" He laughed with no humor. "Are you going to kill me?"

"No. But somebody else might."

He took a step back. "What does that mean?"

"When I was drugged, I may have told Pilar that you set her up on the Barcelona murders."

Eddie blinked twice. "You're...you're crazy."

"Let's sit and talk, Eddie." Cynthia walked toward the couch, and he followed like a puppy.

After they sat, she said, "At this point, I don't care whether you did or didn't set her up. What matters is that I might have told Pilar. After talking with Paulson, I suspected you had some secret level-six that you used to manipulate evidence. It's the only explanation that makes sense."

Eddie looked at the floor.

"Like I said, I don't care if it's true. But if Pilar thinks it's true...well, she branded us, so there's no telling..."

Eddie wiped sweat with a handkerchief, but more took its place.

Cynthia laid her hand on Eddie's. "There *is* a sixth level, right?"

Eddie resisted at first, but when Cynthia kept hold, he spoke. "You've been a good friend to Maria, and you warned me about Pilar, so I'll tell you the truth. You have to promise to keep it confidential."

Cynthia nodded.

"Level-six was supposed to be a temporary secret. I thought I could out-do Pilar by holding back the sixth level. I always wanted to impress her. With my plan, when I announced a miracle breakthrough, we'd have been able to charge big increases when we bumped every customer up a level of functionality."

"So what happened?"

"Ambition and..."

"What?"

"*NightOwl*."

Cynthia moved her hand toward her throat.

Eddie saw the flinch. "In the process of breaking down the functions of *NightOwl*, I learned how to apply its masking concepts so that level-six SCOPE became invisible.

"I started experimenting. Level-six picked up encrypted messages that Root hadn't told Paulson about—the ones concerning Edward

Smythe being at that estate whenever *NightOwl* codes were altered. *After the fact*, I knew Root had allowed the London mission to proceed under false pretenses. Later, I pieced together why Root wanted the mission to fail—to bring down Paulson. But that was after the disaster in Barcelona.

"Root was hiding his handiwork from Paulson by using a bug that I missed in the security logic. Root was sharp. If I had fixed the bug, he would have known I was on to him.

"I knew that Root had to be stopped, so I decided to use the magic of invisible level-six to alter documents, recordings, and time stamps."

"Why turn against Pilar?" Cynthia asked.

"It's complicated. I'd had a crush on her for years, but she just used me. Suddenly, I saw a chance to eliminate all the people between me and the top. Paulson's heart was shaky—I had all his medical files—so I knew he wouldn't be around the business much longer. Root was guilty as sin, and Pilar aligned with Root instead of me. So, I nailed them both. I never would have let her go to jail. I intended to release further evidence that would finger Root as having created the bogus evidence to implicate her. That would have put Pilar in the clear, but by then, of course, I'd have been in charge.

"Then Pilar murdered Root. Open and shut—or so I thought—so there was no need to correct anything. Convicted murderers get what they deserve." Eddie wiped his brow again. "Pilar called me this morning—invited me to dinner tonight."

Cynthia's nostrils flared. "One fucking day after she burns your girlfriend and you—"

"I didn't say I'd go yet, but—"

Cynthia shot optical daggers at him. "But what?"

"I could wear a wire. I'll meet her. Play up to her. Get her to admit what she did."

"We know what she did."

"Yeah, but you said she would pretend it was a sisterhood thing, right? This way we could get the truth on record—old fashioned tape is admissible in court. We can make her pay for what she did to all three of you."

Cynthia shook her head. "No more revenge."

"Not revenge. Justice…and self-preservation. Stop her before she comes after me."

"What makes you think she won't be coming after you tonight?"

"I'll take precautions." He rose. "I have to call Pilar."

Cynthia stood and clamped onto his wrist again. "Why are you doing this?"

"I may not be capable of helping heal Maria's scars, but I can help put away that whacko."

Cynthia let him go. "Maria's still beautiful. She'll always be beautiful, no matter what. Don't you see that?"

He pursed his lips. "Give me some time—time to get used to it."

"Her healing can't wait. I'll make sure she regains her self-esteem, with or without your help."

Cynthia watched Eddie leave. She would have to do it alone. If only Joanie wasn't moving to Arizona. As soon as Cynthia closed the door, she hurried upstairs, her abdomen and buttock burning with every step.

Cynthia knocked on Maria's door. No answer. She entered anyway.

Wigs were strewn around the room like a teenager's clothes. Maria's eyes were moist and red. She stared in the mirror at her burn and bald head. "I look like a fuckin' Martian." Her shoulders sagged. "I'm sorry. The wigs are really nice. I just…"

"It's okay."

"I know that I'll heal…or I can use makeup, and that it won't look this bad forever…" She sniffled. "Shit. If I just weren't so damn vain."

Cynthia embraced Maria, cheek-to-good-cheek, running one hand over the smooth head as if it were a giant gemstone. "We'll take it day-by-day, Ree. Day-by-day. First, let's put on the stocking, okay? I'll help you."

Maria rolled her eyes. "Oh, boy. Twenty-three hours a day breathing out of holes in an ugly nylon mask that's so tight I can't chew food…and for only a year. Why cry about that?"

"Glad you still have a sense of humor. Ready?"

Maria nodded. Cynthia pulled the stocking tight around Maria's chin and velcroed the seam up the back of her head. They both winced.

* * *

Thirty minutes after getting Eddie's call, Pilar Ibanez was on the firing line at an indoor shooting range. While examining her target, she fondled the heated barrel of a Glock 9-mm. Pilar thought about her loss of reputation—being forced out of Paulson Electronics by the plea-bargain. In hindsight, she never should have partnered with Duane Root. One mistake, plus unbelievably bad luck, and her life was in shambles.

The three women who had framed her had been punished. She assumed her final target would be Jerry Paulson, but Cynthia's confession had included a surprise: Eduardo Juarez, not Paulson, had ruined Pilar's life. This was a break because she didn't have the means to penetrate Paulson's citadel. Eddie, on the other hand, could be reached. She thought about the emerald dress she would wear tonight—how she would seduce Eddie.

Pilar fired off another clip—all bull's-eyes.

Entering the Spanish restaurant, Pilar smelled onions, cloves, garlic, and roasted red peppers—she licked her lips. While Bruce Swenson frisked her in the lobby, she teased him. "Keep going, Bruce. You're getting warmer. A little higher."

When she made her entrance into the dining room, every man in the restaurant was envious of Eduardo Juarez. In preparing for this dinner, she had taken particular care with her make-up.

Juarez stood. "You look marvelous."

"Thank you. I'm so glad you agreed to meet. From your friend's greeting out there, a girl might think you didn't trust her."

The table talk was awkward until Pilar steered the conversation toward their early days at Paulson Electronics. Good memories led to better rapport. During the entrée, she easily deflected Juarez's efforts to incriminate her, so he backed off—temporarily. By dessert, they were discussing personal matters.

"Do you remember how we used to sneak off and have lunch together in the Bunker?" Pilar asked.

Juarez nodded. "I remember. But I'm a little confused. You must have known what I wanted?"

"I knew," she said. "But I was married. I loved my husband and had to respect the commitment."

"So why did you lead me on?"

"It was an ego trip to be coveted by such an intelligent man." After a pause, she murmured, "It still is."

"What do you want?"

She smiled. "I was hoping we might start having lunch together again."

"Why should fidelity be different for me?"

"You're not married, and even if you were, I don't impose my values on others. So if you're still interested, I'm here."

"I'll think about it," Juarez said. "But why did you do that horrible thing to her? If you admire me as much as you say, why?"

"Why did you frame me?"

He blinked. "I don't know what you're talking about."

She remained silent until he looked away, unable to hide his nervous eyes. Satisfied, Pilar said, "I'm sorry. All I ever really wanted was your love."

Eddie shook his head at her gall. "Why did you do it? Burn them?"

She pulled her head back a few inches. "It was a voluntary sisterhood thing, in honor of Charisse White. It was her birthday—"

"Bullshit. Give me the real reason."

Her eyes widened. "I don't know what you mean."

"You need help," he said.

"I need *you*."

He waved to the waiter. "Check, please."

"Eddie, will you please take me home?"

He hesitated, rubbing where the itchy wire was taped to his chest. "Okay."

She smiled, but her happiness was short-lived. Eddie escorted her home with Bruce Swenson sharing the back of the limo. Neither Pilar nor Eddie would get what they wanted.

Pilar flung her purse on the hall table as soon as she slammed her front door. "That prick!" she spat, adding, "That bitch," not because Maria had done anything, but because Juarez had refused to cheat on her. "That bitch! That little Burrito Bitch!"

Even in the presence of the bodyguard, Pilar had thrown herself at Eddie in the limo, placing his hand on her thigh and pressing her torso against his arm, squeezing her breast within an eyelash of popping out of her dress. He had looked but not touched.

Pleading for him to come in for a nightcap, she showed her desperation. Worse than not wanting her, Juarez had pitied her. He kept saying she needed help.

"That fuckin' prick!" In cursing him, Pilar was really berating herself for misjudging Juarez and overestimating her own charms. She looked in the mirror. Sex appeal hadn't been enough to entice Eddie away from a maimed girlfriend. She picked up a cordless phone and fired it at the mirror, splitting the glass into jagged shards.

After calming down, she thought about ways to get even. Branding an "80" onto his head wouldn't be enough anymore, but that was a relief—although she had observed the Portuguese doctor in action, she had been anxious about drugging and branding Juarez herself. Now she had an idea that required help of a different sort than that which Eddie meant. She stooped to retrieve the phone and punched in Josh Eggars's number.

* * *

"I was surprised to hear from you," Eggars said to Pilar as they faced each other in an empty warehouse parking lot the next night. The flat gray of dusk made him look like a film noir character. Tall and lean, he had a hungry look that never went away. The scar curling below his right eye was at home on his craggy face.

"I have a job for you," Pilar told him.

"I'm listening."

"I'm planning retribution for a person who set me up. I'd like you and Hammer to help."

"A contract job?"

"Yes, but mainly backup."

Eggars tilted his head. "You want to make the kill yourself?"

Pilar nodded. "It's personal."

"Don't you think you're out of your league?"

"I've been taking shooting lessons, and anyway, you'll need me to get close to the target. I might as well be useful."

He shrugged. "Who's the mark?"

"Eduardo Juarez."

"The rich electronics big-shot?"

Pilar smiled. "The very same."

"You're crazy, sister. That guy's got security up the ying-yang."

"Not all the time. I know how to get at him when he'll only have one bodyguard."

"Yeah? And how's that?"

"Mr. Juarez has taken a fancy to a Pocono hunting and fishing club. Matching the hatch and all that crap. He goes as a guest of one of his bodyguards, David Smathers. While he's there, he has minimal security."

Eggars licked his lip. "How minimal?"

"The club's a rich man's retreat, so the access road is gated and guarded twenty-four-seven. There are fences at obvious places, but the club has thousands of acres, so there are ways in. I can get us to a remote dirt road that's a two-mile hike through the woods to the Smathers cottage where Juarez stays."

Eggars scratched his chin. "If the place is a club, it must be crawling with people, huh?"

"In season, yes, but the clubhouse shuts down on Labor Day. After that, attendance is sporadic, the staff, reduced. Juarez and Smathers are going up with Smathers's girlfriend the second weekend in December, so the place'll be almost deserted."

Eggars picked at a scab on his knuckle. "What about the woman?"

"Her name is Cynthia James. She's as dangerous as Smathers, so to improve the odds, we'll go into the house when she's not there."

Eggars laughed. "What tells me that you know when that will be?"

"You're catching on. I know everything about them. I may have lost my job, but I still have friends. Cynthia James runs each morning at daybreak. She's a fanatic. After she leaves the house, we'll go in and take out Juarez and Smathers. If we do our job properly—while she's out—we'll never come near her. So, are you interested?"

"Depends on the money."

"Thirty-five for you; thirty for Hammer. I want Hammer because he's the best in the business at kicking in doors. You'll get an extra five for sub-contracting him."

Eggars grinned. "Speaking of Hammer, he has a rifle trained on you. I told him if you tried anything, he should kill you."

Pilar narrowed her eyes. "And I've left a sealed envelope with my lawyer. If anything happens to me, she has instructions to open it. Inside is the evidence that will convict you, Hammer, and your two partners for murdering Charisse White's team."

Eggars looked amused. "A fine working relationship built on mutual distrust." She didn't laugh. He studied her for a moment. "You know, thirty is too little for what you're asking. Fifty is the going rate."

"I think you'll both do it at a discount because of what I know." She leaned against her car and waited.

"Not enough."

"Suit yourself," she said, turning to open her car door. "There are other contract men."

"Wait...work's a little scarce."

"So we have a deal?" When Eggars hesitated, Pilar added, "Here's an advance."

Eggars looked inside the envelope then laughed. "I was afraid you wanted revenge for what happened to your people in Barcelona."

"That's of minimal importance now. Losing my job and reputation has changed my outlook. Anyway, your team did a professional job. I want pros working for *me* now."

Eggars held out his hand. "Deal."

She shook, her eyes glowing like emeralds. "Remember, the James woman goes free and the genius is mine. I'll blow his brains out."

40

THE COTTAGE

Locating reflective trail-markers with a flashlight, Pilar Ibanez led Josh Eggars and Hammer Hardin on a round-about trail through the forest. The route bypassed the Fox Lake security gate and avoided roads. It was 4:00 a.m. Sunday, and Pilar was impatient to be in position outside the Smathers cottage before dawn. It was cold, and Pilar walked briskly to keep her blood pumping. She paused to locate the next trail marker then tugged the zipper on her leather jacket before moving on.

Pilar had scouted the trail personally, but she had never walked it at night. In the dark, all the trees and rock formations looked alike; she wandered off the path several times. The men were convinced they were lost, but Pilar kept leading them east, and they reached the house on schedule. Huddling out of earshot from the cottage, they waited for the sunrise.

Cynthia's alarm went off with a series of shrill buzzes; she slapped the snooze button. The ceiling fan chilled the room the way she liked. It was still dark at 6:30 a.m., so she decided to cuddle for a few snooze cycles. When she pressed her backside into David's thighs, he instinctively wrapped his arms around her, his body warm and reassuring. In his torpor, David slid his hand under her T-shirt, feeling for something soft above a girdle-stocking that squeezed her abdomen and buttocks flat.

When the snooze alarm buzzed for the third time, Cynthia rolled over and kissed David, who tried to pull her back. "After," she whispered. "You know how cranky I get when I miss my run."

He playfully swatted her rear as she got out of bed, drawing a wince.

"Sorry, Cyn. I keep forgetting."

"It's okay. I want to forget, too." She popped three ibuprofens and dressed in the bathroom. It was almost four weeks since the branding, and the pain was minimal. Okay, it still hurt like a bitch, but she told David it was minimal so he would let her run. At least she'd gotten off narcotics after the first week.

"Be sure to take the pager," David reminded her when she crawled onto the bed to kiss him goodbye. "There may be a few hunters, so wear orange." He tried to pull her under the covers, but she wriggled free. "I've loved you since the day we met," he said. She smiled and held his kiss longer than usual. If Cynthia didn't leave now, she'd end up back in bed.

"You're making waffles, remember?" she teased.

"Yeah. Last time I'll ever bet the Sundance Kid in Skeet."

In the mud room, she pulled on thin cotton gloves and an orange ski cap, then an orange vest over her lucky gray sweatshirt. Before going out the door, she picked up a pair of binoculars and the pager, which she clipped to the waistband of her stretch pants. After locking the door, she slipped the key into her sock. Outside, the chill was like a series of pinpricks on her abdomen; she relished the sting. Cool air poured into her lungs.

After stretching, Cynthia jogged for two minutes down trail number one. She spied three deer in the distance. Within a few hours, men with rifles could be stalking these beautiful creatures. She stopped and focused her binoculars, watching them browse for a minute. "Get away! Shoo!" They spooked, bounding toward safety—she hoped.

David tossed in bed, knowing he wouldn't be able to get back to sleep. He might as well get up and make the waffle batter. Then he'd be free to enjoy Cynthia's charms when she returned—and still get breakfast on the table by nine.

Eddie Juarez docked the pay of any bodyguard he caught without a weapon, so David picked up his pager, put his shoulder holster on over his T-shirt, then sweatpants over his gym shorts. Knowing it would be cold, he donned a bathrobe and slippers before shuffling to the kitchen.

The three hunters stalking Eduardo Juarez had watched Cynthia's departure. When she had been gone for two minutes, they pulled down their ski masks. Tiny vapor clouds shot from their mouths as they crept over the forest floor, leaves crunching underfoot. Pilar gave hand-signals, and they made their final approach from the garage side, keeping out of window sightlines. Carrying walkie-talkies and pistols equipped with silencers, they closed in on the house, Pilar and Hammer toward the main door, with Eggars moving in on the screened porch.

Eggars crouched, reviewing the floor plan in his head. When he heard the first noise, he would break through the screen door and crawl across the porch. Juarez's bedroom window would be on his left. Eggars would smash through the French doors and enter the living room, looking toward Smathers's bedroom door off the far side of the house. Eggars held his foot to keep it from tapping.

On the other side of the house, Hammer crawled below the kitchen window, across a narrow porch connecting the garage to the front door. Pilar followed him. He was nimble for his bulk. The kitchen light came on, surprising him and Pilar. Hammer peeked through the glass and saw David standing, back to the door, looking inside the refrigerator. Hammer and Pilar exchanged hand signals until she tapped her watch and pointed three times at the door. Hammer silently worked open the storm door's latch then positioned his feet. He raised one leg and eased open the storm door just enough to ram his foot through the main door.

He splintered the jamb around the lock with one driving kick. The door swung open. Hammer leveled his weapon at David's back.

Hearing the crack behind him, David crouched and spun, drawing his piece in the process. Armed with Kevlar-piercing bullets, he aimed for the center of the chest.

Hammer's first silent shot went over David's ducking shoulder; the second went into the ceiling because David had fired two quick rounds into Hammer's chest. David's gunshots reverberated through the house. The heap at the bottom of the doorway was Hammer, his right leg twitching.

"Eddie! Lock the door!" David yelled, looking for more attackers. He slapped his hand at the emergency button on the pager clipped to his sweatpants. Staying low he moved two steps toward Hammer's body.

Pilar crouched, below the kitchen window three feet from Hammer, still hidden from David's view. David's gunshots had startled her. When Hammer's head bounced off the stone floor of the porch, she froze, heart pounding.

While Pilar considered what to do, Eggars reacted to the shots by banging open the porch door then kicking in the French doors to the living room. David turned and fired toward Eggars. At the sound of a shot and breaking glass, Pilar stepped into the doorway, straddling Hammer's body. She aimed with two hands and delivered three silenced rounds into the center of David's back.

He pitched forward onto the tiled kitchen floor.

Eggars and Pilar converged on the door to Juarez's bedroom. As Pilar walked by David's body, she fired an insurance round into his skull.

Eggars saw Hammer down and stepped toward him, but Pilar grabbed his collar. "Leave him," she hissed. "We have to get Juarez!" With two emeralds shining through the black ski mask, Pilar was a deranged alien.

Eggars kicked in the bedroom door. Eddie Juarez fired out. He didn't hit anything, but his shots made the assailants dive away from the door, one to each side. For a few seconds, all were motionless, listening, before Eddie called, "David?"

"Your bodyguard's dead," Eggars shouted back. "Give it up!"

Pilar made some hand signals, but Eggars shook his head. So Pilar dove from the right side of the open door to the left, drawing a wild round from Eddie.

"Shut up and listen," Pilar whispered. "He's in the left corner, behind the bed. Get to the porch; stay low and break the picture window. When he reacts, I'll shoot him from the doorway."

Eggars slithered onto the porch. Pilar stood to the left of the open bedroom door, waiting for the sound of breaking glass, her heart hammering.

What the hell was keeping Eggars, Pilar thought.

It seemed an eternity before she heard the window shatter. At the crash, she stepped into the bedroom doorway. Juarez had taken the bait, turning away from the door, his head and shoulders clearly visible. Pilar fired three times with her Glock, hitting Juarez in the chest, neck, and shoulder. Pilar walked to Juarez's body and put two insurance slugs into Eddie's brain.

She picked up shell casings on her way to the front door where Eggars knelt by Hammer's body. She shoved Eggars's shoulder. "Leave him. He's dead."

"We can't leave him. He's a link to me."

"That's your problem. He's too heavy."

"We could take their car."

"We'd never get past the gate," Pilar snarled. "We go back the way we came, by trails. Let's go!"

Pilar tugged at Eggars's collar, but he remained kneeling and yanked off his ski mask. "I think he's breathing," Eggars said, feeling for a pulse.

She shook her head at Eggars's futility. She aimed and fired a bullet into Hammer's head, splattering blood into Eggar's face. "*Now* he's dead." Pilar just saved $15,000.

Cynthia had heard what sounded like gunshots seconds before David's page vibrated on her hip. She turned and sprinted toward the cottage. Knowing that she should keep adrenaline in check, she didn't run as fast as she could. Her abdomen and buttock throbbed, but she ran on.

Moments later, she heard two more shots from the direction of the cottage, then a few seconds later, another shot. Her legs burned and her lungs begged for oxygen, but she ran faster.

Cynthia climbed the last of the stone steps that rose from a boggy ravine to the ledge where the cottage looked over the lake. She saw that the picture window between the guest bedroom and the screen porch was shattered. She moved low across the stone floor to the splintered French doors. She heard voices—a man and a woman arguing.

Overcoming fear, Cynthia peeked inside and saw David lying face down on the floor, his blood forming a shiny pool on the tile. Her guts burned in an instant, leaving ashes.

She saw black-garbed people tangled in the doorway on the far side of David's body. Two people were moving—one with a ski mask. The one without a mask looked as if he had red war paint smeared on his face. He aimed a gun at Cynthia's head. She pulled back a split-second before a bullet splintered the molding inches from her ear.

She scrambled back across the porch and bolted for the trail. Taking the stone steps six at a bound, she tumbled in a crash-landing at the bottom and forward-rolled onto her feet.

"Shit! She saw my face," Eggars said after firing at Cynthia's head. "We have to get her."

Eggars pursued Cynthia out the porch door, gun in hand. Pilar took Eggars's shell casing and jammed Hammer's gun into the back of her belt before following, thinking that at least they would be heading in the right direction. "Keep your walkie-talkie on," Pilar called to Eggars.

Heading west on trail number one, Cynthia called on her adrenaline. She would stick to the trail until a fork 200 yards ahead. Cynthia looked back. One assassin was gaining on her; it was the man with war paint. Tiring quickly, Cynthia gauged that she had a minute or so before the man caught her. Her orange vest made a distinctive target, but she made no effort to remove it.

Thud. A bullet sent bark chips flying into her right cheek. The man had to have stopped to aim, giving Cynthia a few more seconds. She had to use those seconds wisely.

Back in her old neighborhood games of guns, Mike Jones had been the best at setting ambushes. She wondered…in her predicament, what would Mike do?

The winding trail and density of trees kept trunks between Cynthia and her pursuer. She sprinted over a steep rise without drawing a shot. The fork was a few strides ahead. Because of the rise, Cynthia would be out of sight when she made her decision. Knowing the terrain, she went right, onto the secondary trail away from the clubhouse. It had more turns and changes in elevation. If the man went left, a rocky ridge between the trails would block her from his vision. Still running, she looked back when she reached the end of the only straight section of trail. Nothing. The man had taken the left-hand path, but the slower runner might go right. As her heart pounded and thighs burned, Cynthia decided on a plan but had to find the right tree quickly—her muscles were cramping.

Mike Jones had taught her that people rarely look up, so Cynthia would climb a tree, but none of the mature trees had branches low enough. She would have to find a double-trunked tree with the right orientation. If her memory was accurate, there was one that might do around the next bend. Too tired to wait for something better, she flipped the binoculars to her back and made a running jump.

She shimmied, clawed, and wedged her way skyward, scraping skin on the jagged bark. She scrambled up ten feet without hearing shouts or footsteps. Wedged in the "V," she braced her back against one trunk, her feet against the other. Her thighs burned the way they did taking the moguls down Cascade at Killington. While her chest heaved, she waited for one of the killers to pass under her tree.

Out of respect, Pilar wanted Cynthia to get away. Better still, Cynthia would kill Eggars, thereby saving another $17,500. That thought put Pilar on full alert as she made her way toward the car. Scanning both sides of the trail, Pilar squinted through the ski mask, Glock at the ready. Walking quickly, she concentrated on tree trunks and boulders near the trail. Pilar wouldn't remove the itchy mask until she was in the car. At her current pace, that would be 45 minutes. If Eggars didn't catch up by then, Pilar would leave without him.

Cynthia's wait in the tree was less than a minute. She heard footsteps—walking not running—then a woman's muffled voice. "I'm maybe two hundred yards past the fork. Let her go. Talk to me! Over."

The man's voice responded, but Cynthia couldn't make out the crackling words. She held her breath so strained panting wouldn't give her position away. Her lungs craved oxygen and heaved in spastic lurches. Cynthia heard feet swishing through leaves under the tree. There would be one chance.

Cynthia gauged the lead and jumped, although her descent was more like a fall from her awkward position. Her foot scraped bark in pushing away from the tree, and the woman below flinched at the noise but had no time to move.

Cynthia kicked at the back of the woman's head, making solid contact, and fell hard on her left elbow and hip. The masked woman was down, her groan muffled in the leaves; she was woozy but not out. Coming to her knees, the woman shook her head and ripped off the ski mask. Even from behind, Cynthia knew who it was. Pilar groped through the leaves for her gun before remembering Hammer's in her belt. She straightened her waist and reached behind for the gun.

Cynthia lunged at Pilar's back.

Eggars's walkie-talkie crackled; the voice from Pilar's unit was faint. "She's dead, but I'm hurt. Get over here and help me. Over."

Eggars frowned. He had heard no gunshots. Then he remembered their silencers. "On my way. Over." Eggars moved at an easy trot, back to the fork and then toward his partner in crime. When he recognized Pilar's jacket and ski mask, he slowed for a moment. He waved from fifty yards and trotted on. Cynthia's orange cap and vest were visible in the carpet of leaves. He slowed to walk the last few yards, looking at Pilar where she leaned against a tree, staring at the body. Eggars laughed—the brightly-colored vest was supposed to *protect* the wearer from hunters. He stopped and looked down at the body.

Eggars was saying, "Don't you think it's ironic that—" when the woman raised a gun with both arms. *Phut-phut.* Eggars's last thought was that Pilar had betrayed him.

There was silence. Two corpses lay at Cynthia's feet. After a few seconds, she pulled off the ski mask.

She felt numb as she rolled Pilar over with her foot to see the wide-eyed death mask. The binoculars' strap was still wrapped around Pilar's throat. Cynthia turned to the man, whose face was nothing but a mangled mass of red. Cynthia was empty—David was lying dead in the house.

Switching clothes was another of Mike Jones's neighborhood tricks. Cynthia would have to track Mike down and thank him. She limped toward the cottage in a fog, sensing that Eddie was dead, as well as David. Aching all over, she wondered if she had any narcotic pain-pills left from the first week after the branding.

With both hips throbbing, the trail was a marathon, the stone steps an Everest.

Eventually, she dragged herself up the last three steps to the porch, and across the stone floor.

Inside the cottage, the grizzly scene was as she feared. Gray matter oozed from David's and Eddie's bloody skulls. No doctor was needed to confirm death. Cynthia sobbed as she knelt by David's head and held his limp hand. She stroked his hair the way a child tries to revive a dead pet. When she looked at her blood-stained hand, it twitched as if controlled by a drunken puppeteer.

She was ashamed for having fled. Her guts rolled and knotted. She lunged to the kitchen sink with a spasm of dry heaves. Mouth open, head hanging, she leaned on her aching elbow and cried.

When she looked out through the window, she saw a man in an orange vest staring at her house, or more particularly, at the body in the doorway. The man saw her through the kitchen window and scurried away. Her body was a mass of pain. She labored to her bathroom and searched futilely for narcotics. She settled for ibuprofen, washing down four with sloppy gulps of tap water. She thought about swallowing the whole bottle, but there were only three pills left—not enough.

The mirror reflected a tormented person.

Two people were responsible for this tragedy. Cynthia forgave Pilar, but not herself. Gathering a semblance of composure, she hobbled to the phone, called 911, then the club manager. She heard conversation outside and pulled up the shade to see the skittish man and two other hunters drawn by the gunshots—or maybe the scent of death. Cynthia limped to the door and told them to stand back. It was a crime scene.

The rest of the day would be full of interviews with the police and phone calls—so many phone calls. Most of them would be emotionless, executed with dull efficiency—to her lawyer, funeral home, church, Paulson Electronics, and others, whose grief could not match her own. But before those calls, she had to make the hardest one of her life. She had to tell Maria that Eddie was dead.

41

JUSTICE

Paula Consolasio's office was stuffy with grief.

"I don't know what to say," Paula admitted when Cynthia finished gutting out the story. "I'm so terribly sorry."

"I've come to a decision," Cynthia said, drying her eyes. "I've concealed something important. When I tell you, you'll be disappointed in me, but you won't be shocked.

"In May last year, a man named Alexander Gates disappeared in Tennessee from the steamboat *Louisiana Lady*. I was a bartender on the cruise, and I flirted with both Alex and his brother Thomas. Yes, *the* Thomas Gates. I've been a suspect and material witness in the missing person case. I lied to the police about that night. I've decided to go back to Tennessee and tell the truth."

"The truth about what?" Paula asked.

Cynthia told her therapist what had happened on the Tennessee River and what she was going to do.

After absorbing Cynthia's plan, Paula asked, "Why now?"

"I need to get this weight off my shoulders. The amnesty for what I did on the river is expiring. I never knew there was a limit, but I got a letter that…well, it's time to be accountable."

When they shook hands in the waiting room, Paula said, "You can call me from Tennessee, if it comes to that… We can work out a phone schedule."

"I'd like that. Now I have to write a letter to Thomas and tell Maria."

* * *

Cynthia forced a smile. "Your hair looks good today," she said to Maria. They were in the condo's kitchen, putting away dishes that afternoon.

Maria patted her wig. "I always wanted a new hairstyle every day."

Cynthia laughed. "It's good to hear you joke. How's the pain?"

"Better. I'm better all around. And your butt and gut?"

"Tolerable."

"At least nobody can see your stockings."

The silence could have been awkward, but Maria's eyes made it comfortable.

Cynthia kissed the stocking over Maria's good cheek. "It's time, Ree."

"Time for what?"

"The truth about Alexander Gates and the Tennessee River. Sit down. We both should sit down." They sat across from each other at the kitchen table. Maria was unable to take her eyes off Cynthia.

Cynthia inhaled as if taking a hit of marijuana. "My mother was young when she had me, and she looked great for any age. She met Alex Gates on a river cruise up the Saint Lawrence a few years ago. It was her first vacation without me—I was finally on my own. She and Alex had an affair. She called me from Montreal, telling me she was in love with a man who had the most wonderful eyes. She described a locket he had given her. The next day, a maid found her body on the bed in his cabin, her head cracked by two cannon balls that rolled off an overhead shelf by accident. At least that's what the Canadian police said."

"Cannon balls?" Maria said.

"Yeah. The Gates family foundation has a collection of artillery ammunition—largest in the world. Alex bought cannon balls whenever he traveled. The ones that killed my mother were from the Battle of Quebec. He said he had them on the shelf because the cabins were so tiny and the shelf was just the right size."

"But you thought otherwise."

"Yeah. But he had an alibi—another woman said he was jogging on shore with her when it happened—but he lied about the locket. When it was found around my mom's neck, he said she must have stolen it."

"What was his motive?"

"I wasn't sure. Mom was a clerk with the SEC, and he was involved in risky hedge funds, so there may have been conflict there, but his only proven offense was that he was a womanizer...." Cynthia lost her train of thought.

"So what happened?" Maria asked.

"I kind of flipped out in a controlled sort of way. I stalked him. A friend of mine discovered his vacation plans when he hit on her—at a Hooters, no less—and I got the bartender job on the *Louisiana Lady* so I could get near him.

"On the cruise, both he and his brother flirted with me; I used their sibling rivalry to... Well, I came on to Alex the last night with the intention of killing him. I had an elaborate plan worked out to crack him in the jaw with one of his precious cannon balls. I figured that would be justice."

Maria leaned forward. "What happened?"

"I gave him a note to lure him outside—asking him to bring two cannon balls. But he had such great eyes—the kind that talked. We kissed in the breezeway at the stern of the boat. It was the first time in ten years I'd been turned on by a man."

Cynthia fanned herself with a napkin. "I couldn't go through with it. I don't know if I lost my nerve, or if I really thought it had been an accident, or if he just charmed the pants off me. Anyway, I was kissing him like there was no tomorrow—ten years of suppressed erotic energy ready to blow. My head was spinning; we lost our balance. I think he tripped over my bag, and the paddlewheel may have hit a log or the bottom—the channel was shallow there.... Whatever, we teetered, and he grabbed me to keep me from falling. I grabbed him and pulled him down. Our feet came out from under us. He rotated under me like...he was protecting me. We fell hard, with me on top of him. There was a thud."

Cynthia jerked her head as if she heard it again. "Our heads banged together. I was knocked out. When I came to, Alex wasn't moving. One of the cannon balls was next to his head. The back of his skull was rounded in. I felt bone fragments. He wasn't breathing. No pulse." Cynthia's eyes glazed; she turned away from Maria. "I couldn't think rationally...but I was thinking—like a criminal. In my plan, I had intended to weigh his body down with cannon balls and dump him into the river. I had two zippered tote bags and electric cords to tie them to his body.

"I should have called for help, but all I could think about was how it would look—me having brought extension cords and the bags. And the cannon balls. I figured I'd be convicted no matter what I said.

"I panicked. There were a hundred things I could have done... should have done... but all I could think about was the plan I had been rehearsing. I had exercised on the bike machine at three a.m. every day to establish a natural pattern. I had lured him out on the deck where the paddlewheel wash would cover any noise. I timed it between the watchman's rounds. I had picked a spot near a gate in the railing." Cynthia wiped away a trickle of tears.

Maria, eyes glistening, moved to the chair next to Cynthia's. "I'm so sorry, Cyn. Are you—"

They hugged. "I was so scared of going to jail, that I started doing what I had planned. I put on gloves and disposed of the body."

Cynthia eased out of the embrace. "I probably would have been caught if the deck crew wasn't so thorough. In the dim light, I couldn't possibly have wiped up every drop of blood, but the crew washed down the deck the way they do every morning so that when the police came on board that evening, they didn't find anything."

"It wasn't murder," Maria said.

"The police wouldn't have believed me."

Maria patted Cynthia's hand. "I believe you."

"Even though you know I'm an assassin?"

Maria nodded. "Even though."

"Do you know why I...?"

"What?"

Cynthia stretched her neck, reaching for a memory. "Thomas tracked me down and accused me of having something to do with his brother's disappearance—he thought Alex was dead. It was like he *knew*, you know?"

"And?"

"And I sold myself...figuratively. I seduced him. It sucked, but I faked it and became his girlfriend so he wouldn't go to the police. In time, I cared enough for him to kid myself into thinking we had a future. When I learned about the amnesty deal, I broke up with him. Then I found David and..."

There was a tense silence. "So what does your future hold now?" Maria's voice was thin and dry, as it had been the first few days after the branding.

"Prison. I'm going to tell the truth to the detective in Chattanooga."

"Why?"

"Peace of mind, I guess, though it won't bring back David or Eddie."

Maria bit her lip. "How will going to jail give you peace of mind? You didn't murder Alex Gates."

"Legally, maybe not, but he'd be alive if I hadn't plotted to kill him. I have to take responsibility for that."

"How much time?"

"My lawyer says anywhere from three years to life."

Maria covered her mouth. Her eyes expanded—almost as big as their holes in the stocking. "What will I do without you?"

"What will I do without *you*?" Cynthia thought of twenty things she wanted to add, but none were right. She tried to smile, but that didn't work either. Maria always knew what to say, so Cynthia waited.

"What about our plans for the school?" Maria finally asked, picking at her nails.

"I can't expect you to wait for me."

"When are you going?"

"Today—this afternoon—right after I call Joanie. I hate to drop this on you, but you're taking me to the airport, not the auto shop."

"Shit," Maria said. "Why didn't you tell me sooner?"

"If I told you before the last minute, we might have slept together for the wrong reasons."

Maria touched her facial stocking. "Even with this?"

Cynthia nodded. "You're beautiful."

Maria's jaw relaxed—almost into a smile.

They held eye contact. Cynthia smelled pine air freshener, heard the ticking of the wall clock, saw Maria's blouse swell every third second, felt her own heart accelerate.

Maria slid her hand across Cynthia's face the way a blind person would. "I want to remember what you feel like, not just what you look like."

Cynthia kissed Maria's finger—an appetizer—and reveled at the connection deep inside, where butterflies fluttered. Maria leaned toward Cynthia, who saw only parted lips, not the stocking that surrounded them. Cynthia closed her eyes and melted.

Their kiss tasted like warm dessert. It was different than kissing a man. Not better—different. Cynthia gently sucked—the same as a drowsy baby.

Nipples hardening, Cynthia knew that Maria was enjoying the same sensation, but neither lifted a hand. Confirmation of the inevitable wouldn't improve the moment. They let the kiss recede like a spent wave, its succulence lingering as moisture does on the sand.

Cynthia licked her lips. The sweetness might have to last for years.

* * *

"Welcome back to Chattanooga." Detective Taylor ushered Cynthia into the coffee room and offered her a chair. "So what's so important that I had to bring a tape recorder?" He thumped the machine onto a rectangular table.

Cynthia lowered herself into a molded plastic chair the way a churchgoer sits in a pew. "I'm here to turn myself in, give a statement."

Taylor blinked, refocusing his eyes. "Come again?"

"I'm here to confess to multiple felonies. You've caught me."

Taylor scratched his head and sat down facing her, elbows on the table. "I don't get the game."

Cynthia pointed at the tape recorder. "Turn that on, okay?"

He measured her as if she were prey. "You're not under arrest so you're not protected by Miran—"

"I know. Anything I say can and will be used against me."

"You could have a lawyer present."

She shook her head. "Turn it on before I lose my nerve."

Taylor pushed "Play" and "Record," half-expecting a lawyer to burst through the door, shouting, "April Fools." Taylor recited the date—December eighteenth—and other boiler plate information. "We're at the Chattanooga Police Station. Present are Ms. Cynthia James and Detective James Taylor. Ms. James?"

Cynthia settled herself in the chair. "Here's what really happened that night—the last night of the Civil War cruise. I had given Alexander Gates a note telling him I would knock on his window shortly after three. I implied he could sleep with me and in doing so win a contest against his brother. I was the judge. My intention was to kill Alex because I believed he had been responsible—through negligence or murder—for my mother's death."

"Your mother was Karen Smith, right?" Taylor asked.

"Yes. My note requested that Alex bring two of his cannon balls with him when he came to meet me. I destroyed the note after he read it. His room's window opened on the breezeway at the stern where I was riding the exercise bike. Right after the security watch went by, I knocked on Alex's window, and he came out with the cannon balls. I had two zippered tote bags and a couple of extension cords in my exercise bag. My plan was to flirt—distract him—then smash his jaw with a cannon ball. I would zip the cannon balls into the tote bags as ballast and tie them around his neck and ankles."

Cynthia paused for a drink of water, sweat beading on her brow. "I was nervous and began to doubt myself when he put the cannon balls on the deck, gazed into my eyes, and held my waist. I was dizzy and confused. I couldn't stop staring at his eyes. He had the most amazing eyes, the kind that make a woman—any woman—think she's the most desirable creature on earth. He didn't have a leer the way I expected. He had *giving* eyes. At that instant, I realized I had wanted him to be guilty so badly that I had assumed too much. I had no proof that he had taken my mother's life."

Perspiration glistened—not just on Cynthia's forehead, but on all her exposed skin. She gulped the rest of the glass of water, dribbling some down her chin. Taylor refilled her glass from a pitcher while she wiped her mouth with the back of her hand. "I was really nervous, not because of my plan, which was forgotten, but because I didn't trust men. Part of me wanted to kiss him, but part of me was scared out of my wits. I was so nervous.

"When he kissed me, I closed my eyes and went up on my toes, just like in sappy movies. I was dizzy—excited and flushed. It all happened so fast. I lost my balance. Maybe the boat bumped something, or maybe I was just light-headed. He reached to steady me. I grabbed his shoulders. He tripped over my bag. We lost our balance and fell hard. Going down, he spun under me as if he was my safety net. There was a thud when his head hit a cannon ball on the deck with all my weight on top of him—we cracked heads. I was out for a few seconds—maybe longer. Finally, I got to my knees, but he didn't move.

"The back of his head was dented. He had no pulse and wasn't breathing. I panicked." Cynthia eyes glazed. She shook her head. "I stopped thinking about him and whether he could be saved. From the ballast bags and cords, everyone would conclude that I'd murdered him. Of course, I could have tossed them overboard.... Hindsight. Anyway, I couldn't think of what to do that would save myself except to dispose of the body. I'm sorry and ashamed of what I did. If I'd had time to regain my composure..."

Cynthia looked to Taylor for support, but he turned away. She shook her head clear and pushed on. "I was on automatic pilot—I went to my plan. There were gloves in my bag; I put them on and emptied his pockets, then dragged his body to the railing. My adrenaline made him feel light. I put a cannon ball in each tote bag and tied the bag handles to his neck and ankles. I used my towel to wipe up the blood and stuffed it into one of the tote bags before zipping up. I opened the gate in the railing and shoved him into the river." Her memory recalled a splash, barely audible over the wash of the paddlewheel. She shivered and looked at Taylor, who nodded as if he had known all along.

She downed another half-glass of water. "I hopped on the bike and peddled until the watch came around at three-twenty, but inside, I was a wild animal, bent on survival. The original plan had been to make it seem like he got off the boat normally. It was about three-twenty-five when I snuck into his cabin and packed his bags to put them outside his door. When I saw the ammunition crate, I almost died. In all my brilliant planning, I had messed up, big time. Now, I had to fill the empty space.

"Lucky for me, he had kept newspapers. I turned on the water in his sink to muffle the sound, and I stuffed crumbled sheets into the crate. Then I set his luggage outside the door. I put personal items he was likely to carry in his pockets—his wallet and key ring—into a plastic bag with an ashtray for weight. I left his cabin key on the bureau and threw the plastic bag into the river. Then I walked around the deck and put his tipping envelopes into the box by the purser's office. And that's it. I went down to my cabin, took a shower, and lay down, just like I did every morning after exercising. I was sure I'd be caught.

"I want to be clear, Detective. I wasn't crazy. I knew that disposing of the body was wrong. I'm very sorry. The death was an accident." She exhaled, indicating she was done.

Taylor looked at her with an expression she couldn't quite read—maybe superiority. "You didn't seem panicky when I questioned you. I wrote in my notes that you were cool as a cucumber. Why didn't you tell the truth then?"

"Self-preservation. And I wasn't cool at all. You know Poe's story, *The Tell-Tale Heart*?"

"Sure."

Cynthia shrugged. "That's what I felt like, so I acted...as if I was playing the *femme fatale* in a Hollywood melodrama. Anyway, once I pushed Alex over the side, I was committed. It was too late to change my story."

"But you're here today. What's different?"

She forced a smile. "The mirror."

"What mirror?"

"The mirror I look into—every day." They measured each other. "I'm a better person than I was then—far from perfect, but better and hoping to be better still someday. I can't be the person I want with what I did hanging over me."

Taylor slipped his Pentel between his teeth. "After all your previous lies, why should I believe this version?"

She shrugged. "I didn't have to come here...."

"Even if everything you said today is true, you're still guilty of felonies."

"And I'm throwing myself on the mercy of the court."

He frowned. "I'm not the court, you know. The final charges won't be up to me."

"Then I'll throw myself on the mercy of the D.A. That's where my lawyer is right now."

Taylor furrowed his brow, as if weighing a choice of words. "So you want to plea-bargain?"

"Yes, I want to make a deal."

"A deal implies give and take. What do you have to offer?"

Cynthia put her elbows on the table and leaned forward. "My lawyer is telling the D.A., but I think you know the gist—patriotic actions in service of the country."

Taylor turned off the tape recorder with a snort of disgust.

Cynthia leaned back, eyes wide. "What?"

"Patriotic service?" Taylor oozed cynicism. "Do you really believe that load of crap?"

"Aren't you a patriot, Detective?"

"Not your kind." Taylor tapped his Pentel on the table. "Your so-called patriotism is a myth."

Her eyes narrowed.

"That's right—a myth." He leaned forward, his gaze sharpening. "Your vision of patriotism assumes that we're better than everyone else—that we're so much better we have moral *carte-blanche* to do anything we want. You go beyond loving your country—the real definition of patriotism—to arrogance. My country, right or wrong."

"What about the founding fathers?" Cynthia asked.

"I love my country, but the founders were revolutionaries. Loyalists were the real patriots, and they lost everything."

Cynthia leaned back a few inches.

Taylor wagged his pen at her. "Your patriotism is made-up hooey for people with low self-esteem who need to hide behind a flag. I believe in what's real and what's good: hard work, pride mixed with modesty, respect for *everyone's* heritage, love of one's fellow man, and a society of law. If every person does the best they can within the law, day-in and day-out, they don't have to wave the flag—the pride is inside. That's what patriotism is. Real patriots don't have to act like they're better than their enemies."

"So you admit we have enemies."

Taylor smiled. "Of course. The bad guys. I—"

"Like terrorists," she interrupted. "They attacked the country *you* love—killed people like you and me—so I helped stop them. Aren't they bad guys?"

"The worst kind," Taylor said. "I know all about bad guys. I try to put them in jail every day." He slapped his shield on the table.

Cynthia didn't flinch. "So I'm a bad guy?"

"Yes…" Taylor softened his glare. "And no."

In a moment of silence, the tension in her face eased.

He noticed and made a show of filling her glass with water.

"Thank you, Detective." She sipped. "You know, you can't judge me until you've walked a mile in my shoes—had a loved one cut down in a senseless act of terror."

He sucked on his pen...then removed it. "Maybe you need others—luckier people, like me, to hold you accountable when tragedy makes your blood boil."

She exhaled out her nose and almost smiled. "Murdering terrorists have forfeited their right to society's justice."

Taylor fixed his eyes on hers. "I keep my demons bottled up in a locked room, Ms. James. I only let them out when I'm chopping wood or at the practice range."

He held eye contact until she looked at her shoes and took another sip of water.

He rolled the pen between his fingers. "Let's change the subject. You'll be interested to know that I used SCOPE to do some investigating about a group called Sabah Al Khair, also known as *Eighteen Ninety-Eight*. I believe you're familiar with them. I learned about a raid on an island where five brothers went down in a blaze of gunfire. Plus another raid on the Garden State Spring Water Company. I also found evidence of what they planned to do to reservoirs and why they didn't." His eyes twinkled. "I drink water, too, so thank you."

Cynthia stretched her neck and looked at Taylor. There was something admirable about him—something respectable. She was envious.

"Where were we?" she asked.

"The myth of patriotism. What you did was heroic and a public service...and against the law. Vengeance plus murder doesn't equal patriotism."

"Sometimes it's necessary to stop terrorists who want to kill us. It's proactive self-defense." She waited for his response, nervous without knowing why.

He smiled, softening like a teddy bear. "Maybe you are a patriot, Ms. James. I'll think about your point."

"Fair enough, Detective. Can we get back to the case? I came to set things right—to pay my debt to society. Alexander Gates didn't deserve to die."

After an awkward pause, Taylor said, "If you want to make things right, what about that murder in Boston?"

She frowned. "Someone else already confessed to that crime."

He chuckled. "You've got balls, Ms. James. Whether or not your story is another pack of lies, you've got balls. And I think the D.A. may deal with you. He fancies himself the flag-waving kind of patriot."

"I hope you'll remind him about Abe Sachs."

"Ah." He nodded and tipped an imaginary cap. "Mr. Sachs is where he belongs—in prison. I'll put in a good word for you at sentencing. By the way, what kind of deal are you looking for?"

"My lawyer says the best I can hope for is reckless endangerment and obstruction of justice. Maybe a stiff fine and anywhere from five to twenty-five years. With my service—patriotic or not—maybe I'll get the five. If so, I could be out in three."

"That would be a damn good deal. The D.A.'s office might push for manslaughter, even if they believe you—or first-degree murder if they don't."

She looked at her nails. "I like my hand."

He squinted. "You want to go to jail?"

"No. What I mean is: I like who I am now more than who I used to be. I'll take my chances."

He smiled—not like a cop. "You said earlier that I caught you, but we both know that's not what this is."

"Yet here I am, about to be arrested." Cynthia felt tears forming. She wished they had met under different circumstances—maybe as volunteers or in a classroom.

"What's next?" she asked.

"We'll check the *Louisiana Lady*'s logs and dredge the river where she was between three and three-twenty—looking for bones."

"No. I mean, what's next right now?"

"Even though your fate is up to the D.A., we have to play out our scene. Procedures, you know. I have to—"

"I know."

"I'll arrest you before I resume questioning."

She stood and turned around, crossing her wrists behind her back. Her spine was jelly, but she willed herself to remain upright, head high.

Taylor touched her shoulder. "That won't be necessary. Sit."

He restarted the tape recorder. "Cynthia James, you're under arrest for reckless endangerment and obstruction of justice. You have the right to remain silent...."

EPILOGUE

It was a good morning.

The airliner banked into its final descent, giving Cynthia James a glorious view of the Atlantic Ocean, endless in her angle of vision through a tiny window—no land, no point of reference but the horizon.

The jet leveled off, and she searched for her favorite landmark in New York Harbor—the Statue of Liberty—small but growing larger as the plane approached a Newark touchdown. It had been too long since she had seen Lady Liberty. Three years, six months, and seventeen days in the Tennessee Prison for Women had been worse than her lost decade, but the sentence had passed. Now free on parole, she was only 32, with a clear conscience ahead of her.

Deplaning into the terminal, her eyes were drawn to a TV monitor—flames and smoke on CNN. She squinted to read the scrolling headline. A terrorist bomb had killed 35 people and burned hundreds more in Berlin. It was a bittersweet realization that brought a bittersweet song to mind. Cynthia hung her satchel over a shoulder and hummed *American Pie* as she rolled a carry-on suitcase down the long concourse. She missed the CNN follow-up story, an uplifting report about an organization called *Liberty for All* that was rushing burn doctors and supplies to Germany.

When Cynthia saw Maria's beaming face in the crowd outside security, she hurried the last few yards. They embraced so tightly that Cynthia felt she was breathing the air in Maria's lungs.

They released and smiled, verifying that there was no glass or table between them.

Cynthia traced her finger down Maria's cheek. "The scar's gone."

"Almost," Maria chuckled. "I still have to work some magic." She feathered her fingers through the prison bob haircut then caressed Cynthia's neck. "Your ruby studs have faded to pink rosebuds. I'm glad you didn't wear a turtleneck. How are your butt and gut?"

Cynthia laughed. "The eighties are still visible, but they don't hurt any more…. I've missed you. The visits weren't enough."

They hugged again. Cynthia reveled in the warmth, oblivious to the stream of travelers sweeping past them. "Thanks for watching my place all this time," she said. "I can never repay you."

"We'll think of something."

Cynthia stretched her neck. "Take me home. I've been without a home too long."

Maria squeezed Cynthia's hand. "I'll take your shoulder-bag."

They burst outside and bounced toward the parked car, one step away from skipping.

"Oh, I almost forgot," Maria said. "I signed the papers. The studio lease starts on the first."

"I still can't believe you waited for me—you've given me a shot at doing something good."

Maria's eyes danced. "That's what partners do. The school will be good for both of us. I'm looking forward to something new—something we do together." Maria stopped walking. "Wait. I have a sketch of the sign. Here."

Cynthia stood her suitcase on end. She unfolded the paper and focused on the letters: *J&L School of Self-Defense.*

Cynthia James inhaled fresh air and smiled.

Printed in the United States
37855LVS00009B/34-39